P9-EEU-605

3 5674 05824288 5

Praise for #1 *New York Times* bestselling author

NORA ROBERTS

"Roberts's style has a fresh, contemporary snap."

—*Kirkus Reviews*

"With clear-eyed, concise vision and a sure pen, Roberts nails her characters and settings with awesome precision, drawing readers into a vividly rendered world of family-centered warmth and unquestionable magic."

—*Library Journal*

SHERWOOD FOREST LIBRARY
7117 W. SEVEN MILE RD.
DETROIT, MI 48221

—*Chicago Tribune*

"Roberts' bestselling novels are some of the best in the romance genre."

—*USA TODAY*

"When it comes to compelling, entertaining tales, Roberts is peerless."

—*RT Book Reviews*

JAN ' ' 2018   SF

Also available from Silhouette Books
and Harlequin Books by

NORA ROBERTS

THE MacGREGORS: ROBERT & CYBIL
Love is the biggest gamble…

THE MacGREGORS: DANIEL & IAN
Every great story has a beginning…

THE MacGREGORS: ALAN & GRANT
Passion ignites in restless hearts…

THE MacGREGORS: SERENA & CAINE
Charmed lives and fated romances…

REBELLION
Danger, secrets and love in the Scottish Highlands…

A ROYAL INVITATION
Love and duplicity in a Mediterranean paradise…

* * *

Be sure to look for more Nora Roberts titles
at your local stores, or contact our
Harlequin Reader Service Center:
USA: 3010 Walden Avenue
PO Box 1325, Buffalo, NY 14269
Canada: PO Box 609, Fort Erie, Ontario L2A 5X3
Visit Silhouette Books at www.Harlequin.com

NORA ROBERTS

I'LL ALWAYS HAVE YOU

Published by Silhouette Books
America's Publisher of Contemporary Romance

If you purchased this book without a cover you should be aware
that this book is stolen property. It was reported as "unsold and
destroyed" to the publisher, and neither the author nor the
publisher has received any payment for this "stripped book."

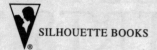

SILHOUETTE BOOKS

I'll Always Have You

ISBN-13: 978-0-373-28233-3

Recycling programs
for this product may
not exist in your area.

Copyright © 2017 by Harlequin Books S.A.

The publisher acknowledges the copyright holder
of the individual works as follows:

Once More with Feeling
Copyright © 1983 by Nora Roberts

Reflections
Copyright © 1983 by Nora Roberts

All rights reserved. Except for use in any review, the reproduction
or utilization of this work in whole or in part in any form by any
electronic, mechanical or other means, now known or hereinafter
invented, including xerography, photocopying and recording, or in
any information storage or retrieval system, is forbidden without
the written permission of the editorial office, Silhouette Books,
195 Broadway, New York, NY 10007 U.S.A.

This is a work of fiction. Names, characters, places and incidents are
either the product of the author's imagination or are used fictitiously, and
any resemblance to actual persons, living or dead, business establishments,
events or locales is entirely coincidental.

This edition published by arrangement with Harlequin Books S.A.

For questions and comments about the quality of this book, please contact us
at CustomerService@Harlequin.com.

® and TM are trademarks of Harlequin Books S.A., used under license.
Trademarks indicated with ® are registered in the United States Patent
and Trademark Office, the Canadian Intellectual Property Office and in
other countries.

Visit Silhouette Books at www.Harlequin.com

Printed in U.S.A.

CONTENTS

ONCE MORE
WITH FEELING

To Ran,
for all the songs yet unwritten,
for all the songs yet unsung.

Chapter 1

He stood out of view as he watched her. His first thought was how little she had changed in five years. Time, it seemed, hadn't rushed or dragged but had merely hung suspended.

Raven Williams was a small, slender woman who moved quickly, with a thin, underlying nervousness that was unaccountably appealing. She was tanned deep gold from the California sun, but at twenty-five her skin was as smooth and dewy soft as a child's. She pampered it when she remembered and ignored it when she forgot. It never seemed to make any difference. Her long hair was thick and straight and true black. She wore it simply, parted in the center. The ends brushed her hips and it swirled and floated as she walked.

Her face was pixielike, with its cheekbones well-defined and the chin slightly pointed. Her mouth smiled easily, but her eyes reflected her emotions. They were smoky gray and round. Whatever Raven felt would be reflected there. She had an overwhelming need to love and be loved. Her own need was one of the reasons for her tremendous success. The other was her voice—the rich, dark, velvet voice that had catapulted her to fame.

Raven always felt a little strange in a recording studio: insulated, sealed off from the rest of the world by the glass and the soundproofing. It had been more than six years since she had cut her first record, but she was still never completely comfortable in a studio. Raven was made for the stage, for the live audience that pumped the blood and heat into the music. She considered the studio too tame, too mechanical. When she worked in the studio, as she did now, she thought of it exclusively as a job. And she worked hard.

The recording session was going well. Raven listened to a playback with a single-mindedness that blocked out her surroundings. There was only the music. It was good, she decided, but it could be better. She'd missed something in the last song, left something out. Without knowing precisely what it was, Raven was certain she could find it. She signaled the engineers to stop the playback.

"Marc?"

A sandy-haired man with the solid frame of a light-weight wrestler entered the booth. "Problem?" he said simply, touching her shoulder.

"The last number, it's a little…" Raven searched for the word. "Empty," she decided at length. "What do you think?" She respected Marc Ridgely as a musician and depended on him as a friend. He was a man of few words who had a passion for old westerns and Jordan almonds. He was also one of the finest guitarists in the country.

Marc reached up to stroke his beard, a gesture, Raven had always thought, that took the place of several sentences. "Do it again," he advised. "The instrumental's fine."

She laughed, producing a sound as warm and rich as her singing voice. "Cruel but true," she murmured, slipping the headset back on. She went back to the microphone. "Another vocal on 'Love and Lose,' please," she instructed the engineers. "I have it on the best authority that it's the singer, not the musicians." She saw Marc grin before she turned to the mike. Then the music washed over her.

Raven closed her eyes and poured herself into the song. It was a slow, aching ballad suited to the smoky depths of her voice. The lyrics were hers, ones she had written long before. It had only been recently that she had felt strong enough to sing them publicly. There was only the music in her head now, an arrangement of notes she herself had produced. And as she added her voice, she knew that what had been missing before had been her emotions. She had restricted them on the other recordings, afraid to risk them. Now she let them out. Her voice flowed with them.

An ache passed through her, a shadow of a pain buried for years. She sang as though the words would bring her relief. The hurt was there, still with her when the song was finished.

For a moment there was silence, but Raven was too dazed to note the admiration of her colleagues. She pulled off the headset, suddenly sharply conscious of its weight.

"Okay?" Marc entered the booth and slipped his arm around her. He felt her tremble lightly.

"Yes." Raven pressed her fingers to her temple a moment and gave a surprised laugh. "Yes, of course. I got a bit wrapped up in that one."

He tilted her face to his, and in a rare show of public affection for a shy man, kissed her. "You were fantastic."

Her eyes warmed, and the tears that had threatened were banished. "I needed that."

"The kiss or the compliment?"

"Both." She laughed and tossed her hair behind her back. "Stars need constant admiration, you know."

"Where's the star?" a backup vocalist wanted to know.

Raven tried for a haughty look as she glanced over. "You," she said ominously, "can be replaced." The vocalist grinned in return, too used to Raven's lack of pretentions to be intimidated.

"Who'd carry you through the session?"

Raven turned to Marc. "Take that one out and shoot him," she requested mildly, then looked up at the booth. "That's a wrap," she called out before her eyes locked on the man now standing in full view behind the glass.

The blood drained from her face. The remnants of emotion from the song surged back in full force. She nearly swayed from the power of it. "Brandon." It was a thought to be spoken aloud but only in a whisper. It was a dream she thought had finally run its course. Then his eyes were on hers, and Raven knew it was real. He'd come back.

Years of performing had taught her to act. It was always an effort for her to slip a mask into place, but by the time Brand Carstairs had come down from the booth, Raven wore a professionally untroubled face. She'd deal with the storm inside later.

"Brandon, it's wonderful to see you again." She held out both hands and tilted her face up to his for the expected, meaningless kiss of strangers who happen to be in the same business.

Her composure startled him. He'd seen her pale, seen the shock in her eyes. Now she wore a façade she'd never had before. It was slick, bright and practiced. Brand realized he'd been wrong; she *had* changed.

"Raven." He kissed her lightly and took both her hands. "You're more beautiful than anyone has a right to be." There was the lightest touch of brogue in his speech, a mist of Ireland over the more formal British. Raven allowed herself a moment to look at him, really look at him.

He was tall and now, as always, seemed a bit too thin. His hair was as dark as her own but waved where hers was needle straight. It was thick and full over his ears and down to the collar of his shirt. His face hadn't changed; it was still the same face that drove girls and women to scream and swoon at his concerts. It was raw-boned and tanned, more intriguing than handsome, as the features were not altogether even. There was something of the dreamer there, from his mother's Irish half. Perhaps that was what drew women to him, though they were just as fascinated by the occasional British reserve. And the eyes. Even now Raven felt the pull of his large, heavy-lidded aquamarine eyes. They were unsettling eyes for as easygoing a man as Brand Carstairs. The blue and green seemed constantly at odds. But it was the charm he wore so easily that tilted the scales, Raven realized. Charm and blatant sex appeal were an irresistible combination.

"You haven't changed, have you, Brandon?" The

question was quiet, the first and only sign of Raven's distress.

"Funny." He smiled, not the quick, flashing grin he was capable of, but a slow, considering smile. "I thought the same of you when I first saw you. I don't suppose it's true of either of us."

"No." God, how she wished he would release her hands. "What brings you to L.A., Brandon?"

"Business, love," he answered carelessly, though his eyes were taking in every inch of her face. "And, of course, the chance to see you again."

"Of course." Her voice was coldly polite, and the smile never reached her eyes.

The sarcasm surprised him. The Raven he remembered hadn't known the meaning of the word. She saw his brow lift into consideration. "I do want to see you, Raven," Brand told her with his sudden, disarming sincerity. "Very much. Can we have dinner?"

Her pulse had accelerated at his change of tone. Just reflex, just an old habit, she told herself and struggled to keep her hands passive in his. "I'm sorry, Brandon," she answered with perfect calm. "I'm booked." Her eyes slipped past him in search of Marc, whose head was bent over his guitar as he jammed with another musician. Raven could have sworn with frustration. Brand followed the direction of her gaze. Briefly his eyes narrowed.

"Tomorrow, then," he said. His tone was still light and casual. "I want to talk to you." He smiled as to an old friend. "I'll just drop by the house awhile."

"Brandon," Raven began and tugged on her hands.

"You still have Julie, don't you?" Brand smiled and

held on to her hands, unaware of—or ignoring—her resistance.

"Yes, I…"

"I'd like to see her again. I'll come by around four. I know the way." He grinned, then kissed her again, a quick, friendly brushing of lips before he released her hands, turned and walked away.

"Yes," she murmured to herself. "You know the way."

An hour later Raven drove through the electric gates that led to her house. The one thing she hadn't allowed Julie or her agent to thrust on her was a chauffeur. Raven enjoyed driving, having control of the low, sleek foreign car and indulging from time to time in an excess of speed. She claimed it cleared her head. It obviously hadn't done the job, she thought as she pulled up in front of the house with a short, peevish squeal of the brakes. Distracted, she left her purse sitting on the seat beside her as she sprang from the car and jogged up the three stone steps that led to the front door. It was locked. Her frustration only mounted when she was forced to go back and rip the keys from the ignition.

Slamming into the house, Raven went directly to the music room. She flung herself down on the silk-covered Victorian sofa and stared straight ahead without seeing anything. A gleaming mahogany grand piano dominated the room. It was played often and at odd hours. There were Tiffany lamps and Persian rugs and a dime-store flowerpot with a struggling African violet. An old, scarred music cabinet was filled to overflowing. Sheet music spilled onto the floor. A priceless Fabergé box sat next to the brass unicorn she had found in a thrift shop and had fallen in love with. One wall was crowded with awards: Grammys, gold and platinum records, plaques and statues and the keys to a few cities. On another was the framed sheet music from the first song she had written and a breathtaking Picasso. The sofa on which she sat had a bad spring.

It was a strange hodgepodge of cultures and tastes and uniquely Raven's own. She would have thought *eclectic* a pretentious word. She had allowed Julie her exacting taste everywhere else in the house, but here she had expressed herself. Raven needed the room the same way she needed to drive her own car. It kept her sane and helped her remember exactly who Raven Williams was. But the room, like the drive, hadn't calmed her nerves. She walked to the piano.

She pounded out Mozart fiercely. Like her eyes, her music reflected her moods. Now it was tormented, volatile. Even when she'd finished, anger seemed to hover in the air.

"Well, I see you're home." Julie's voice, mild and unruffled, came from the doorway. Julie walked into the room as she had walked into Raven's life: poised and confident. When Raven had met her nearly six years before, Julie had been rich and bored, a partygoer born into old money. Their relationship had given them both something of importance: friendship and a dual dependence. Julie handled the myriad details attached to Raven's career. Raven gave Julie a purpose that the glittery world of wealth had lacked.

"Didn't the recording go well?" Julie was tall and blond, with an elegant body and that exquisitely casual California chic.

Raven lifted her head, and the smile fled from Julie's

face. It had been a long time since she'd seen that help-less, ravaged look. "What happened?"

Raven let out a long breath. "He's back."

"Where did you see him?" There was no need for Julie to ask for names. In all the years of their associa-tion only two things had had the power to put that look on Raven's face. One of them was a man.

"At the studio." Raven combed her fingers through her hair. "He was up in the booth. I don't know how long he'd been there before I saw him."

Julie pursed her lightly tinted lips. "I wonder what Brand Carstairs is doing in California."

"I don't know." Raven shook her head. "He said busi-ness. Maybe he's going to tour again." In an effort to release the tension, she rubbed her hand over the back of her neck. "He's coming here tomorrow."

Julie's brows rose. "I see."

"Don't turn secretary on me, Julie," Raven pleaded. She shut her eyes. "Help me."

"Do you want to see him?" The question was prac-tical. Julie, Raven knew, was practical. She was orga-nized, logical and a stickler for details—all the things Raven wasn't. They needed each other.

"No," Raven began almost fiercely. "Yes..." She swore then and pressed both hands to her temples. "I don't know." Now her tone was quiet and weary. "You know what he's like, Julie. Oh, God, I thought it was over. I thought it was finished!"

With something like a moan, she jumped from the stool to pace around the room. She didn't look like a star in jeans and a simple linen blouse. Her closet held everything from bib overalls to sables. The sables were for the performer; the overalls were for her.

"I'd buried all the hurts. I was so sure." Her voice was low and a little desperate. It was still impossible for her to believe that she had remained this vulnerable after five years. She had only to see him again, and she felt it once more. "I knew sooner or later that I'd run into him somewhere." She ran her fingers through her hair as she roamed the room. "I think I'd always pictured it would be in Europe—London—probably at a party or a benefit. I'd have expected him there; maybe that would have been easier. But today I just looked up and there he was. It all came back. I didn't have any time to stop it. I'd been singing that damn song that I'd written right after he'd left." Raven laughed and shook her head. "Isn't that wild?" She took a deep breath and repeated softly, wonderingly, "Isn't that wild?"

The room was silent for nearly a full minute before Julie spoke. "What are you going to do?"

"Do?" Raven spun back to her. Her hair flew out to follow the sudden movement. "I'm not going to *do* anything. I'm not a child looking for happily-ever-after anymore." Her eyes were still dark with emotion, but her voice had grown gradually steadier. "I was barely twenty when I met Brandon, and I was blindly in love with his talent. He was kind to me at a time when I badly needed kindness. I was overwhelmed by him and with my own success."

She lifted a hand to her hair and carefully pushed it behind her shoulders. "I couldn't cope with what he wanted from me. I wasn't ready for a physical relationship." She walked to the brass unicorn and ran a fingertip down its withers. "So he left," she said softly. "And I was hurt. All I could see—maybe all I wanted to see—was that he didn't understand, didn't care enough to want to know why I said no. But that was unrealistic." She turned to Julie then with a frustrated sigh. "Why don't you say something?"

"You're doing fine without me."

"All right, then." Raven thrust her hands in her pockets and stalked to the window. "One of the things I've learned is that if you don't want to get hurt, you don't get too close. You're the only person I've never applied that rule to, and you're the only one who hasn't let me down." She took a deep breath.

"I was infatuated with Brandon years ago. Perhaps it was a kind of love, but a girl's love, easily brushed aside. It was a shock seeing him today, especially right after I finished that song. The coincidence was..." Raven pushed the feelings away and turned back from the window. "Brandon will come over tomorrow, and he'll say whatever it is that he has to say, then he'll go. That'll be the end of it."

Julie studied Raven's face. "Will it?"

"Oh, yes." Raven smiled. She was a bit weary after the emotional outburst but more confident. She had regained her control. "I like my life just as it is, Julie. He's not going to change it. No one is, not this time."

Chapter 2

Raven had dressed carefully, telling herself it was because of the fittings she had scheduled and the luncheon meeting with her agent. She knew it was a lie, but the smart, sophisticated clothes made her feel confident. Who could feel vulnerable dressed in a St. Laurent?

Her coat was white silk and full cut with batwing sleeves that made it seem almost like a cape. She wore it over matching pants with an orchid cowlneck blouse and a thick, gold belt. With the flat-brimmed hat and the carefully selected earrings, she felt invulnerable. You've come a long way, she had thought as she had studied herself in the bedroom mirror.

Now, standing in Wayne Metcalf's elaborate fitting room, she thought the same thing again—about both of them. Wayne and Raven had started the rise to fame together, she scratching out a living singing in seamy clubs and smoky piano bars and he waiting tables and sketching designs no one had the time to look at. But Raven had looked and admired and remembered.

Wayne had just begun to eke out a living in his trade when plans had begun for Raven's first concert tour. The first professional decision she made without advice was the choice of her costume designer. She had never regretted it. Like Julie, Wayne was a friend close enough to know something about Raven's early personal life. And like Julie, he was fiercely, unquestionably loyal.

Raven wandered around the room, a much plusher room, she mused, than the first offices of Metcalf Designs. There'd been no carpet on that floor, no signed lithographs on laquered walls, no panoramic view of Beverly Hills. It had been a cramped, airless little room above a Greek restaurant. Raven could still remember the strange, heavy aromas that would seep through the walls. She could still hear the exotic music that had vibrated through the bare wood floor.

Raven's star had not risen with that first concert tour, it had rocketed. The initial taste of fame had been so heady and so quick, she had hardly had the time to savor it all: tours, rehearsals, hotel rooms, reporters, mobs of fans, unbelievable amounts of money and impossible demands. She had loved it, although the traveling had sometimes left her weak and disoriented and the fans could be as frightening as they were wonderful. Still she had loved it.

Wayne, deluged with offers after the publicity of that first tour, had soon moved out of the one-room office above the *moussaka* and *souvlaki*. He'd been Raven's designer for six years, and although he now had a large staff and a huge workload, he still saw to every detail of her designs himself.

While she waited for him, Raven wandered to the bar and poured herself a ginger ale. Through all the years of luncheon meetings, elegant brunches and recording sessions, she had never taken more than an occasional drink. In this respect, at least, she would control her life.

The past, she mused, was never very far away, at least not while she still had to worry about her mother. Raven shut her eyes and wished that she could shut off her thoughts as easily. How long had it been that she had lived with that constant anxiety? She could never remember a life without it. She had been very young when she had first discovered that her mother wasn't like other mothers. Even as a little girl, she had hated the oddly sweet smell of the liquor on her mother's breath that no mints could disguise, and she had dreaded the flushed face, the first slurred, affectionate, then angry tones that had drawn mocking stares or sympathetic glances from friends and neighbors.

Raven pressed her fingers against her brow. So many years. So much waste. And now her mother had disappeared again. Where was she? In what sordid hotel room had she holed herself up in to drink away what was left of her life? Raven made a determined effort to push her mother out of her mind, but the terrible images, the frightful scenes, played on in her mind.

It's my life! I have to get on with it, Raven told herself, but she could feel the bitter taste of sorrow and guilt rise in her throat. She started when the door across swung open and Wayne walked in.

He leaned against the knob. "Beautiful!" he said admiringly, surveying her. "Did you wear that for me?"

She made a sound that was somewhere between a laugh and a sob as she moved across the room to hug him. "Of course. Bless you!"

"If you were going to dress up for me, you might at least have worn something of mine," he complained but returned the embrace. He was tall, a thin reed of a man who had to bend over to give her the quick kiss. Not yet thirty, he had a scholarly attractive face with hair and eyes the same rich shade of brown. A small white scar marred his left eyebrow and gave him, he preferred to think, a rakish profile.

"Jealous?" Raven grinned and drew away from him. "I thought you were too big for that."

"You're never too big for that." He released her, then made his way across to the bar. "Well, at least take off your hat and coat."

Raven obliged, tossing them aside with a carelessness that made Wayne wince. He gazed at her for a long moment as he poured out a Perrier. She grinned again and did a slow model's turn. "How am I holding up?" she demanded.

"I should have seduced you when you were eighteen." He sighed and drank the sparkling water. "Then I wouldn't be constantly regretting that you slipped through my fingers."

She came back for her ginger ale. "You had your chance, fella."

"I was too exhausted in those days." He lifted his scarred brow in a practiced gesture that always amused her. "I get more rest now."

"Too late," she told him and touched her glass to his. "And you're much too busy with the model-of-the-week contest."

"I only date all those skinny girls for the publicity." He reached for a cigarette and lit it elegantly. "I'm basically a very retiring man."

"The brilliance of the pun I could make is terrifying, but I'll pass."

"Wise," he concluded, then blew out a delicate trail of smoke. "I hear Brand Carstairs is in town."

Raven's smile fled, then returned. "He never could keep a low profile."

"Are you okay?"

She shrugged her shoulders. "A minute ago I was beautiful, now you have to ask if I'm okay?"

"Raven." Wayne laid a hand on top of hers. "You folded up when he left. I was there, remember?"

"Of course I remember." The teasing note left her voice. "You were very good to me, Wayne. I don't think I would have made it without you and Julie."

"That's not what I'm talking about, Raven. I want to know how you feel now." He turned her hand over and laced his fingers through hers. "I could renew my offer to go try to break all his bones, if you like."

Touched and amused, she laughed. "I'm sure you're a real killer, Wayne, but it isn't necessary." The straightening of her shoulders was unconscious, a gesture of pride that made Wayne smile. "I'm not going to fold this time."

"Are you still in love with him?"

She hadn't expected such a direct question. Dropping her gaze, she took a moment to answer. "A better question is, did I ever love him?"

"We both already know the answer to that one," Wayne countered. He took her hand when she would have turned away. "We've been friends a long time. What happens to you matters to me."

"Nothing's going to happen to me." Her eyes were back on his, and she smiled. "Absolutely nothing. Brandon is the past. Who knows better than I that you can't run away from the past, and who knows better how to cope with it?" She squeezed his hand. "Come on, show me the costumes that are going to make me look sensational."

After a quick, final glance at her face, Wayne walked over to a gleaming Chippendale table and pushed the button on an intercom. "Bring in Ms. Williams's designs."

Raven had approved the sketches, of course, and the fabrics, but still the completed designs took her by surprise. They had been created for the spotlights. She knew she'd sparkle on stage. It felt odd wearing blood red and silver sequins in Wayne's brightly lit, elegant room with mirrors tossing her image back at her from all angles. But then, she remembered, it was an odd business.

Raven stared at the woman in the mirrors and listened with half an ear to Wayne's mumbling as he tucked and adjusted. Her mind could not help but wander. Six years before, she'd been a terrified kid with an album shooting off the top of the charts and a whirlwind concert tour to face. It had all happened so fast: the typical overnight success—not counting the years she had struggled in smoke-choked dives. Still, she'd been young to make a name for herself and determined to prove she wasn't a one-shot fluke. The romance with Brand Carstairs, while she had still been fresh, hot news, hadn't hurt her career. For a brief time it had made her the crown princess of popular music. For more than six months their faces appeared on every magazine cover, dominating the newsstands. They'd laughed about it, Raven remembered, laughed at the silly, predictable headlines: "Raven and Brand Plan Love Nest"; "Williams and Carstairs Make Their Own Music."

Brand had complained about his billing. They had ignored the constant flare and flash of cameras because they had been happy and saw little else but each other. Then, when he had gone, the pictures and headlines had continued for a long time—the cold, cruel words that flashed the intimacies of private hurts for the public eye. Raven no longer looked at them.

Over the months and years, she had grown from the crown princess to a respected performer and celebrity in her own right. That's what's important, she reminded herself. Her career, her life. She'd learned about priorities the hard way.

Raven slipped into the glistening black jumpsuit and found it fit like a second skin. Even her quiet breathing sent sequins flashing. Light streaked out from it at the slightest movement. It was, she decided after a critical survey, blisteringly sexy.

"I'd better not gain a quarter of an ounce before the tour," she remarked, turning to view her slim, sleek profile. Thoughtfully, she gathered her hair in her hand and tossed it behind her back. "Wayne..." He was kneeling at her feet, adjusting the hem. His answer was a grunt. "Wayne, I don't know if I have the nerve to wear this thing."

"This thing," he said mildly as he rose to pluck at the sleeve, "is fantastic."

"No artistic snub intended," she returned and smiled as he stepped back to survey her up and down in his concentrated, professional gaze. "But it's a bit..." She glanced at herself again. "Basic, isn't it?"

"You've got a nice little body, Raven." Wayne examined his creation from the rear. "Not all my clients could wear this without a bit of help here and there. Okay, take it off. It's perfect just as it is."

"I always feel like I've been to the doctor when I've finished here," she commented as she slipped back into her white slacks and orchid blouse. "Who knows more about our bodies' secrets than our dressmakers?"

"Who else knows more about *your* secrets, darling?" he corrected absently as he made notes on each one of the costumes. "Women tend to get chatty when they're half-dressed."

"Oh, what lovely gossip do you know?" Fastening her belt, Raven walked to him, then leaned companionably on his shoulder. "Tell me something wonderfully indiscreet and shocking, Wayne."

"Babs Curtin has a new lover," he murmured, still intent on his notes.

"I said shocking," Raven complained. "Not predictable."

"I've sworn an oath of secrecy, written in dressmaker's chalk."

"I'm very disappointed in you." Raven left his side to fetch her coat and hat. "I was certain you had feet of clay."

"Lauren Chase just signed to do the lead in *Fantasy.*"

Raven stopped on her way to the door and whirled. "What?" She dashed back across the room and yanked the notebook from Wayne's hand.

"Somehow I thought that would get your attention," Wayne observed dryly.

"When? Oh, Wayne," she went on before he could answer. "I'd give several years of my young life for a chance to write that score. Lauren Chase…oh, yes, she's so right for it. Who's doing the score, Wayne?" Raven gripped his shoulders and closed her eyes. "Go ahead, tell me, I can take it."

"She doesn't know. You're cutting off the circulation, Raven," he added, disengaging her hands.

"Doesn't know!" she groaned, crushing the hat down on her head in a way that made Wayne swear and adjust it himself. "That's worse, a thousand times worse! Some faceless, nameless songwriter who couldn't possibly know what's right for that fabulous screenplay is even now sitting at a piano making unforgivable mistakes."

"There's always the remote possibility that whoever's writing it has talent," he suggested and earned a lethal glare.

"Whose side are you on?" she demanded and flung the coat around her shoulders.

He grinned, grabbed her cheeks and gave her a resounding kiss. "Go home and stomp your feet, darling. You'll feel better."

She struggled not to smile. "I'm going next door and buy a Florence DeMille," she threatened him with the name of a leading competitor.

"I'll forgive you that statement," Wayne said with a hefty sigh. "Because along with my feet of clay I've a heart of gold."

She laughed and left him with her rack of costumes and his notebook.

The house was quiet when Raven returned. The faint scent of lemon oil and pine told her that the house had just been cleaned. As a matter of habit, she peeked into her music room and was satisfied that nothing there had been disturbed. She liked her disorganization just as it was. With the idle thought of making coffee, Raven wandered toward the kitchen.

She had bought the house for its size and rambling openness. It was the antithesis of the small, claustrophobic rooms she had grown up in. And it smelled clean, she decided. Not antiseptic; she would have hated that, but there was no lingering scent of stale cigarettes, no sickly sweet odor of yesterday's bottle. It was her house, as her life was hers. She'd bought them both with her voice.

Raven twirled once around the room, pleased with herself for no specific reason. I'm happy, she thought, just happy to be alive.

Grabbing a rose from a china vase, she began to sing as she walked down the hall. It was the sight of Julie's long, narrow bare feet propped up on the desk in the library that stopped her.

Raven hesitated, seeing Julie was on the phone, but was quickly gestured inside.

"I'm sorry, Mr. Cummings, but Ms. Williams has a strict policy against endorsements. Yes, I'm sure it's a marvelous product." Julie lifted her eyes from her pink-tinted toenails and met Raven's amused grin. She rolled her eyes to the ceiling, and Raven settled cross-legged in an overstuffed leather chair. The library, with its warm, mahogany paneling and stately furnishings, was Julie's domain. And, Raven thought, snuggling down more comfortably, it suited her.

"Of course, I'll see she gets your offer, but I warn you, Ms. Williams takes a firm stand on this." With one last exasperated glance at the ceiling, Julie hung up. "If you didn't insist on being nice to everybody who calls you, I could have thought of a few different words for that one," Julie snapped.

"Trouble?" Raven asked, sniffing her rose and smiling.

"Get smart and I'll tell them you'll be thrilled to endorse his Earth Bubble Shampoo." She laced her fingers behind her head as she made the threat.

"Mercy," Raven pleaded, then kicked off her elegant, orchid-toned shoes. "You look tired," she said, watching Julie stretch her back muscles. "Been busy?"

"Just last-minute nonsense to clear things for the tour." A shrug dismissed the complications she had handled. "I never did ask you how the recording went. It's finished, isn't it?"

"Yeah." Raven took a deep breath and twirled her rose by the stem. "It went perfectly. I haven't been happier with a session since the first one. Something just clicked."

"You worked hard enough on the material," Julie remarked, thinking of the endless nights Raven had spent writing and arranging.

"Sometimes I still can't believe it." She spoke softly, the words hardly more than thoughts. "I listen to a playback, and it's all there, the strings, the brass, the rhythm and backups, and I can't believe it's me. I've been so incredibly lucky."

"Talented," Julie corrected.

"Lots of people have talent," Raven reminded her. "But they're not sitting here. They're still in some dreary piano bar, waiting. Without luck, they're never going to be anywhere else."

"There are also things like drive, perseverance, guts." Raven's persistent lack of self-confidence infuriated

Julie. She'd been with her almost from the beginning of Raven's start in California six years before. She'd seen the struggles and the disappointments. She knew about the fears, insecurities and work behind the glamour. There was nothing about Raven Williams that Julie didn't know.

The phone interrupted her thoughts on a lecture on self-worth. "It's your private line," she said as she pressed the button. "Hello." Raven tensed but relaxed when she saw Julie smile. "Hi, Henderson. Yes, she's right here, hold on. Your illustrious agent," Julie stated as she rose. She slipped her feet back into her sandals. Raven got up from her chair just as the doorbell chimed.

"I guess that's Brandon." With admirable ease, she flopped into the chair that Julie had just vacated. "Would you tell him I'll be along in a minute?"

"Sure." Julie turned and left as Raven's voice followed her down the hall.

"I left it where? In your office? Henderson, I don't know why I ever bother carrying a purse."

Julie smiled. Raven had a penchant for losing things: her purse, her shoes, her passport. Vital or trivial, it simply didn't matter. Music and people filled Raven's thoughts, and material objects were easily forgotten.

"Hello, Brand," Julie said as she opened the front door. "Nice to see you again." Her eyes were cool, and her mouth formed no smile.

"Hello, Julie."

There was warmth in his greeting. She sensed it and ignored it. "Come in," she invited. "Raven's expecting you; she'll be right out."

"It's good to be here again. I've missed this place."

"Have you?" Her tone was sharp.

His grin turned into a look of appraisal. Julie was a long-stemmed woman with a sleek cap of honey-blond hair and direct brown eyes. She was closer to Brand's age than Raven's and was the sort of woman he was usually attracted to: smart, sophisticated and coolly sexy. Yet, there could never have been anything between them but friendship. She was too fiercely devoted to Raven. Her loyalty, he saw, was unchanged.

"Five years is a long time, Julie."

"I'm not sure it's long enough," she countered. Old resentments came simmering back to the surface. "You hurt her."

"Yes, I know." His gaze didn't falter at the confession, and there was no plea for understanding in his eyes. The lack of it touched off respect in Julie, but she dismissed it. She shook her head as she looked at him.

"So," she said softly, "you've come back."

"I've come back," he agreed, then smiled. "Did you think I wouldn't?"

"She didn't," Julie retorted, annoyed with herself for warming to him. "That's what matters."

"Julie, Henderson's sending over my purse." Raven came down the hall toward them in her quick, nervous stride. "I told him not to bother; I don't think there's anything in it but a comb and an expired credit card. Hello, Brandon." She offered her hands as she had at the recording studio, but now she felt more able to accept his touch.

She hadn't bothered to put her shoes back on or to repaint her mouth. Her smile was freer, more as he remembered it. "Raven." Brand brought her hands to his lips. Instantly she stiffened, and Brand released her. "Can we talk in the music room?" His smile was easy, friendly. "I was always comfortable in there."

"Of course." She turned toward the doorway. "Would you like something to drink?"

"I'd have some tea." He gave Julie his quick, charming grin. "You always made a good cup of tea."

"I'll bring it in." Without responding to the grin, Julie moved down the hall toward the kitchen. Brand followed Raven into the music room.

He touched her shoulder before she could cross to the sofa. It was a gesture that asked her to wait. Turning her head, Raven saw that he was giving the room one of his long, detailed studies. She had seen that look on his face before. It was a curious aspect of what seemed like a casual nature. There was an intensity about him at times that recalled the tough London street kid who'd once fought his way to the top of his profession. The key to his talent seemed to be in his natural gift for observation. He saw everything, remembered everything. Then he translated it into lyric and melody.

The fingers on her shoulder caressed once, almost absently, and brought back a flood of memories. Raven would have moved away, but he dropped the hand and turned to her. She had never been able to resist his eyes.

"I remember every detail of this room. I've pictured it from time to time when I couldn't do anything but think of you." He lifted his hand again to brush the back of it against her cheek.

"Don't." She shook her head and stepped away.

"It's difficult not to touch you, Raven. Especially here. Do you remember the long evenings we spent here? The quiet afternoons?"

He was moving her—with just his voice, just the steady spell of his eyes. "It was a long time ago, Brandon."

"It doesn't seem so long ago at the moment. It could be yesterday; you look the same."

"I'm not," she told him with a slight shake of her head. He saw her eyes darken before she turned away. "If I had known this was why you wanted to see me, I wouldn't have let you come. It's over, Brandon. It's been over for a long time."

"Is it?" Raven hadn't realized he was so close behind her. He turned her in his arms and caught her. "Show me, then," he demanded. "Just once."

The moment his mouth touched hers, she was thrown back in time. It was all there—the heat, the need, the loving. His lips were so soft, so warm; hers parted with only the slightest pressure. She knew how he would taste, how he would smell. Her memory was sharper than she had thought. Nothing was forgotten.

He tangled his fingers in the thickness of her hair, tilting her head further back as he deepened the kiss. He wanted to luxuriate in her flavor, in her scent, in her soft, yielding response. Her hands were trapped between their bodies, and she curled her fingers into the sweater he wore. The need, the longing, seemed much too fresh to have been dormant for five years. Brand held her close but without urgency. There was a quiet kind of certainty in the way he explored her mouth. Raven responded, giving, accepting, remembering. But when she felt the pleasure drifting toward passion, she resisted. When she struggled, he loosened his hold but didn't release her. Raven stared up at him with a look he well remembered but had never been able to completely decipher.

"It doesn't seem it's altogether finished after all," he murmured.

"You never did play fair, did you?" Raven pushed out of his arms, furious and shaken. "Let me tell you something, Brandon. I won't fall at your feet this time. You hurt me before, but I don't bruise so easily now. I have no intention of letting you back into my life."

"I think you will," he corrected easily. "But perhaps not in the way you mean." He paused and caught her hair with his fingers. "I can apologize for kissing you, Raven, if you'd like me to lie."

"Don't bother. You've always been good at romance. I rather enjoyed it." She sat down on the sofa and smiled brightly up at him.

He lifted a brow. It was hardly the response he had expected. He drew out a cigarette and lit it. "You seem to have grown up in my absence."

"Being an adult has its advantages," Raven observed. The kiss had stirred more than she cared to admit, even to herself.

"I always found your naiveté charming."

"It's difficult to remain naive, however charming, in this business." She leaned back against the cushion, relaxing deliberately. "I'm not wide-eyed and twenty anymore, Brandon."

"Tough and jaded are you, Raven?"

"Tough enough," she returned. "You gave me my first lesson!"

He took a deep drag on his cigarette, then considered the glowing tip of it. "Maybe I did," he murmured. "Maybe you needed it."

"Maybe you'd like me to thank you," she tossed back, and he looked over at her again.

"Perhaps." He walked over, then dropped down beside her on the sofa. His laugh was sudden and unexpected. "Good God, Raven, you've never had this bloody spring fixed."

The tension in her neck fled as she laughed with him. "I like it that way." She tossed her hair behind her back. "It's more personal."

"To say nothing of uncomfortable."

"I never sit on that spot," she told him.

"You leave it for unsuspecting guests, I imagine." He shifted away from the defective spring.

"That's right. I like people to feel at home."

Julie brought in a tea tray and found them sitting companionably on the sofa. Her quick, practiced glance found no tension on Raven's face. Satisfied, she left them again.

"How've you been, Brandon? Busy, I imagine." Raven crossed her legs under her and leaned over to pour the tea. It was a move Brandon had seen many times. Almost savagely, he crushed out his cigarette.

"Busy enough." He understated the five albums he had released since she'd last seen him and the three grueling concert tours. There'd been more than twenty songs with his name on the copyright in the past year.

"You've been living in London?"

"Mostly." His brow lifted, and she caught the gesture as she handed him his tea.

"I read the trades," she said mildly. "Don't we all?"

"I saw your television special last month." He sipped his tea and relaxed against the back of the sofa. His eyes were on her, and she thought them a bit more green than blue now. "You were marvelous."

"Last month?" She frowned at him, puzzled. "It wasn't aired in England, was it?"

"I was in New York. Did you write all the songs for the album you finished up yesterday?"

"All but two." Shrugging, she took up her own china cup. "Marc wrote 'Right Now' and 'Coming Back.' He's got the touch."

"Yes." Brand eyed her steadily. "Does he have you, too?" Raven's head whipped around. "I read the trades," he said mildly.

"That comes under a more personal heading." Her eyes were dark with anger.

"More bluntly stated, none of my business?" he asked, sipping again.

"You were always bright, Brandon."

"Thanks, love." He set down his cup. "But my question was professional. I need to know if you have any entanglements at the moment."

"Entanglements are usually personal. Ask me about my dancing lessons."

"Later, perhaps. Raven, I need your undivided devotion for the next three months." His smile was engaging. Raven fought his charm.

"Well," she said and set her cup beside his. "That's bluntly stated."

"No indecent proposal at the moment," he assured her. Settling back in the hook of the sofa's arm, he sought her eyes. "I'm doing the score for *Fantasy*. I need a partner."

Chapter 3

To say she was surprised would have been a ridiculous understatement. Brand watched her eyes widen. He thought they were the color of peat smoke. She didn't move but simply stared at him, her hands resting lightly on her knees. Her thoughts had been flung in a thousand different directions, and she was trying to sit calmly and bring them back to order.

Fantasy. The book that had captured America's heart. A novel that had been on the bestseller list for more than fifty weeks. The sale of its paperback rights had broken all records. The film rights had been purchased as well, and Carol Mason, the author, had written the screenplay herself. It was to be a musical; *the* musical of the nineties. Speculation had been buzzing for months on both coasts as to who would write the score. It would be the coup of the decade, the chance of a lifetime. The plot was a dream, and the reigning box-office queen had the lead. And the music… Raven already had half-formed songs in her head. Carefully she reached back and poured more tea. Things like this don't just fall in your lap, she reminded herself. Perhaps he means something entirely different.

"You're going to score *Fantasy,*" she said at length, cautiously. Her eyes met his again. His were clear, confident, a little puzzled. "I just heard that Lauren Chase had been signed. Everywhere I go, people are wondering who's going to play Tessa, who's going to play Joe."

"Jack Ladd," Brand supplied, and the puzzlement in Raven's eyes changed to pure pleasure.

"Perfect!" She reached over to take his hands. "You're going to have a tremendous hit. I'm very happy for you."

And she was. He could see as well as hear the absolute sincerity. It was typical of her to gain genuine pleasure from someone else's good fortune, just as it was typical of her to suffer for someone else's misfortune. Raven's feelings ran deep, and he knew she'd never been afraid to show emotion. Her unaffectedness had always been a great part of her appeal. For the moment, she had forgotten to be cautious with Brand. She smiled at him as she held his hands.

"So that's why you're in California," she said. "Have you already started?"

"No." He seemed to consider something for a moment, then his fingers interlaced with hers. Her hands were narrow-boned and slender, with palms as soft as a child's. "Raven, I meant what I said. I need a partner. I need you."

She started to remove her hands from his, but he tightened his fingers. "I've never known you to need anyone,

Brandon," she said, not quite succeeding in making her tone light. "Least of all me."

His grip tightened quickly, causing Raven's eyes to widen at the unexpected pain. Just as quickly, he released her. "This is business, Raven."

She lifted a brow at the temper in his voice. "Business is usually handled through my agent," she said. "You remember Henderson."

He gave her a long, steady look. "I remember everything." He saw the flash of hurt in her eyes, swiftly controlled. "Raven," his tone was gentler now. "I'm sorry."

She shrugged and gave her attention back to her tea. "Old wounds, Brandon. It does seem to me that if there was a legitimate offer, Henderson would have gotten wind of it."

"There's been an offer," Brand told her. "I asked him to let me speak to you first."

"Oh?" Her hair had drifted down, curtaining her face, and she flipped it behind her back. "Why?"

"Because I thought that if you knew we'd be working together, you'd turn it down."

"Yes," she agreed. "You're right."

"And that," he said without missing a beat, "would be incredibly soft-headed. Henderson knows that as well as I do."

"Oh, does he?" Raven rose, furious. "Isn't it marvelous the way people determine my life? Did you two decide I was too feeble-brained to make this decision on my own?"

"Not exactly." Brand's voice was cool. "We did agree that left to yourself, you have a tendency to be emotional rather than sensible."

"Terrific. Do I get a leash and collar for Christmas?"

"Don't be an idiot," Brand advised.

"Oh, so now I'm an idiot?" Raven turned away to pace the room. She had the same quicksilver temper he remembered. She was all motion, all energy. "I don't know how I've managed all this time without your pretty compliments, Brandon." She whirled back to him. "Why in the world would you want an emotional idiot as a collaborator?"

"Because," Brandon said and rose, "you're a hell of a writer. Now shut up."

"Of course," she said, seating herself on the piano bench. "Since you asked so nicely."

Deliberately he took out another cigarette, lit it and blew out a stream of smoke, all the while his eyes resting on her face. "This is an important project, Raven," he said. "Let's not blow it. Because we were once very close, I wanted to talk to you face-to-face, not through a mediator, not through a bloody telephone wire. Can you understand that?"

She waited a long moment before answering. "Maybe."

Brand smiled and moved over to her. "We'll add stubborn to those adjectives later, but I don't want you mad again."

"Then let me ask you something before you say anything I'll have to get mad about." Raven tilted her head and studied his face. "First, why do you want a collaborator on this? Why share the glory?"

"It's also a matter of sharing the work, love. Fifteen songs."

She nodded. "All right, number two, then. Why me, Brandon? Why not someone who's scored a musical before?"

He answered her by walking around her and slipping down on the piano bench beside her. Without speaking, he began to play. The notes flooded the room like ghosts. "Remember this?" he murmured, glancing over and into her eyes.

Raven didn't have to answer. She rose and walked away. It was too difficult to sit beside him at the same piano where they had composed the song he now played. She remembered how they had laughed, how warm his eyes had been, how safe she had felt in his arms. It was the first and only song they had written and recorded together.

Even after he had stopped playing, she continued to prowl the room. "What does 'Clouds and Rain' have to do with anything?" she demanded. He had touched a chord in her; he heard it in the tone of her voice. He felt a pang of guilt at having intentionally peeled away a layer of her defense.

"There's a Grammy over there and a gold record, thanks to that two minutes and forty-three seconds, Raven. We work well together."

She turned back to look at him. "We did once."

"We will again." Brand stood and came to her but this time made no move to touch her. "Raven, you know how important this could be to your career. And you must realize what you'd be bringing to the project. *Fantasy* needs your special talents."

She wanted it. She could hardly believe that something she wanted so badly was being offered to her. But how would it be to work with him again, to be in constant close contact? Would she be able to deal with it? Would she be sacrificing her personal sanity for professional gain? *But I don't love him anymore,* she reminded herself. Raven caught her bottom lip between her teeth in a gesture of indecision. Brand saw it.

"Raven, think of the music."

"I am," she admitted. "I'm also thinking of you—of us." She gave him a clear, candid look. "I'm not sure it would be healthy for me."

"I can't promise not to touch you." He was annoyed, and his voice reflected it in its crisp, concise tone. "But I can promise not to push myself on you. Is that good enough?"

Raven evaded the question. "If I agreed, when would we start? I've a tour coming up."

"I know, in two weeks. You'll be finished in six, so we could start the first week in May."

"I see." Her mouth turned up a bit as she combed her fingers through her hair. "You've looked into this thoroughly."

"I told you, it's business."

"All right, Brandon," she said, conceding his point. "Where would we work? Not here," she said quickly. There was a sudden pressure in her chest. "I won't work with you here."

"No, I thought not. I have a place," he continued when Raven remained silent. "It's in Cornwall."

"Cornwall?" Raven repeated. "Why Cornwall?"

"Because it's quiet and isolated, and no one, especially the press, knows I have it. They'll be all over us when they hear we're working together, especially on this project. It's too hot an item."

"Couldn't we just rent a small cave on the coast somewhere?"

He laughed and caught her hair in his hand. "You

know how poor the acoustics are in a cave. Cornwall's incredible in the spring, Raven. Come with me."

She lifted a hand to his chest to push back, not certain if she was about to agree or decline. He could still draw too much from her too effortlessly. She needed to think, she decided; a few days to put it all in perspective.

"Raven."

She turned to see Julie in the doorway. "Yes?"

"There's a call for you."

Vaguely annoyed, Raven frowned at her. "Can't it wait, Julie? I..."

"It's on your private line."

Brand felt her stiffen and looked down curiously. Her eyes were completely blank.

"I see." Her voice was calm, but he detected the faintest of tremors.

"Raven?" Without thinking, he took her by the shoulders and turned her to face him. "What is it?"

"Nothing." She drew out of his arms. There was something remote about her now, something distant that puzzled him. "Have some more tea," she invited and smiled, but her eyes remained blank. "I'll be back in a minute."

She was gone for more than ten, and Brand had begun to pace restlessly through the room. Raven was definitely no longer the malleable young girl she had been five years before; he knew that. He wasn't at all certain she would agree to work with him. He wanted her—for the project and yes, for himself. Holding her, tasting her again, had stirred up much more than memories. She fascinated him and always had. Even when she had been so young, there had been an air of secrecy about her. There still was. It was as if she kept certain parts of herself locked in a closet out of reach. She had held him off five years before in more than a physical sense. It had frustrated him then and continued to frustrate him.

But he was older, too. He'd made mistakes with her before and had no intention of repeating them. Brand knew what he wanted and was determined to get it. Sitting back at the piano, he began to play the song he had written with Raven. He remembered her voice, warm and sultry, in his ear. He was nearly at the end when he sensed her presence.

Glancing up, Brand saw her standing in the doorway. Her eyes were unusually dark and intense. Then he realized it was because she was pale, and the contrast accentuated the gray of her irises. Had the song disturbed her that much? He stopped immediately and rose to go to her.

"Raven..."

"I've decided to do it," she interrupted. Her hands were folded neatly in front of her, her eyes direct.

"Good." He took her hands and found them chilled. "Are you all right?"

"Yes, of course." She removed her hands from his, but her gaze never faltered. "I suppose Henderson will fill me in on all the details."

Something about her calm disturbed him. It was as if she'd set part of herself aside. "Let's have dinner, Raven." The urge to be with her, to pierce her armor, was almost overwhelming. "I'll take you to the Bistro; you always liked it there."

"Not tonight, Brandon, I...have some things to do."

"Tomorrow," he insisted, knowing he was pushing but unable to prevent himself. She looked suddenly weary.

"Yes, all right, tomorrow." She gave him a tired smile.

"I'm sorry, but I'll have to ask you to leave now, Brandon. I didn't realize how late it was."

"All right." Bending toward her, he gently kissed her. It was an instinctive gesture, one that demanded no response. He felt the need to warm her, protect her. "Seven tomorrow," he told her. "I'm at the Bel-Air; you only have to call me."

Raven waited until she heard the front door shut behind her. She pressed the heel of her hand to her brow and let the tide of emotions rush through her. There were no tears, but a blinding headache raged behind her eyes. She felt Julie's hand on her shoulder.

"They found her?" Julie asked, concerned. Automatically she began kneading the tension from Raven's shoulders.

"Yes, they found her." She let out a long, deep breath. "She's coming back."

Chapter 4

The sanitarium was white and clean. The architect, a good one, had conceived a restful building without medical overtones. The uninformed might have mistaken it for an exclusive hotel snuggled in California's scenic Ojai. It was a proud, elegantly fashioned building with several magnificent views of the countryside. Raven detested it.

Inside, the floors were thickly carpeted, and conversation was always low-key. Raven hated the controlled silence, the padded quiet. The staff members wore street clothes and only small, discreet badges to identify themselves, and they were among the best trained in the country, just as the Fieldmore Clinic was the best detoxification center on the west coast. Raven had made certain of its reputation before she had brought her mother there for the first time over five years before.

Raven waited in Justin Karter's paneled, book-lined, tasteful office. It received its southern exposure through a wide, thick-paned window. The morning sunlight beamed in on a thriving collection of leafy green plants. Raven wondered idly why her own plants seemed always to put up only a halfhearted struggle for life, one they usually lost. Perhaps she should ask Dr. Karter what his secret was. She laughed a little and rubbed her fingers on the nagging headache between her brows.

How she hated these visits and the leathery, glossy smell of his office. She was cold and cupped her elbows, hugging her arms across her midriff. Raven was always cold in the Fieldmore Clinic, from the moment she walked through the stately white double doors until long after she walked out again. It was a penetrating cold that went straight to the bone. Turning away from the window, she paced nervously around the room. When she heard the door open, she stopped and turned around slowly.

Karter entered, a small, youthful man with a corn-colored beard and healthy pink cheeks. He had an earnest face, accentuated by tortoise-rimmed glasses and a faint smattering of freckles. Under other circumstances, Raven would have liked his face, even warmed to it.

"Ms. Williams." He held out a hand and took hers in a quick, professional grip. It was cold, he realized, and as fragile as he remembered. Her hair was pinned up at the nape of her neck, and she looked young and pale in the dark tailored suit. This woman was far different from the vibrant, laughing entertainer he had watched on television a few weeks before.

"Hello, Dr. Karter."

It always amazed him that the rich, full-toned voice

belonged to such a small, delicate-looking woman. He had thought the same years before when she had been hardly more than a child. He was an ardent fan but had never asked her to sign any of the albums in his collection. It would, he knew, embarrass them both.

"Please sit down, Ms. Williams. Could I get you some coffee?"

"No, please." She swallowed. Her throat was always dry when she spoke to him. "I'd like to see my mother first."

"There are a few things I'd like to discuss with you."

He watched her moisten her lips, the only sign of agitation. "After I've seen her."

"All right." Karter took her by the arm and led her from the room. They walked across the quiet, carpeted hallway to the elevators. "Ms. Williams," he began. He would have liked to have called her Raven. He thought of her as Raven, just as the rest of the world did. But he could never quite break through the film of reserve she slipped on in his presence. It was, Karter knew, because he knew her secrets. She trusted him to keep them but was never comfortable with him. She turned to him now, her great, gray eyes direct and expressionless.

"Yes, Doctor?" Only once had Raven ever broken down in his presence, and she had promised herself she would never do so again. She would not be destroyed by her mother's illness, and she would not make a public display of herself.

"I don't want you to be shocked by your mother's appearance." They stepped into the elevator together, and he kept his hand on her arm. "She had made a great deal of progress during her last stay here, but she left prematurely, as you know. Over the past three months, her condition has...deteriorated."

"Please," Raven said wearily, "don't be delicate. I know where she was found and how. You'll dry her out again, and in a couple of months she'll leave and it'll start all over. It never changes."

"Alcoholics fight a continuing battle."

"Don't tell me about alcoholics," she shot back. The reserve cracked, and the emotion poured through. "Don't preach to me about battles." She stopped herself, then, shaking her head, pressed her fingers to the concentrated source of her headache. "I know all about alcoholics," she said more calmly. "I haven't your dedication or your optimism."

"You keep bringing her back," he reminded Raven softly.

"She's my mother." The elevator doors slid open, and Raven walked through them.

Her skin grew colder as they moved down the hallway. There were doors on either side, but she refused to think of the people beyond them. The hospital flavor was stronger here. Raven thought she could smell the antiseptic, the hovering medicinal odor that always made a hint of nausea roll in her stomach. When Karter stopped in front of a door and reached for a knob, Raven laid a hand on top of his.

"I'll see her alone, please."

He sensed her rigid control. Her eyes were calm, but he had seen the quick flash of panic in them. Her fingers didn't tremble on his hand but were stiff and icy. "All right. But only a few minutes. There are complications we need to discuss." He took his hand from the knob. "I'll wait for you here."

Raven nodded and twisted the knob herself. She took a moment, struggling to gather every ounce of strength, then walked inside.

The woman lay in a hospital bed on good linen sheets, dozing lightly. There was a tube feeding liquid into her through a needle in her arm. The drapes were drawn, and the room was in shadows. It was a comfortable room painted in soft blue with an ivory carpet and a few good paintings. With her fingers dug into the leather bag she carried, Raven approached the bed.

Raven's first thought was that her mother had lost weight. There were hollows in her cheeks, and her skin had the familiar unhealthy yellow cast. Her dark hair was cropped short and streaked liberally with gray. It had been lovely hair, Raven remembered, glossy and full. Her face was gaunt, with deathly circles under the eyes and a mouth that seemed dry and pulled in. The helplessness stabbed at Raven, and for a minute she closed her eyes against it. She let them fall while she looked down on the sleeping woman. Without a sound, without moving, the woman in bed opened her eyes. They were dark and gray like her daughter's.

"Mama." Raven let the tears roll freely. "Why?"

By the time Raven got to her front door, she was exhausted. She wanted bed and oblivion. The headache was still with her, but the pain had turned into a dull, sickening throb. Closing the door behind her, she leaned back on it, trying to summon the strength to walk up the stairs.

"Raven?"

She opened her eyes and watched Julie come down the hall toward her. Seeing Raven so pale and beaten,

Julie slipped an arm around her shoulders. Her concern took the form of a scolding. "You should have let me go with you. I should never have let you go alone." She was already guiding Raven up the stairs.

"My mother, my problem," Raven said tiredly.

"That's the only selfish part of you," Julie said in a low, furious voice as they entered Raven's bedroom. "I'm supposed to be your friend. You'd never let me go through something like this alone."

"Please, don't be angry with me." Raven swayed on her feet as Julie stripped off the dark suit jacket. "It's something I feel is my responsibility, just mine. I've felt that way for too long to change now."

"I am angry with you." Julie's voice was tight as she slipped the matching skirt down over Raven's hips. "This is the only thing you do that makes me genuinely angry with you. I can't stand it when you do this to yourself." She looked back at the pale, tired face. "Have you eaten?" Raven shook her head as she stepped out of the skirt. "And you won't," she concluded, brushing Raven's fumbling hands away from the buttons of the white lawn blouse. She undid them herself, then pushed the material from Raven's shoulders. Raven stood, unresisting.

"I'm having dinner with Brandon," Raven murmured, going willingly as Julie guided her toward the bed.

"I'll call him and cancel. I can bring you up something later. You need to sleep."

"No." Raven slipped between the crisp, cool sheets. "I want to go. I need to go," she corrected as she shut her eyes. "I need to get out; I don't want to think for a while. I'll rest now. He won't be here until seven."

Julie walked over to pull the shades. Even before the room was darkened, Raven was asleep.

* * *

It was some minutes past seven when Julie opened the door to Brandon. He wore a stone-colored suit with a navy shirt open at the throat. He looked casually elegant, Julie thought. The nosegay of violets was charming rather than silly in his hands. He lifted a brow at the clinging black sheath she wore.

"Hello, Julie. You look terrific." He plucked one of the violets out of the nosegay and handed it to her. "Going out?"

Julie accepted the flower. "In a little while," she answered. "Raven should be down in a minute. Brand…" Hesitating, Julie shook her head, then turned to lead him into the music room. "I'll fix you a drink. Bourbon, isn't it? Neat."

Brand caught her arm. "That isn't what you were going to say."

She took a deep breath. "No." For a moment longer she hesitated, then began, fixing him with her dark brown eyes. "Raven's very important to me. There aren't many like her, especially in this town. She's genuine, and though she thinks she has, she hasn't really developed any hard edges yet. I wouldn't like to see her hurt, especially right now. No, I won't answer any questions," she said, anticipating him. "It's Raven's story, not mine. But I'm going to tell you this: She needs a light touch and a great deal of patience. You'd better have them both."

"How much do you know about what happened between us five years ago, Julie?" Brandon asked.

"I know what Raven told me."

"One day you ought to ask me how I felt and why I left."

"And would you tell me?"

"Yes," he returned without hesitation. "I would."

"I'm sorry!" Raven came dashing down the stairs in a filmy flutter of white. "I hate to be late." Her hair settled in silky confusion over the shoulders of the thin voile dress as she stopped at the foot of the stairs. "I couldn't seem to find my shoes."

There was a becoming blush of color on her cheeks, and her eyes were bright and full of laughter. It passed through Brand's mind quickly, and then was discarded, that she looked a little too bright, a little too vibrant.

"Beautiful as ever." He handed her the flowers. "I've never minded waiting for you."

"Ah, the golden Irish tongue," she murmured as she buried her face in the violets. "I've missed it." Raven held the flowers up to her nose while her eyes laughed at him over them. "And I believe I'll let you spoil me tonight, Brandon. I'm in a mood to be pampered."

He took her free hand in his. "Where do you want to go?"

"Anywhere. Everywhere." She tossed her head. "But dinner first. I'm starving."

"All right, I'll buy you a cheeseburger."

"Some things do stay the same," she commented before she turned to Julie. "You have fun, and don't worry about me." She paused a moment, then smiled and kissed her cheek. "I promise I won't lose my key. And say hello to…" She hesitated as she walked toward the door with Brandon. "Who is it tonight?"

"Lorenzo," Julie answered, watching them. "The shoe baron."

"Oh, yes." Raven laughed as they walked into the cool, early spring air. "Amazing." She tucked her arm through Brandon's. "Julie's always having some millionaire fall in love with her. It's a gift."

"Shoe baron?" Brand questioned as he opened the car door for Raven.

"*Mmm.* Italian. He wears beautiful designer suits and looks as though he should be stamped on the head of a coin."

Brand slid in beside her and in an old reflex gesture brushed the hair that lay on her shoulder behind her back. "Serious?"

Raven tried not to be moved by the touch of his fingers. "No more serious than the oil tycoon or the perfume magnate." The leathery smell of the upholstery reminded her abruptly of Karter's office. Quickly she pushed away the sensation. "What are you going to feed me, Brandon?" she asked brightly—too brightly. "I warn you, I'm starving."

He circled her throat with his hand so that she had no choice but to meet his eyes directly. "Are you going to tell me what's wrong?"

He'd always seen too much too quickly, she thought. It was one of the qualities that had made him an exceptional songwriter.

Raven placed her hand on top of his. "No questions, Brandon, not now."

She felt his hesitation. Then he turned his hand over and gripped hers. Slowly, overriding her initial resistance, he brought her palm to his lips. "Not now," he agreed, watching her eyes. "I can still move you," he murmured and smiled as though the knowledge pleased him. "I can feel it."

Raven felt the tremors racing up her arms. "Yes." She

drew her hand from his but kept her eyes steady. "You can still move me. But things aren't the same anymore."

He grinned, a quick flash of white teeth, then started the engine. "No, things aren't the same anymore."

As he pulled away, she had the uncomfortable impression that they had said the same words but meant two different things.

Dinner was quiet and intimate and perfect. They ate in a tiny old inn they had once discovered by chance. Here, Brand knew, there would be no interruptions for autographs, no greetings and drinks from old acquaintances. Here there would be just the two of them, a man and a woman amidst candlelight, wine, fine food, and an intimate atmosphere.

As the evening wore on, Raven's smile became more spontaneous, less desperate, and the unhappiness he had seen deep in her eyes before now faded. Though he noticed the transition, Brand made no comment.

"I feel like I haven't eaten in a week," Raven managed between bites of the tender roast beef that was the house speciality.

"Want some of mine?" Brand offered his plate.

Raven scooped up a bit of baked potato; her eyes seemed to laugh at him. "We'll have them wrap it up so I can take it home. I want to leave room for dessert. Did you see that pastry tray?"

"I suppose I could roll you to Cornwall," Brand considered, adding some burgundy to his glass.

Raven laughed, a throaty sound that appealed and aroused. "I'll be a bag of bones by the time we go to Cornwall," she claimed. "You know what those whirlwind tours can do." She shook her head as he offered her more wine.

"One-night stands from San Francisco to New York." Brand lifted his glass as Raven gave him a quizzing look. "I spoke to Henderson." He twirled a strand of her hair around his finger so absently, Raven was certain he was unaware of the gesture. She made no complaint. "If it's agreeable with you, I'll meet you in New York at the end of the tour. We'll fly to England from there."

"All right." She took a deep breath, having finally reached her fill of the roast beef. "You'd better set it up with Julie. I haven't any memory for dates and times. Are you staying in the States until then?"

"I'm doing a couple of weeks in Vegas." He brushed his fingers across her cheek, and when she would have resisted, he laid his hand companionably over hers. "I haven't played there in quite a while. I don't suppose it's changed."

She laughed and shook her head. "No. I played there, oh, about six months ago, I guess. Julie won a bundle at the baccarat table. I was a victim of the slots."

"I read the reviews. Were you as sensational as they said?" He smiled at her while one finger played with the thin gold bracelet at her wrist.

"Oh, I was much more sensational than they said," she assured him.

"I'd like to have seen you." His finger drifted lazily to her pulse. He felt it jump at his touch. "It's been much too long since I've heard you sing."

"You heard me just the other day in the studio," she pointed out. She took her hand from his to reach for her wine. He easily took her other one. "Brandon," she began, half-amused.

"I've heard you over the radio as well," he continued, "but it's not the same as watching you come alive at a concert. Or," he smiled as his voice took on that soft, intimate note she remembered, "listening to you when you sing just for me."

His tone was as smooth as the burgundy she drank. Knowing how easily he could cloud her brain, she vowed to keep their conversation light. "Do you know what I want right now?" She lowered her own voice as she leaned toward him, but he recognized the laughter in her eyes.

"Dessert," he answered.

"You know me so well, Brandon." She smiled.

She wanted to go dancing. By mutual consent, when they left the restaurant they avoided the popular, trendy spots in town and found a crowded, smoky hole-in-the-wall club with a good band, much like the dozens they had both played in at the beginnings of their respective careers. They thought they wouldn't be recognized there. For almost twenty minutes they were right.

"Excuse me, aren't you Brand Carstairs?" The toothy young blonde stared up at Brand in admiration. Then she glanced at Raven. "And Raven Williams."

"Bob Muldroon," Brand returned in a passable Texas drawl. "And my wife Sheila. Say howdy, Sheila," he instructed as he held her close and swayed on the postage-sized dance floor.

"Howdy," Raven said obligingly.

"Oh, Mr. Carstairs." She giggled and thrust out a cocktail napkin and a pencil. "Please, I'm Debbie. Could you write, 'To my good friend Debbie'?"

"Sure." Brand gave her one of his charming smiles

and told Raven to turn around. He scrawled quickly, using her back for support.

"And you, too, Raven," Debbie asked when he'd finished. "On the other side."

It was typical of her fans to treat her informally. They thought of her as Raven. Her spontaneous warmth made it difficult for anyone to approach her with the awe normally reserved for superstars. Raven wrote on her side of the napkin when Brand offered his back. When she had finished, she noted that Debbie's eyes were wide and fixed on Brand. The pulse in her throat was jumping like a jackhammer. Raven knew what fantasies were dancing in the girl's mind.

"Here you are, Debbie." She touched her hand to bring the girl back to reality.

"Oh." Debbie took the napkin, looked at it blankly a moment, then smiled up at Brand. "Thanks." She looked at Raven, then ran a hand through her hair as if she had just realized what she had done. "Thanks a lot."

"You're welcome." Brand smiled but began to edge Raven toward the door.

It was too much to expect that the incident had gone unnoticed or that no one else would recognize them. For the next fifteen minutes they were wedged between the crowd and the door, signing autographs and dealing with a barrage of questions. Brand made certain they weren't separated from each other as he slowly maneuvered a path through the crowd.

They were jostled and shoved a bit but he judged the crowd to be fairly civilized. It was still early by L.A. standards, and there hadn't been too much drinking yet. Still he wanted her out. This type of situation was notoriously explosive; the mood could change abruptly. One overenthusiastic fan and it could all be different. And ugly. Raven signed and signed some more while an occasional hand reached out to touch her hair. Brand felt a small wave of relief as he finally drew her out into the fresh air. Only a few followed them out of the club, and they were able to make their way to Brand's car with just a smattering of extra autographs.

"Damn it. I'm sorry." He leaned across her to lock her door. "I should have known better than to have taken you there."

Raven took a long breath, combing her hair back from her face with her fingers as she turned to him. "Don't be silly; I wanted to go. Besides, the people were nice."

"They aren't always," he muttered as the car merged with Los Angeles traffic.

"No." She leaned back, letting her body relax. "But I've been pretty lucky. Things have only gotten out of hand once or twice. It's the hype, I suppose, and it's to be expected that fans sometimes forget we're flesh and blood."

"So they try to take little chunks of us home with them."

"That," Raven said dryly, "can be a problem. I remember seeing a film clip of a concert you gave, oh, seven or eight years ago." She leaned her elbow on the back of the seat now and cupped her cheek in her palm. "A London concert where the fans broke through the security. They seemed to swallow you whole. It must have been dreadful."

"They loved me enough to give me a couple of broken ribs."

"Oh, Brandon." She sat up straight now, shocked. "That's terrible. I never knew that."

He smiled and moved his shoulders. "We played it down. It did rather spoil my taste for live concerts for a while. I got over it." He turned, heading toward the hills. "Security's tighter these days."

"I don't know if I'd be able to face an audience after something like that."

"Where else would you get the adrenaline?" he countered. "We need it, don't we? That instant gratification of applause." He laughed and pulled her over beside him. "Why else do we do it, Raven? Why else are there countless others out there scrambling to make it? Why did you start up the road, Raven?"

"To escape," she answered before she had time to think. She sighed and relaxed against his shoulder when he didn't demand an explanation. "Music was always something I could hold on to. It was constant, dependable. I needed something that was wholly mine." She turned her head a bit to study his profile. "Why did you?"

"For most of the same reasons, I suppose. I had something to say, and I wanted people to remember I said it."

She laughed. "And you were so radical at the start of your career. Such pounding, demanding songs. You were music's bad boy for some time."

"I've mellowed," he told her.

"'Fire Hot' didn't sound mellow to me," she commented. "Wasn't that the lead cut on your last album?"

He grinned, glancing down at her briefly. "I have to keep my hand in."

"It was number one on the charts for ten consecutive weeks," she pointed out. "That isn't bad for mellow."

"That's right," he agreed as if he'd just remembered. "It knocked off a little number of yours, didn't it? It was kind of a sweet little arrangement, as I recall. Maybe a bit heavy on the strings, but…"

She gave him an enthusiastic punch on the arm.

"Raven," Brand complained mildly. "You shouldn't distract me when I'm driving."

"That sweet little arrangement went platinum."

"I said it was sweet," he reminded her. "And the lyrics weren't bad. A bit sentimental, maybe, but…"

"I like sentimental lyrics," she told him, giving him another jab on the arm. "Not every song has to be a blistering social commentary."

"Of course not," he agreed reasonably. "There's always room for cute little ditties."

"Cute little ditties," Raven repeated, hardly aware that they had fallen back into one of their oldest habits by debating each other's work. "Just because I don't go in for showboating or lyrical trickery," she began. But when he swung off to the side of the road, she narrowed her eyes at him. "What are you doing?"

"Pulling over before you punch me again." He grinned and flicked a finger down her nose. "Showboating?"

"Showboating," she repeated. "What else do you call that guitar and piano duel at the end of 'Fire Hot'?"

"A classy way to fade out a song," he returned, and though she agreed with him, Raven made a sound of derision.

"I don't need the gadgetry. My songs are…"

"Overly sentimental."

She lifted a haughty brow. "If you feel my music is overly sentimental and cute, how do you imagine we'll work together?"

"Perfectly," he told her. "We'll balance each other, Raven, just as we always did."

"We're going to have terrible fights," she predicted.

"Yes, I imagine we will."

"And," she added, failing to suppress a smile, "you won't always win."

"Good. Then the fights won't be boring." He pulled her to him, and when she resisted, he cradled her head on his shoulder again. "Look," he ordered, pointing out the window, "why is it cities always look better at night from above?"

Raven looked down on the glittering Los Angeles skyline. "I suppose it's the mystique. It makes you wonder what's going on and you can't see how fast it's moving. Up here it's quiet." She felt his lips brush her temple. "Brandon." She drew away, but he stopped her.

"Don't pull away from me, Raven." It was a low, murmured request that shot heat up her spine. "Don't pull away from me."

His head lowered slowly, and his lips nibbled at hers, hardly touching, but the hand at the back of her neck was firm. He kept her facing him while he changed the angle of the kiss. His lips were persuasive, seductive. He kissed the soft, dewy skin of her cheeks, the fragile, closed eyelids, the scented hair at her temple. She could feel herself floating toward him as she always had, losing herself to him.

Her lips parted so that when his returned, he found them inviting him to explore. The kiss deepened, but slowly, as if he savored the taste of her on his tongue. Her hand slid up his chest until she held him and their bodies touched. He murmured something, then pressed his mouth against the curve of her neck. Her scent rose and enveloped him.

She moaned when he took her breast, a sound of both

hunger and protest. His mouth came back to hers, plundering now as he responded to the need he felt flowing from her. She was unresisting, as open and warm as a shaft of sunlight. Her body was yearning toward him, melting irresistibly. She thought his hand burned through the thin fabric of her dress and set fire to her naked skin. It had been so long, she thought dizzily, so long since she had felt anything this intensely, needed anything this desperately. Her whole being tuned itself to him.

"Raven." His mouth was against her ear, her throat, the hollow of her cheek. "Oh, God, I want you." The kiss was urgent now, his hands no longer gentle. "So long," he said, echoing her earlier thought. "It's been so long. Come back with me. Let me take you back with me to the hotel. Stay with me tonight."

Passion flooded her senses. His tongue trailed over her warmed skin until he came again to her mouth. Then he took possession. The heat was building, strangling the breath in her throat, suffocating her. There was a fierce tug of war between fear and desire. She began to struggle.

"No." She took deep gulps of air. "Don't."

Brand took her by the shoulders and with one quick jerk had her face turned back up to his. "Why?" he demanded roughly. "You want me, I can feel it."

"No." She shook her head, and her hands trembled as she pushed at his chest. "I don't. I can't." Raven tried to deepen her breathing to steady it. "You're hurting me, Brandon. Please let me go."

Slowly he relaxed his fingers, then released her. "The same old story," he murmured. Turning away from her, he carefully drew out a cigarette and lit it. "You still give until I'm halfway mad, then pull away from me."

He took a long, deep drag. "I should have been better prepared for it."

"You're not fair. I didn't start this; I never wanted…"

"You wanted," he tossed back furiously. "Damn it, Raven, you wanted. I've had enough women to know when I'm holding one who wants me."

She stiffened against the ache that was speeding through her. "You're better off with one of your many women, Brandon. I told you I wouldn't fall at your feet this time, and I meant it. If we can have a professional relationship, fine." She swallowed and straightened the hair his fingers had so recently caressed. "If you can't work with things on that level, then you'd best find another partner."

"I have the one I want." He tossed his cigarette through the open window. "We'll play it your way for a while, Raven. We're both professionals, and we both know what this musical's going to do for our careers." He started the engine. "I'll take you home."

Chapter 5

Raven hated to be late for a party, but there was no help for it. Her schedule was drum tight. If it hadn't been important that she be there, to rub elbows with Lauren Chase and a few other principals from the cast and crew of *Fantasy,* she'd have bowed out. There were only two days left before the start of her tour.

The truth was, Raven had forgotten about the party. Rehearsals had run over, then she had found herself driving into Beverly Hills to window shop. She hadn't wanted to buy anything but had simply wanted to do something mindless. For weeks there had been nothing but demand after demand, and she could look forward only to more of the same in the weeks to come. She would steal a few hours. She didn't want to think about her mother and the clean white sanitarium or song lists and cues or her confusion over Brand as she browsed through the treasures at Neiman Marcus and Gucci. She looked at everything and bought nothing.

Arriving home, she was met by a huge handwritten note from Julie tacked on her bedroom door.

Party at Steve Jarett's. I know—you forgot. IMPORTANT! Get your glad rags together, babe, and go. Out with Lorenzo for dinner, we'll see you there. J.

Raven swore briefly, rebelled, then capitulated before she stalked to the closet to choose an outfit. An hour later she was cruising fast through the Hollywood Hills. It was important that she be there.

Steve Jarett was directing *Fantasy*. He was, at the moment, the silver screen's boy wonder, having just directed three major successes in a row. Raven wanted *Fantasy* to be his fourth as much as he did.

The party would be crowded, she mused, and looked wistfully at the open, star-studded sky. And noisy. Abruptly she laughed at herself. Since when did a noisy, crowded party become a trial by fire? There had been a time when she had enjoyed them. And there was no denying that the people who haunted these parties were fascinating and full of incredible stories. Raven could still be intrigued. It was just that… She sighed, allowing herself to admit the real reason she had dragged her feet. Brandon would be there. He was bound to be.

Would he bring a date? she wondered. Why wouldn't he? She answered herself shortly, downshifting as she took a curve. Unless he decided to wait and take his pick from the women there. Raven sighed again, seeing the blaze of lights that told her she was approaching Jarett's house. It was ridiculous to allow herself to get tied up in knots over something that had ended years before.

Her headlights caught the dull gleam of sturdy iron gates, and she slowed. The guard took her name, checked his list, then admitted her. She could hear the music before she was halfway up the curving, palm-lined drive.

There was a white-jacketed teenager waiting to hand her out of the Lamborghini. He was probably a struggling actor or an aspiring screenwriter or cinematographer, Raven thought as she smiled at him.

"Hi, I'm late. Do you think I can slip in without anybody noticing?"

"I don't think so, Ms. Williams, not looking like that."

Raven lifted her brows, surprised that he had recognized her so quickly in the dim light. But even if he had missed the face and hair, she realized, he would never have mistaken the voice.

"That's a compliment, isn't it?" she asked.

"Yes, ma'am," he said so warmly that she laughed.

"Well, I'm going to do my best, anyway. I don't like entrances unless they're on stage." She studied the sprawling, white brick mansion. "There must be a side door."

"Around to the left." He pointed. "There's a set of glass doors that lead into the library. Go through there and turn left. You should be able to slip in without being noticed."

"Thanks." She went to take a bill out of her purse, discovered she had left it in the car and leaned in the window to retrieve it. After a moment's search, she found a twenty and handed it to him.

"Thank *you!* Raven," he enthused as she turned away.

Then he called to her, "Ms. Williams?" Raven turned back with a half smile. "Would you sign it for me?"

She tossed back her hair. "The bill?"

"Yeah."

She laughed and shook her head. "A fat lot of good it would do you then. Here." She dug into her bag again and came up with a slip of paper. One side was scrawled on, a list of groceries Julie had given her a few weeks before, but the other side was blank. "What's your name?" she demanded.

"Sam, Sam Rheinhart."

"Here, Sam Rheinhart," she said. Dashing off a quick line on the paper, she gave him the autograph. He stared after her, the twenty in one hand and the grocery list in the other, as she rushed off.

Raven found the glass doors without trouble. Though they were closed, the sounds of the party came clearly through. There were groups of people out back listening to a very loud rock band and drifting around by the pool. She stayed in the shadows. She wore an ankle-length skirt and a dolman-sleeve pullover in a dark plum color with silver metallic threads running through which captured the moonlight. Entering through the library, she gave herself a moment to adjust to the darkness before groping her way to the door.

There was no one in the hall immediately outside. Pleased with herself, Raven stepped out and gravitated slowly toward the focus of noise.

"Why, Raven!" It was Carly Devers, a tiny blond fluff of an actress with a little-girl voice and a rapier sharp talent. Though they generally moved in different circles, Raven liked her. "I didn't know you were here."

"Hi, Carly." They exchanged obligatory brushes of

the cheek. "Congratulations are in order, aren't they? I heard you were being signed as second lead in *Fantasy*."

"It's still in the working stage, but it looks like it. It's a gem of a part, and of course, working with Steve is *the* thing to do these days." As she spoke, she gave Raven a piercing look with her baby blue eyes. "You look fabulous," she said. Raven knew she meant it. "And of course, congratulations are in order for you as well, aren't they?"

"Yes, I'm excited about doing the score."

Carly tilted her head, and a smile spread over her face. "I was thinking more about Brand Carstairs than the score, darling." Raven's smile faded instantly. "Oops." Carly's smile only widened. "Still tender." There was no malice in her amusement. She linked her arm with Raven's. "I'd keep your little collaboration very tight this time around, Raven. I'm tempted to make a play for him myself, and I guarantee I'm not alone."

"What happened to Dirk Wagner?" Raven reminded herself to play it light as they drew closer to the laughter and murmurs of the party.

"Old news, darling, do try to keep up." Carly laughed, a tinkling bell of a sound that Raven could not help but respond to. "Still, I don't make it a habit to tread on someone else's territory."

"No signs posted, Carly," Raven said carelessly.

"Hmm." Carly tossed back a lock of silver-blond hair. A waiter passed by with a tray of glasses, and she neatly plucked off two. "I've heard he's a marvelous lover," she commented, her eyes bright and direct on Raven's.

Raven returned the look equably and accepted the offered champagne. "Have you? But then, I imagine that's old news, too."

"Touché," Carly murmured into her glass.

"Is Brandon here?" she asked, trying to prove to herself and her companion that the conversation meant nothing.

"Here and there," Carly said ambiguously. "I haven't decided whether he's been trying to avoid the flocks of females that crawl around him or if he's seeking them out. He doesn't give away much, does he?"

Raven uttered a noncommittal sound and shrugged. It was time, she decided, to change the subject. "Have you seen Steve? I suppose I should fight my way through and say hello."

It was a typical enough party, Raven decided. Clothes ranged from Rive Gauche to Salvation Army. There was a steady drum beat from the band by the pool underlying the talk and laughter. The doors to the terrace were open wide, letting out the clouds of smoke and allowing the warm night air to circulate freely. The expansive lawns were ablaze with colored lights. Raven was more interested in the people but gave the room itself a quick survey.

It was decorated stunningly in white—walls, furniture, rugs—with a few vivid green accents slashed here and there. Raven decided it was gorgeous and that she couldn't have lived in it in a million years. She'd never be able to put her feet up on the elegant, free-form glass coffee table. She went back to the people.

Her eyes sought out Julie with her handsome Italian millionaire. She spotted Wayne with one of his bone-thin models hanging on his arm. Raven decided that the rumors that he would design the costumes for *Fantasy* must be true. There were others Raven recognized: producers, two major stars whom she had watched countless times in darkened theaters, a choreographer she knew only by face and reputation, a screenwriter she had met before socially and several others whom she knew casually or not at all. She and Carly were both drawn into the vortex of the party.

There were dozens of greetings to exchange, along with hand-kissing and cheek-brushing, before Raven could begin to inch her way back toward the edges. She was always more comfortable with one or two people at a time than with a crowd, unless she was onstage. At a touch on her arm, she turned and found herself facing her host.

"Well, hello." Raven smiled, appreciating the chance for a tête-à-tête.

"Hi. I was afraid you weren't going to make it."

Raven realized she shouldn't have been surprised that he had noticed her absence in the crowds of people. Steve Jarett noticed everything. He was a small, slight man with a pale, intense face and dark beard who looked ten years younger than his thirty-seven years. He was considered a perfectionist, often a pain when shooting, but the maker of beautiful films. He had a reputation for patience—enough to cause him to shoot a scene over and over and over again until he got precisely what he wanted. Five years before, he had stunned the industry with a low-budget sleeper that had become the unchallenged hit of the year. His first film had received an Oscar and had opened all the doors that had previously been firmly shut in his face. Steve Jarett held the keys now and knew exactly which ones to use.

He held both of her hands and studied her face. It was he who had insisted on Brand Carstairs as the writer of the original score for *Fantasy* and he who had approved the choice of Raven Williams as collaborator. *Fantasy* was his first musical, and he wasn't going to make any mistakes.

"Lauren's here," he said at length. "Have you met her?"

"No, I'd like to."

"I'd like you to get a real feel for her. I've copies of all of her films and records. You might study them before you begin work on the score."

Raven's brow rose. "I don't think I've missed any of her movies, but I'll watch them again. She is the core of the story."

He beamed suddenly, unexpectedly. "Exactly. And you know Jack Ladd."

"Yes, we've worked together before. You couldn't have picked a better Joe."

"I'm making him work off ten pounds," Jarett said, plucking a canape from a tray. "He has some very unflattering things to say about me at the moment."

"But he's taking off the ten pounds," Raven observed.

Jarett grinned. "Ounce by ounce. We go to the same gym. I keep reminding him Joe's a struggling writer, not a fulfilled hedonist."

Raven gave a low, gurgling laugh and popped a bite of cheese into her mouth. "Overweight or not, you're assembling a remarkable team. I don't know how you managed to wrangle Larry Keaston into choreographing. He's been retired for five years."

"Bribes and perseverance," Jarett said easily, glancing over to where the trim, white-haired former dancer lounged in a pearl-colored armchair. "I'm talking him into doing a cameo." He grinned at Raven again. "He's pretending dignified reluctance, but he's dying to get in front of the cameras again."

"If you can even get him to do a time step on film, you'll have the biggest coup of the decade," Raven observed and shook her head. And he'd do it, she thought. He has the touch.

"He's a big fan of yours," Jarett remarked and watched Raven's eyes widen.

"Of mine? You're joking."

"I am not." He gave Raven a curious look. "He wants to meet you."

Raven stared at Jarett, then again at Larry Keaston. Such things never ceased to amaze her. How many times, as a child, had she watched his movies on fuzzy black and white TV sets in cramped rooms while she had waited for her mother to come home? "You don't have to ask me twice," she told Jarett. She linked her arm in his.

Time passed quickly as Raven began enjoying herself. She talked at length with Larry Keaston and discovered her girlhood idol to be personable and witty. He spoke in a string of expletives delivered in his posh Boston accent. Though she spoke briefly with Jack Ladd, she had yet to meet Lauren Chase when she spotted Wayne drinking quietly in a corner.

"All alone?" she asked as she joined him.

"Observing the masses, my dear," he told her, sipping lightly from his whiskey and soda. "It's amazing how intelligent people will insist on clothing themselves in inappropriate costumes. Observe Lela Marring," he suggested, tilting his head toward a towering brunette in a narrow, pink minidress. "I have no idea why a woman would care to wear a place mat in public."

Raven suppressed a giggle. "She has very nice legs."

"Yes, all five feet of them." He swerved his line of

vision. "Then, of course, there's Marshall Peters, who's trying to start a new trend. Chest hair and red satin."

Raven followed the direction of his gaze and this time did giggle. "Not everyone has your savoir-faire, Wayne."

"Of course not," he agreed readily and took out one of his imported cigarettes. "But surely, taste."

"I like the way you've dressed your latest protégée," Raven commented, nodding toward the thin model speaking to a current hot property in the television series game. The model was draped in cobwebby black and gold filigree lace. "I swear, Wayne, she can't be more than eighteen. What do you find to talk about?"

He gave Raven one of his long, sarcastic looks. "Are you being droll, darling?"

She laughed in spite of herself. "Not intentionally."

He gave her a pat on the cheek and lifted his glass again. "I notice Julie has her latest conquest with her, a Latin type with cheekbones."

"Shoes," Raven said vaguely, letting her eyes drift around the room. They rested in disbelief on a girl dressed in skin-tight leather pants and a spangled sweatshirt who wore heart-shaped glasses over heavily kohl-darkened eyes. Knowing Wayne would be horrified, she started to call his attention to her when she spotted Brand across the room.

His eyes were already on hers. Raven realized with a jolt that he had been watching her for some time. It had been at just such a party that they had first met, with noise and laughter and music all around them. Their eyes had found each other's then also.

It had been Raven's first Hollywood party, and she had been unashamedly overwhelmed. There had been people there whom she had known only as voices over the radio or faces on the screen. She had come alone then, too, but in that case it had been a mistake. She hadn't yet learned how to dodge and twist.

She remembered she had been cornered by an actor, though oddly she couldn't recall his name or his face. She hadn't had the experience to deal with him and was slowly being backed against the wall when her eyes had met Brand's. Raven remembered how he had been watching her then, too, rather lazily, a half smile on his mouth. He must have seen the desperation in her eyes, because his smile had widened before he had started to weave his way through the crowd toward her. With perfect aplomb, Brand had slid between Raven and the actor, then had draped his arm over her shoulders.

"Miss me?" he had asked, and he had kissed her lightly before she could respond. "There're some people outside who want to meet you." He had shot the actor an apologetic glance. "Excuse us."

Before another word could be exchanged, he had propelled Raven through the groups of people and out to a terrace. She could still remember the scent of orange blossoms that had drifted from an orchard nearby and the silver sprinkle of moonlight on the flagstone.

Of course Raven had recognized him and had been flustered. She had managed to regain her poise by the time they were alone in the shadows on the terrace. She had brushed a hand through her hair and smiled at him. "Thanks."

"You're welcome." It had been the first time he had studied her in his direct, quiet fashion. She could still remember the sensation of gentle intrusion. "You're not quite what I expected."

"No?" Raven hadn't known exactly how to take that.

"No." He'd smiled at her. "Would you like to go get some coffee?"

"Yes." The agreement had sprung from her lips before she had given it a moment's thought.

"Good. Let's go." Brand had held out his hand. After a brief hesitation, Raven had put hers into it. It had been as simple as that.

"Raven...Raven."

She was tossed back into the present by the sound of Wayne's voice and his hand on her arm.

"Yes...what?" Blandly Raven looked up at him.

"Your thoughts are written all over your face," he murmured. "Not a wise move in a room full of curious people." Taking a fresh glass of champagne from a tray, he handed it to her. "Drink up."

She was grateful for something to do with her hands and took the glass. "I was just thinking," she said inadequately, then made a sound of frustration at Wayne's dry look. "So," she tried another tactic, "it seems we'll be working on the same project."

"Old home week?" he said with a crooked grin.

She shot him a direct look. "We're professionals," she stated, aware that they both knew whom she was speaking of.

"And friends?" he asked, touching a finger to her cheek.

Raven inclined her head. "We might be; I'm a friendly sort of person."

"Hmm." Wayne glanced over her shoulder and watched Brand approach. "At least he knows how to dress," he murmured, approving of Brand's casual but perfectly cut slate-colored slacks and jacket. "But are you sure Cornwall's necessary? Couldn't you try Sausalito?"

Raven laughed. "Is there anything you don't know?"

"I certainly hope not. Hello, Brand, nice to see you again."

Raven turned, smiling easily. The jolt of the memory had passed. "Hello, Brandon."

"Raven." His eyes stayed on her face. "You haven't met Lauren Chase."

With an effort Raven shifted her eyes from his. "No." She smiled and looked at the woman at his side.

Lauren Chase was a slender wisp of a woman with a thick mane of dark, chestnut hair and sea-green eyes. There was something ethereal about her. Perhaps, Raven thought, it was that pale, almost translucent skin or the way she had of walking as though her feet barely touched the ground. She had a strong mouth that folded itself in at the corners and a long, slender neck that she adorned with gold chains. Raven knew she was well into her thirties and decided she looked it. This was a woman who needn't rely on dewy youth for her beauty.

She had been married twice. The first divorce had become an explosive affair that had received a great deal of ugly press. Her second marriage was now seven years old and had produced two children. Raven recalled there was little written about Lauren Chase's current personal life. Obviously, she had learned to guard her privacy.

"Brand tells me you're going to put the heart in the music." Lauren's voice was full and rich.

"That's quite a responsibility." Raven shot Brand a glance. "Generally Brand considers my lyrics on the sentimental side; often I consider him a cynic."

"Good." Lauren smiled. "Then we should have a score with some meat in it. Steve's given me final word on my own numbers."

Raven lifted a brow. She wasn't altogether certain if this had been a warning or a passing remark. "Then I suppose we should keep you up to date on our progress," she said agreeably.

"By mail and phone," Lauren said, slanting a glance at Brand, "since you're traipsing off halfway around the world to write."

"Artistic temperament," Brand said easily.

"No question, he has it," Raven assured her.

"You should know, I suppose." Lauren lifted a shoulder. Abruptly she fixed Raven with a sharp, straight look. "I want a lot out of this score. This is the one I've been waiting for." It was both a challenge and a demand.

Raven met the look with a slow nod. Lauren Chase was, she decided, the perfect Tessa. "You'll get it."

Lauren touched her upper lip with the tip of her tongue and smiled again. "Yes, I do believe I will at that. Well," she said, turning to Wayne and linking her arm through his, "why don't you get me a drink and tell me about the fabulous costumes you're going to design for me?"

Raven watched them move away. "That," she murmured, toying with the stem of her glass, "is a woman who knows what she wants."

"And she wants an Oscar," Brand remarked. Raven's eyes came back to his. "You'll remember she's been nominated three times and edged out three times. She's determined it isn't going to happen again." He smiled then, fingering the dangling amethyst Raven wore at her ear. "Wouldn't you like to bag one yourself?"

"That's funny, I'd forgotten we could." She let the thought play in her mind. "It sounds good, but we'd better get the thing written before we dream up an acceptance speech."

"How're rehearsals going?"

"Good. Very good." She sipped absently at her champagne. "The band's tight. You leave for Vegas soon, don't you?"

"Yes. Did you come alone?"

She glanced back at him, confused for a moment. "Here? Why, yes. I was late because I'd forgotten about it altogether, but Julie left me a note. Did she introduce you to Lorenzo?"

"No, we haven't crossed paths tonight." As she had begun to search the crowd for Julie, Brand took her chin to bring her eyes back to his. "Will you let me take you home?"

Her expression shifted from startled to wary. "I have my car, Brandon."

"That isn't an answer."

Raven felt herself being drawn in and struggled. "It wouldn't be a good idea."

"Wouldn't it?" She sensed the sarcasm before he smiled, bent down and kissed her. It was a light touch—a tease, a promise or a challenge? "You could be right." He touched her earring again and set it swinging. "I'll see you in a few weeks," he said with a friendly grin, then turned and merged back into the crowd.

Raven stared after him, hardly realizing she had touched her lips with her tongue to seek his taste.

Chapter 6

The theater was dark and quiet. The sound of Raven's footsteps echoed, amplified by the excellent acoustics. Very soon the quiet would be shattered by stagehands, grips, electricians, all the many backstage people who would put together the essential and hardly noticed details of the show. Voices would bounce, mingling with hammering and other sounds of wood and metal. The noise would have a hollow, empty tone, almost like her footsteps. But it was an important sound, an appealing sound, which Raven had always enjoyed.

But she enjoyed the quiet, too and often found herself roaming an empty theater long before she was needed for rehearsals, hours before the fans started to line up outside the main doors. The press would be there then, with their everlasting, eternal questions. And Raven wasn't feeling too chummy with the press at the moment. Already she'd seen a half dozen different stories about herself and Brandon—speculation about their pending collaboration on *Fantasy* and rehashes of their former relationship. Old pictures had been dredged up and reprinted. Old questions were being asked again. Each time it was like bumping the same bruise.

Twice a week she put through a call to the Fieldmore Clinic and held almost identical conversations with Karter. Twice a week he transferred her to her mother's room. Though she knew it was foolish, Raven began to believe all the promises again, all the tearful vows. She began to hope. Without the demands of the tour to keep her occupied and exhausted, she knew she would have been an emotional wreck. Not for the first time in her life, she blessed her luck and her voice.

Mounting the stage, Raven turned to face an imaginary audience. The rows of seats seemed to roll back like a sea. But she knew how to navigate it, had known from the first moment of her first concert. She was an innate performer, just as her voice was natural and untrained. The hesitation, the uncertainty she felt now, had to do with the woman, not the singer. The song had hovered in her mind, but she still paused and considered before bringing it into play. Memories, she felt, could be dangerous things. But she needed to prove something to herself, so she sang. Her voice lifted, drifting to the far corners of the theater; her only accompaniment was her imagination.

Through the clouds and the rain
You were there,
And the sun came through to find us.

Oversentimental? She hadn't thought so when the words had been written. Now Raven sang what she hadn't sung in years. Two minutes and forty-three seconds that bound her and Brand together. Whenever it had played on the radio, she had switched it off, and never, though the requests had been many, had she ever incorporated it in an album or in a concert. She sang it now as a kind of test, remembering the drifting, almost aching harmony of her own low tones combined with Brand's clean, cool voice. She needed to be able to face the memory of working with him if she was to face the reality of doing so. The tour had reached its halfway point. There were only two weeks remaining.

It didn't hurt the way she had been afraid it would; there was no sharp slap across the face. There was more of a warm ache, almost pleasant, somehow sexual. She remembered the last time she had been in Brand's arms in the quiet car in the hills above L.A.

"I've never heard you sing that."

Caught off guard, Raven swung around to stage right, her hand flying in quick panic to her throat. "Oh, Marc!" On a laugh, she let out a long breath. "You scared the wits out of me. I didn't know anyone was here."

"I didn't want you to stop. I've only heard the cut you and Carstairs made of that." He came forward now out of the shadows, and she saw he had an acoustic guitar slung over his shoulder. It was typical; she rarely saw him without an instrument in his hands or close by. "I've always thought it was too bad you never used it again; it's one of your best. But I guess you didn't want to sing it with anyone else."

Raven looked at him with genuine surprise. Of course, that had been the essential reason, but she hadn't real-

ized it herself until that moment. "No, I guess I didn't."
She smiled at him. "I guess I still don't. Did you come
here to practice?"

"I called your room. Julie said you'd probably be
here." He walked to her, and since there were no chairs,
he sat on the floor. Raven sat with him. She crossed her
legs in the dun-colored trousers and let her hair fall over
the soft shoulders of her topaz angora sweater. She was
relaxed with him, ready to talk or jam like any musician.

Raven smiled at Marc as he went through a quick,
complicated lick. "I'm glad you came by. Sometimes I
have to get the feel of the theater before a performance.
They all begin to run together at this part of a tour."
Raven closed her eyes and tilted her head, shaking her
hair back. "Where are we, Kansas City? God, I hate the
thought of getting back on that airplane. Shuttle here,
shuttle there. It always hits me like this at the halfway
point. In a couple of days I'll have my second wind."

Marc let her ramble while he played quick, quiet runs
on the guitar. He watched her hands as they lay still on
her knees. They were very narrow, and although they
were tanned golden brown, they remained fragile. There
was a light tracing of blue vein just under the skin. The
nails were not long but well-shaped and painted in some
clear, hardening polish with a blush of pink. There were
no rings. Because they were motionless, he knew she
was relaxed. Whatever nerves he had sensed when he
had first spoken to her were stilled now.

"It's been going well, I think," she continued. "The
Glass House is a terrific warm-up act, and the band's
tight, even though we lost Kelly. The new bass is good,
don't you think?"

"Knows his stuff," Marc said briefly. Raven grinned and reached over to tug his beard.

"So do you," she said. "Let me try."

Agreeably Marc slipped the strap over his head, then handed Raven his guitar. She was a better-than-average player, although she took a great deal of ribbing from the musicians in her troupe whenever she attempted the guitar. Periodically she threatened them with a bogus plan to incorporate her semiskillful playing into the act.

Still she liked to make music with the six strings. It soothed her. There was something intimate about holding an instrument close, feeling its vibrations against your own body. After hitting the same wrong note twice, Raven sighed, then wrinkled her nose at Marc's grin.

"I'm out of practice," she claimed, handing him back his Gibson.

"Good excuse."

"It's probably out of tune."

He ran quickly up and down the scales. "Nope."

"You might be kind and lie." She changed position, putting her feet flat on the floor and lacing her hands over her knees. "It's a good thing you're a musician. You'd have made a lousy politician."

"Too much traveling," he said as his fingers began to move again. He liked the sound of her laughter as it echoed around the empty theater.

"Oh, you're right! How can anyone remain sane going from city to city day after day? And music's such a stable business, too."

"Sturdy as a crap table."

"You've a gift for analogy," she told him, watching the skill of his fingers on the strings. "I love to watch you play," she continued. "It's so effortless. When Brandon was first teaching me, I…" but the words trailed off. Marc glanced up at her face, but his fingers never faltered. "I—it was difficult," she went on, wondering what had made her bring up the matter, "because he was left-handed, and naturally his guitar was, too. He bought me one of my own, but watching him, I had to learn backwards." She laughed, pleased with the memory. Absently she lifted a hand to toy with the thick, dangling staff of her earring. "Maybe that's why I play the way I do. I'm always having to twist it around in my head before it can get to my fingers."

She lapsed into silence while Marc continued to play. It was soothing and somehow intimate with the two of them alone in the huge, empty theater. But his music didn't sound lonely as it echoed. She began to sing with it quietly, as though they were at home, seated on a rug with the walls close and comforting around them.

It was true that the tour had tired her and that the midway point had her feeling drained. But the interlude here was lifting her, though in a different way than the audience would lift her that night. This wasn't the quick, dizzying high that shot endurance back into her for the time she was on stage and in the lights. This was a steadying hand, like a good night's sleep or a home-cooked meal. She smiled at Marc when the song was over and said again, "I'm glad you came."

He looked at her, and for once his hands were silent on the strings. "How long have I been with you, Raven?"

She thought back to when Marc had first become a semiregular part of her troupe. "Four—four and a half—years."

"Five this summer," he corrected. "It was in August, and you were rehearsing for your second tour. You had on baggy white pants and a T-shirt with a rainbow on it. You were barefoot. You had a lost look in your eyes. Carstairs had gone back to England about a month before."

Raven stared at him. She had never heard him make such a long speech. "Isn't it strange that you would remember what I was wearing? It doesn't sound very impressive."

"I remember because I fell in love with you on the spot."

"Oh, Marc." She searched for something to say and found nothing. Instead, she reached up and took his hand. She knew he meant exactly what he said.

"Once or twice I've come close to asking you to live with me."

Raven let out a quick breath. "Why didn't you?"

"Because it would have hurt you to have said no and it would have hurt me to hear it." He laid the guitar across his lap and leaning over it, kissed her.

"I didn't know," she murmured, pressing both of his hands to her cheeks. "I should have. I'm sorry."

"You've never gotten him out of your head, Raven. It's damn frustrating competing with a memory." Marc squeezed her hands a moment, then released them. "It's also safe. I knew you'd never make a commitment to me, so I could avoid making one to you." He shrugged his well-muscled shoulders. "I think it always scared me that you were the kind of woman who would make a man give everything because you asked for nothing."

Her brows drew together. "Am I?"

"You need someone who can stand up to you. I'd never have been able to. I'd never have been able to say no or shout at you or make crazy love. Life's nothing without things like that, and we'd have ended up hurting each other."

She tilted her head and studied him. "Why are you telling me all this now?"

"Because I realized when I watched you singing that I'll always love you but I'll never have you. And if I did, I'd lose something very special." He reached across to touch her hair. "A fantasy that warms you on cold nights and makes you feel young again when you're old. Sometimes might-have-beens can be very precious."

Raven didn't know whether to smile or to cry. "I haven't hurt you?"

"No," he said so simply she knew he spoke the truth. "You've made me feel good. Have I made you uncomfortable?"

"No." She smiled at him. "You've made me feel good."

He grinned, then rose and held out a hand to her. "Let's go get some coffee."

Brand changed into jeans in his dressing room. It was after two in the morning, but he was wide-awake, still riding on energy left over from his last show. He'd go out, he decided, and put some of it to use at the blackjack table. He could grab Eddie or one of the other guys from the band and cruise the casinos.

There'd be women. Brand knew there'd be a throng of them waiting for him when he left the privacy of his dressing room. He could take his pick. But he didn't want a woman. He wanted a drink and some cards and some action; anything to use up the adrenaline speeding through his system.

He reached for his shirt, and the mirror reflected his

naked torso. It was tight and lean, teetering on being thin, but there were surprising cords of muscles in the arms and shoulders. He'd had to use them often when he'd been a boy on the London streets. He always wondered if it had been the piano lessons his mother had insisted on that had saved him from being another victim of the streets. Music had opened up something for him. He hadn't been able to get enough, learn enough. It had been like food, and he had been starving.

At fifteen Brand had started his own band. He was tough and cocky and talked his way into cheap little dives. There had been women even then; not just girls, but women attracted by his youthful sexuality and arrogant confidence. But they'd only been part of the adventure. He had never given up, though the living had been lean in the beer-soaked taverns. He had pulled his way up and made a local reputation for himself; both his music and his personality were strong.

It had taken time. He had been twenty when he had cut his first record, and it had gone nowhere. Brand had recognized that its failure had been due to a combination of poor quality recording, mismanagement and his own see-if-I-care attitude. He had taken a few steps back, found a savvy manager, worked hard on arrangements and talked himself into another recording session.

Two years later he had bought his family a house in the London suburbs, pushed his younger brother into a university and set off on his first American tour.

Now, at thirty, there were times he felt he'd never been off the merry-go-round. Half his life had been given over to his career and its demands. He was tired of wandering. Brand wanted something to focus his life, something to center it. He knew he couldn't give up music, but it wasn't enough by itself anymore. His family wasn't enough, and neither was the money or the applause.

He knew what he wanted. He had known five years before, but there were times he didn't feel as sure of himself as he had when he had been a fifteen-year-old punk talking his way past the back door of a third-rate nightclub. A capacity crowd had just paid thirty dollars a head to hear him, and he knew he could afford to take every cent he made on that two-week gig and throw it away on one roll of the dice. He had an urge to do it. He was restless, reckless, running on the same nerves he had felt the night he'd taken Raven home from their dinner date. He'd only seen her once after that—at Steve Jarett's house. Almost immediately afterward he had flown to Las Vegas to begin polishing his act.

It was catching up with him now—the tension, the anger, the needs. Not for the first time, Brand wondered whether his unreasonable need for her would end if he could have her once, just once. With quick, impatient movements, he thrust the tail of his shirt into the waist of his jeans. He knew better, but there were times he wished it could be. He left the dressing room looking for company.

For an hour Brand sat at the blackjack table. He lost a little, won a little, then lost it again. His mind wasn't on the cards. He had thought the noise, the bright lights, the rich smell of gambling was what he had wanted. There was a thin, intense woman beside him with a huge chunk of diamond on her finger and sapphires around her neck. She drank and lost at the same steady rhythm. Across the table was a young couple he pegged as honeymooners. The gold band on the girl's finger looked brilliantly new and untested. They were giddy with winning what Brand figured was about thirty dollars. There was something touching in their pleasure and in the soft, exchanged looks. All around them came the endless chinkity-chink of the slots.

Brand found himself as restless as he had been an hour before in his dressing room. A half-empty glass of bourbon sat at his elbow, but he left it as he rose. He didn't want the casino, and he felt an enormous surge of envy for the man who had his woman and thirty dollars worth of chips.

When he entered his suite, it was dark and silent, a sharp contrast to the world he had just left. Brand didn't bother hitting the switches as he made his way into the bedroom. Taking out a cigarette, he sat on the bed before lighting it. The flame made a sharp hiss and a brief flare. He sat with the silence, but the adrenaline still pumped. Finally he switched on the small bedside lamp and picked up the phone.

Raven was deep in sleep, but the ringing of the phone shot panic through her before she was fully awake. Her heart pounded in her throat before the mists could clear. She'd grown up with calls coming in the middle of the night. She forgot where she was and fumbled for the phone with a sense of dread and anticipation.

"Yes...hello."

"Raven, I know I woke you. I'm sorry."

She tried to shake away the fog. "Brandon? Is something wrong? Are you all right?"

"Yes, I'm fine. Just unbelievably inconsiderate."

Relaxing, Raven sank back on the pillows and tried to orient herself. "You're in Vegas, aren't you?" The dim light told her it was nearing dawn. He was two hours behind her. Or was it three? She couldn't for the life of her remember what time zone she was in.

"Yes, I'm in Vegas through next week."

"How's the show going?"

It was typical of her, he mused, not to demand to know why the hell he had called her in the middle of the night. She would simply accept that he needed to talk. He drew on the cigarette and wished he could touch her. "Better than my luck at the tables."

She laughed, comfortably sleepy. The connection was clean and sharp; he didn't sound hundreds of miles away. "Is it still blackjack?"

"I'm consistent," he murmured. "How's Kansas?"

"Where?" He laughed, pleasing her. "The audience was fantastic," she continued, letting her mind wander back to the show. "Has been straight along. That's the only thing that keeps you going on a tour like this. Will you be there in time for the show in New York? I'd love you to hear the warm-up act."

"I'll be there." He lay back on the bed as some of the superfluous energy started to drain. "Cornwall is sounding more and more appealing."

"You sound tired."

"I wasn't; I am now. Raven…"

She waited, but he didn't speak. "Yes?"

"I missed you. I needed to hear your voice. Tell me what you're looking at," he demanded, "what you see right now."

"It's dawn," she told him. "Or nearly. I can't see any buildings, just the sky. It's more mauve than gray and the light's very soft and thin." She smiled; it had been a long time since she had seen a day begin. "It's really lovely, Brandon. I'd forgotten."

"Will you be able to sleep again?" He had closed his eyes; the fatigue was taking over.

"Yes, but I'd rather go for a walk, though I don't think Julie would appreciate it if I asked her to come along."

Brand pried off his shoes, using the toe of one foot, then the other. "Go back to sleep, and we'll walk on the cliffs one morning in Cornwall. I shouldn't have woken you."

"No, I'm glad you did." She could hear the change; the voice that had been sharp and alert was now heavy. "Get some rest, Brandon. I'll look for you in New York."

"All right. Good night, Raven."

He was asleep almost before he hung up. Fifteen hundred miles away, Raven laid her cheek on the pillow and watched the morning come.

Chapter 7

Raven tried to be still while her hair was being twisted and knotted and groomed. Her dressing room was banked with flowers; they had been arriving steadily for more than two hours. And it was crowded with people. A tiny little man with sharp, black eyes touched up her blusher. Behind her, occasionally muttering in French, was the nimble-fingered woman who did her hair. Wayne was there, having business of his own here in New York. He'd told Raven that he'd come to see his designs in action and was even now in deep discussion with her dresser. Julie opened the door to another flower delivery.

"Have I packed everything? You know, I should have told Brandon to give me an extra day in town for shopping. There're probably a dozen things I need." Raven turned in her seat and heard the swift French oath as her partially knotted hair flew from the woman's fingers. "Sorry, Marie. Julie, did I pack a coat? I might need one." Slipping the card from the latest arrangement of flowers, she found it was from a successful television producer with whom she'd worked on her last TV special. "They're from Max.... There's a party tonight. Why don't you go?" She handed the card to Julie and allowed her lip liner to be straightened by the finicky makeup artist.

"Yes, you packed a coat, your suede, which you could need this early in the spring. And several sweaters," Julie said distractedly, checking her list. "And maybe I will."

"I can't believe this is it, the last show. It's been a good tour, hasn't it, Julie?" Raven turned her head and winced at the sharp tug on her hair.

"I can't remember you ever getting a better response or deserving one more...."

"And we're all glad it's over," Raven finished for her.

"I'm going to sleep for a week." Julie found space for the flowers, then continued to check off things in her notebook. "Not everyone has your constant flow of energy."

"I love playing New York," she said, tucking up her legs to the despair of her hairdresser.

"You must hold still!"

"Marie, if I hold still much longer, I'm going to explode." Raven smiled at the makeup artist as he fussed around her face. "You always know just what to do. It looks perfect; I feel beautiful."

Recognizing the signal, Julie began nudging people from the room. Eventually they went, and soon only Julie and Wayne were left. The room quieted considerably; now the walls hummed gently with the vibrations of the warm-up act. Raven let out a deep sigh.

"I'll be so glad to have my face and body and hair back," she said and sprawled in the chair. "You should have seen what he made me put all over my face this morning."

"What was it?" Wayne asked absently as he smoothed the hem of one of her costumes.

"Green," she told him and shuddered.

He laughed and turned to Julie. "What are you going to do when this one takes off to the moors?"

"Cruise the Greek Islands and recuperate." She pushed absently at the small of her back. "I've already booked passage on the ninth. These tours are brutal."

"Listen to her." Raven sniffed and peered at herself critically in the glass. "She's the one who's held the whip and chair for four weeks. He certainly makes me look exotic, doesn't he?" She wrinkled her nose and spoiled the effect.

"Into costume," Julie commanded.

"See? Orders, orders." Obediently Raven rose.

"Here." Wayne lifted the red and silver dress from the hanger. "Since I nudged your dresser along, I'll be your minion."

"Oh, good, thanks." She stepped out of her robe and into the dress. "You know, Wayne," she continued as he zipped her up, "you were right about the black number. It gets a tremendous response. I never know if they're applauding me or the costume after that set."

"Have I ever let you down?" he demanded as he tucked a pleat.

"No." She turned her head to smile at him over her shoulder. "Never. Will you miss me?"

"Tragically." He kissed her ear.

There was a brief, brisk knock at the door. "Ten minutes, Ms. Williams."

She took a long breath. "Are you going to go out front?"

"I'll stay back with Julie." He glanced over at her, lifting a brow in question.

"Yes, thanks. Here, Raven, don't forget these wonderfully gaudy earrings." She watched Raven fasten one. "Really, Wayne, they're enough to make me shudder, but they're fabulous with that dress."

"Naturally."

She laughed, shaking her head. "The man's ego," she said to Raven, "never ceases to amaze me."

"As long as it doesn't outdistance the talent," he put in suavely.

"New York audiences are tough." Raven spoke quickly, her voice jumping suddenly with nerves and excitement. "They scare me to death."

"I thought you said you loved playing New York." Wayne took out a cigarette and offered one to Julie.

"I do, especially at the end of a tour. It keeps you sharp. They're really going to know if I'm not giving them everything. How do I look?"

"The dress is sensational," Wayne decided. "You'll do."

"Some help you are."

"Let's go," Julie urged. "You'll miss your cue."

"I never miss my cue." Raven fussed with the second earring, stalling. He'd said he'd be here, she told herself. *Why isn't he?* He could have gotten the time mixed up, or he could be caught in traffic. Or he could simply have forgotten that he'd promised to be here for the show.

The quick knock came again. "Five minutes, Ms. Williams."

"Raven." Julie's voice was a warning.

"Yes, yes, all right." She turned and gave them both a flippant smile. "Tell me I'm wonderful when it's over, even if I wasn't. I want to end the tour feeling marvelous."

Then she was dashing for the door and hurrying down the hall where the sounds of the warm-up band were no longer gentle; now they shook the walls.

"Ms. Williams, Ms. Williams! Raven!"

She turned, breaking the concentration she'd been building and looked at the harried stage manager. He thrust a white rose into her hand.

"Just came back for you."

Raven took the bud and lifted it, wanting to fill herself with the scent. She needed no note or message to tell her it was from Brand. For a moment she simply dreamed over it.

"Raven." The warm-up act had finished; the transition to her own band would take place on the darkened stage quickly. "You're going to miss your cue."

"No, I'm not." She gave the worried stage manager a kiss, forgetful of her carefully applied lipstick. Twirling the rose between her fingers, she took it with her. They were introducing her as she reached the wings.

Big build-up; don't let the audience cool down. They were already cheering for her. *Thirty seconds; take a breath.* Her band hit her introduction. Music crashed through the cheers. *One, two, three!*

She ran out, diving into a wave of applause.

The first set was hot and fast, staged to keep the audience up and wanting more. She seemed to be a ball of flame with hundreds of colored lights flashing around her. Raven knew how to play to them, play with them, and she pumped all her energy into a routine she had done virtually every night for four weeks. Enthusiasm and verve kept it fresh. It was hot under the lights, but she didn't notice. She was wrapping herself in the audience, in the music. The costume sizzled and sparked. Her voice smoked.

It was a demanding forty minutes, and when she rushed offstage during an instrumental break, she had less than three minutes in which to change costumes. Now she was in white, a brief, shimmering top covered with bugle beads matched with thin harem pants. The pace would slow a bit, giving the audience time to catch their breath. The balance was in ballads, the slow trembling ones she did best. The lighting was muted, soft and moody.

It was during a break between songs, when she traditionally talked to the audience, that someone in the audience spotted Brand in their midst. Soon more people knew, and while Raven went on unaware of the disturbance, the crowd soon became vocal. Shielding her eyes, she could just make out the center of the commotion. Then she saw him. It seemed they wanted him up on stage.

Raven was a good judge of moods and knew the value of showmanship. If she didn't invite Brand on stage, she'd lose the crowd. They had already taken the choice out of her hands.

"Brandon." Raven spoke softly into the mike, but her voice carried. Though she couldn't see his eyes with the spotlight in her own, she knew he was looking at her. "If you come up and sing," she told him, lightly, "we might get you a refund on your ticket." She knew he'd grin at that. There was an excited rush of applause and cheers as he rose and came to the stage.

He was all in black: trim, well-cut slacks and a casual polo sweater. The contrast was striking as he stood beside her. It might have been planned. Smiling at her, he spoke softly, out of the range of the microphone. "I'm sorry, Raven, I should have gone backstage. I wanted to watch you from out front."

She tilted her head. It was, she discovered, more wonderful to see him than she had imagined. "You're the one being put to work. What would you like to do?"

Before he could answer, the demands sprang from the crowd. Once the idea formed, it was shouted over and over with growing enthusiasm. Raven's smile faded. "Clouds and Rain."

Brand took her wrist and lifted the rose she held. "You remember the words, don't you?"

It was a challenge. A stagehand rushed out with a hand mike for Brand.

"My band doesn't know it," she began.

"I know it." Marc shifted his guitar and watched them. The crowd was still shouting when he gave the opening chords. "We'll follow you."

Brand kept his hand on Raven's wrist and lifted his own mike.

Raven knew how it needed to be sung: face-to-face, eye to eye. It was a caress of a song, meant for lovers. The audience was silent now. Their harmony was close, intricate. Raven had once thought it must be like making love. Their voices flowed into each other. And she forgot the audience, forgot the stage and for a moment forgot the five years.

There was more intimacy in singing with him than she had ever allowed in any other aspect of their relationship. Here she could not resist him. When he sang to her, it was as if he told her there wasn't anyone else, had never been anyone else. It was more moving than a kiss, more sexual than a touch.

When they finished, their voices hung a moment, locked together. Brand saw her lips tremble before he brought her close and took them.

They might have been on an island rather than on stage, spotlighted for thousands. She didn't hear the tumultuous applause, the cheers, the shouting of their names. Her arms went around him, one hand holding the mike, the other the rose. Cameras flashed like fireworks, but she was trapped in a velvet darkness. She lost all sense of time; her lips might have moved on his for hours or days or only seconds. But when he drew her away, she felt a keener sense of loss than any she had ever known before. Brand saw the confusion in her eyes, the dazed desire, and smiled.

"You're better than you ever were, Raven." He kissed her hand. "Too bad about those sentimental numbers you keep sticking into the act."

Her brows rose. "Try to boost your flagging career by letting you sing with me, and you insult me." Her balance was returning as they took a couple of elaborate bows, hands linked.

"Let's see if you can carry the rest on your own, love. I've warmed them back up for you." He kissed her again, but lightly now, on the cheek, before he waved to the audience and strolled offstage left.

Raven grinned at his back, then turned to her audience. "Too bad he never made it, isn't it?"

* * *

Raven should have been wrung dry after the two hours were over. But she wasn't. She'd given them three encores, and though they clamored for more, Brand caught her hand as she hesitated in the wings.

"They'll keep you out there all night, Raven." He could feel the speed of her pulse under his fingers. Because he knew how draining two hours onstage could be, he urged her back down the hall toward her dressing room.

There were crowds of people jammed in together in the hallway, congratulating her, touching her. Now and then a reporter managed to elbow through to shoot out a question. She answered, and Brandon tossed off remarks with quick charm while steering her determinedly toward her dressing room. Once inside, he locked the door.

"I think they liked me," she said gravely, then laughed and spun away from him. "I feel so good!" Her eyes lit on the bucket of ice that cradled a bottle. "Champagne?"

"I thought you'd need to console yourself after a flop like that." Brand moved over and drew out the bottle. "You'll have to open the door soon and see people. Do try to put on a cheerful front, love."

"I'll do my best." The cork popped, and the white froth fizzed a bit over the mouth of the bottle.

Brand poured two glasses to the rim and handed her one. "I meant it, Raven." He touched his glass to hers. "You were never better."

Raven smiled, bringing the glass to her lips. Again, he felt the painful thrust of desire. Carefully Brand took the glass from her, then set both it and his own down again. "There's something I didn't finish out there tonight."

She was unprepared. Even though he drew her close

slowly and took his time bringing his mouth to hers, Raven wasn't ready. It was a long, deep, kiss that mingled with the champagne. His mouth was warm on hers, seeking. His hands ran over her hips, snugly encased in the thin black jumpsuit, but she could sense he was under very tight control.

His tongue made a thorough, lengthy journey through the moist recesses of her mouth, and she responded in kind. But he wanted her to do more than give; he wanted her to want more. And she did, feeling the pull of need, the flash of passion. She could feel the texture of his long, clever fingers through the sheer material of her costume, then flesh to flesh as he brought them up to caress the back of her neck.

Her head was swimming with a myriad of sensations: excitement and power still clinging from her performance; the heady, heavy scent of mixed flowers which crowded the air; the firm press of his body against her; and desire, more complex, more insistent than she had been prepared for.

"Brandon," she murmured against his lips. She wanted him, wanted him desperately, and was afraid.

Brand drew her away, then carefully studied her face. Her eyes were like thin glass over her emotions. "You're beautiful, Raven, one of the most beautiful women I know."

She was unsteady and tried to find her balance without clinging to him. She stepped back, resting her hand on the table that held their glasses. "One of the most?" she challenged, lifting her champagne.

"I know a lot of women." He grinned as he lifted his own glass. "Why don't you take that stuff off your face so I can see you?"

"Do you know how long I had to sit still while he troweled this stuff on?" Moving to the dressing table, she scooped up a generous glob of cold cream. Her blood was beginning to settle. "It's supposed to make me glamorous and alluring." She slathered it on.

"You make me nervous when you're glamorous, and you'd be alluring in a paper sack."

She lifted her eyes to his in the mirror. His expression was surprisingly serious. "I think that was a compliment." She smeared the white cream generously over her face and grinned. "Am I alluring now?"

Brand grinned back, then slowly let his eyes roam down her back to focus on her snugly clad bottom. "Raven, don't fish. The answer is obvious."

She began to tissue off the cream and with it the stage makeup. "Brandon. It was good to sing with you again." After removing the last of the cream from her face, Raven toyed with the stem of her champagne glass. "I always felt very special when I sang with you. I still do." He watched her chew for a moment on her bottom lip as if she was unsure about what she should say. "I imagine they'll play up that duet in the papers. They'll probably make something else out of it, especially— especially with the way we ended it."

"I like the way we ended it." Brand came over and laid his hands on her shoulders. "It should always be ended that way." He kissed the back of her neck while his eyes smiled into hers in the glass. "Are you worried about the press, Raven?"

"No, of course not. But, Brandon…"

"Do you know," he interrupted, brushing the hair away from her neck with the back of his hand, "no one else calls me that but my mother. Strange." He bent, nuzzling his lips into the sensitive curve of her neck. "You affect me in an entirely different way."

"Brandon…"

"When I was a boy," he continued, moving his lips up to her ear, "and she called me Brandon, I knew that was it. Whatever crime I'd committed had been found out. Justice was about to strike."

"I imagine you committed quite a few crimes." She forced herself to speak lightly. When she would have moved away, he turned her around to face him.

"Too many to count." He leaned to her, but instead of the kiss she expected and prepared for, he caught her bottom lip between his teeth. She clutched at his shirt as she struggled for breath and balance. Their eyes were open and on each other's, but his face dimmed, then faded, as passion clouded her vision.

Brand released her, then gave her a quick kiss on the nose. Raven ran a hand through her hair, trying to steady herself. He was tossing her back and forth too swiftly, too easily.

"Do you want to change before we let anyone in?" he asked. When she could focus again, Raven saw he was drinking champagne and watching her. There was an odd look on his face, as if, she thought, he were a boxer checking for weaknesses, looking for openings.

"I—yes." Raven brought herself back. "Yes, I think I would, but…" She glanced around the dressing room. "I don't know what I did with my clothes."

He laughed, and the look was gone from his face. Relieved, Raven laughed with him. They began to search through the flowers and sparkling costumes for her jeans and tennis shoes.

Chapter 8

It was late when they arrived at the airport. Raven was still riding on post-performance energy and chattered about everything that came into her head. She looked up at a half-moon as she and Brand transferred from limo to plane. The private jet wasn't what she had been expecting, and studying the comfortably lush interior of the main cabin helped to allay the fatigue of yet one more flight.

It was carpeted with a thick, pewter-colored shag and contained deep, leather chairs and a wide, plush sofa. There was a padded bar at one end and a doorway at the other which she discovered led into a tidy galley. "You didn't have this before," she commented as she poked her head into another room and found the bath, complete with tub.

"I bought it about three years ago." Brand sprawled

on the sofa and watched her as she explored. She looked different than she had a short time before. Her face was naked now, and he found he preferred it that way. Makeup seemed to needlessly gloss over her natural beauty. She wore faded jeans and sneakers, which she immediately pried off her feet. An oversize yellow sweater left her shapeless. It made him want to run his hands under it and find her. "Do you still hate to fly?"

Raven gave him a rueful grin. "Yes. You'd think after all this time I'd have gotten over it, but…" She continued to roam the cabin, not yet able to settle. If she had to, Raven felt she could give the entire performance again. She had enough energy.

"Strap in," Brand suggested, smiling at the quick, nervous gestures. "We'll get started, then you won't even know you're in the air."

"You don't know how many times I've heard that one." Still she did as he said and waited calmly enough while he told the pilot they were ready. In a few minutes they were airborne, and she was able to unstrap and roam again.

"I know the feeling," Brand commented, watching her. She turned in silent question. "It's as though you still have one last burst of energy to get rid of. It's the way I felt that night in Vegas when I called and woke you up."

She caught back her hair with both hands. "I feel I should jog for a few miles. It might settle me down."

"How about some coffee?"

"Yes." She wandered over to a porthole and pressed her nose against it. It was black as pitch outside the glass. "Yes, coffee would be nice, then you can tell me what marvelous ideas you have forming for the score. You've probably got dozens of them."

"A few." She heard the clatter of cups. "I imagine you've some of your own."

"A few," she said, and he chuckled. Turning away from the dark window, she saw him leaning against the opening between the galley and the main cabin. "How soon do you think we'll start to fight?"

"Soon enough. Let's wait at least until we're settled into the house. Is Julie going back to L.A., or have you tied up all your loose ends there?"

A shadow visited her face. Raven thought of the one brief visit she had paid to her mother since the start of the tour. They had had a day's layover in Chicago, and she had used the spare time to make the impossible flight to the coast and back. There had been the inevitable interview with Karter and a brief, emotional visit with her mother. Raven had been relieved to see that the cast had gone from her mother's skin and that there was more flesh to her face. There had been apologies and promises and tears, just as there always were, Raven thought wearily. And as she always did, she had begun to believe them again.

"I never seem to completely tie up the loose ends," she murmured.

"Will you tell me what's wrong?"

She shook her head. She couldn't bear to dwell on unhappiness now. "No, nothing, nothing really." The kettle sang out, and she smiled. "Your cue," she told him.

He studied her for a moment while the kettle spit peevishly behind him. Then, turning, he went back into the galley to fix the coffee. "Black?" he asked, and she gave an absent assent.

Sitting on the sofa, Raven let her head fall back while the energy began to subside. It was almost as if she could feel it draining. Brand recognized the signs as soon as he came back into the room. He set down her mug of coffee, then sipped thoughtfully from his own as he watched her. Sensing him, Raven slowly opened her eyes. There was silence for a moment; her body and her mind were growing lethargic.

"What are you doing?" she murmured.

"Remembering."

Her lids shuttered down, concealing her eyes and their expression. "Don't."

He drank again, letting his eyes continue their slow, measured journey over her. "It's a bit much to ask me not to remember, Raven, isn't it?" It was a question that expected no answer, and she gave it none. But her lids fluttered up again.

He didn't have her full trust, nor did he believe he had ever had it. That was the root of their problems. He studied her while he stood and drank his coffee. There was high, natural color in her cheeks, and her eyes were dark and sleepy. She sat, as was her habit, with her legs crossed under her and her hands on her knees. In contrast to the relaxed position, her fingers moved restlessly.

"I still want you. You know that, don't you?"

Again Raven left his question unanswered, but he saw the pulse in her throat begin to thump. When she spoke, her voice was calm. "We're going to work together, Brandon. It's best not to complicate things."

He laughed, not in mockery but in genuine amusement. She watched his eyes lose their brooding intensity and light. "By all means, let's keep things simple." After draining his coffee, he walked over and sat beside her. In a smooth, practiced move, he drew her against his side. "Relax," he told her, annoyed when she resisted.

"Give me some credit. I know how tired you are. When are you going to trust me, Raven?"

She tilted her head until she could see him. Her look was long and eloquent before she settled into the crook of his shoulder and let out a long sigh. Like a child, she fell asleep quickly, and like that of a child, the sleep was deep. For a long moment he stayed as he was, Raven curled against his side. Then he laid her down on the sofa, watching as her hair drifted about her.

Rising, Brand switched off the lights. In the dark he settled into one of the deep cabin chairs and lit a cigarette. Time passed as he sat gazing out at a sprinkle of stars and listening to Raven's soft, steady breathing. Unable to resist, he rose, and moving to her, lay down beside her. She stirred when he brushed the hair from her cheek, but only to snuggle closer to him. Over the raw yearning came a curiously sweet satisfaction. He wrapped his arm around her, felt her sigh, then slept.

It was Brand who awoke first. As was his habit, his mind and body came together quickly. He lay still and allowed his eyes to grow accustomed to the darkness. Beside him, curled against his chest, Raven slept on.

He could make out the curve of her face, the pixie sharp features, the rain straight fall of hair. Her leg was bent at the knee and had slipped between his. She was soft and warm and tempting. Brand knew he had experience enough to arouse her into submission before she was fully awake. She would be drowsy and disoriented.

The hazy gray of early dawn came upon them as he watched her. He could make out her lashes now, a long sweep of black that seemed to weigh her lids down. He wanted her, but not that way. Not the first time. Asleep, she sighed and moved against him. Desire rippled along his skin. Carefully Brand shifted away from her and rose.

In the kitchen he began to make coffee. A glance at his watch and a little arithmetic told him they'd be landing soon. He thought rather enthusiastically about breakfast. The drive from the airport to his house would take some time. He remembered an inn along the way where they could get a good meal and coffee better than the instant he was making.

Hearing Raven stir, he came to the doorway and watched her wake up. She moaned, rolled over and unsuccessfully tried to bury her face. Her hand reached out for a pillow that wasn't there, then slowly, on a disgusted sigh, she opened her eyes. Brand watched the stages as her eyes roamed the room. First came disinterest, then confusion, then sleepy understanding.

"Good morning," he ventured, and she shifted her eyes to him without moving her head. He was grinning at her, and his greeting was undeniably cheerful. She had a wary respect for cheerful risers.

"Coffee," she managed and shut her eyes again.

"In a minute." The kettle was beginning to hiss behind him. "How'd you sleep?"

Dragging her hands through her hair, she made a courageous attempt to sit up. The light was still gray but now brighter, and she pressed her fingers against her eyes for a moment. "I don't know yet," she mumbled from behind her hands. "Ask me later."

The whistle blew, and as Brand disappeared back into the galley, Raven brought her knees up to her chest and buried her face against them. She could hear him talking to her, making bright, meaningless conversation, but her mind wasn't yet receptive. She made no attempt to listen or to answer.

"Here, love." As Raven cautiously raised her head, Brand held out a steaming mug. "Have a bit, then you'll feel better." She accepted with murmured thanks. He sat down beside her. "I've a brother who wakes up ready to bite someone's—anyone's—head off. It's metabolism, I suppose."

Raven made a noncommittal sound and began to take tentative sips. It was hot and strong. For some moments there was silence as he drank his own cream-cooled coffee and watched her. When her cup was half empty, she looked over and managed a rueful smile.

"I'm sorry, Brandon. I'm simply not at my best in the morning. Especially early in the morning." She tilted her head so that she could see his watch, made a brave stab at mathematics, then gave up. "I don't suppose it matters what time it actually is," she decided, going back to the coffee. "It'll take me days to adjust to the change, anyway."

"A good meal will set you up," he told her, lazily sipping at his own coffee. "I read somewhere where drinking yeast and jogging cures jet lag, but I'll take my chances with breakfast."

"Yeast?" Raven grimaced into her mug, then drained it. "I think sleep's a better cure, piles of it." The mists were clearing, and she shook back her hair. "I guess we'll be landing soon, won't we?"

"Less than an hour, I'd say."

"Good. The less time I spend awake on a plane, the less time I have to think about being on one. I slept like a rock." With another sigh, Raven stretched her back, letting her shoulders lift and fall with the movement. "I made poor company." Her system was starting to hum again, though on slow speed.

"You were tired." Over the rim of his cup he watched the subtle movements of her body beneath the oversize sweater.

"I turned off like a tap," she admitted. "It happens that way sometimes after a concert." She lifted one shoulder in a quick shrug. "But I suppose we'll both be better today for the rest. Where did you sleep?"

"With you."

Raven closed her mouth on a yawn, swallowed and stared at him. "What?"

"I said I slept with you, here on the couch." Brand made a general gesture with his hand. "You like to snuggle."

She could see he was enjoying her dismayed shock. His eyes were deep blue with amusement as he lifted his cup again. "You had no right..." Raven began.

"I always fancied being the first man you slept with," he told her before draining his cup. "Want some more coffee?"

Raven's face flooded with color; her eyes turned dark and opaque. She sprang up, but Brand managed to pluck the cup from her hand before she could hurl it across the room. For a moment she stood, breathing hard, watching him while he gave her his calm, measuring stare.

"Don't flatter yourself," she tossed out. "You don't know how many men I've slept with."

Very precisely, he set down both coffee cups, then looked back up at her. "You're as innocent as the day you were born, Raven. You've barely been touched by a man, much less been made love to."

Her temper flared like a rocket. "You don't know

anything about who I've been with in the last five years, Brandon." She struggled to keep from shouting, to keep her voice as calm and controlled as his. "It's none of your business how many men I've slept with."

He lifted a brow, watching her thoughtfully. "Innocence isn't something to be ashamed of, Raven."

"I'm not…" She stopped, balling her fists. "You had no right to—" She swallowed and shook her head as fury and embarrassment raced through her. "—While I was asleep," she finished.

"Do what while you were asleep?" Brandon demanded, lazing back on the sofa. "Ravish you?" His humor shimmered over the old-fashioned word and made her feel ridiculous. "I don't think you'd have slept through it, Raven."

Her voice shook with emotion. "Don't laugh at me, Brandon."

"Then don't be such a fool." He reached over to the table beside him for a cigarette, then tapped the end of it against the surface without lighting it. His eyes were fixed on hers and no longer amused. "I could have had you if I'd wanted to, make no mistake about it."

"You have colossal nerve, Brandon. Please remember that you're not privy to my sex life and that you wouldn't have had me because I don't want you. I choose my own lovers."

She hadn't realized he could move so fast. The indolent slouch on the sofa was gone in a flash. He reached up, seizing her wrist, and in one swift move had yanked her down on her back, trapping her body with his. Her gasp of surprise was swallowed as his weight pressed down on her.

Never, in all the time they had spent together past and

present, had Raven seen him so angry. An iron taste of fear rose in her throat. She could only shake her head, too terrified to struggle, too stunned to move. She had never suspected he possessed the capacity for violence she now read clearly on his face. This was far different from the cold rage she had seen before and which she knew how to deal with. His fingers bit into her wrist while his other hand came to circle her throat.

"How far do you think I'll push?" he demanded. His voice was harsh and deep with the hint of Ireland more pronounced. Her breathing was short and shallow with fear. Lying completely still, she made no answer. "Don't throw your imaginary string of lovers in my face, or, by God, you'll have a real one quickly enough whether you want me or not." His fingers tightened slightly around her throat. "When the time comes, I won't need to get you drunk on champagne or on exhaustion to have you lie with me. I could have you now, this minute, and after five minutes of struggle you'd be more than willing." His voice lowered, trembling along her skin. "I know how to play you, Raven, and don't you forget it."

His face was very close to hers. Their breathing mixed, both swift and strained, the only sound coming from the hum of the plane's engines. The fear in her eyes leaped out, finally penetrating his fury. Swearing, Brand pushed himself from her and rose. Her eyes stayed on his as she waited for what he would do next. He stared at her, then turned sharply away, moving over to a porthole.

Raven lay where she was, not realizing she was massaging the wrist that throbbed from his fingers. She watched him drag a hand through his hair.

"I slept with you last night because I wanted to be close to you." He took another long, cleansing breath. "It was nothing more than that. I never touched you. It was an innocent and rather sweet way to spend the night." He curled his fingers into a fist, remembering the frantic flutter of her pulse under his hand when he had circled it around her throat. It gave him no pleasure to know he had frightened her. "It never occurred to me that it would offend you like this. I apologize."

Raven covered her eyes with her hand as the tears began. She swallowed sobs, not wanting to give way to them. Guilt and shame washed over her as fear drained. Her reaction to Brand's simple, affectionate gesture had been to slap his face. It had been embarrassment, she knew, but more, her own suppressed longing for him that had pushed her to react with anger and spiteful words. She'd tried to provoke him and had succeeded. But more, she knew now she had hurt him. Rising from the sofa, she attempted to make amends.

Though she walked over to stand behind him, Raven didn't touch him. She couldn't bear the thought that he might stiffen away from her.

"Brandon, I'm so sorry." She dug her teeth into her bottom lip to keep her voice steady. "That was stupid of me, and worse, unkind. I'm terribly ashamed of the way I acted. I wanted to make you angry; I was embarrassed, I suppose, and…" The words trailed off as she searched for some way to describe the way she had felt. Even now something inside her warmed and stirred at the knowledge that she had lain beside him, sharing the intimacy of sleep.

Raven heard him swear softly, then he rubbed a hand over the back of his neck. "I baited you."

"You're awfully good at it," she said, trying to make light of what had passed between them. "Much better than I am. I can't think about what I'm saying when I'm angry."

"Obviously, neither can I. Look, Raven," Brand began and turned. Her eyes were huge, swimming with restrained tears. He broke off what he had been about to say and moved to the table for his cigarettes. After lighting one, he turned back to her. "I'm sorry I lost my temper. It's something I don't do often because it's a nasty one. And you've got a good aim with a punch, Raven, and it reminded me of the last time we were together five years ago."

She felt her stomach tighten in defense. "I don't think either of us should dwell on that."

"No." He nodded slowly. His eyes were calm again and considering. Raven knew he was poking into her brain. "Not at the moment, in any case. We should get on with today." He smiled, and she felt each individual muscle in her body relax. "It seems we couldn't wait until we settled in before having a fight."

"No." She answered his smile. "But then I've always been impatient." Moving to him, Raven rose on her toes and pressed her lips tightly to his. "I'm really sorry, Brandon."

"You've already apologized."

"Yes, well, just remember the next time, it'll be your turn to grovel."

Brand tugged on her hair. "I'll make some more coffee. We should have time for one more cup before we have to strap in."

When he had gone into the galley, Raven stood where she was a moment. The last time, she thought, five years ago.

She remembered it perfectly: each word, each hurt.

And she remembered that the balance of the fault then had also been hers. They'd been alone; he'd wanted her. She had wanted him. Then everything had gone wrong. Raven remembered how she had shouted at him, near hysteria. He'd been patient, then his patience had snapped, though not in the way it had today. Then, she remembered, he'd been cold, horribly, horribly cold. Comparing the two reactions, Raven realized she preferred the heat and violence to the icy disdain.

Raven could bring the scene back with ease. They'd been close, and the desire had risen to warm her. Then it was furnace hot and she was smothering, then shouting at him not to touch her. She'd told him she couldn't bear for him to touch her. Brand had taken her at her word and left her. Raven could easily remember the despair, the regret and confusion—and the love for him outweighing all else.

But when she had gone to find him the next morning, he had already checked out of his hotel. He had left California, left her, without a word. And there'd been no word from him in five years. No word, she mused, but for the stories in every magazine, in every newspaper. No word but for the whispered comments at parties and in restaurants whenever she would walk in. No word but for the constant questions, the endless speculation in print as to why they were no longer an item—why Brand Carstairs had begun to collect women like trophies.

So she had forced him out of her mind. Her work, her talent and her music had been used to fill the holes he had left in her life. She'd steadied herself and built a life with herself in control again. That was for the best, she had decided. Sharing the reins was dangerous. And, she mused, glancing toward the galley, it would still be dangerous. *He* would still be dangerous.

Quickly Raven shook her head. Brandon was right, she told herself. It was time to concentrate on today. They had work to do, a score to write. Taking a deep breath, she walked to the galley to help him with the coffee.

Chapter 9

Raven fell instantly in love with the primitive countryside of Cornwall. She could accept this as the setting
for Arthur's Camelot. It was easy to imagine the clash
of swords and the glint of armor, the thundering gallop
of swift horses.

Spring was beginning to touch the moors, the green
blooms just now emerging. Here and there was the faintest touch of pink from wild blossoms. A fine, constant
drizzling mist added to the romance. There were houses,
cottages really, with gardens beginning to thrive. Lawns
were a tender, thin green, and she spotted the sassy yellow of daffodils and the sleepy blue of wood hyacinths.
Brand drove south toward the coast and cliffs and Land's
End.

They had eaten a country breakfast of brown eggs,
thick bacon and oat cakes and had set off again in the

little car Brand had arranged to have waiting for them at the airport.

"What's your house like, Brandon?" Raven asked as she rummaged through her purse in search of something to use to secure her hair. "You've never told me anything about it."

He glanced at her bent head. "I'll let you decide for yourself when you see it. It won't be long now."

Raven found two rubber bands of differing sizes and colors. "Are you being mysterious, or is this your way of avoiding telling me the roof leaks."

"It might," Brand considered. "Though I don't recall being dripped on. The Pengalleys would see to it; they're quite efficient about that sort of thing."

"Pengalleys?" Raven began to braid her hair.

"Caretakers," he told her. "They've a cottage a mile or so off from the house. They kept an eye on the place, and she does a bit of housekeeping when I'm in residence. He does the repairs."

"Pengalley," she murmured, rolling the name over on her tongue.

"Cornishmen, tried and true," Brand remarked absently.

"I know!" Raven turned to him with a sudden smile. "She's short and a bit stout, not fat, just solidly built, with dark hair pulled back and a staunch, rather disapproving face. He's thinner and going gray, and he tipples a bit from a flask when he thinks she's not looking."

Brand quirked a brow and shot her another brief glance. "Very clever. Just how did you manage it?"

"It had to be," Raven shrugged as she secured one braid and started on the next, "if any gothic novel I've ever read had a dab of truth in it. Are there any neighbors?"

"No one close by. That's one of the reasons I bought it."

"Antisocial?" she asked, smiling at him.

"Survival instinct," Brand corrected. "Sometimes I have to get away from it or go mad. Then I can go back and slip into harness again and enjoy it. It's like recharging." He felt her considering look and grinned. "I told you I'd mellowed."

"Yes," she said slowly, "you did." Still watching him, Raven twisted the rubber band around the tip of the second braid. "Yet you've still managed to put out quite a bit. All the albums, the double one last year; all but five of the songs were yours exclusively. And the songs you wrote for Cal Ripley—they were the best cuts on his album."

"Did you think so?" he asked.

"You know they were," she said, letting the rubber band snap into place.

"Praise is good for the ego, love."

"You've had your share now." She tossed both braids behind her back. "What I was getting at was that for someone who's so mellow, you're astonishingly productive."

"I do a lot of my writing here," Brand explained. "Or at my place in Ireland. More here, actually, because I've family across the channel, so there's visiting to be done if I'm there."

Raven gave him a curious look. "I thought you still lived in London."

"Primarily, but if I've serious work or simply need to be alone, I come here. I've family in London as well."

"Yes." Raven looked away again out into the misty landscape. "I suppose large families have disadvantages."

Something in her tone made him glance over again,

but her face was averted. He said nothing, knowing from experience that any discussion of Raven's family was taboo. Occasionally in the past, he had probed, but she had always evaded him. He knew that she had been an only child and had left home at seventeen. Out of curiosity, Brand had questioned Julie. Julie knew all there was to know about Raven, he was certain, but she had told him nothing. It was yet another mystery about Raven which alternately frustrated and attracted Brand. Now he put the questions in the back of his mind and continued smoothly.

"Well, we won't be troubled by family or neighbors. Mrs. Pengalley righteously disapproves of show people, and will keep a healthy distance."

"Show people?" Raven repeated and turning back to him, grinned. "Have you been having orgies again, Brand?"

"Not for at least three months," he assured her and swung onto a back road. "I told you I'd mellowed. But she knows about actors and actresses, you see, because as Mr. Pengalley tells me, she makes it her business to read everything she can get her hands on about them. And as for musicians, *rock* musicians, well..." He let the sentence trail off meaningfully, and Raven giggled.

"She'll think the worst, I imagine," she said cheerfully.

"The worst?" Brand cocked a brow at her.

"That you and I are carrying on a hot, illicit love affair."

"Is that the worst? It sounds rather appealing to me."

Raven colored and looked down at her hands. "You know what I meant."

Brand took her hand, kissing it lightly. "I know what

you meant." The laugh in his voice eased her embarrassment. "Will it trouble you to be labeled a fallen woman?"

"I've been labeled a fallen woman for years," she re-
turned with a smile, "every time I pick up a magazine.
Do you know how many affairs I've had with people
I've never even spoken to?"

"Celebrities are required to have overactive libidos,"
he murmured. "It's part of the job."

"Your press does yours credit," she observed dryly.

Brand nodded gravely. "I've always thought so. I
heard about a pool going around London last year. They
were betting on how many women I'd have in a three-
month period. The British," he explained, "will bet on
anything."

Raven allowed the silence to hang for a moment.
"What number did you take?"

"Twenty-seven," he told her, then grinned. "I thought
it best to be conservative."

She laughed, enjoying him. He would have done it,
too, she reflected. There was enough of the cocky street
kid left in him. "I don't think I'd better ask you if you
won."

"I wish you wouldn't," he said as the car began to
climb up a macadam drive.

Raven saw the house. It was three stories high,
formed of sober, Cornish stone with shutters of deep,
weathered green and a series of stout chimneys on the
roof. She could just make out thin puffs of smoke before
they merged with the lead-colored sky.

"Oh, Brandon, how like you," she cried, enchanted.
"How like you to find something like this."

She was out of the car before he could answer. It was
then that she discovered the house had its back to the

sea. There were no rear doors, she learned as she dashed quickly to the retaining wall on the left side. The cliff sheared off too close to the back of the house to make one practical. Instead, there were doors on the sides, set deep in Cornish stone.

Raven could look down from the safety of a waist-high wall and watch the water foam and lash out at jagged clumps of rock far below. The view sent a thrill of terror and delight through her. The sea roared below, a smashing fury of sound. Raven stood, heedless of the chill drizzle, and tried to take it all in.

"It's fabulous. Fabulous!" Turning, she lifted her face, studying the house again. Against the stone, in a great tangle of vines, grew wild roses and honeysuckles. They were greening, not yet ready to bloom, but she could already imagine their fragrance. A rock garden had been added, and among the tender green shoots was an occasional flash of color.

"You might find the inside fabulous, too," Brand ventured, laughing when she turned her wet face to him. "And dry."

"Oh, Brandon, don't be so unromantic." She turned a slow circle until she faced the house again. "It's like something out of *Wuthering Heights.*"

He took her hand. "Unromantic or not, mate, I want a bath, a hot one, and my tea."

"That does have a nice sound to it," she admitted but hung back as he pulled her to the door. She thought the cliffs wonderfully jagged and fierce. "Will we have scones? I developed a taste for them when I toured England a couple years ago. Scones and clotted cream— why does that have to sound so dreadful?"

"You'll have to take that up with Mrs. Pengalley,"

Brand began as he placed his hand on the knob. It opened before he could apply any pressure.

Mrs. Pengalley looked much as Raven had jokingly described her. She was indeed a sturdily built woman with dark hair sternly disciplined into a sensible bun. She had dark, sober eyes that passed briefly over Raven, took in the braids and damp clothing, then rested on Brandon without a flicker of expression.

"Good morning, Mr. Carstairs, you made good time," she said in a soft, Cornish burr.

"Hullo, Mrs. Pengalley, it's good to see you again. This is Ms. Williams, who'll be staying with me."

"Her room's ready, sir. Good morning, Miss Williams."

"Good morning, Mrs. Pengalley," said Raven, a trifle daunted. This, she was sure, was what was meant by "a formidable woman." "I hope I haven't put you to too much trouble."

"There's been little to do." Mrs. Pengalley's dark eyes shifted to Brand again. "There be fires laid, and the pantry's stocked, as you instructed. I've done you a casserole for tonight. You've only to heat it when you've a mind to eat. Mr. Pengalley laid in a good supply of wood; the nights're cool, and it's been damp. He'll be bringing your bags in now. We heard you drive up."

"Thanks." Brand glanced over, seeing that Raven was already wandering around the room. "We're both in need of a hot bath and some tea, then we should do well enough. Is there anything you want in particular, Raven?"

She glanced back over at the sound of her name but hadn't been attentive to the conversation. "I'm sorry. What?"

He smiled at her. "Is there anything you'd like before Mrs. Pengalley sees to tea?"

"No." Raven smiled at the housekeeper. "I'm sure everything's lovely."

Mrs. Pengalley inclined her head, her body bending not an inch. "I'll make your tea, then." As she swept from the room, Raven shot Brand a telling glance. He grinned and stretched his back.

"You continually amaze me, Brandon," she murmured, then went back to her study of the room.

It was, Raven knew, the room in which they would be doing most of their work over the next weeks. A grand piano, an old one which, she discovered on a quick testing run, had magnificent tone, was set near a pair of narrow windows. Occasional rag rugs dotted the oak-planked floor. The drapes were cream-colored lace and obviously handworked. Two comfortable sofas, both biscuit-colored, and a few Chippendale tables completed the furniture.

A fire crackled in the large stone fireplace. Raven moved closer to examine the pictures on the mantel.

At a glance, she could tell she was looking at Brand's family. There was a teenage boy in a black leather jacket whose features were the same as Brand's though his dark hair was a bit longer and was as straight as Raven's. He wore the same cocky grin as his brother. A woman was next; Raven thought her about twenty-five and astonishingly pretty with fair hair and slanted green eyes and a true English rose complexion. For all the difference in coloring, however, the resemblance to Brand was strong enough for Raven to recognize his sister. She was in another picture along with a blond man and two boys. Both boys had dark hair and the Carstairs mischief gleaming in their eyes. Raven decided Brand's sister had her hands full.

Raven studied the picture of Brand's parents for some time. The tall, thin frame had been passed down from his father, but it seemed only one of the children had inherited his fair, English looks. Raven judged it to be an old snapshot—twenty, perhaps twenty-five, years old. It had been painstakingly staged, with the man and woman dead center, standing straight in their Sunday best. The woman was dark and lovely. The man looked a bit self-conscious and ill at ease having to pose, but the woman beamed into the camera. Her eyes bespoke mischief and her mouth a hint of the cockiness so easily recognized in her children.

There were more pictures: family groups and candid shots, with Brand in several of them. The Carstairses were very much a family. Raven felt a small stir of envy. Shaking it off, she turned back to Brand and smiled.

"This is quite a group." She flicked her fingers behind her toward the mantel. "You're the oldest, aren't you? I think I read that somewhere. The resemblance is remarkable."

"Sweeney genes from my mother's side," Brand told her, looking beyond her shoulder at the crowded grouping of frames. "The only one they slipped up on a bit was Alison." He ran a hand through his damp hair and came to stand beside her. "Let me take you upstairs, love, and get you settled in. The grand tour can wait until we're dry." He slipped an arm around her. "I'm glad you're here, Raven. I've never seen you with things that are mine before. And hotel rooms, no matter how luxurious, are never home."

Later, lounging in a steaming tub, Raven thought over

Brand's statement. It was part of the business of being an entertainer to spend a great many nights in hotel rooms, albeit luxury suites, in their positions, but they were hotel rooms nonetheless. Home was a place for between concerts and guest appearances, and to her, it had become increasingly important over the years. It seemed the higher she rose, the more she needed a solid base. She realized it was the same with Brand.

They'd both been on the road for several weeks. He was home now, and somehow Raven knew already that she, too, would be at home there. For all its age and size, there was something comforting in the house. Perhaps, Raven mused as she lazily soaped a leg, it's the age and size. Continuity was important to her, as she felt she'd had little of it in her life, and space was important for the same reason.

Raven had felt an instant affinity for the house. She liked the muffled roar of the sea outside her window and the breathtaking view. She liked the old-fashioned porcelain tub with the curved legs and the oval, mahogany-framed mirror over the tiny pedestal sink.

Rising from the tub, she lifted a towel from the heated bar. When she had dried herself, she wrapped a thick, buff-colored towel around her before letting down her hair. The two braids fell from where she had pinned them atop of her head. Absently, as she wandered back into the bedroom, she began to undo them.

Her luggage still sat beside an old brass chest, but she didn't give much thought to unpacking. Instead she walked to the window seat set in the south wall and knelt on the padded cushion.

Below her the sea hurled itself onto the rocks, tossed up by the wind. There was a sucking, drawing sound before it crashed back onto the shingles and cliffs. Like the sky, they were gray, except for where the waves crested in stiff, white caps. The rain drizzled still, with small drops hitting her window to trail lazily downward. Placing her arms on the wide sill, Raven rested her chin on them and lost herself in dreamy contemplation of the scene below.

"Raven."

She heard Brand's call and the knock and answered both absently. "Yes, come in."

"I thought you might be ready to go downstairs," he said.

"In a minute. What a spectacular view this is! Come look. Does your room face the sea like this? I think I could sit here watching it forever."

"It has its points," he agreed and came over to stand behind her. He tucked his hands into his pockets. "I didn't know you had such a fondness for the sea."

"Yes, always, but I've never had a room where I felt right on top of it before. I'm going to like hearing it at night." She smiled over her shoulder at him. "Is your house in Ireland on the coast, too?"

"No, it's more of a farm, actually. I'd like to take you there." He ran his fingers through her hair, finding it thick and soft and still faintly damp. "It's a green, weepy country, and as appealing as this one, in a different way."

"That's your favorite, isn't it?" Raven smiled up at him. "Even though you live in London and come here to do work, it's the place in Ireland that's special."

He returned the smile. "If it wasn't that there'd have been Sweeneys and Hardestys everywhere we looked, I'd have taken you there. My mother's family," he explained, "are very friendly people. If the score goes well, perhaps we can take a bit of a vacation there when we're done."

Raven hesitated. "Yes...I'd like that."

"Good." The smile turned into a grin. "And I like your dress."

Puzzled, Raven followed his lowered glance. Stunned, she gripped the towel at her breasts and scrambled to her feet. "I didn't realize...I'd forgotten." She could feel the color heating her cheeks. "Brandon, you might have said something."

"I just did," he pointed out. His eyes skimmed down to her thighs.

"Very funny," Raven retorted and found herself smiling. "Now, why don't you clear out and let me change?"

"Must you? Pity." He hooked his hand over the towel where it met between her breasts. The back of his fingers brushed the swell of her bosom. "I was just thinking I liked your outfit." Without touching her in any other way, he brought his mouth down to hers.

"You smell good," he murmured, then traced just the inside of her mouth with his tongue. "Rain's still in your hair."

A roaring louder than the sea began in her brain. Instinctually she was kissing him back, meeting his tongue with hers, stepping closer and rising on her toes. Though her response was quick and giving, he kept the kiss light. She sensed the hunger and the strength under tight control.

Under the towel, his finger swept over her nipple, finding it taut with desire. Raven felt a strong, unfamiliar ache between her thighs. She moaned with it as each muscle in her body went lax. He lifted his face and waited until her eyes opened.

"Shall I make love to you, Raven?"

She stared at him, aching with the churn of rising needs. He was putting the decision in her hands. She should have been grateful, relieved, yet at that moment she found she would have preferred it if he had simply swept her away. For an instant she wanted no choice, no voice, but only to be taken.

"You'll have to be sure," he told her quietly. Lifting her chin with his finger, he smiled. His eyes were a calm blue-green. "I've no intention of making it easy for you."

He dropped his hand. "I'll wait for you downstairs, though I still think it's a pity you have to change. You're very attractive in a towel."

"Brandon," she said when he was at the door. He turned, lifting a brow in acknowledgment. "What if I'd said yes?" Raven grinned, feeling a bit more steady with the distance between them. "Wouldn't that have been a bit awkward with Mrs. Pengalley still downstairs?"

Leaning against the door, he said lazily, "Raven, if you'd said yes, I wouldn't give a damn if Mrs. Pengalley and half the country were downstairs." He shut the door carefully behind him.

Chapter 10

Both Raven and Brand were anxious to begin. They started the day after their arrival and soon fell into an easy, workable routine. Brand rose early and was usually finishing up a good-sized breakfast by the time Raven dragged herself downstairs. When she was fortified with coffee, they started their morning stretch, working until noon and Mrs. Pengalley's arrival. While the housekeeper brought in the day's marketing and saw to whatever domestic chores needed to be seen to, Brand and Raven would take long walks.

The days were balmy, scented with sea spray and spring. The land was rugged, even harsh, with patches of poor ground covered with heather not yet in bloom. The pounding surf beat against towering granite cliffs. Hardy birds built their nests in the crags. Their cries could be heard over the crash of the waves. Standing high, Raven could see down to the village with its neat rows of cottages and white church spire.

They'd work again in the afternoon with the fire sizzling in the grate at their backs. After dinner they went over the day's work. By the end of the week they had a loosely based outline for the score and the completed title song.

They didn't work without snags. Both Raven and Brand felt too strongly about music for any collaboration to run smoothly. But the arguments seemed to stimulate both of them; and the final product was the better for them. They were a good team.

They remained friends. Brand made no further attempt to become Raven's lover. From time to time Raven would catch him staring intently at her. Then she would feel the pull, as sensual as a touch, as tempting as a kiss. The lack of pressure confused her and drew her more effectively than his advances could have. Advances could be refused, avoided. She knew he was waiting for her decision. Underneath the casualness, the jokes and professional disagreements, the air throbbed with tension.

The afternoon was long and a bit dreary. A steady downpour of rain kept Raven and Brand from walking the cliffs. Their music floated through the house, echoing in corners here and there and drifting to forgotten attics. They'd built the fire high with Mr. Pengalley's store of wood to chase away the dampness that seemed to seep through the windows. A tray of tea and biscuits that they had both forgotten rested on one of the Chippendale tables. Their argument was reaching its second stage.

"We've got to bring up the tempo," Raven insisted. "It just doesn't work this way."

"It's a mood piece, Raven."

"Not a funeral dirge. It drags this way, Brandon. People are going to be nodding off before she finishes singing it."

"Nobody falls asleep while Lauren Chase is singing," Brand countered. "This number is pure sex, Raven, and she'll sell it."

"Yes, she will," Raven agreed, "but not at this tempo." She shifted on the piano bench so that she faced him more directly. "All right, Joe's fallen asleep at the typewriter in the middle of the chapter he's writing. He's already believing himself a little mad because of the vivid dreams he's having about his character Tessa. She seems too real, and he's fallen in love with her even though he knows she's a product of his own imagination, a character in a novel he's writing, a fantasy. And now, in the middle of the day, he's dreaming about her again, and this time she promises to come to him that night."

"I know the plot, Raven," Brand said dryly.

Though she narrowed her eyes, Raven checked her temper. She thought she detected some fatigue in his voice. Once or twice she'd been awakened in the middle of the night by his playing. "'Nightfall' is hot, Brandon. You're right about it being pure sex, and your lyrics are fabulous. But it still needs to move."

"It moves." He took a last drag on his cigarette before crushing it out. "Chase knows how to hang on to a note."

Raven made a quick sound of frustration. Unfortunately he was usually right about such things. His instincts were phenomenal. This time, however, she was certain that her own instincts—as a songwriter and as a woman—were keener. She knew the way the song had to be sung to reap the full effect. The moment she had read Brand's lyrics, she had known what was needed. The song had flowed, completed, through her head.

"I know she can hang on to a note, and she can handle choreography. She'll be able to do both and still do the song at the right tempo. Let me show you." She began to play the opening bars. Brand shrugged and rose from the bench.

Raven moved the tempo to *andante* and sang to her own accompaniment. Her voice wrapped itself around the music. Brand moved to the window to watch the rain. It was the song of a temptress, full of implicit, wild promises.

Raven's voice flowed over the range of notes, then heated when it was least expected until Brand felt a tight knot of desire in the pit of his stomach. There was something not quite earthy in the melody she had created. The quicker tempo made a sharp contrast, much more effective than the pace Brand had wanted. She ended abruptly in a raspy whisper without any fade-out. She tossed her hair, then shot him a look over her shoulder.

"Well?" There was a half smile on her face.

He had his back to her and kept his hands tucked into his pockets. "You have to be right now and again, I suppose."

Raven laughed, spinning around on the bench until she faced the room. "You've a way with compliments, Brandon. It sets my heart fluttering."

"She doesn't have your range," he murmured. Then, making an impatient movement, he wandered over to the teapot. "I don't think she'll get as much out of the low scale as you do."

"Mmm." Raven shrugged as she watched him pour out a cup of tea. "She's got tremendous style, though;

she'll milk every ounce out of it." He set the tea down again without touching it and roamed to the fire. As she watched him, a worried frown creased Raven's brow. "Brandon, what's wrong?"

He threw another log on the already roaring fire. "Nothing, just restless."

"This rain's depressing." She rose to go to the window. "I've never minded it. Sometimes I like a dreary, sleepy day. I can be lazy without feeling guilty. Maybe that's what you should do, Brandon, be lazy today. You've got that marvelous chessboard in the library. Why don't you teach me to play?" She lifted her hands to his shoulders and feeling the tension, began to knead absently. "Of course, that might be hard work. Julie gave up playing backgammon with me. She says I haven't any knack for strategy."

Raven broke off when Brand turned abruptly around and removed her hands from his shoulders. Without speaking, he walked away from her. He went to the liquor cabinet and drew out a bottle of bourbon. Raven watched as he poured three fingers into a glass and drank it down.

"I don't think I've the patience for games this afternoon," he told her as he poured a second drink.

"All right, Brandon," she said. "No games." She walked over to stand in front of him, keeping her eyes direct. "Why are you angry with me? Certainly not because of the song."

The look held for several long moments while the fire popped and sizzled in the grate. Raven heard a log fall as the one beneath it gave way.

"Perhaps it's time you and I talked," Brandon said as he idly swirled the remaining liquor in the glass. "It's dangerous to leave things hanging for five years; you never know when they're going to fall."

Raven felt a ripple of disquiet but nodded. "You may be right."

Brand gave her a quick smile. "Should we be civilized and sit down or take a few free swings standing up?"

She shrugged. "I don't think there's any need to be civilized. Civilized fighting never clears the air."

"All right," he began but was interrupted by the peal of the bell. Setting down his glass, Brand shot her a last look, then went to answer.

Alone, Raven tried to control her jitters. There was a storm brewing, she knew, and it wasn't outside the windows. Brand was itching for a fight, and though the reason was unclear to her, Raven found herself very willing to oblige him. The tension between them had been glossed over in the name of music and peace. Now, despite her nerves, she was looking forward to shattering the calm. Hearing his returning footsteps, she walked back to the tea tray and picked up her cup.

"Package for you." Brand gestured with it as he came through the doorway. "From Henderson."

"I wonder what he could be sending me," she murmured, already ripping off the heavy packing tape. "Oh, of course." She tossed the wrappings carelessly aside and studied the album jacket. "They're sample jackets for the album I'm releasing this summer." Without glancing at him, Raven handed Brand one of the covers, then turned to another to read the liner notes.

For the next few minutes Brand studied the cover picture without speaking. Again, a background of white, Raven sitting in her habitual cross-legged fashion. She was looking full into the camera with only a tease of a smile on her lips. Her eyes were very gray and very direct. Over her shoulders and down to her knees, her hair spilled—a sharp contrast against the soft-focused white of the background. The arrangement appeared to be haphazard but had been cleverly posed nonetheless. She appeared to be nude, and the effect was fairly erotic.

"Did you approve this picture?"

"Hmm?" Raven pushed back her hair as she continued to read. "Oh, yes, I looked over the proofs before I left on tour. I'm still not completely sure about this song order, but I suppose it's a bit late to change it now."

"I always felt Henderson was above packaging you this way."

"Packaging me what way?" she asked absently.

"As a virgin offering to the masses." He handed her the cover.

"Brandon, really...how ridiculous."

"I don't think so," he said. "I think it's an uncannily apt description: virgin white, soft focus, and you sitting naked in the middle of it all."

"I'm not naked," she retorted indignantly. "I don't do nudes."

"The potential buyer isn't supposed to know that, though, is he?" Brand leaned against the piano and watched her through narrowed eyes.

"It's provocative, certainly. It's meant to be." Raven frowned down at the cover again. "There's nothing wrong with that. I'm not a child to be dressed up in Mary Janes and a pink pinafore, Brandon. This is business. There's nothing extreme about this cover. And I'm more modestly covered than I would be on a public beach."

"But not more decently," he said coldly. "There's a difference."

Color flooded her face, now a mixture of annoyance and embarrassment. "It's not indecent. I've never posed for an indecent picture. Karl Straighter is one of the finest photographers in the business. He doesn't shoot indecent pictures."

"One man's art is another's porn, I suppose."

Her eyes widened as she lowered the jackets to the piano bench. "That's a disgusting thing to say," she whispered. "You're being deliberately horrible."

"I'm simply giving you my opinion," he corrected, lifting a brow. "You don't have to like it."

"I don't need your opinion. I don't need your approval."

"No," he said and crushed out his cigarette. "You bloody well don't, do you? But you're going to have it in any case." He caught her by the arm when she would have turned away. The power of the grip contrasted the cool tone and frosty eyes.

"Let go of me," Raven demanded, putting her hand on top of his and trying unsuccessfully to pry it from her arm.

"When I'm finished."

"You have finished." Her voice was abruptly calm, and she stopped her frantic attempts to free herself. Instead she faced him squarely, emotion burning in her eyes. "I don't have to listen to you when you go out of your way to insult me, Brandon. I won't listen to you. You can prevent me from leaving because you're stronger than I am, but you can't make me listen." She swallowed but managed to keep her voice steady. "I run my own life. You're entitled to your opinion, certainly, but you're not entitled to hurt me with it. I don't want to talk to you now; I just want you to let me go."

He was silent for so long, Raven thought he would refuse. Then, slowly, he loosened his grip until she could slip her arm from his fingers. Without a word she turned and left the room.

Perhaps it was the strain of her argument with Brand or the lash of rain against the windows or the sudden fury of thunder and lightning. The dream formed out of a vague montage of childhood remembrances that left her with impressions rather than vivid pictures. Thoughts and images floated and receded against the darkness of sleep. There were rolling sensations of fear, guilt, despair, one lapping over the other while she moaned and twisted beneath the sheets, trying to force herself awake. But she was trapped, caught fast in the world just below consciousness. Then the thunder seemed to explode inside her head, and the flash of lightning split the room with a swift, white flash. Screaming, Raven sat up in bed.

The room was pitch dark again when Brand rushed in; he found his way to the bed by following the sounds of Raven's wild weeping. "Raven. Here, love." Even as he reached her, she threw herself into his arms and clung. She was trembling hard, and her skin was icy. Brand pulled the quilt up over her back and cuddled her. "Don't cry, love, you're safe here." He patted and stroked as he would for a child frightened of a storm. "It'll soon be over."

"Hold me." She pressed her face into his bare shoulder. "Please, just hold me." Her breathing was quick, burning her throat as she struggled for air. "Oh, Brandon, such an awful dream."

He rocked her and laid a light kiss on her temple.

"What was it about?" The telling, he recalled from child-hood, usually banished the fear.

"She'd left me alone again," Raven murmured, shuddering so that he drew her closer in response. The words came out as jumbled as her thoughts, as tumbled as the dream. "How I hated being alone in that room. The only light was from the building next door—one of those red neon lights that blinks on and off, on and off, so that the dark was never still. And so much noise out on the street, even with the windows closed. Too hot…too hot to sleep," she murmured into his shoulder. "I watched the light and waited for her to come back. She was drunk again." She whimpered, her fingers opening and closing against his chest. "And she'd brought a man with her. I put the pillow over my head so I wouldn't hear."

Raven paused to steady her breath. It was dark and quiet in Brand's arms. Outside, the storm rose in high fury.

"She fell down the steps and broke her arm, so we moved, but it was always the same. Dingy little rooms, airless rooms that smelled always of gin no matter how you scrubbed. Thin walls, walls that might as well not have existed for the privacy they gave you. But she always promised that this time, this time it'd be different. She'd get a job, and I'd go to school…but always one day I'd come home and there'd be a man and a bottle."

She wasn't clinging any longer but simply leaning against him as if all passion were spent. Lightning flared again, but she remained still.

"Raven." Brand eased her gently away and tilted her face to his. Tears were still streaming from her eyes, but her breathing was steadier. He could barely make out the shape of her face in the dark. "Where was your father?"

He could see the shine of her eyes as she stared at him. She made a soft, quiet sound as one waking. He knew the words had slipped from her while she had been vulnerable and unaware. Now she was aware, but it was too late for defenses. The sigh she made was an empty, weary sound.

"I don't know who he was." Slowly she drew out of Brand's arms and rose from the bed. "She didn't, either. You see, there were so many."

Brand said nothing but reached into the pocket of the jeans he had hastily dragged on and found a pack of matches. Striking one, he lit the bedside candle. The light wavered and flickered, hardly more than a pulse beat in the dark. "How long," he asked and shook out the match, "did you live like that?"

Raven dragged both hands through her hair, then hugged herself. She knew she'd already said too much for evasions. "I don't remember a time she didn't drink, but when I was very young, five or six, she still had some control over it. She used to sing in clubs. She had big dreams and an average voice, but she was very lovely... once."

Pausing, Raven pressed her fingers against her eyes and wiped away tears. "By the time I was eight, she was...her problem was unmanageable. And there were always men. She needed men as much as she needed to drink. Some of them were better than others. One of them took me to the zoo a couple of times...."

She trailed off and turned away. Brand watched the candlelight flicker over the thin material of her nightgown.

"She got steadily worse. I think part of it was from the frustration of having her voice go. Of course, she abused it dreadfully with smoking and drinking, but the more it deteriorated, the more she smoked and drank. She ruined her voice and ruined her health and ruined any chance she had of making something of herself. Sometimes I hated her. Sometimes I know she hated herself."

A sob escaped, but Raven pushed it back and began to wander the room. The movement seemed to make it easier, and the words tumbled out quicker, pressing for release. "She'd cry and cling to me and beg me not to hate her. She'd promise the moon, and more often than not, I'd believe her. 'This time'—that was one of her favorite beginnings. It still is." Raven let out a shaky sigh. "She loved me when she wasn't drinking and forgot me completely when she was. It was like living with two different women, and neither one of them was easy. When she was sober, she expected an average mother-and-daughter relationship. Had I done my homework? Why was I five minutes late getting home from school? When she was drunk, I was supposed to keep the hell out of her way. I remember once, when I was twelve, she went three months and sixteen days without a drink. Then I came home from school and found her passed out on the bed. She'd had an audition that afternoon for a gig at this two-bit club. Later she told me she'd just wanted one drink to calm her nerves. Just one…" Raven shivered and hugged herself tighter. "It's cold," she murmured.

Brand rose and stooped in front of the fire. He added kindling and logs to the bed of coals in the grate. Raven walked to the window to watch the fury of the storm over the sea. Lightning still flashed sporadically, but the violence of the thunder and the rain were dying.

"There were so many other times. She was working as a cocktail waitress in this little piano bar in Houston. I was sixteen then. I always came by on payday so I could make certain she didn't spend the money before I bought food. She'd been pretty good then. She'd been working about six weeks straight and had an affair going with the manager. He was one of the better ones. I used to play around at the piano if the place was empty. One of my mother's lovers had been a musician; he'd taught me the basics and said I had a good ear. Mama liked hearing me play." Her voice had quieted. Brand watched her trail a finger down the dark pane of window glass.

"Ben, the manager, asked me if I wanted to play during the lunch hour. He said I could sing, too, as long as I kept it soft and didn't talk to the customers. So I started." Raven sighed and ran a hand over her brow. Behind her came the pop and crackle of flame. "We left Houston for Oklahoma City. I lied about my age and got a job singing in a club. It was one of Mama's worst periods. There were times I was afraid to leave her alone, but she wasn't working then, and…" She broke off with a sound of frustration and rubbed at an ache in her temple. She wanted to stop, wanted to block it all out, but she knew she had come too far. Pressing her brow against the glass, she waited until her thoughts came back into order.

"We needed the money, so I had to risk leaving her at night. I suppose we exchanged roles for a time," she murmured. "The thing I learned young, but consistently forgot, was that an alcoholic finds money for a bottle. Always, no matter what. One night during my second set she wove her way into the club. Wayne was working there and caught onto the situation quickly. He managed to quiet her down before it got too ugly. Later he helped me get her home and into bed. He was wonderful: no lectures, no pity, no advice. Just support."

Raven turned away from the window again and wandered to the fire. "But she came back again, twice more, and they let me go. There were other towns, other clubs, but it was the same then and hardly matters now. Just before I turned eighteen I left her." Her voice trembled a bit, and she took a moment to steady it. "I came home from work one night, and she was passed out at the kitchen table with one of those half-gallon jugs of wine. I knew if I didn't get away from her I'd go crazy. So I put her to bed, packed a bag, left her all the money I could spare and walked out. Just like that." She covered her face with her hands a moment, pressing her fingers into her eyes. "It was like being able to breathe for the first time in my life."

Raven roamed back to the kitchen. She could see the vague ghost of her own reflection. Studying it, listening to the steady but more peaceful drum of rain, she continued. "I worked my way to L.A., and Henderson saw me. He pushed me. I'm not certain what my ambition was before I signed with him. Just to survive, I think. One day and then the next. Then there were contracts and recording sessions and the whole crazy circus. Doors started opening. Some of them were trap doors, I've always thought." She gave a quick, wondering laugh. "God, it was marvelous and scary and I don't believe I could ever go through those first few months again. Anyway, Henderson got me publicity, and the first hit single got me more. And then I got a call from a hospital in Memphis."

Raven turned and began to pace. The light silk of her nightgown clung, then swirled, with her movements. "I had to go, of course. She was in pretty bad shape. Her latest lover had beaten her and stolen what little money she had. She cried. Oh, God, all the same promises. She was sorry; she loved me. Never again, never again. I was the only decent thing she'd ever done in her life." The tears were beginning to flow again, but this time Raven made no attempt to stop them. "As soon as she could travel, I brought her back with me. Julie had found a sanitarium in Ojai and a very earnest young doctor. Justin Randolf Karter. Isn't that a marvelous name, Brandon?" Bitterness spilled out with the tears. "A marvelous name, a remarkable man. He took me into his tasteful, leather-bound office and explained the treatment my mother would receive."

Whirling, Raven faced Brand, her shoulders heaving with sobs. "I didn't want to know! I just wanted him to do it. He told me not to set my hopes too high, and I told him I hadn't any hopes at all. He must have found me cynical, because he suggested several good organizations I could speak to. He reminded me that alcoholism is a disease and that my mother was a victim. I said the hell she was; *I* was the victim!" Raven forced the words out as she hugged herself tightly. "*I* was the victim; *I* had had to live with her and deal with her lies and her sickness and her men. It was so safe, so easy, for him to be sanctimonious and understanding behind that tidy white coat. And I *hated* her." The sobs came in short, quick jerks as she balled her hands and pressed them against her eyes. "And I loved her." Her breath trembled in and out as everything she had pent up over the weeks of her mother's latest treatment poured through her. "I still love her," she whispered.

Weary, nearly spent, she turned to the fire, resting her palms on the mantel. "Dr. Karter let me shout at him, then he sat with me when I broke down. I went home, and they started her treatment. Two days later I met you."

Raven didn't hear him move, didn't know he stood behind her, until she felt his hands on her shoulders. Without speaking she turned and went into his arms. Brand held her, feeling the light tremors while he stared down at the licking, greedy flames. Outside, the storm had become only a patter of rain against the windows.

"Raven, if you had told me, I might have been able to make things easier for you."

She shook her head, then buried her face against his chest. "No, I didn't want it to touch that part of my life. I just wasn't strong enough." Taking a deep breath, she pulled back far enough to look in his eyes. "I was afraid that if you knew you wouldn't want anything to do with me."

"Raven." There was hurt as well as censure in his voice.

"I know it was wrong, Brandon, even stupid, but you have to understand: everything seemed to be happening to me at once. I needed time. I needed to sort out how I was going to live my life, how I was going to deal with my career, my mother, everything." Her hands gripped his arms as she willed him to see through her eyes. "I was nobody one day and being mobbed by fans the next. My picture was everywhere. I heard myself every time I turned on the radio. You know what that's like."

Brand brushed her hair from her cheek. "Yes, I know what that's like." As he spoke, he could feel her relax with a little shudder.

"Before I could take a breath, Mama walked back into my life. Part of me hated her, but instead of realizing that it was a normal reaction and dealing with it, I felt an unreasonable guilt. And I was ashamed. No," she shook her head, anticipating him, "there's no use telling me I had no need to be. That's an intellectual statement, a practical statement; it has nothing to do with emotion. I don't expect you to understand that part of it. You've never had to deal with it. She's my mother. It isn't possible to completely separate myself from that, even knowing that the responsibility for her problem isn't mine." Raven gave him one last, long look before turning away. "And on top of everything that was happening to me, I fell in love with you." The flames danced and snapped as she watched. "I loved you," she murmured so quietly he strained to hear, "but I couldn't be your lover."

Brand stared at her back, started to reach for her, then dropped his hands to his sides. "Why?"

Only her head turned as she looked over her shoulder at him. Her face was in shadows. "Because then I would be like her," she whispered, then turned away again.

"You don't really believe that, Raven." Brand took her shoulders, but she shook her head, not answering. Firmly he turned her to face him, making a slow, thorough study of her. "Do you make a habit of condemning children for their parents' mistakes?"

"No, but I…"

"You don't have the right to do it to yourself."

She shut her eyes on a sigh. "I know, I know that, but…"

"There're no buts on this one, Raven." His fingers tightened until she opened her eyes again. "You know who you are."

There was only the sound of the sea and the rain and fire. "I wanted you," she managed in a trembling voice, "when you held me, touched me. You were the first man I'd ever wanted." She swallowed, and again he felt the shudder course through her. "Then I'd remember all those cramped little rooms, all those men with my mother...." She broke off and would have turned away again if his hands hadn't held her still.

Brand removed his hands from her arms, then slowly, his eyes still on hers, he used them to frame her face. "Sleeping with a stranger is different from making love with someone you care for."

Raven moistened her lips. "Yes, I know that, but..."

"Do you?" The question stopped her. She could do no more than let out a shaky breath. "Let me show you, Raven."

Her eyes were trapped by his. She knew he would release her if she so much as shook her head. Fear was tiny pinpoints along her skin. Need was a growing warmth in her blood. She lifted her hands to his wrists. "Yes."

Again Brand gently brushed the hair away from her cheeks. When her face was framed by his hands alone, he lowered his head and kissed her eyes closed. He could feel her trembling in his arms. Her hands still held his wrists, and her fingers tightened when he brought his mouth to hers. His was patient, waiting until her lips softened and parted.

The kisses grew deeper, but slowly, now moister until she swayed against him. His fingers caressed, his mouth roamed. Firelight flickered over them in reds and golds, casting its own shadows. Raven could feel the heat from it through the silk she wore, but it was the glow inside of her which built and flamed hot.

Brand lowered his hands to her shoulders, gently massaging as he teased her lower lip with his teeth. Raven felt the gown slip down over her breasts, then cling briefly to her hips before it drifted to the floor. She started to protest, but he deepened the kiss. The thought spiraled away. Down the curve of her back, over the slight flare of her hips, he ran his hands. Then he picked her up in his arms. With her mind spinning, she sank into the mattress. When Brand joined her, the touch of his naked body against hers jolted her, bringing on a fresh surge of doubts and fears.

"Brandon, please, I..." The words were muffled, then died inside his mouth.

Easily, his hands caressed her, stroking without hurry. Somewhere in the back of her mind she knew he held himself under tight control. But her mind had relaxed, and her limbs were heavy. His mouth wandered to her throat, tasting, giving pleasure, arousing by slow, irresistible degrees. He worked her nipple with his thumb, and she moaned and moved against him. Brand allowed his mouth to journey downward, laying light, feathering kisses over the curve of her breast. Lightly, very lightly, he ran his tongue over the tip. Raven felt the heat between her thighs, and tangling her fingers in his hair, pressed him closer. She arched and shuddered not from fear but from passion.

Heat unlike anything she had ever known or imagined was building inside her. She was still aware of the flicker of the fire and candlelight on her closed lids, of the soft brush of linen sheets against her back, of the faint, pleasant smell of woodsmoke. But these sensations were dim, while her being seemed focused on the liquefying touch of his tongue over her skin, the feathery brush of his fingers on her thighs. Over the hiss of rain and fire, she heard him murmur her name, heard her own soft, mindless response.

Her breath quickened, and her mouth grew hungry. Suddenly desperate, she drew his face back to hers. She wrapped her arms around him tightly as the pressure of the kiss pushed her head deep into the pillow. Brand lay across her, flesh to flesh, so that her breasts yielded to his chest. Raven could feel the light mat of his hair against her skin.

His hand lay on her stomach and drifted down as she moved under him. There was a flash of panic as he slid between her thighs, then her breath caught in a heady rush of pleasure. He was still patient, his fingers gentle and unhurried as they gradually increased her rhythm.

For Raven, there was no world beyond the firelit room, beyond the four-poster bed. His mouth took hers, his tongue probing deeply, then moving to her ear, her throat, her neck and back to her lips. All the while, his hands and fingers were taking her past all thought, past all reason.

Then he was on top of her, and she opened for him, ready to give, to receive. She was too steeped in wonder to comprehend his strict, unwavering control. She knew only that she wanted him and urged him to take her. There was a swift flash of pain, dulled by a pleasure too acute to be measured. She cried out, but the sound was muffled against his mouth, then all was lost on wave after wave of delight.

Chapter 11

With her head in the curve of Brand's shoulder, Raven watched the fire. Her hand lay over his heart. She could feel its quick, steady rhythm under her palm.

The room was quiet, and outside, the rain had slackened to a murmur. Raven knew she would remember this moment every time she lay listening to rain against windows. Brand's arm was under her, curled over her back with his hand loosely holding her arm. Since he had rolled from her and drawn her against his side, he had been silent. Raven thought he slept and was content to lie with him, watching the fire and listening to the rain. She shifted her head, wanting to look at him and found he wasn't asleep. She could see the sheen of his eyes as he stared at the ceiling. Raven lifted a hand to his cheek.

"I thought you were asleep."

Brand caught her hand and pressed it to his lips. "No,

I…" Looking down at her, he broke off, then slowly brushed a tear from her lash with his thumb. "I hurt you."

"No." Raven shook her head. For a moment she buried her face in the curve of his neck, where she could feel his warmth, smell his scent. "Oh, no, you didn't hurt me. You made me feel wonderful. I feel…free." She looked up at him again and smiled. "Does that sound foolish?"

"No." Brand ran his fingers through the length of her hair, pushing it back when it would have hidden her face from him. Her skin was flushed. In her eyes he could see the reflected flames from the fire. "You're so beautiful."

She smiled again and kissed him. "I've always thought the same about you."

He laughed, drawing her closer. "Have you?"

She lay half across him, heated flesh to heated flesh. "Yes, I always thought you'd make a remarkably lovely girl, and I see by your sister's picture that I was right."

He lifted a brow. "Strange, I never realized the direction of your thoughts. Perhaps it's best I didn't."

Raven gave one of her low, rich chuckles and pressed her lips against the column of his throat. She loved the way his tones could become suddenly suavely British. "I'm sure you make a much better man."

"That's comforting," he said dryly as he began to stroke her back, "under the circumstances." His fingers lingered at her hip to caress.

"I'm sure I like you much better this way." Raven kissed the side of his throat again, working her way to his ear. Under her breast she felt the sudden jump and scramble of his heartbeat. "Brandon…" She sighed, nuzzling his ear. "You're so good to me, so kind, so gentle."

She heard him groan before he rolled over, reversing their positions. His eyes were heated and intense and very green, reminding her of the moment he had held her like this on the plane. Now again her pulse began to hammer, but not with fear.

"Love isn't always kind, Raven," he said roughly. "It isn't always gentle."

His mouth came down on hers crushingly, urgently, as all the restraints he had put on himself snapped. There was no patience in him now, only passion. Where before he had taken her up calmly, easily, now he took her plummeting at a desperate velocity. Her mouth felt bruised and tender from his, yet she learned hunger incited hunger. Raven wanted more, and still more, so she caught him closer.

Demanding, possessing, he took his hands over her. "So long," she heard him mutter. "I've wanted you for so long." Then his teeth found the sensitive area of her neck, and she heard nothing. She plunged toward the heat and the dark.

Brand felt her give and respond and demand. He was nearly wild with need. He wanted to touch all of her, taste all of her. He was as desperate as a starving man and as ruthless. Where before, responding to her innocence, he had been cautious, now he took what he had wanted for too many years. She was his as he had dreamed she would be: soft and yielding, then soft and hungry beneath him.

He could hear her moan, feel the bite of her fingernails in his shoulders as he took his mouth down the curve of her breast. The skin of her stomach was smooth and quivered under his tongue. He slipped a hand between her thighs, and she strained against him so that he knew she was as desperate as he. Yet he wouldn't take her, not yet. He felt an impossible greed. His tongue moved to follow the path of his hands. All the years he'd wanted her, all the frustrated passion, burst out, catching them both in the explosion. Not knowing the paths, Raven went where he led her and learned that desire was deeper, stronger, than anything she had known possible.

He was pulling her down—down until the heat was too intense to bear. But she wanted more. His hands were rough, bruising her skin. But she craved no gentleness. She was steeped in passion too deep for escape. She called out for him, desperately, mindlessly, for him to take her. She knew there couldn't be more; they'd gone past all the rules. Pleasure could not be sharper; passion could not be darker than it was at that moment.

Then he was inside her, and everything that had gone before paled against the color and the heat.

His mouth was buried at her neck. From far off he heard her gasps for breath merge with his own. They moved together like lightning, so that he could no longer think. There was only Raven. All passion intensified, concentrated, until he thought he would go mad from it. The pain of it shot through him, then flowed from him, leaving him weak.

They lay still, with Brand over her, his face buried in her hair. His breathing was ragged, and he gave no thought to his weight as he relaxed completely. Beneath him Raven shuddered again and again with the release of passion. She gripped his shoulders tightly, not wanting him to move, not wanting to relinquish the unity. If he had shown her the tenderness and compassion of loving the first time, now he had shown her darker secrets.

A log fell in the grate, scattering sparks against the screen. Brand lifted his head and looked down at her. His eyes were heavy, still smoldering, as they lowered to her swollen mouth. He placed a soft kiss on them, then, shifting his weight, prepared to rise.

"No, don't go." Raven took his arm, sitting up as he did.

"Only to bank the fire."

Bringing her knees to her chest, Raven watched as Brand stacked the fire for the night. The light danced over his skin as she stared, entranced. The ripple of muscles was surprising in one so lean. She saw them in his shoulders, his back, his thighs. The passion in the cool, easygoing man was just as surprising, but she knew the feel of it now, just as she knew the feel of the muscles. He turned and looked at her with the fire leaping at his back. They studied each other, both dazed by what had passed between them. Then he shook his head.

"My God, Raven, I want you again."

She held her arms out to him.

There was a brilliant ribbon of sunlight across Raven's eyes. It was a warm, red haze. She allowed her lids to open slowly before turning to Brand.

He slept still, his breathing deep and even. She had to suppress the urge to brush his hair away from his face because she didn't want to wake him. Not yet. For the first time in her life she woke to look at her lover's face. She felt a warm, settled satisfaction.

He *is* beautiful, she thought, remembering how he had been faintly distressed to hear her say so the night before. *And I love him.* Raven almost said the words aloud as she let herself think them. I've always loved him, right from the beginning, all through the years in between— and even more now that we're together. But no mistakes this time. She closed her eyes tight on the sudden fear that he could walk out of her life again. *No demands, no pressures.* We'll just be together; that's all I need.

She dropped her eyes to his mouth. It had been tender in the night, she remembered, then hungry, almost brutal. She hadn't realized how badly he had wanted her, or she him, until the barriers had shattered. *Five years, five empty years!* Raven pushed the thought away. There was no yesterday, no tomorrow; only the present.

Suddenly she smiled, thinking of the enormous breakfasts he habitually ate. She would usually stumble into the kitchen for coffee as he was cleaning off a plate. Cooking wasn't her best thing, she mused, but it would be fun to surprise him. His arm was tossed around her waist, holding her against him so that their bodies had warmed each other even in sleep. Carefully Raven slipped out from under it. Padding to the closet, she found a robe, then left Brand sleeping to go downstairs.

The kitchen was washed in sunlight. Raven went straight to the percolator. First things first, she decided. Strangely, she was wide-awake, there was none of the drowsy fogginess she habitually used coffee to chase away. She felt vital, full of energy, very much the way she felt when finishing a live concert, she realized as she scooped out coffee. Perhaps there was a parallel. Raven fit the lid on the pot, then plugged it in. She had always felt that performing for an audience was a bit like making love: sharing yourself, opening your emotions, pulling down the barriers. That's what she had done with Brand. The thought made her smile, and she was singing as she rummaged about for a frying pan.

Upstairs, Brand stirred, reached for her and found her gone. He opened his eyes to see that the bed beside him was empty. Quickly he pushed himself up and scanned the room. The fire was still burning. It had been late when he had added the last logs. The drapes were open to the full strength of the sun. It spilled across the bed and onto the floor. Raven's nightgown lay where it had fallen the night before.

Not a dream, he told himself, tugging a hand through his hair. They'd been together last night, again and again until every ounce of energy had been drained. Then they had slept, still holding each other, still clinging. His eyes drifted to the empty pillow beside him again. *But where—where the devil is she now?* Feeling a quick flutter of panic, he rose, tugged on his jeans and went to find her.

Before Brand reached the bottom of the stairs, her voice drifted to him.

Every morning when I wake,
I'll see your eyes.
And there'll only be the love we make,
No more goodbyes.

He recognized the song as the one he had teased her about weeks before when they had sat in his car in the hills above Los Angeles. The knot in his stomach untied itself. He walked down the hall, listening to the husky, morning quality of her voice, then paused in the doorway to watch her.

Her movements suited the song she sang: cheerful, happy. The kitchen was filled with morning noises and scents. There was the popping rhythm of the percolator as the coffee bubbled on the burner, the hiss and sizzle of the fat sausage she had frying in a cast-iron skillet, the clatter of crockery as she searched for a platter. Her hair was streaming down her back, still tumbled from the night, while the short terry robe she wore rode high up on her thighs as she stretched to reach the top shelf of a cupboard.

Raven stopped singing for a moment to swear good-naturedly about her lack of height. After managing to get a grip on the platter, she lowered her heels back to the floor and turned. She gave a gasp when she spotted Brand, dropped the fork she held and just managed to save the platter from following it.

"Brandon!" Raven circled her throat with her hand a moment and took a deep breath. "You scared me! I didn't hear you come down."

Brand didn't answer her smile. He didn't move but only looked at her. "I love you, Raven."

Her eyes widened, and her lips trembled open, then shut again. The words, she reminded herself, mean so many different things. It was important not to take a simple statement and deepen its meaning. Raven kept her voice calm as she stooped to pick up the fork. "I love you, too, Brandon."

He frowned at the top of her head, then at her back as she turned away to the sink. She turned on the tap to rinse off the fork. "You sound like my sister. I've already two of those; I don't need another."

Raven took her time. She turned off the tap, composed her face into a smile, then turned. "I don't think of you as a brother, Brandon." The tension at the back of her neck made it difficult to move calmly back to the cupboard for cups and saucers. "It isn't easy for me to tell you how I feel. I needed your support, your compassion. You helped me last night more than I can say."

"Now you make me sound like a bloody doctor. I

said I love you, Raven." There was a snap of anger in the words this time. When Raven turned back to him, her eyes were eloquent.

"Brandon, you don't have to feel obligated…" She broke off as his eyes flared. Storming into the room, he flicked off the gas under the smoking sausage, then yanked the percolator cord from the wall. Coffee continued to pop for a few moments, then subsided weakly.

"Don't tell me what I have to do!" he shouted. "I know what I have to do." He grabbed her by the shoulders and shook her. "I *have* to love you. It's not an obligation, it's a fact, it's a demand, it's a terror."

"Brandon…"

"Shut up," he commanded. He pulled her close, trapping the dishes she held between them before he kissed her. She tasted the desperation, the temper. "Don't tell me you love me in that calm, steady voice." Brand lifted his head only to change the angle of the kiss. His mouth was hard and insistent before it parted from hers. "I need more than that from you, Raven, much more than that." His eyes blazed green into hers. "I'll have more, damn it!"

"Brandon." She was breathless, dizzy, then laughing. This was no dream. "The cup's digging a permanent hole in my chest. Please, let me put the dishes down." He said something fierce about the dishes, but she managed to pull away from him enough to put them on the counter. "Oh, Brandon!" Immediately Raven threw her arms around his neck. "You have more; you have everything. I was afraid—and a fool to be afraid—to tell you how much I love you." She placed her hands on his cheeks, holding his face away from her so that he could read what was in her eyes. "I love you, Brandon."

Quick and urgent, their lips came together. They clung still when he swept her up in his arms. "You'll have to do without your coffee for a while," he told her as she pressed a kiss to the curve of his neck. She only murmured an assent as he began to carry her down the hall.

"Too far," she whispered.

"Mmm?"

"The bedroom's much too far away."

Brand turned his head to grin at her. "Too far," he agreed, taking a sharp right into the music room. "Entirely too far." They sank together on a sofa. "How's this?" He slipped his hands beneath the robe to feel her skin.

"We've always worked well together here." Raven laughed into his eyes, running her fingers along the muscles of his shoulders. It was real, she thought triumphantly, kissing him again.

"The secret," Brand decided, then dug his teeth playfully into her neck, "is a strong melody."

"It's nothing without the proper lyric."

"Music doesn't always need words." He switched to the other side of her neck as his hand roamed to her breast.

"No," she agreed, finding that her own hands refused to be still. They journeyed down his back and up again. "But harmony—two strong notes coming together and giving a bit to each other."

"Melding," he murmured. "I'm big on melding." He loosened the belt of her robe.

"Oh, Brandon!" she exclaimed suddenly, remembering. "Mrs. Pengalley...she'll be here soon."

"This should certainly clinch her opinion of show people," he decided as his mouth found her breast.

"Oh, no, Brandon, stop!" She laughed and moaned and struggled.

"Can't," he said reasonably, trailing his lips back up to her throat. "Savage lust," he explained and bit her ear. "Uncontrollable. Besides," he said as he kissed her, then moved to her other ear, "it's Sunday, her day off."

"It is?" Raven's mind was too clouded to recall trivial things like days of the week. "Savage lust?" she repeated as he pushed the robe from her shoulders. "Really?"

"Absolutely. Shall I show you?"

"Oh, yes," she whispered and brought his mouth back to hers. "Please do."

A long time later Raven sat on the hearth rug and watched Brand stir up the fire. She had reheated the coffee and brought it in along with the sausages. Brand had pulled a sweater on with his jeans, but she still wore the short, terry robe. Holding a coffee cup in both hands, she yawned and thought that she had never felt so relaxed. She felt like a cat sitting in her square of sunlight, watching Brand fix a log onto snapping flames. He turned to find her smiling at him.

"What are you thinking?" He stretched out on the floor beside her.

"How happy I am." She handed him his coffee, leaning over to kiss him as he took it. It all seemed so simple, so right.

"How happy?" he demanded. He smiled at her over the rim of the cup.

"Oh, somewhere between ecstatic and delirious, I think." She sought his hand with hers. Their fingers linked. "Bordering on rapturous."

"Just bordering on?" Brand asked with a sigh. "Well, we'll work on it." He shook his head, then kissed her hand. "Do you know you nearly drove me mad in this room yesterday?"

"Yesterday?" Raven tossed her hair back over her shoulder with a jerk of her head. "What are you talking about?"

"I don't suppose you'll ever realize just how arousing your voice is," he mused as he sipped his coffee and studied her face. "That might be part of the reason—that touch of innocence with a hell-smoked voice."

"I like that." Raven reached behind her to set down her empty cup. The movement loosened the tie of her robe, leaving it open to brush the curve of her breasts. "Do you want one of these sausages? They're probably awful."

Brand lifted his eyes from the smooth expanse of flesh that the shift of material had revealed. He shook his head again and laughed. "You make them sound irresistible."

"A starving man can't be picky," she pointed out. Raven plucked one with her fingers and handed it over. "They're probably greasy."

He lifted a brow at this but took a bite. "Aren't you going to have one?"

"No. I know better than to eat my own cooking." She handed him a napkin.

"We could go out to eat."

"Use your imagination," she suggested, resting her hands on her knees. "Pretend you've already eaten. It always works for me."

"My imagination isn't as good as yours." Brand finished off the sausage. "Maybe if you tell me what I've had."

"An enormous heap of scrambled eggs," she decided,

narrowing her eyes. "Five or six, at least. You really should watch your cholesterol. And three pieces of toast with that dreadful marmalade you pile on."

"You haven't tried it," he reminded her.

"I imagined I did," she explained patiently. "You also had five slices of bacon." She put a bit of censure in her voice, and he grinned.

"I've a healthy morning appetite."

"I don't see how you could eat another bite after all that. Coffee?" Raven reached for the pot.

"No, I imagine I've had enough."

She laughed and leaning over, linked her arms around his neck. "Did I really drive you mad, Brandon?" She found the taste of her own power delicious and sweet.

"Yes." He rubbed her nose with his. "First it was all but impossible to simply be in the same room with you, wanting you as I did. Then that song." He gave a quiet laugh, then drew back to look at her. "Music doesn't always soothe the savage beast. And then that damn album jacket. I had to be furious, or I'd have thrown you down on the rug then and there."

He saw puzzlement, then comprehension, dawn in her eyes. "Is that why you…" She stopped, and the smile grew slowly. Raven tilted her head and ran the tip of her tongue over her teeth. "I suppose that now that you've had your way with me, I won't drive you mad anymore."

"That's right." He kissed her lightly. "I can take you or leave you." Brand set down his empty cup, then ruffled her hair, amused by her wry expression. "It's noon," he said with a glance at the clock. "We'd best get to it if we're going to get any work done today. That novelty number we were toying with, the one for the second female lead—I'd an idea for that."

"Really?" Raven unhooked her hands from behind his neck. "What sort of idea?"

"We might bounce up the beat, a bit of early forties jive tempo, you know. It'd be a good contrast to the rest of the score."

"*Hmmm,* could be a good dance number." Raven slipped her hands under his sweater and ran them up his naked chest. She smiled gently at the look of surprise that flickered in his eyes. "We need a good dance number there."

"That's what I was thinking," Brand murmured. The move had surprised him, and the light touch of her fingers sent a dull thud of desire hammering in his stomach. He reached for her, but she rose and moved to the piano.

"Like this, then?" Raven played a few bars of the melody they had worked with, using the tempo he had suggested. "A little boogie-woogie?"

"Yes." He forced his attention to the bouncing, repetitive beat but found his blood beating with it. "That's the idea."

She looked back over her shoulder and smiled at him. "Then all we need are the lyrics." She experimented a moment longer, then went to the coffeepot. "Cute and catchy." Raven drank, smiling down at Brand. "With a chorus."

"Any ideas?"

"Yes." She set down the cup. "I have some ideas." Raven sat down beside him, facing him, and thoughtfully brushed the hair back from his forehead. "If they're going to cast Carly, as it appears they're going to do, we need something to suit that baby-doll voice of hers. Her songs should be a direct foil for Lauren's." She pressed her lips lightly to his ear. "Of course, the chorus could carry the meat of it." Again she slipped a hand under his sweater, letting her fingertips toy with the soft mat of hair on his chest. She slid her eyes up to his. "What do you think?"

Brand took her arm and pulled her against him, but she turned her head so that the kiss only brushed her cheek. "Raven," he said after a laughing moan. But when she trailed her finger down to his stomach, she felt him suck in air. Again he moaned her name and crushed her against him.

Raven tilted her head back for the kiss. It was deep and desperate, but when he would have urged her down, she shifted so that her body covered his. She buried her mouth at his neck and felt the pulse hammering against her lips. Her hands were still under his sweater so that she was aware of the heating of his skin. He tugged at her robe, but she only pressed harder against him, lodging the fabric between them. She nipped at the cord of his neck.

"Raven." His voice was low and husky. "For God's sake, let me touch you."

"Am I driving you mad, Brandon?" she murmured, nearly delirious with her own power. Before he could answer, she brought her lips to his and took her tongue deep into his mouth. Slowly she hiked up his sweater, feeling the shudders of his skin as she worked it over his chest and shoulders. Even as she tossed it aside, Raven began journeying down his chest, using her lips and tongue to taste him.

It was a new sensation for her: the knowledge that he was as vulnerable to her as she was to him. There was harmony between them and the mutual need to make the music real and full. Before, he had guided her, but now she was ready to experiment with her own skill. She wanted to toy with tempos, to take the lead. She wanted to flow *pianissimo,* savoring each touch, each taste. Now it was her turn to teach him as he had taught her.

His skin was hot under her tongue. He was moving beneath her, but the first wave of desperation had passed into a drugged pleasure. Her fingers weren't shy but rather sought curiously, stroking over him to find what excited, what pleased. His taste was something she knew now she would starve without. She could feel his fingers in her hair tightening as his passion built. As she had the night before, she sensed his control, but now the challenge of breaking it excited her.

His stomach was taut and tightened further when she glided over it. She heard his breathing catch. Finding the snap to his jeans, she undid it, then began to tug them down over his hips. The rhythm was gathering speed.

Then her mouth was on his, ripping them both far beyond the gentle pace she had initiated. She was suddenly starving, trembling with the need. Pushing herself up, Raven let the robe fall from her shoulders. Her hair tumbled forward to drape her breasts.

"Touch me." Her eyes were heavy but locked in his. "Touch me now."

Brand's fingers tangled in her hair as they sought her flesh. When she would have swayed back down to him, he held her upright, wanting to watch the pleasure and passion on her face. Her eyes were blurred with it. The need built fast and was soon too great.

"Raven." There was desperate demand in his voice as he took her hips.

She let him guide her, then gave a sharp gasp of pleasure. Their bodies fused in a soaring rhythm, completely

tuned to each other. Raven shuddered from the impact.
Then, drained, she lowered herself until she lay prone on
him. He brought his arms around her to hold her close
as the two of them flowed from passion to contentment.

Tangled with him, fresh from loving in a room quiet
and warm, Raven gave a long, contented sigh. "Brandon," she murmured, just wanting to hear the sound of
his name.

"Hmm?" He stroked her hair, seemingly lost somewhere in a world between sleep and wakefulness.

"I never knew it could be like this."

"Neither did I."

Raven shifted until she could look at his face. "But
you've been with so many women." She curled up at
his side, preparing to rest her head in the curve of his
shoulder.

Brand rose on his elbow, then tilted her face up to
his. He studied her softly flushed cheeks, the swollen
mouth and drowsy eyes. "I've never been in love with
my lover before," he told her quietly.

For a moment there was silence. Then she smiled.
"I'm glad. I suppose I've never been sure of that until
now."

"Be sure of it." He kissed her, hard and quick and
possessively.

She settled against him again but shivered, then
laughed. "A few moments ago I'd have sworn I'd never
be cold again."

Grinning, Brand reached for her robe. "I seriously
doubt we'll get any work done unless you get dressed.
In fact, I'd suggest unattractive clothes."

After tugging her arms through the sleeves, Raven

put her hands on his shoulders. Her eyes were light and full of mischief. "Do I distract you, Brandon?"

"You might put it that way."

"I'll probably be tempted to try all the time, now that I know I can." Raven kissed him, then gave a quick shrug. "I won't be able to help myself."

"I'll hold you to that." Brand lifted a brow. "Would you like to start now?"

She gave his hair a sharp tug. "I don't think that's very flattering. I'm going to go see about those unattractive clothes."

"Later," he said, pulling her back when she started to rise.

Raven laughed again, amazed with what she saw in his eyes. "Brandon, really!"

"Later," he said again and pressed her back gently to the floor.

Chapter 12

Summer came to Cornwall in stages. Cool mornings turned to warm afternoons that had bees humming outside the front windows. The stinging chill of the nights mellowed. The first scent of honeysuckle teased the air. Then the roses, lush wild roses, began to bloom. And all through the weeks the countryside blossomed, Raven felt that she, too, was blooming. She was loved.

Throughout her life, if anyone had asked her what one thing she wanted most, Raven would have answered, "To be loved." She had starved for it as a child, had hungered as an adolescent when she had been shuffled from town to town, never given the opportunity to form lasting friendships and affections. It was this need, in part, that had made her so successful as a performer. Raven was willing to let the audience love her. She never felt herself beyond their reach when she stood in the spotlight. And they knew it. The love she had gained from her audiences had filled an enormous need. It had filled her but had not satisfied her as much, she discovered, as Brand's love.

As the weeks passed, she forgot the demands and responsibilities of the performer and became more and more in tune with the woman. She had always known herself; it had been important early that she grasp an identity. But for the first time in her life Raven focused on her womanhood. She explored it, discovered it, enjoyed it.

Brand was demanding as a lover, not only in the physical sense but in an emotional one as well. He wanted her body, her heart, her thoughts, with no reservations. His need for an absolute commitment was the only shadow in the summery passing of days. Raven found it impossible not to hold parts of herself in reserve. She'd been hurt and knew how devastating pain could be when you loved without guard. Her mother had broken her heart too many times to count, with always a promise of happiness after the severest blow. Raven had learned to cope with that, to guard against it to some extent.

She had loved Brand before, naively perhaps, but totally. When he had walked out of her life, Raven had thought she would never be whole again. For five years she had insulated herself against the men who had touched her life. They could be friends—loving friends—but never lovers. The wounds had healed, but the scar had been a constant reminder to be careful. She had promised herself that no man would ever hurt her as Brand Carstairs had. And Raven discovered the vow she had made still held true. He was the only man who would ever have the power to hurt her. That realization was enough to both exhilarate and frighten.

There was no doubt that he had awakened her physically. Her fears had been swept away by the tides of love. Raven found that in this aspect of their relationship she could indeed give herself to Brand unreservedly. Knowing she could arouse him strengthened her growing confidence as a woman. She learned her passions were as strong and sensitive as his. She had kept them restricted far too long. If Brand could heat her blood with a look, Raven was aware he was just as susceptible to her. There was nothing of the cool, British reserve in his lovemaking; she thought of him as all Irish then, stormy and passionate.

One morning he woke her at dawn by strewing the bed with wild rosebuds. The following evening he surprised her with iced champagne while she bathed in the ancient footed tub. At night he could be brutally passionate, waking and taking her with a desperate urgency that allowed no time for surprise, protest or response. At times he appeared deliriously happy; at others she would catch him studying her with an odd, searching expression.

Raven loved him, but she could not yet bring herself to trust him completely. They both knew it, and they both avoided speaking of it.

Seated next to Brand at the piano, Raven experimented with chords for the opening bars of a duet. "I really think a minor mode with a raised seventh." She frowned thoughtfully. "I imagine a lot of strings here, a big orchestration of violins and cellos." She played more, hearing the imagined arrangement rather than the solitary piano. "What do you think?" Raven turned her head to find Brand looking down at her.

"Go ahead," he suggested, drawing on a cigarette. "Play the lot."

She began, only to have him interrupt during a bridge. "No." He shook his head. "That part doesn't fit."

"That was your part," she reminded him with a grin.

"Genius is obliged to correct itself," he returned, and Raven gave an unladylike snort. He looked down his very straight British nose. "Had you a comment, then?"

"Who, me? I never interrupt genius."

"Wise," he said and turned back to spread his own fingers over the keys. "Like this." Brand played the same melody from the beginning, only altering a few notes on the bridge section.

"Did you change something?"

"I realize your inferior ear might not detect the subtlety," he began. She jammed her elbow into his ribs. "Well said," he murmured, rubbing the spot. "Shall we try again?"

"I love it when you're dignified, Brandon."

"Really?" He lifted an inquiring brow. "Now, where was I?"

"You were about to demonstrate the first movement from Tchaikovsky's Second Symphony."

"Ah." Nodding, Brand turned back to the keys. He ran through the difficult movement with a fluid skill that had Raven shaking her head.

"Show-off," she accused when he finished with a flourish.

"You're just jealous."

With a sigh she lifted her shoulders. "Unfortunately, you're right."

Brand laughed and put his hand palm to palm with hers. "I have the advantage in spread."

Raven studied her small, narrow-boned hand. "It's a good thing I didn't want to be a concert pianist."

"Beautiful hands," Brand told her, making one of his sudden and completely natural romantic gestures by lifting her fingers to his lips. "I'm quite helplessly in love with them."

"Brandon." Disarmed, Raven could only look at him. A tremble of warmth shot up her spine.

"They always smell of that lotion you have in the little white pot on the dresser."

"I didn't think you'd notice something like that." She shivered in response when his lips brushed the inside of her wrist.

"There's nothing about you I don't notice." He kissed her other wrist. "You like your bath too hot, and you leave your shoes in the most unexpected places. And you always keep time with your left foot." Brand looked back up at her, keeping one hand entwined with hers while he reached up with the other to brush the hair from her shoulder. "And when I touch you like this, your eyes go to smoke." He ran a fingertip gently over the point of her breast and watched her irises darken and cloud. Very slowly he leaned over and touched his lips to hers. Lazily he ran his finger back and forth until her nipple was taut and straining against the fabric of her blouse.

Her mouth was soft and opened willingly. Raven tilted her head back, inviting him to take more. Currents of pleasure were already racing along her skin. Brand drew her closer, one hand lingering at her breast.

"I can feel your bones melt," he murmured. His mouth grew hungrier, his hand more insistent. "It drives me

crazy." His fingers drifted from her breast to the top
button of her blouse. Even as he loosened it, the phone
shrilled from the table across the room. He swore, and
Raven gave a laugh and hugged him.

"Never mind, love," she said on a deep breath. "I'll
remind you where you left off this time, too." Slipping
out of his arms, she crossed the room to answer. "Hello."

"Hello, I'd like to speak with Brandon Carstairs,
please," a voice said.

Raven smiled at the musical lilt in the voice and wondered vaguely how one of Brand's fans had gotten ac-
cess to his number. "Mr. Carstairs is quite busy at the
moment." She grinned over at him and got both a grin
and a nod of approval before he crossed to her. He began
to distract her by kissing her neck.

"Would you ask him to call his mother when he's
free?"

"I beg your pardon?" Raven stifled a giggle and tried
to struggle out of Brand's arms.

"His mother, dear," the voice repeated. "Ask him to
call his mother when he has a minute, won't you? He
has the number."

"Oh, please, Mrs. Carstairs, wait! I'm sorry." Wide-
eyed, she looked up at Brand. "Brandon's right here.
Your mother," Raven said in a horrified whisper that
had him grinning again. Still holding her firmly to his
side, he accepted the receiver.

"Hullo, Mum." Brand kissed the top of Raven's head,
then chuckled. "Yes, I was busy. I was kissing a beautiful woman I'm madly in love with." The color rising
in Raven's cheeks had him laughing. "No, no, it's all
right, love, I intend to get back to it. How are you? And
the rest?"

Raven nudged herself free of Brand's arm. "I'll make some tea," she said quietly, then slipped from the room.

Mrs. Pengalley had left the kitchen spotlessly clean, and Raven spent some time puttering around it aimlessly while the kettle heated on the stove. She found herself suddenly hungry, then remembered that she and Brand had worked straight through lunch. She got out the bread, deciding to make buttered toast fingers to serve with the tea.

Afternoon tea was one of Brand's rituals, and Raven had grown fond of it. She enjoyed the late afternoon breaks in front of the fireplace with tea and biscuits or scones or buttered toast. They could be any two people then, Raven mused, two people sitting in front of a fireplace having unimportant conversations. The kettle sang out, and she moved to switch off the flame.

Raven went about the mechanical domestic tasks of brewing tea and buttering toast, but her thoughts kept drifting back to Brand. There had been such effortless affection in his voice when he had spoken to his mother, such relaxed love. And Raven had felt a swift flash of envy. It was something she had experienced throughout childhood and adolescence, but she hadn't expected to feel it again. Raven reminded herself she was twenty-five and no longer a child.

The chores soothed her. She loaded the tray and started back down the hall with her feelings more settled. When she heard Brand's voice, she hesitated, not wanting to interrupt his conversation. But the weight of the tray outbalanced her sense of propriety.

He was sunk into one of the chairs by the fire when Raven entered. With a smile he gestured her over so that she crossed the room and set the tray on the table beside him. "I will, Mum, perhaps next month. Give everyone my love." He paused and smiled again, taking Raven's hand. "She's got big gray eyes, the same color as the dove Shawn kept in the coop on the roof. Yes, I'll tell her. Bye, Mum. I love you."

Hanging up, Brand glanced at the ladened tea tray, then up at Raven. "You've been busy."

She crouched down and began pouring. "I discovered I was starving." She watched with the usual shake of her head as he added milk to his tea. That was one English habit Raven knew she would never comprehend. She took her own plain.

"My mother says to tell you you've a lovely voice over the phone." Brand picked up a toast finger and bit into it.

"You didn't have to tell her you'd been kissing me," Raven mumbled, faintly embarrassed. Brand laughed, and she glared at him.

"Mum knows I have a habit of kissing women," he explained gravely. "She probably knows I've occasionally done a bit more than that, but we haven't discussed that particular aspect of my life for some time." He took another bite of toast, studying Raven's face. "She wants to meet you. If the score keeps going along at this pace, I thought we might drive up to London next month."

"I'm not used to families, Brandon," she said. Raven reached for her cup, but he placed his hand over hers, waiting until she looked back up at him.

"They're easy people, Raven. They're important to me. You're important to me. I want them to know you."

She felt her stomach tighten, and lowered her eyes.

"Raven." Brand gave a short, exasperated sigh. "When are you going to talk to me?"

She couldn't pretend not to understand him. She could

only shake her head and avoid the subject a little while longer. The time when they would have to return to California and face reality would come soon enough. "Please, tell me about your family. It might help me get used to being confronted with all of them if I know a bit more than I've read in the gossip columns." Raven smiled. Her eyes asked him to smile back and not to probe. Not yet.

Brand struggled with a sense of frustration but gave in. He could give her a little more time. "I'm the oldest of five." He gestured toward the mantel. "Michael's the distinguished-looking one with the pretty blond wife. He's a solicitor." Brand smiled, remembering the pleasure it had given him to send his brother to a good university. He'd been the first Carstairs to receive that sort of education. "There was nothing distinguished about him at all as a boy," Brand remarked. "He liked to give anyone within reach a bloody nose."

"Sounds like a good lawyer," Raven observed dryly. "Please go on."

"Alison's next. She graduated from Oxford at the top of her class." He watched Raven glance up at the photo of the fragile, lovely blonde. "An amazing brain," Brand continued, smiling. "She does something incomprehensible with computers and has a particular fondness for rowdy rugby matches. That's where she met her husband."

Raven shook her head, trying to imagine the delicate-looking woman shouting at rugby games or programming sophisticated computers. "I suppose your other brother's a physicist."

"No, Shawn's a veterinarian." Affection slipped into Brand's voice.

"Your favorite?"

He tilted his head as he reached for more tea. "If one has a favorite among brothers and sisters, I suppose so. He's simply one of the nicest people I know. He's incapable of hurting anyone. As a boy he was the one who always found the bird with the broken wing or the dog with a sore paw. You know the type."

Raven didn't, but she murmured something and continued to sip at her tea. Brand's family was beginning to fascinate her. Somehow, she had thought that people raised in the same house under the same circumstances would be more the same. These people seemed remarkably diverse. "And your other sister?"

"Moray." He grinned. "She's in school yet, claims she's going into finance or drama. Or perhaps," he added, "anthropology. She's undecided."

"How old is she?"

"Eighteen. She thinks your records are smashing, by the way, and had them all the last time I was home."

"I believe I'll like her," Raven decided. She let her gaze sweep the mantel again. "Your parents must be very proud of all of you. What does your father do?"

"He's a carpenter." Brand wondered if she was aware of the wistful look in her eyes. "He still works six days a week, even though he knows money isn't a problem anymore. He has a great deal of pride." He paused a moment, stirring his tea, his eyes on Raven. "Mum still hangs sheets out on a line, even though I bought her a perfectly good dryer ten years ago. That's the sort of people they are."

"You're very lucky," Raven told him and rose to wander about the room.

"Yes, I know that." Brand watched her move around

the room with her quick, nervous stride. "Though I doubt I thought a great deal about it while I was growing up. It's very easy to take it all for granted. It must have been very difficult for you."

Raven lifted her shoulders, then let them fall. "I survived." Walking to the window, she looked out on the cliffs and the sea. "Let's go for a walk, Brandon. It's so lovely out."

He rose and walked to her. Taking her by the shoulders, Brand turned her around to face him. "There's more to life than surviving, Raven."

"I survived intact," she told him. "Not everyone does."

"Raven, I know you call home twice a week, but you never tell me anything about it." He gave her a quick, caring shake. "Talk to me."

"Not about that, not now, not here." She slipped her arms around him and pressed her cheek to his chest. "I don't want anything to touch us here—nothing from the past, nothing from tomorrow. Oh, there's so much ugliness, Brandon, so many responsibilities. I want time. Is that so wrong?" She held him tighter, suddenly possessive. "Can't this be our fantasy, Brandon? That there isn't anybody but us? Just for a little while."

She heard him sigh as his lips brushed the crown of her head. "For a little while, Raven. But fantasies have to end, and I want the reality, too."

Raven lifted her face, then framed his with her hands. "Like Joe in the script," she reflected and smiled. "He finds his reality in the end, doesn't he?"

"Yes." Brand bent to kiss her and found himself lingering over it longer than he had intended. "Proving dreams come true," he murmured.

"But I'm not a dream, Brandon." She took both of his hands in hers while her eyes smiled at him. "And you've already brought me to life."

"And without magic."

Raven lifted a brow. "That depends on your point of view," she countered. "I still feel the magic." Slowly she lifted his hand to the neckline of her blouse. "I think you were here when we left off."

"So I was." He loosened the next button, watching her face. "What about that walk?"

"Walk? In all that rain?" Raven glanced over to the sun-filled window. "No." Shaking her head, she looked back at Brand. "I think we'd better stay inside until it blows over."

He ran his finger down to the next button, smiling at her while he toyed with it. "You're probably right."

Chapter 13

Mrs. Pengalley made it a point to clean the music room first whenever Raven and Brand left her alone in the house. It was here they spent all their time working— if what show people did could be considered work. She had her own opinion on that. She gathered up the cups, as she always did, and sniffed them. Tea. Now and again she had sniffed wine and occasionally some bourbon, but she was forced to admit that Mr. Carstairs didn't seem to live up to the reputation of heavy drinking that show people had. Mrs. Pengalley was the smallest bit disappointed.

They lived quietly, too. She had been sure when Brand had notified her to expect him to be in residence for three months that he would have plans to entertain. Mrs. Pengalley knew what sort of entertainment show business people went in for. She had waited for the fancy cars to start arriving, the fancy people in their outrageous clothes. She had told Mr. Pengalley it was just a matter of time.

But no one had come, no one at all. There had been no disgraceful parties to clean up after. There had only been Mr. Carstairs and the young girl with the big gray eyes who sang as pretty as you please. But of course, Mrs. Pengalley reminded herself, she was in *that* business, too.

Mrs. Pengalley walked over to shake the wrinkles from the drapes at the side window. From there she could see Raven and Brand walking along the cliffs. Always in each other's pockets, she mused and sniffed to prevent herself from smiling at them. She snapped the drape back into place and began dusting off the furniture.

And how was a body supposed to give anything a proper dusting, she wanted to know, when they were always leaving their papers with the chicken scratchings on them all over everywhere? Picking up a piece of staff paper, Mrs. Pengalley scowled down at the lines and notes. She couldn't make head nor tail out of the notations; she scanned the words instead.

Loving you is no dream/I need you here to hold on to/Wanting you is everything/Come back to me.

She clucked her tongue and set the paper back down. Fine song, that one, she thought, resuming her dusting. Doesn't even rhyme.

Outside, the wind from the sea was strong, and Brand slipped his arm around Raven's shoulders. Turning her swiftly to face him, he bent her backward and gave her a long, lingering kiss. She gripped his shoulders for balance, then stared at him when his mouth lifted.

"What," she began and let out a shaky breath, "was that for?"

"For Mrs. Pengalley," he answered easily. "She's peeking out the music room window."

"Brandon, you're terrible." His mouth came down to hers again. Her halfhearted protest turned into total response. With a quiet sound of pleasure, Brand deepened the kiss and dragged her closer to him. Raven could feel the heat of the sun on her skin even as the sea breeze cooled it. The wind brought them the scent of honeysuckle and roses.

"That," he murmured as his mouth brushed over her cheeks, "was for me."

"Have any other friends?" Raven asked.

Laughing, Brand gave her a quick hug and released her. "I suppose we've given her enough to cluck her tongue over today."

"So that's what you want me for." Raven tossed her head. "Shock value."

"Among other things."

They wandered to the sea wall, for some moments looking out in comfortable silence. Raven liked the cliffs with their harsh faces and sheer, dizzying drop. She liked the constant, boiling noise of the sea, the screaming of the gulls.

The score was all but completed, with only a few minor loose ends and a bit of polishing to be done. Copies of completed numbers had been sent back to California. Raven knew they were drawing out a job that could be finished quickly. She had her own reasons for procrastinating, though she wasn't wholly certain of Brand's. She didn't want to break the spell.

Raven wasn't sure precisely what Brand wanted from

her because she hadn't permitted him to tell her yet. There were things, she knew, that had to be settled between them—things that could be avoided for the time being while they both simply let themselves be consumed by love. But the time would come when they would have to deal with the everyday business of living.

Would their work be a problem? That was one of the questions Raven refused to ask herself. Or if she asked it, she refused to answer. Commitments went with their profession, time-consuming commitments that made it difficult to establish any sort of a normal life. And there was so little privacy. Every detail of their relationship would be explored in the press. There would be pictures and stories, true and fabricated. The worst kind, Raven mused, were those with a bit of both. All of this, she realized, could be handled with hard work and determination if the love was strong enough. She had no doubt theirs was, but she had other doubts.

Would she ever be able to rid herself of the nagging fear that he might leave her again? The memory of the hurt kept her from giving herself to Brand completely. And her feelings of responsibility to her mother created yet another barrier. This was something she had always refused to share with anyone. She couldn't even bring herself to share it with the person she cared for most in the world. Years before, she had made a decision to control her own life, promising herself she would never depend too heavily on anything or anyone. Too often she had watched her mother relinquish control and lose.

If she could have found a way, Raven would have prolonged the summer. But more and more, the knowledge that the idyll was nearly at an end intruded into her thoughts. The prelude to fantasy was over. She hoped the fantasy would become a reality.

Brand watched Raven's face as she leaned her elbows on the rough stone wall and looked out to sea. There was a faraway look in her eyes that bothered him. He wanted to reach her, but their time alone together was slipping by rapidly. A cloud slid across the sun for a moment, and the light shifted and dimmed. He heard Raven sigh.

"What are you thinking?" he demanded, catching her flying hair in his hand.

"That of all the places I've ever been, this is the best." Raven tilted her head to smile up at him but didn't alter her position against the wall. "Julie and I took a break in Monaco once, and I was sure it was the most beautiful spot on earth. Now I know it's the second."

"I knew you'd love it if I could ever get you here," Brand mused, still toying with the ends of her hair. "I had some bad moments thinking you'd refuse. I'm not at all sure I could have come up with an alternate plan."

"Plan?" Raven's forehead puckered over the word. "I don't know what you mean. What plan?"

"To get you here, where we could be alone."

Raven straightened away from the wall but continued looking out to sea. "I thought we came here to write a score."

"Yes." Brand watched the flight of a bird as it swooped down over the waves. "The timing of that was rather handy."

"Handy?" Raven felt the knot start in her stomach. The clouds shifted over the sun again.

"I doubt you'd have agreed to work with me again if the project hadn't been so tempting," he said. Brand frowned up at a passing cloud. "You certainly wouldn't have agreed to live with me."

"So you dangled the score in front of my nose like a meaty bone?"

"Of course not. I wanted to work with you on the project the moment it was offered to me. It was all just a matter of timing, really."

"Timing and planning," she said softly. "Like a chess game. Julie's right; I've never been any good at strategy." Raven turned away, but Brand caught her arm before she could retreat.

"Raven?"

"How could you?" She whirled back to face him. Her eyes were dark and hot, her cheeks flushed with fury. Brand narrowed his eyes and studied her.

"How could I what?" he asked coolly, releasing her arm.

"How could you use the score to trick me into coming here?" She dragged at her hair as the wind blew it into her face.

"I'd have used anything to get you back," Brand said. "And I didn't trick you, Raven. I told you nothing but the truth."

"Part of the truth," she continued.

"Perhaps," he agreed. "We're both rather good at that, aren't we?" He didn't touch her, but the look he gave her became more direct. "Why are you angry? Because I love you or because I made you realize you love me?"

"Nobody *makes* me do anything!" She balled her hands into fists as she whirled away. "Oh, I detest being maneuvered. I run my own life, make my own decisions."

"I don't believe I've made any for you."

"No, you just led me gently along by the nose until I *chose* what was best for myself." Raven turned back again, and now her voice was low and vibrant with anger. "Why couldn't you have been honest with me?"

"You wouldn't have let me anywhere near you if I'd been completely honest. I had experience with you before, remember?"

Raven's eyes blazed. "Don't tell me what I would've done, Brandon. You're not inside my head."

"No, you've never let me in there." He pulled out a cigarette, cupped his hands around a match and lit it. Before speaking, he took a long, contemplative drag. "We'll say I wasn't in the mood to be taking chances, then. Will that suit you?"

His cool, careless tone fanned her fury. "You had no right!" she tossed at him. "You had no right to arrange my life this way. Who said I had to play by your rules, Brandon? When did you decide I was incapable of planning for myself?"

"If you'd like to be treated as a rational adult, perhaps you should behave as one," he suggested in a deceptively mild tone. "At the moment I'd say you're being remarkably childish. I didn't bring you here under false pretenses, Raven. There was a score to be written, and this was a quiet place to do it. It was also a place I felt you'd have the chance to get used to being with me again. I wanted you back."

"*You* felt. *You* wanted!" Raven tossed back her hair. "How incredibly selfish! What about *my* feelings? Do you think you can just pop in and out of my life at your convenience?"

"As I remember, I was pushed out."

"You left me!" The tears came from nowhere and

blinded her. "Nothing's ever hurt me like that before. Nothing!" Tears of hurt sprang to her eyes. "I'll be damned if you'll do it to me again. You went away without a word!"

"You mightn't have liked the words I wanted to say." Brand tossed the stub of his cigarette over the wall. "You weren't the only one who was hurt that night. How the hell else could I be rational unless I put some distance between us? I couldn't have given you the time you seemed to need if I'd stayed anywhere near you."

"Time?" Raven repeated as thoughts trembled and raced through her mind. "You gave me time?"

"You were a child when I left," he said shortly. "I'd hoped you'd be a woman when I came back."

"You had hoped…" Her voice trailed off into an astonished whisper. "Are you telling me you stayed away, giving me a chance to—to grow up?"

"I didn't see I had any choice." Brand dug his hands into his pockets as his brows came together.

"Didn't you?" She remembered her despair at his going, the emptiness of the years. "And of course, why should you have given me one? You simply took it upon yourself to decide for me."

"It wasn't a matter of deciding." He turned away from her, knowing he was losing his grip on his temper. "It was a matter of keeping sane. I simply couldn't stay near you and not have you."

"So you stayed away for five years, then suddenly reappeared, using my music as an excuse to lure me into bed. You didn't give a damn about the quality of *Fantasy*. You just used it—and the talent and sweat of the performers—for your own selfish ends."

"That," he said in a deadly calm voice, "is beyond

contempt." Turning, he walked away. Within moments Raven heard the roar of an engine over the sound of the sea.

She stood, watching the car speed down the lane. If she had meant to deal a savage blow, she had succeeded. The shock of her own words burned in her throat. She shut her eyes tightly.

Even with her eyes closed, she could see clearly the look of fury on Brand's face before he had walked away. Raven ran a shaking hand through her hair. Her head was throbbing with the aftereffects of temper. Slowly she opened her eyes and stared out at the choppy green sea.

Everything we've had these past weeks was all part of some master plan, she thought. Even as she stood, the anger drained out of her, leaving only the weight of unhappiness.

She resented the fact that Brand had secretly placed a hand on the reins of her life, resented that he had offered her the biggest opportunity in her career as a step in drawing her to him. And yet… Raven shook her head in frustration. Confused and miserable, she turned to walk back to the house.

Mrs. Pengalley met her at the music room door. "There's a call for you, miss, from California." She had watched the argument from the window with a healthy curiosity. Now, however, the look in the gray eyes set her maternal instincts quivering. She repressed an urge to smooth down Raven's hair. "I'll make you some tea," she said.

Raven walked to the phone and lifted the receiver. "Yes, hello."

"Raven, it's Julie."

"Julie." Raven sank down in a chair. She blinked back

fresh tears at the sound of the familiar voice. "Back from the isles of Greece?"

"I've been back for a couple weeks, Raven."

Of course. She should have known that. "Yes, all right. What's happened?"

"Karter contacted me because he wasn't able to reach you this morning. Some trouble on the line or something."

"Has she left again?" Raven's voice was dull.

"Apparently she left last night. She didn't go very far." Hearing the hesitation in Julie's voice, Raven felt the usual tired acceptance sharpen into apprehension.

"Julie?" Words dried up, and she waited.

"There was an accident, Raven. You'd better come home."

Raven closed her eyes. "Is she dead?"

"No, but it's not good, Raven. I hate having to tell you over the phone this way. The housekeeper said Brand wasn't there."

"No." Raven opened her eyes and looked vaguely around the room. "No, Brandon isn't here." She managed to snap herself back. "How bad, Julie? Is she in the hospital?"

Julie hesitated again, then spoke quietly. "She's not going to make it, Raven. I'm sorry. Karter says hours at best."

"Oh, God." Raven had lived with the fear all her life, yet it still came as a shock. She looked around the room again a little desperately, trying to orient herself.

"I know there's no good way to tell you this, Raven, but I wish I could find a better one."

"What?" She brought herself back again with an enormous effort. "No, I'm all right. I'll leave right away."

"Shall I meet you and Brand at the airport?"

The question drifted through Raven's mind. "No. No, I'll go straight to the hospital. Where is she?"

"St. Catherine's, intensive care."

"Tell Dr. Karter I'll be there as soon as I can. Julie…"

"Yes?"

"Stay with her."

"Of course I will. I'll be here."

Raven hung up and sat staring at the silent phone.

Mrs. Pengalley came back into the room carrying a cup of tea. She took one look at Raven's white face and set it aside. Without speaking, she went to the liquor cabinet and took out the brandy. After pouring out two fingers, she pressed the snifter on Raven.

"Here now, miss, you drink this." The Cornish burr was brisk.

Raven's eyes shifted to her. "What?"

"Drink up, there's a girl."

She obeyed as Mrs. Pengalley lifted the glass to her lips. Instantly Raven sucked in her breath at the unexpected strength of the liquor. She took another sip, then let out a shaky sigh.

"Thank you." She lifted her eyes to Mrs. Pengalley again. "That's better."

"Brandy has its uses," the housekeeper said righteously.

Raven rose, trying to put her thoughts in order. There were things to be done and no time to do them. "Mrs. Pengalley, I have to go back to America right away. Could you pack some things for me while I call the airport?"

"Aye." She studied Raven shrewdly. "He's gone off to cool his heels, you know. They all do that. But he'll be back soon enough."

Realizing Mrs. Pengalley spoke of Brand, Raven dragged a hand through her hair. "I'm not altogether certain of that. If Brandon's not back by the time I have to go to the airport, would you ask Mr. Pengalley to drive me? I know it's an inconvenience, but it's terribly important."

"If that's what you want." Mrs. Pengalley sniffed. Young people, she thought, always flying off the handle. "I'll pack your things, then."

"Thank you." Raven glanced around the music room, then picked up the phone.

An hour later she hesitated at the foot of the stairs. Everything seemed to have happened at once. She willed Brand to return, but there was no sign of his car in the driveway. Raven struggled over writing a note but could think of nothing to say on paper that could make up for the words she had thrown at him. And how could she say in a few brief lines that her mother was dying and she had to go to her?

Yet there wasn't time to wait until he returned. She knew she couldn't risk it. Frantically she pulled a note pad from her purse. "Brandon," she wrote quickly, "I had to go. I'm needed at home. Please, forgive me. I love you, Raven."

Dashing back into the music room, she propped the note against the sheet of staff paper on top of the pile on the piano. Then, hurrying from the room, she grabbed her suitcases and ran outside. Mr. Pengalley was waiting in his serviceable sedan to drive her to the airport.

Chapter 14

Five days passed before Raven began thinking clearly again. Karter had been right about there only being a matter of hours. Raven had had to deal not only with grief but also with an unreasonable guilt that she hadn't been in time. The demand of details saved her from giving in to the urge to sink into self-pity and self-rebuke. She wondered once, during those first crushing hours, if that was why people tied so many traditions and complications to death: to keep from falling into total despair.

She was grateful that Karter handled the police himself in a way that ensured the details would be kept out of the papers.

After the first busy days there was nothing left but to accept that the woman she had loved and despised was gone. There was no more she could do. The disease had beaten them, just as surely as if it had been a cancer. Gradually she began to accept her mother's death as the result of a long, debilitating illness. She didn't cry, knowing she had already mourned, knowing it was time to put away the unhappiness. She had never had control of her mother's life; she needed the strength to maintain control of her own.

A dozen times during those days Raven phoned the house in Cornwall. There was never an answer. She could almost hear the hollow, echoing sounds of the ring through the empty rooms. More than once she considered simply getting on a plane and going back, but she always pushed the thought aside. He wouldn't be there waiting for her.

Where could he be? she wondered again and again. *Where would he have gone? He hasn't forgiven me.* And worse, she thought again and again, *he'll never forgive me.*

After hanging up the phone a last time, Raven looked at herself in her bedroom mirror. She was pale. The color that had drained from her face five days ago in Cornwall had never completely returned. There was too much of a helpless look about her. Raven shook her head and grabbed her blusher. Borrowed color, she decided, was better than none at all. She had to start somewhere.

Yes, she thought again, still holding the sable brush against her cheek. I've got to start somewhere. Turning away from the mirror, Raven again picked up the phone.

Thirty minutes later she came downstairs wearing a black silk dress. She had twisted her hair up and was setting a plain, stiff-brimmed black hat over it as she stepped into the hall.

"Raven?" Julie came out of the office. "Are you going out?"

"Yes, if I can find that little envelope bag and my car

keys. I think they're inside it." She was already poking into the hall closet.

"Are you all right?"

Raven drew her head from the closet and met Julie's look. "I'm better," she answered, knowing Julie wouldn't be satisfied with a clichéd reply. "The lecture you gave me after the funeral, about not blaming myself? I'm trying to put it into practice."

"It wasn't a lecture," Julie countered. "It was simply a statement of facts. You did everything you could do to help your mother; you couldn't have done any more."

Raven sighed before she could stop herself. "I did everything I knew how to do, and I suppose that's the same thing." She shook off the mood as she shut the closet door. "I *am* better, Julie, and I'm going to be fine." She smiled, then, glimpsing a movement, looked beyond Julie's shoulder. Wayne stepped out of the office. "Hello, Wayne, I didn't know you were here."

He moved past Julie. "Well, I can definitely approve of that dress," he greeted her.

"And so you should," Raven returned dryly. "You charged me enough for it."

"Don't be a philistine, darling. Art has no price." He flicked a finger over the shoulder of the dress. "Where are you off to?"

"Alphonso's. I'm meeting Henderson for lunch."

Wayne touched Raven's cheek with a fingertip. "A bit heavy on the blush," he commented.

"I'm tired of looking pale. Don't fuss." She placed a hand on each of his cheeks, urging him to bend so that she could kiss him. "You've been a rock, Wayne. I haven't told you how much I appreciate your being here the last few days."

"I needed to escape from the office."

"I adore you." She lowered her hands to meet his arms and squeezed briefly. "Now, stop worrying about me." Raven shot a look past his shoulder to Julie. "You, too. I'm meeting Henderson to talk over plans for a new tour."

"New tour?" Julie frowned. "Raven, you've been working nonstop for over six months. The album, the tour, the score." She paused. "After all of this you need a break."

"After all this the thing I need least is a break," Raven corrected. "I want to work."

"Then take a sabbatical," Julie insisted. "A few months back you were talking about finding a mountain cabin in Colorado, remember?"

"Yes." Raven smiled and shook her head. "I was going to write and be rustic, wasn't I? Get away from the glitter-glamour and into the woods." Raven grinned, recalling the conversation. "You said something about not being interested in anything more rustic than a margarita at poolside."

Julie lifted a thin, arched brow. "I've changed my mind. I'm going shopping for hiking boots."

Wayne's comment was a dubious *"hmmm."*

Raven smiled. "You're sweet," she said to Julie as she kissed her cheek. "But it isn't necessary. I need to do something that takes energy, physical energy. I'm going to talk to Henderson about a tour of Australia. My records do very well there."

"If you'd just talk to Brand…" Julie began, but Raven cut her off.

"I've tried to reach him; I can't." There was something

final and flat in the statement. "Obviously he doesn't want to talk to me. I'm not at all sure I blame him."

"He's in love with you," Wayne said from behind her. Raven turned and met the look. "A few thousand people saw the sparks flying the night of your concert in New York."

"Yes, he loves me, and I love him. It doesn't seem to be enough, and I can't quite figure out why. No, please." She took his hand, pressing it between both of hers. "I have to get my mind off it all for a while. I feel as if I had been having a lovely picnic and got caught in a landslide. The bruises are still a bit sore. I could use some good news," she added, glancing from one of them to the other, "if the two of you are ever going to decide to tell me."

Raven watched as Wayne and Julie exchanged glances. She grinned, enjoying what she saw. "I've been noticing a few sparks myself. Isn't this a rather sudden situation?"

"Very," Wayne agreed, smiling at Julie over Raven's head. "It's only been going on for about six years."

"Six years!" Raven's brows shot up in amazement.

"I didn't choose to be one of a horde," Wayne said mildly, lighting one of his elegant cigarettes.

"And I always thought he was in love with you," Julie stated, letting her gaze drift from Raven to Wayne.

"With *me?*" Raven laughed spontaneously for the first time in days.

"I fail to see the humour in that," Wayne remarked from behind a nimbus of smoke. "I'm considered by many to be rather attractive."

"Oh, you are," she agreed, then giggled and kissed his cheek. "Madly so. But I can't believe anyone could think you were in love with me. You've always dated those rather alarmingly beautiful models with their sculpted faces and long legs."

"I don't think we need bring all that up at the moment," Wayne retorted.

"It's all right." Julie smiled sweetly and tucked her hair behind her ear. "I haven't any problem with Wayne's checkered past."

"When did all this happen, please?" Amused, Raven cut into their exchange. "I turn my back for a few weeks, and I find my two best friends making calf's eyes at each other."

"I've never made calf's eyes at anyone," Wayne remonstrated, horrified. "Smoldering glances, perhaps." He lifted his rakishly scarred brow.

"When?" Raven repeated.

"I looked up from my deck chair the first morning out on the cruise," Julie began, "and who do you suppose is sauntering toward me in a perfectly cut Mediterranean white suit?"

"Really?" Raven eyed Wayne dubiously. "I'm not certain whether I'm surprised or impressed."

"It seemed like a good opportunity," he explained, tapping his expensive ashes into a nearby dish, "if I could corner her before she charmed some shipping tycoon or handy sailor."

"I believe I charmed a shipping tycoon a few years ago," Julie remarked lazily. "And as to the sailor..."

"Nevertheless," Wayne went on, shooting her a glance. "I decided a cruise was a very good place to begin winning her over. It was," he remarked, "remarkably simple."

"Oh?" Julie's left brow arched. "Really?"

Wayne tapped out his cigarette, then moved over to gather her in his arms. "A piece of cake," he added carelessly. "Of course, women habitually find me irresistible."

"It would be safer if they stopped doing so. I might be tempted to wring their necks," Julie cooed, winding her arms around his neck.

"The woman's going to be a trial to live with." Wayne kissed her as though he'd decided to make the best of it.

"I can see you two are going to be perfectly miserable together. I'm so sorry." Walking over, Raven slipped an arm around each of them. "You will let me give you the wedding?" she began, then stopped. "That is, are you having a wedding?"

"Absolutely," Wayne told her. "We don't trust each other enough for anything less encumbering." He gave Julie a flashing grin that inexplicably made Raven want to weep.

Raven hugged them both again fiercely. "I needed to hear something like this right now. I'm going to leave you alone. I imagine you can entertain yourselves while I'm gone. Can I tell Henderson?" she asked. "Or is it a secret?"

"You can tell him," Julie said, watching as Raven adjusted her hat in the hall mirror. "We're planning on taking the plunge next week."

Raven's eyes darted up to Julie's in the mirror. "My, you two move fast, don't you?"

"When it's right, it's right."

Raven smiled in quick agreement. "Yes, I suppose it is. There's probably champagne in the refrigerator, isn't there, Julie?" She turned away from the mirror. "We can have a celebration drink when I get back. I'll just be a couple of hours."

"Raven." Julie stopped her as she headed for the door. Raven looked curiously over her shoulder. "Your purse." Smiling, Julie retrieved it from a nearby table. "You won't forget to eat, will you?" she demanded as she placed it in Raven's hand.

"I won't forget to eat," Raven assured her, then dashed through the door.

Within the hour Raven was seated in the glassed-in terrace room of Alphonso's toying with a plate of scampi. There were at least a dozen people patronizing the restaurant whom she knew personally. A series of greetings had been exchanged before she had been able to tuck herself into a corner table.

The room was an elaborate jungle, with exotic plants and flowers growing everywhere. The sun shining through the glass and greenery gave the terrace a warmth and glow. The floor was a cool ceramic tile, and there was a constant trickle of water from a fountain at the far end of the room. Raven enjoyed the casual elegance, the wicker accessories and the pungent aromas of food and flowers that filled the place. Now, however, she gave little attention to the terrace room as she spoke with her agent.

Henderson was a big, burly man whom Raven had always thought resembled a logjammer rather than the smooth, savvy agent he was. He had a light red thatch of hair that curled thinly on top of his head and bright merry blue eyes that she knew could sharpen to a sword's point. There was a friendly smattering of freckles over his broad, flat-featured face.

He could smile and look genial and none too bright. It was one of his best weapons. Raven knew Henderson was as sharp as they came, and when necessary, he could be hard as nails. He was fond of her, not only because she made him so rich, but because she never resented having done so. He couldn't say the same about all of his clients.

Now Henderson allowed Raven to ramble on about ideas for a new tour, Australia, New Zealand, promotion for the new album that was already shooting up the charts a week after its release. He ate his veal steadily, washing it down with heavy red wine while Raven talked and sipped occasionally from her glass of white wine.

He noticed she made no mention of the *Fantasy* score or of her time in Cornwall. The last progress report he had received from her had indicated the project was all but completed. The conversations he had had with Jarett had been enthusiastic. Lauren Chase had approved each one of her numbers, and the choreography had begun. The score seemed to be falling into place without a hitch.

So Henderson had been surprised when Raven had returned alone so abruptly from Cornwall. He had expected her to phone him when the score was completed, then to take the week or two she had indicated she and Brand wanted to relax and do nothing. But here she was, back early and without Brand.

She chattered nervously, darting from one topic to another. Henderson didn't interrupt, only now and again making some noncommittal sounds as he attended to his meal. Raven talked nonstop for fifteen minutes, then began to wind down. Henderson waited, then took a long swallow of wine.

"Well, now," he said, patting his lips with a white linen napkin. "I don't imagine there should be any problem setting up an Australian tour." His voice suited his looks.

"Good." Raven pushed the scampi around on her plate. She realized she had talked herself out. Spearing a bit of shrimp, she ate absently.

"While it's being set up, you could take yourself a nice little vacation somewhere."

Raven's brows rose. "No, I thought you could book me on the talk-show circuit, dig up some guest shots here and there."

"Could do that, too," he said genially. "After you take a few weeks off."

"I want gigs, not a few weeks off." Her brows lowered suspiciously. "Have you been talking to Julie?"

He looked surprised. "No, about what?"

"Nothing." Raven shook her head, then smiled. "Gigs, Henderson."

"You've lost weight, you know," he pointed out and shoveled in some more veal. "It shows in your face. Eat."

Raven gave an exasperated sigh and applied herself to her lunch. "Why does everyone treat me like a dim-witted child?" she mumbled, swallowing shrimp. "I'm going to start being temperamental and hard to get along with until I get some star treatment." Henderson said something quick and rude between mouthfuls which she ignored. "What about Jerry Michaels? Didn't I hear he was lining up a variety special for the fall? You could get me on that."

"Simplest thing in the world," Henderson agreed. "He'd be thrilled to have you."

"Well?"

"Well what?"

"Henderson." Resolutely, Raven pushed her plate aside. "Are you going to book me on the Jerry Michaels show?"

"No." He poured more wine into his glass. The sun shot through it, casting a red shadow on the tablecloth.

"Why?" Annoyance crept into Raven's tone.

"It's not for you." Henderson lifted a hand, palm up, as she began to argue. "I know who's producing the show, Raven. It's not for you."

She subsided a bit huffily, but she subsided. His instincts were the best in the field. "All right, forget the Michaels gig. What, then?"

"Want some dessert?"

"No, just coffee."

He signaled the waiter, then, after ordering blueberry cheesecake for himself and coffee for both of them, he settled back in his chair. "What about *Fantasy?*"

Raven twirled her wineglass between her fingers. "It's finished," she said flatly.

"And?"

"And?" she repeated, looking up. His merry blue eyes were narrowed. "It's finished," she said again. "Or essentially finished. I can't foresee any problem with the final details. Brandon or his agent will get in touch with you if there are, I'm sure."

"Jarett will probably need the two of you off and on during the filming," Henderson said mildly. "I wouldn't consider myself finished with it for a while yet."

Raven frowned into the pale golden liquid in her glass. "Yes, you're right, of course. I hadn't thought about it. Well…" She shook her head and pushed the wine away. "I'll deal with that when the times comes."

"How'd it go?"

She looked at Henderson levelly, but her thoughts drifted. "We wrote some of the best music either one of us has ever done. That I'm sure of. We work remarkably well together. I was surprised."

"You didn't think you would?" Henderson eyed the blueberry cheesecake the waiter set in front of him.

"No, I didn't think we would. Thank you," this to the waiter before she looked at Henderson again. "But everything else apart, we did work well together."

"You'd worked well together before," he pointed out. "'Clouds and Rain.'" He saw her frown but continued smoothly. "Did you know sales on that have picked up again after your New York concert? You got yourself a lot of free press, too."

"Yes," Raven mumbled into her coffee. "I'm sure we did."

"I've had a lot of questions thrown at me during the last weeks," he continued blandly, even when her eyes lifted and narrowed. "From the inside," he said with a smile, "as well as the press. I was at a nice little soiree just last week. You and Brand were the main topic of conversation."

"As I said, we work well together." Raven set down her cup. "Brandon was right; we are good for each other artistically."

"And personally?" Henderson took a generous bite of cheesecake.

"Well." Raven lifted a brow. "You certainly get to the point."

"That's all right, you don't have to answer me." He swallowed the cake, then broke off another piece. "You can tell *him*."

"Who?"

"Brand," Henderson answered easily and added cream to his coffee. "He just walked in."

Raven whirled around in her chair. Instantly her eyes locked on Brand's. With the contact came a wild, swift surge of joy. Her first instinct was to spring from the table and run to him. Indeed, she had pushed the chair back, preparing to do so, when the expression on his face cut through her initial spring of delight. It was ice-cold fury. Raven sat where she was, watching as he weaved his way through the crowded restaurant toward her. There were casual greetings along the way which he ignored. Raven heard the room fall silent.

He reached her without speaking once or taking his eyes from her. Raven's desire to hold out a hand to him was also overcome. She thought he might strike it away. The look in his eyes had her blood beating uneasily. Henderson might not have been sitting two feet away.

"Let's go."

"Go?" Raven repeated dumbly.

"Now." Brand took her hand and yanked her to her feet. She might have winced at the unexpected pressure if she hadn't been so shocked by it.

"Brandon…"

"Now," he repeated. He began to walk away, dragging her behind him. Raven could feel the eyes following them. Shock, delight, anxiety all faded into temper.

"Let go of me!" she demanded in a harsh undertone. "What's the matter with you? You can't drag me around like this." She bumped into a lunching comedian, then skirted around him with a mumbled apology as Brand continued to stalk away with her hand in his. "Brandon, stop this! I will not be dragged out of a public restaurant."

He halted then and turned so that their faces were very close. "Would you prefer that I say what I have to say to you here and now?" His voice was clear and cool in the dead silence of the room. It was very easy to see the violence of temper just beneath the surface. Raven could feel it in the grip of his hand on hers. They were spotlighted again, she thought fleetingly, but hardly in the manner in which they had been in New York. She took a deep breath.

"No." Raven struggled for dignity and kept her voice lowered. "But there isn't any need to make a scene, Brandon."

"Oh, I'm in the mood for a scene, Raven," he tossed back in fluid British tones that carried well. "I'm in the mood for a bloody beaut of a scene."

Before she could comment, Brand turned away again and propelled her out of the restaurant. There was a Mercedes at the curb directly outside. He shoved her inside it, slamming the door behind her.

Raven straightened in the seat, whipping her head around as he opened the other door. "Oh, you're going to get one," she promised and ripped off her hat to throw it furiously into the back seat. "How *dare* you…"

"Shut up. I mean it." Brand turned to her as she started to speak again. "Just shut up until we get where we're going, otherwise I might be tempted to strangle you here and be done with it."

He shot away from the curb, and Raven flopped back against her seat. I'll shut up, all right, she thought on wave after wave of anger. I'll shut up. It'll give me time to think through exactly what I have to say.

Chapter 15

By the time Brand stopped the car in front of the Bel-Air, Raven felt she had her speech well in order. As he climbed out of his side, she climbed out of hers, then turned to face him on the sidewalk. But before she could speak, he had her arm in a tight grip and was pulling her toward the entrance.

"I told you not to drag me."

"And I told you to shut up." He brushed past the doorman and into the lobby. Raven was forced into an undignified half-trot in order to keep up with his long-legged stride.

"I will *not* be spoken to like that," she fumed and gave her arm an unsuccessful jerk. "I will *not* be carted through a hotel lobby like a piece of baggage."

"I'm tired of playing it your way." Brand turned, grabbing both of her shoulders and dragging her against him.

His fingers bit into her skin and shocked her into silence. "My game now, my rules."

His mouth came down hard on hers. It was a kiss of rage. His teeth scraped across her lips, forcing them open so that he could plunder and seek. He held her bruisingly close, as if daring her to struggle.

When Brand pulled away, he stared at her for a long, silent moment, then swore quickly, fiercely. Turning, he pulled her to the elevators.

Though she was no longer certain if it was fear or anger, Raven was trembling with emotion as they took the silent ride up. Brand could feel the throbbing pulse as he held her arm. He swore again, pungently, but she didn't glance at him. As the doors slid open, he pulled her into the hall and toward the penthouse.

There were no words exchanged between them as he slid the key into the lock. He released her arm as he pushed the door open. Without protest, Raven walked inside. She moved to the center of the room.

The suite was elegant, even lush, in a dignified, old-fashioned style with a small bricked fireplace and a good, thick carpet. Behind her the door slammed—a final sound—and she heard Brand toss the key with a faint metallic jingle onto a table. Raven drew a breath and turned around.

"Brandon..."

"No, I'll do the talking first." He crossed to her, his eyes locked on hers. "My rules, remember?"

"Yes." She lifted her chin. Her arm throbbed faintly where his fingers had dug into it. "I remember."

"First rule, no more bits and pieces. I won't have you closing parts of yourself off from me anymore." They were standing close. Now that the first dazed shock and surprise were passing, Raven noticed signs of strain and fatigue on his face. His words were spilling out so quickly, she couldn't interrupt. "You did the same thing to me five years ago, but then we weren't lovers. You were always holding out, never willing to trust."

"No." She shook her head, scrambling for some defense. "No, that's not true."

"Yes, it's true," he countered and took her by the shoulders again. "Did you tell me about your mother all those years ago? Or how you felt, what you were going through? Did you bring me into your life enough to let me help you, or at least comfort you?"

This was not what she had expected from him. Raven could only press her hand to her temple and shake her head again. "No, it wasn't something…"

"Wasn't something you wanted to share with me." He dropped her arms and stepped away from her. "Yes, I know." His voice was low and furious again as he pulled out a cigarette. He knew he had to do something with his hands or he'd hurt her again. He watched as she unconsciously nursed her arm where he had gripped her. "And this time, Raven, would you have told me anything about it if it hadn't been for the nightmare? If you hadn't been half asleep and frightened, would you have told me, trusted me?"

"I don't know." She made a small sound of confusion. "My mother had nothing to do with you."

Brand hurled the cigarette away before he lit it. "How can you say that to me? How can you stand there and say that to me?" He took a step toward her, then checked himself and stalked to the bar. "Damn you, Raven," he said under his breath. He poured bourbon and drank. "Maybe I should have stayed away," he managed in a calmer tone. "You'd already tossed me out of your life five years ago."

"*I* tossed you out?" This time her voice rose. "You walked out on me. You left me flat because I wouldn't be your lover." Raven walked over to the bar and leaned her palms on it. "You walked out of my house and out of my life, and the only word I had from you was what I read in the paper. It didn't take you long to find other women—several other women."

"I found as many as I could," Brand agreed and drank again. "As quickly as I could. I used women, booze, gambling—anything—to try to get you out of my system." He studied the dregs of liquor in his glass and added thoughtfully, "It didn't work." He set the glass down and looked at her again. "Which is why I knew I had to be patient with you."

Raven's eyes were still dark with hurt. "Don't talk to me about tossing you out."

"That's exactly what you did." Brand grabbed her wrist as she turned to swirl away from him. He held her still, the narrow, mahogany bar between them. "We were alone, remember? Julie was away for a few days."

Raven kept her eyes level. "I remember perfectly."

"Do you?" He arched a brow. Both his eyes and voice were cool again. "There might be a few things you don't remember. When I came to the house that night I was going to ask you to marry me."

Raven could feel every thought, every emotion, pour out of her body. She could only stare at him.

"Surprised?" Brand released her wrist and again reached in his pocket for a cigarette. "Apparently we have two differing perspectives on that night. I *loved* you." The words were an accusation that kept her speechless.

"And God help me, all those weeks we were together I was faithful to you. I never touched another woman." He lit the cigarette, and as the end flared, Raven heard him say softly, "I nearly went mad."

"You never told me." Her voice was weak and shaken. Her eyes were huge gray orbs. "You never once said you loved me."

"You kept backing off," he retorted. "And I knew you were innocent and afraid, though I didn't know why." He gave her a long, steady look. "It would have made quite a lot of difference if I had, but you didn't trust me."

"Oh, Brandon."

"That night," he went on, "you were so warm, and the house was so quiet. I could feel how much you wanted me. It drove me crazy. Good God, I was trying to be gentle, patient, when the need for you was all but destroying me." He ran a tense hand through his hair. "And you were giving, melting, everywhere I touched you. And then—then you were struggling like some terrified child, pushing at me as if I'd tried to kill you, telling me not to touch you. You said you couldn't bear to have me touch you."

He looked back at her, but his eyes were no longer cool. "You're the only woman who's ever been able to hurt me like that."

"Brandon." Raven shut her eyes. "I was only twenty, and there were so many things…"

"Yes, I know now; I didn't know then." His tone was flat. "Though there really weren't so many changes this time around." Raven opened her eyes and started to speak, but he shook his head. "No, not yet. I've not finished. I stayed away to give you time, as I told you before. I didn't see any other way. I could hardly stay, kicking my heels in L.A., waiting for you to make up your mind. I didn't know how long I'd stay away, but during those five years I concentrated on my career. So did you."

Brand paused, spreading his long, elegant hands on the surface of the bar. "Looking back, I suppose that's all for the best. You needed to establish yourself, and I had a surge of productivity. When I started reading about you regularly in the gossip columns I knew it was time to come back." He watched her mouth fall open at that, and her eyes heat. "Get as mad as you damn well like when I've finished," he said shortly. "But don't interrupt."

Raven turned away to search for control. "All right, go on," she managed and faced him again.

"I came to the States without any real plan, except to see you. The solid idea fell into my lap by way of *Fantasy* when I was in New York. I used the score to get you back," he said simply and without apology. "When I stood up in that recording booth watching you again, I knew I'd have used anything, but the score did nicely." He pushed his empty glass aside with his fingertip. "I wasn't lying about wanting to work with you again for professional reasons or about feeling you were particularly right for *Fantasy*. But I would have if it had been necessary. So perhaps you weren't so far wrong about what you said on the cliffs that day." He moved from the bar to the window. "Of course, there was a bit more to it in my mind than merely getting you to bed."

Raven felt her throat burn. "Brandon." She swallowed and shut her eyes. "I've never been more ashamed of anything in my life than what I said to you. Anger is hardly an excuse, but I'd hoped—I'd hoped you'd forgive me."

Brand turned his head and studied her a moment. "Perhaps if you hadn't left, it would have been easier."

"I had to. I told you in the note…"

"What note?" His voice sharpened as he turned to face her.

"The note." Raven was uncertain whether to step forward or back. "I left it on the piano with the music."

"I didn't see any note. I didn't see anything but that you were gone." He let out a long breath. "I dumped all the music into a briefcase. I didn't notice a note."

"Julie called only a little while after you'd left to tell me about the accident."

His eyes shot back to hers again. "What accident?"

Raven stared at him.

"Your mother?" he said, reading it in her eyes.

"Yes. She'd had an accident. I had to get back right away."

He jammed his hands into his pockets. "Why didn't you wait for me?"

"I wanted to; I couldn't." Raven laced her fingers together to prevent her hands from fluttering. "Dr. Karter said it would only be a matter of hours. As it was…" She paused and turned away. "I was too late, anyway."

Brand felt the anger drain from him. "I'm sorry. I didn't know."

Raven didn't know why the simple, quiet statement should bring on the tears she hadn't shed before. They blinded her eyes and clogged her throat so that speech was impossible.

"I went a bit crazy when I got back to the house and found you'd packed and gone." Brand spoke wearily now. "I don't know exactly what I did at first; afterwards I got roaring drunk. The next morning I dumped all the music together, packed some things and took off for the States.

"I stopped off for a couple of days in New York, trying to sort things out. It seems I spend a great deal of time running after you. It's difficult on the pride. In New York I came up with a dozen very logical, very valid reasons why I should go back to England and forget you. But there was one very small, very basic point I couldn't argue aside." He looked at her again. Her back was to him, her head bent so that with her hair pulled up he could see the slender length of her neck. "I love you, Raven."

"Brandon." Raven turned her tear-drenched face toward him. She blinked at the prisms of light that blinded her, then shook her head quickly when she saw him make a move to come to her. "No, please don't. I won't be able to talk if you touch me." She drew in a deep breath, brushing the tears away with her fingertips. "I've been very wrong; I have to tell you."

He stood away from her, though impatience was beginning to simmer through him again. "I had my say," he agreed. "I suppose you should have yours."

"All those years ago," she began. "All those years ago there were things I couldn't say, things I couldn't even understand because I was so—dazzled by everything. My career, the fame, the money, the perpetual spotlight." The words came quickly, and her voice grew stronger with them. "Everything happened at once; there didn't seem to be any time to get used to it all. Suddenly I was in love with Brandon Carstairs." She laughed and brushed at fresh tears. "*The* Brandon Carstairs. You have to understand, one minute you were an image, a name on a record, and the next you were a man, and I loved you."

Raven moistened her lips, moving to stare from the window as Brand had. "And my mother—my mother was my responsibility, Brandon. I've felt that always, and it isn't something that can be changed overnight. You were the genuine knight on a charger. I couldn't—wouldn't talk to you about that part of my life. I was afraid, and I was never sure of you. You never told me you loved me, Brandon."

"I was terrified of you," he murmured, "of what I was feeling for you. You were the first." He shrugged. "But you were always pulling back from me. Always putting up No Trespassing signs whenever I started to get close."

"You always seemed to want so much." She hugged her arms. "Even this time, in Cornwall, when we were so close. It didn't seem to be enough. I always felt you were waiting for more."

"You still put up the signs, Raven." She turned, and his eyes locked on hers. "Your body isn't enough. That isn't what I waited five years for."

"Love should be enough," she tossed back, suddenly angry and confused.

"No." Brand shook his head, cutting her off. "It isn't enough. I want a great deal more than that." He waited a moment, watching the range of expressions on her face. "I want your trust, without conditions, without exceptions. I want a commitment, a total one. It's all or nothing this time, Raven."

She backed away. "You can't own me, Brandon."

A quick flash of fury shot into his eyes. "Damn it, I don't want to own you, but I want you to belong to me. Don't you know there's a difference?"

Raven stared at him for a full minute. She dropped her arms, no longer cold. The tension that had begun to creep up the back of her neck vanished. "I didn't," she said softly. "I should have."

Slowly she crossed to him. She was vividly aware of every detail of his face: the dark, expressive brows drawn together now with thought, the blue-green eyes steady but with the spark of temper, the faint touch of mauve beneath them that told her he'd lost sleep. It came to her then that she loved him more as a woman than she had as a girl. A woman could love without fear, without restrictions. Raven lifted her fingertip to his cheek as if to smooth away the tension.

Then they were locked in each other's arms, mouth to mouth. His hands went to her hair, scattering pins until it tumbled free around them. He murmured something she had no need to understand, then plunged deep again into her mouth. Hurriedly, impatiently, they began to undress each other. No words were needed. They sought only touch, to give, to fulfill.

His fingers fumbled with the zipper of her dress, making him swear and her laugh breathlessly until he pulled her with him to the rug. Then, somehow, they were flesh to flesh. Raven could feel the shudders racing through him to match her own as they touched. His mouth was no more greedy than hers, his hands no less demanding. Their fire blazed clean and bright. Need erupted in them both so that she pulled him to her, desperate to have him, frantic to give.

Raw pleasure shot through her, rocking her again and again as she moved with him. His face was buried in her hair, his body damp to her touch. Air was forcing its way from her lungs in moans and gasps as they took each other higher and faster. Then the urgency passed, and a sweetness took its place.

Time lost all meaning as they lay together. Neither moved nor spoke. Tensions and angers, ecstasies and desperations, had all passed. All that was left was a soft contentment. She could feel his breath move lightly against her neck.

"Brandon," Raven murmured, letting her lips brush his skin.

"Hmm?"

"I think I still had something to say, but it's slipped my mind." She gave a low laugh.

Brand lifted his head and grinned. "Maybe it'll come back to you. Probably wasn't important."

"You're right, I'm sure." She smiled, touching his cheek. "It had something to do with loving you beyond sanity or some such thing and wanting more than anything in the world to belong to you. Nothing important."

Brand lowered his mouth to hers and nipped at her still tender lip. "You were distracted," he mused, seeking her breast with his fingertip.

Raven ran her hands down his back. "I was in a bit of a hurry."

"This time…" He began to taste her neck and shoulder. "This time we'll slow down the tempo. A bit more orchestration, don't you think?" His fingers slid gently and teasingly over the point of her breast.

"Yes, quite a bit more orchestration. Brandon…" Her words were lost on a sound of pleasure as his tongue found her ear. "Once more, with feeling," she whispered.

* * * * *

REFLECTIONS

Chapter 1

The wind had cooled the air. It blew dark clouds across the sky and whistled through the leaves, now hinting at fall. Along the roadside the trees appeared more yellow than green, and touches of flame and scarlet were beginning to show. The day was poised in September, just as summer was turning autumn. The late afternoon sunshine squeezed between the clouds, slanting onto the roadway.

The air smelled of rain. Lindsay walked swiftly, knowing the clouds could win out at any moment. The breeze lifted and tossed the strands of her silvery blond hair, and she pushed at them with annoyance. She would have been wiser to have left it neatly pinned at the nape of her neck, she thought.

Had she not been so pressed for time, Lindsay would have enjoyed the walk. She would have reveled at the hint of fall and the threatening storm. Now, however, she hurried along the roadway wondering what else could go wrong.

In the three years since she had returned to Connecticut to teach, she had experienced some rough moments. But this, she decided, was among the top ten for frustration value. Backed up plumbing in the studio, a forty-five minute lecture from an overeager parent on her child's prowess, two torn costumes and a student with an upset stomach—these minor annoyances had culminated with her temperamental car. It had coughed and moaned as usual when she had turned the ignition, but then it had failed to pull itself together. It simply had sat there shuddering until Lindsay had admitted defeat. This car, she thought with a rueful smile, is about as old as I am, and we're both tired.

After taking a hopeless look under the hood, Lindsay had gritted her teeth and begun the two-and-a-half-mile hike home from the studio.

Of course, she admitted as she trudged along under the shifting sunlight, she could have called someone. She sighed, knowing her temper had set her off. Ten minutes of brisk walking had cooled it. Nerves, she told herself. I'm just nervous about the recital tonight. Not the recital, technically, she corrected, stuffing her hands into her pockets. The girls are ready; rehearsals had been perfect. The little ones are cute enough that mistakes won't matter. It was the times before and after the recitals that distressed Lindsay. And the parents.

She knew that some would be dissatisfied with their children's parts. And more still who would try to pressure her into accelerating the training. Why wasn't their Pavlova on *pointe* yet? Why did Mrs. Jones's ballerina have a bigger part than Mrs. Smith's? Shouldn't Sue move on to the intermediate class?

So often Lindsay's explanations on anatomy, growing bones, endurance and timing met with only more suggestions. Normally, she used a mixture of flattery, stubbornness and intimidation to hold them off. She prided herself on being able to handle overzealous parents. After all, she mused, hadn't her mother been exactly the same?

Above all else, Mae Dunne had wanted to see her daughter on stage. She herself was short-legged, with a small, compact body. But she had possessed the soul of a dancer. Through sheer determination and training, she had secured a place in the *corps de ballet* with a small touring company.

Mae had been nearly thirty when she married. Resigned that she would never be a principal dancer, she had turned to teaching for a short time, but her own frustrations made her a poor instructor. Lindsay's birth had altered everything. She could never be a prima ballerina, but her daughter would.

Lessons for Lindsay had begun at age five with Mae in constant attendance. From that time on, her life had been a flurry of lessons, recitals, ballet shoes and classical music. Her diet had been scrupulously monitored, her height agonized over until it was certain that five-feet-two was all she would achieve. Mae had been pleased. Toe shoes add six inches to a dancer's height, and a tall ballerina has a more difficult time finding partners.

Lindsay had inherited her mother's height, but to Mae's pride, her body was slender and delicate. After a brief, awkward stage, Lindsay had emerged as a teenager with fawnlike beauty: fragile blond hair, ivory

skin, and Viking blue eyes with brows thin and naturally arched. Her bone structure was elegant, masking a
sturdy strength gained from years of training. Her arms
and legs were slim with the long muscles of a classical
dancer. All of Mae's prayers had been answered.

Lindsay looked the part of a ballerina, and she had
the talent. Mae didn't need a teacher to confirm what
she could see for herself. There were the coordination,
the technique, the endurance and the ability. But more,
there was the heart.

At eighteen Lindsay had been accepted into a New
York company. Unlike her mother, she did not remain
in the *corps*. She advanced to soloist, then, the year
she turned twenty, she became a principal dancer. For
nearly two years it seemed that Mae's dreams were reality. Then, without warning, Lindsay had been forced
to give up her position and return to Connecticut.

For three years teaching dance had been her profession. Though Mae was bitter, Lindsay was more phil-
osophical. She was a dancer still. That would never
change.

The clouds shifted again to block out the sun. Lindsay shivered and wished she had remembered her jacket.
It sat in the front seat of her car, where, in the heat of
her temper, she had tossed it. Her arms were now bare,
covered only at the shoulders by a pale blue leotard. She
had pulled on jeans, and her leg warmers helped, but she
thought longingly of the jacket. Because thinking of it
failed to warm her, Lindsay quickened her pace to a jog.
Her muscles responded instantly. There was a fluidity
to the motion, a grace instinctive rather than planned.
She began to enjoy the run. It was her nature to hunt for
pleasure and to find it.

Abruptly, as if a hand had pulled the plug, the rain began. Lindsay stopped to stare up at the churning, black sky. "What else?" she demanded. A deep roar of thunder answered her. With a half laugh, she shook her head. The Moorefield house was just across the street. She decided to do what she should have done initially: ask Andy to drive her home. Hugging her arms, she stepped out into the road.

The rude blast of a horn had her heart bounding to her throat. Her head snapped around, and she made out the dim shape of a car approaching through the curtain of rain. Instantly she leaped out of the way, slipping on the wet pavement and landing with a splash in a shallow puddle.

Lindsay shut her eyes as her pulse quickened. She heard the high squeal of brakes and the skid of tires. Years from now, she thought as the cold wetness soaked through her jeans, I'll laugh at this. But not now. She kicked and sent a small spray of water flying.

"Are you out of your mind?"

Lindsay heard the roar through the rain and opened her eyes. Standing over her was a raging, wet giant. Or a devil, she thought, eyeing him warily as he towered over her. He was dressed in black. His hair was black as well; sleek and wet, it enhanced a tanned, raw-boned face. There was something faintly wicked about that face. Perhaps it was the dark brows that rose ever so slightly at the ends. Perhaps it was the strange contrast of his eyes, a pale green that brought the sea to mind. And at the moment, they were furious. His nose was long and rather sharp, adding to the angular impression of his face. His clothes were plastered against his body by the rain and revealed a firm, well-proportioned frame.

Had she not been so absorbed with his face, Lindsay would have admired it professionally. Speechless, she only stared up at him, her eyes huge.

"Are you hurt?" he demanded when she failed to answer his first question. There was no concern in his voice, only restrained anger. Lindsay shook her head and continued to stare. With an impatient oath, he took her arms and pulled her up, lifting her well off the ground before he set her on her feet. "Don't you look where you're going?" he tossed out, giving her a quick shake before releasing her.

He was not the giant Lindsay had first imagined. He was tall, certainly—perhaps a foot taller than herself—but hardly a bone-crushing giant or satanic apparition. She began to feel more foolish than frightened.

"I'm terribly sorry," she began. She was fully aware that she had been at fault and equally willing to admit it. "I did look, but I didn't..."

"Looked?" he interrupted. The impatience in his tone barely covered a deeper, tightly controlled fury. "Then perhaps you'd better start wearing your glasses. I'm sure your father paid good money for them."

Lightning flashed once, slicing white across the sky. More than the words, Lindsay resented the tone. "I don't wear glasses," she retorted.

"Then perhaps you should."

"My eyes are fine." She pushed clinging hair from her brow.

"Then you certainly should know better than to walk out into the middle of the street."

Rain streamed down her face as she glared at him. She wondered that it didn't turn to steam. "I apologized," she snapped, placing her hands on her hips. "Or had

begun to before you jumped on me. If you expect grov-
eling, you can forget it. If you hadn't been so heavy on
the horn, I wouldn't have slipped and landed in that stupid puddle." She wiped ineffectually at the seat of her
pants. "I don't suppose it occurs to you to apologize?"

"No," he answered evenly, "it doesn't. I'm hardly responsible for your clumsiness."

"Clumsiness?" Lindsay repeated. Her eyes grew
round and wide. *"Clumsiness?"* On the repetition, her
voice broke. To her, there was no insult more vile. *"How
dare you!"*

She would take the dunk in the puddle, she would
take his rudeness, but she would not take that. "You're
the most deplorable excuse for a man I've ever met!"
Her face was aglow with passion now, and she pushed
impatiently at the hair the rain continued to nudge into
her eyes. They shone an impossibly vivid blue against
her flushed skin. "You nearly run me down, frighten me
to death, push me into a puddle, lecture me as if I were
a nearsighted child and now, *now* you have the nerve to
call me *clumsy!*"

A winglike brow raised up at the passion of her
speech. "If the shoe fits," he murmured, then stunned
her by grabbing her arm and pulling her with him.

"Just what are you doing?" Lindsay demanded, trying
for imperviousness and ending on a squeak.

"Getting out of this damn downpour." He opened the
car door on the driver's side and shoved her, without cer-
emony, inside. Automatically, Lindsay scooted across
the seat to accommodate him. "I can hardly leave you
out in the rain." His tone was brusque as he moved in
beside her at the wheel and slammed the door behind
him. The storm battered against the windows.

He dragged his fingers through the thick hank of hair that was now plastered against his forehead, and Lindsay was immediately taken with his hand. It had the wide palm and long-fingered extension of a pianist. She almost felt sympathy for his predicament. But then he turned his head. The look was enough to erase any empathy.

"Where were you going?" he asked. The question was curt, as though it had been put to a child. Lindsay straightened her wet, chilled shoulders.

"Home, about a mile straight down this road."

The brows lifted again as he took a good, long look at her. Her hair hung limp and straight around her face. Her lashes were darkened and curled without the aid of mascara, framing eyes almost shockingly blue. Her mouth pouted, but it obviously did not belong to the child he had first taken her for. Though unpainted, it was clearly a woman's mouth. The naked face had something beyond simple beauty, but before he could define it, Lindsay shivered, distracting him.

"If you're going to go out in the rain," he said mildly as he reached toward the back seat, "you should take care to dress for it." He tossed a tan jacket into her lap.

"I don't need..." Lindsay began, only to break off by sneezing twice. Teeth clenched, she slipped her arms into the jacket as he started the engine. They drove in silence with the rain drumming on the roof.

It occurred to Lindsay all at once that the man was a total stranger. She knew virtually everyone in the small seacoast town by name or by sight, but never had she seen this man. She would hardly have forgotten that face. It was easy, in the slow-moving, friendly atmosphere of Cliffside, to be casual, but Lindsay had also spent several years in New York. She knew the very real dangers of accepting rides from strangers. Surreptitiously, she inched closer to the passenger door.

"A bit late to think of that now," he said quietly.

Lindsay's head snapped around. She thought, but couldn't be certain, that his mouth lifted slightly at the corner. She angled her chin. "Just there," she said coolly, pointing to the left. "The cedar house with the dormers."

The car purred to a halt in front of a white picket fence. Pulling together all her dignity, Lindsay turned to him again. She fully intended to make her thanks frosty.

"You'd better get out of those wet clothes," he advised before she could speak. "And next time, look both ways before you cross the street."

She could only make a strangled sound of fury as she fumbled for the door handle. Stepping back into the torrent of rain, she glared across the seat. "Thanks heaps," she snapped and slammed the door peevishly. She dashed around the back of the car and through the gate, forgetting she still wore a stranger's jacket.

Lindsay stormed into the house. With her temper still simmering, she stood quite still, eyes shut, calling herself to order. The incident had been infuriating, outrageously so, but the last thing she wanted was to have to relate the entire story to her mother. Lindsay was aware that her face was too expressive, her eyes too revealing. Her tendency to so visibly express her feelings had been only another asset in her career. When she danced *Giselle,* she felt as Giselle. The audience could read the tragedy on Lindsay's face. When she danced, she became utterly rapt in the story and in the music. But when her ballet shoes came off and she was Lindsay Dunne again, she knew it was not wise to let her thoughts shout from her eyes.

If she saw that Lindsay was upset, Mae would question her and demand a detailed account, only to criticize in the end. At the moment, the last thing that Lindsay wanted was a lecture. Wet and tired, she wearily began to climb the stairs to the second floor. It was then that she heard the slow, uneven footsteps, a constant reminder of the accident that had killed Lindsay's father.

"Hi! I was just dashing upstairs to change." Lindsay pulled back the wet hair from her face to smile at her mother, who stood at the foot of the stairs. Mae rested her hand on the newel post. Though her carefully coiffed hair had been dyed an ageless blond and her makeup had been skillfully applied, the effect was spoiled by Mae's perpetual expression of dissatisfaction.

"The car was acting up," Lindsay continued before the questioning could begin. "I got caught in the rain before I got a lift. Andy will have to give me a ride back tonight," she added in afterthought.

"You forgot to give him back his jacket," Mae observed. She leaned heavily on the newel post as she looked at her daughter. The damp weather plagued her hip.

"Jacket?" Blankly, Lindsay looked down and saw the wet, too-long sleeves that hung over her arms. "Oh no!"

"Well, don't look so panic-stricken," Mae said testily as she shifted her weight. "Andy can manage without it until tonight."

"Andy?" Lindsay repeated, then made the connection her mother had guessed at. Explanations, she decided, were too complicated. "I suppose so," she agreed casually. Then, descending a step, she laid her hand over her mother's. "You look tired, Mother. Did you rest today?"

"Don't treat me like a child," Mae snapped, and Lindsay immediately stiffened. She drew her hand away.

"I'm sorry." Her tone was restrained, but hurt flickered into her eyes. "I'll just go up and change before dinner." She would have turned, but Mae caught at her arm.

"Lindsay." She sighed, easily reading the emotions in the wide, blue eyes. "I'm sorry; I'm bad-tempered today. The rain depresses me."

"I know." Lindsay's voice softened. It had been a combination of rain and poor tires that had caused her parents' accident.

"And I hate your staying here taking care of me when you should be in New York."

"Mother..."

"It's no use." Mae's voice was sharp again. "Things won't be right until you're where you belong, where you're meant to be." Mae turned, moving down the hall in her awkward, uneven gate.

Lindsay watched her disappear before she turned to mount the stairs. Where I belong, she mused as she turned into her room. Where is that really? Closing the door, she leaned back against it.

The room was big and airy with two wide windows side by side. On the dresser that had been her grandmother's was a collection of shells gathered from a beach barely a mile from the house. Set in a corner was a shelf stacked with books from her childhood. The faded Oriental rug was a prize she had brought back with her when she had closed up her New York apartment. The rocking chair was from the flea market two blocks away, and the framed Renoir print was from a Manhattan art gallery. Her room, she thought, reflected the two worlds in which she had lived.

Over the bed hung the pale pink toe shoes she had worn in her first professional solo. Lindsay walked over to them and lightly fingered the satin ribbons. She remembered sewing them on, remembered the stomach-churning excitement. She remembered her mother's ecstatic face after the performance and her father's gently awed one.

A lifetime ago, she thought as she let the satin fall from her fingers. Back then she had believed that anything was possible. Perhaps, for a time, it had been.

Smiling, Lindsay let herself remember the music, the movement, the magic and the times she had felt her body was without bounds, fluid and free. Reality had come afterward, with unspeakable cramping, bleeding feet, strained muscles. How had it been possible, again and again, to contort her body into the unnatural lines that made up the dance? But she had done it, and she had pushed herself to the limits of ability and endurance. She had given herself over, sacrificing her body and the years. There had been only the dance. It had absorbed her utterly.

Shaking her head, Lindsay brought herself back. That, she reminded herself, was a long time ago. Now, she had other things to think about. She stripped out of the damp jacket, then frowned at it. What do I do with this? she wondered.

The owner's blatant rudeness came back to her. Her frown deepened. Well, if he wants it, he can just come back for it. A quick scan of the material and the label told her it was not a piece of clothing to be carelessly forgotten. But the mistake was hardly her fault, she told herself as she walked to the closet for a hanger. If he hadn't made her so mad, she wouldn't have forgotten to give it back to him.

She hung the jacket in her closet and began to peel off her own wet clothes. She slipped a thick, chenille robe over her shivering skin and closed the closet doors. She told herself to forget the jacket and the man it belonged to. Neither of them, she decided, had anything to do with her.

Chapter 2

It was a different Lindsay Dunne who stood greeting parents two hours later. She wore a high-necked, ruffled lawn blouse with a full, knife-pleated skirt, both in a rain-washed shade of blue. Her hair was neatly braided and coiled at each ear. Her features were calm and composed. Any resemblance to the wet, furious woman of the early evening had vanished. In her preoccupation with the recital, Lindsay had completely forgotten the incident in the rain.

Chairs had been set up in rows from which parents could watch their children's performance. Behind the audience was a table on which coffee and assorted cookies had been arranged. Throughout the room Lindsay could hear the buzz of conversation, and it made her recall the innumerable recitals of her own past. She tried not to hurry through the handshakings and questions, but her mind flitted to the adjoining room, where two dozen girls were busy with tutus and toe shoes.

She was nervous. Underneath the calm, smiling exterior, Lindsay was every bit as nervous as she had been before every one of her own recitals. But she managed to field questions smoothly, knowing almost invariably in advance what they would be. She'd been here before, as a preschooler, a junior, an intermediate and as a senior dancer. Now she was the instructor. Lindsay felt there was no aspect of a recital that she had missed in her lifetime. Yet she was still nervous.

The quiet Beethoven sonata she had placed on the CD player had been an attempt to quiet her own nerves as much as to create atmosphere. It was foolish, she told herself, for a seasoned professional—an established instructor—to be nervous and tense over a simple recital. But there was no help for it. Lindsay's heart was very close to the surface when it came to her school and her students. She wanted badly for the evening to be a success.

She smiled, shaking hands with a father whom she was certain would rather be at home watching a ball game. The finger he eased surreptitiously under his collar made it plain that he was uncomfortable in the restricting tie. If Lindsay had known him better, she would have laughed, then whispered to him to remove it.

Since she had started giving recitals more than two years before, one of Lindsay's main objectives had been to keep the parents at ease. Her rule of thumb was that comfortable parents made a more enthusiastic audience, and a more enthusiastic audience could generate more students for the school. She had founded the school by word of mouth, and it was still a neighbor's recommendation to a neighbor, a satisfied parent's suggestion to an acquaintance, that kept it working. It was her business now, her living as well as her love. She considered herself fortunate to have been able to combine the two for a second time in her life.

Aware that many of the dancers' families had come out of a sense of duty, Lindsay was determined to give them a good time. In each recital, she tried not only to vary the program but to see to it that every dancer had a part especially choreographed for her talent and ability. She knew that not all mothers were as ambitious for their children as Mae, nor were all fathers as supportive as hers had been.

But they came anyway, she thought, looking around her at the group huddled in her studio. They drove out in the rain, giving up a favorite television show or an after-dinner snooze on the sofa. Lindsay smiled, touched again by the perpetually unnoticed selflessness of parents dealing with their children.

It struck her then—strongly, as it did from time to time—how very glad she was to have come home, how very content she was to remain here. Oh, she had loved New York, the continual throb of life, the demands, the undeniable excitement, but the simple pleasure of the close-knit town and the quiet streets more than satisfied her now.

Everyone in the room knew each other, either by sight or by name. The mother of one of the senior dancers had been Lindsay's sitter almost twenty years before. She'd worn a ponytail then, Lindsay remembered as she looked at the woman's short, sculptured hairstyle. It had been a long ponytail tied up with colored yarn. It had swung when she walked, and Lindsay had found it beautiful. Now the memory warmed her and eased her nerves.

Perhaps everyone should leave at some point, then come back to their hometown as an adult, she reflected, whether they settled down there again or not. What a revelation it is to see the things and people we knew as children through an adult's perspective.

"Lindsay."

Lindsay turned to greet a former schoolmate, now the mother of one of her smallest dancers. "Hello, Jackie. You look wonderful."

Jackie was a trim and competent brunette. Lindsay recalled that she had been on an amazing number of committees during their high school years. "We're awfully nervous," Jackie confessed, referring to herself, her daughter and her husband as one.

Lindsay followed Jackie's eyes across the room and spotted the former track star turned insurance executive whom Jackie had married within a year of graduation. He was talking with two elderly couples. All the grandparents are here as well, Lindsay thought with a smile.

"You're supposed to be nervous," Lindsay told her. "It's traditional."

"I hope she'll do well," Jackie said, "for her sake. And she wants so badly to impress her daddy."

"She'll be just fine," Lindsay assured her, giving the nervous hand a squeeze. "And they'll all look wonderful, thanks to the help you gave me with the costumes. I haven't had a chance to thank you yet."

"Oh, that was a pleasure," Jackie assured her. She glanced toward her family again. "Grandparents," she said in an undertone, "can be terrifying."

Lindsay laughed softly, knowing how these particular grandparents doted on the tiny dancer.

"Go ahead, laugh," Jackie invited scornfully, but a self-deprecating smile touched her lips. "You don't have to worry about grandparents yet. Or in-laws," she added, giving the word a purposefully ominous tone. "By the way," Jackie's change of tone put Lindsay on immediate alert. "My cousin Tod...you remember?"

"Yes," Lindsay answered cautiously as Jackie paused.

"He's coming through town in a couple of weeks. Just for a day or so." She gave Lindsay a guileless smile. "He asked about you the last time he phoned."

"Jackie..." Lindsay began, determined to be firm.

"Why don't you let him take you out to dinner?" Jackie continued, cutting off Lindsay's chance to make a clean escape. "He was so taken with you last year. He'll only be in town for a short time. He has a marvellous business in New Hampshire. You know, hardware; I told you."

"I remember," Lindsay said rather shortly. One of the disadvantages of being single in a small town was continually having to dodge matchmaking schemes by well-meaning friends, she thought. The hints and suggestions for partners had been dropped more frequently now that Mae was improving steadily. Lindsay knew that in order to avoid a deluge, she must set a precedent. She must be firm.

"Jackie, you know how busy I am...."

"You're doing a wonderful job here, Lindsay," Jackie said quickly. "The girls all love you, but a woman needs a diversion now and then, doesn't she? There's nothing serious between you and Andy?"

"No, of course not, but..."

"Then there certainly isn't any need to bury yourself."

"My mother…"

"She looked so well when I dropped off the costumes at your house the other day," Jackie went on relentlessly. "It was wonderful to see her up and around. She's finally putting on a bit of weight, I noticed."

"Yes, she is, but…"

"Tod should be in town a week from Thursday. I'll tell him to give you a ring," Jackie said lightly before turning to weave her way through the crowd to her family.

Lindsay watched her retreat with a mixture of irritation and amusement. Never expect to win over someone who won't let you finish a sentence, she concluded. Oh well, she thought, one cousin with a nervous voice and slightly damp palms won't be too bad for an evening. Her social calendar wasn't exactly bulging with appointments, and fascinating men weren't exactly lining up at her front door.

Lindsay pushed the prospective dinner date to the back of her mind. Now wasn't the time to worry about it. Now was the time to think of her students. She walked across the studio to the dressing room. Here, at least, her authority was absolute.

Once inside, she leaned back against the closed door and took a long, deep breath. Before her, pandemonium ruled, but this was the sort of chaos she was immune to. Girls chattered excitedly, helping each other into costumes or trying out steps one final time. One senior dancer calmly executed *pliés* while a pair of five-year-olds played tug of war with a ballet shoe. All around there was the universal backstage confusion.

Lindsay straightened, her voice rising with the gesture. "I'd like your attention, please." The soft tone carried over the chattering and brought all eyes to her.

"We'll begin in ten minutes. Beth, Josey," she addressed two senior dancers with a nod, "if you'd help the little ones." Lindsay glanced at her watch, wondering why the piano accompanist was so late. If worse comes to worst, she would use the CD player.

She crouched to adjust the tights on a young student and dealt with questions and nerves from others.

"Ms. Dunne, you didn't let my brother sit in the front row, did you? He makes faces. Awful ones."

"Second row from the back," Lindsay countered with a mouthful of hairpins as she completed repairs on a tousled coiffure.

"Ms. Dunne, I'm worried about the second set of *jetés*."

"Just like rehearsal. You'll be wonderful."

"Ms. Dunne, Kate's wearing red nail polish."

"Hmm." Lindsay glanced at her watch again.

"Ms. Dunne, about the *fouettés*..."

"Five, no more."

"We really ought to be wearing stage makeup so we don't look washed out," a diminutive dancer complained.

"No," Lindsay said flatly, suppressing a smile. "Monica, thank goodness!" Lindsay suddenly called out with relief as an attractive young woman entered through the back door. "I was about to drag out the CD player."

"Sorry I'm late." Monica grinned cheerfully as she shut the door at her back.

Monica Anderson at twenty was pretty in a healthy, wholesome way. Her bouncy blond hair adorned a face that featured a dash of freckles and large, hopeful, brown eyes. She had a tall, athletic body and the purest heart of anyone Lindsay had ever known. She collected stray cats, listened to both sides of every argument and never thought the worst of anyone, even after being confronted with it. Lindsay liked her for her simple goodness.

Monica also possessed a true gift for piano accompaniment. She kept tempo, playing the classics truthfully, without the embellishments that would detract from the dancers. But she was not, Lindsay thought with a sigh, overly obsessed with punctuality.

"We've got about five minutes," Lindsay reminded her as Monica maneuvered her generously curved body toward the door.

"No problem. I'll go out in just a second. This is Ruth," she continued, gesturing to a girl who stood just to the side of the door. "She's a dancer."

Lindsay's attention shifted from the tall, busty blonde to the finely boned girl. She noted the exotic, almond-shaped eyes and the full, passionate mouth. Ruth's straight, black hair was parted in the center to frame her small, triangular face and hung down just past her shoulder blades. Her features were uneven, and while individually they might have been unremarkable, in combination they were arresting. She was a girl on the brink of womanhood. Though her stance was easy and full of confidence, there was something in the dark eyes that bespoke uncertainty and nervousness. The eyes caused Lindsay's smile to warm as she held out her hand.

"Hello, Ruth."

"I'll go give them a quick overture and quiet things down," Monica interjected, but as she turned to go, Ruth plucked at her sleeve.

"But, Monica…" Ruth protested.

"Oh, Ruth wants to talk to you, Lindsay." She gave

her cheerful, toothy smile and turned once more toward the door. "Don't worry," she said to the younger girl, "Lindsay's very nice. I told you. Ruth's a little nervous," she announced as she backed out the door leading to the studio.

Amused, Lindsay shook her head, but as she turned back, she saw Ruth's heightened color. At ease with strangers herself, she still recognized one who was not. She touched the girl's arm lightly. "There's only one Monica," she stated with a new smile. "Now, if you'll give me a hand lining up the first dancers, we should be able to talk."

"I don't want to be in the way, Ms. Dunne."

In answer, Lindsay gestured behind her to the backstage confusion. "I could use the help."

Lindsay was easily capable of organizing the dancers herself, but she knew, watching Ruth relax, that she had made the right gesture. Intrigued, she watched the way the girl moved, recognizing natural grace and trained style. Lindsay then turned to give her full attention to her students. In a few moments, a restrained hush fell over the room. After opening the door, she gave a quick signal to Monica. The introductory music began, then the youngest of Lindsay's students glided into the studio.

"They're so cute at this stage," she murmured. "There's very little they can do wrong." Already some of the pirouettes had touched off smatterings of applause. "Posture," she whispered to the small dancers. Then to Ruth: "How long have you been studying?"

"Since I was five."

Lindsay nodded while keeping her eyes trained on the tiny performers. "How old are you?"

"Seventeen."

It was stated with such determination that Lindsay lifted a brow.

"Just last month," Ruth added with a tinge of defense. Lindsay smiled but continued to watch the dancers.

"I was five, too. My mother still has my first pair of ballet shoes."

"I saw you dance in *Don Quixote*." The words tumbled out swiftly. Lindsay turned to see Ruth staring at her, her bottom lip trapped between her teeth.

"Did you? When?"

"Five years ago in New York. You were wonderful." The eyes were so filled with awe and admiration that Lindsay lifted a hand to the girl's cheek. Ruth stiffened, but Lindsay, puzzled, smiled nonetheless.

"Thank you. It was always my favorite ballet. So full of flash and fire."

"I'm going to dance Dulcinea one day." Some of the nerves had faded from the voice. Now Ruth's eyes were direct on Lindsay's.

Studying her, Lindsay thought she had never seen more perfect looks for the part. "Do you want to continue your training?"

"Yes." Ruth moistened her lips.

She tilted her head, still studying. "With me?"

Ruth nodded before the word would come. "Yes."

"Tomorrow's Saturday." Lindsay lifted her hand to signal the next group of dancers. "My first class is at ten. Can you come at nine?" The triumphant preschoolers forged back into the dressing room. "I'll want to check the progress of your training to see where to place you. Bring ballet and toe shoes."

Ruth's eyes shimmered with excitement. "Yes, Ms. Dunne. Nine o'clock."

"I'd also like to speak with your parents, Ruth, if one or both of them could come with you."

Monica changed tempo to introduce the next group.

"My parents were killed in an accident a few months ago."

Lindsay heard the quiet pronouncement as she nudged the next group out on stage. Over their heads, her eyes met Ruth's. She saw that the light in them had dimmed. "Oh, Ruth, I'm terribly sorry." Sympathy and distress deepened Lindsay's tone. She knew the feel of tragedy. But Ruth shook her head briskly and avoided the touch of her hand. Suppressing the instinctive need to comfort, Lindsay stood silently while Ruth composed herself. She recognized a very private person, one who was not yet ready to share her emotions.

"I live with my uncle," Ruth continued. There was nothing of her feelings in her voice. It was low and smooth. "We've just moved into the house on the edge of town."

"The Cliff House." Fresh interest sparkled in Lindsay's eyes. "I'd heard it'd been sold. It's a fabulous place." Ruth merely looked off into space. She hates it, Lindsay decided, again feeling a profound tug of sympathy. She hates everything about it. It was difficult to keep her tone practical. "Well, then, perhaps your uncle could come in with you. If it's not convenient, have him phone me. I'm in the book. It's important that I speak with him before we outline your routine."

A sudden smile illuminated Ruth's face. "Thank you, Ms. Dunne."

Lindsay turned away to quiet a pair of youngsters. When she looked again, Ruth had gone.

An odd girl, she mused, obliging one of the little ones

by picking her up. *Lonely.* The word seemed too suitable, and Lindsay nuzzled against the neck of the small child she held. She had had little time for loneliness, but she recognized it. It saddened her to see it reflected in the eyes of one so young.

She wondered what the uncle was like as she watched her intermediate students carry out a short routine from *Sleeping Beauty.* Is he kind? Is he understanding? She thought again of the large, dark eyes and sighed. Monica had found another stray, and Lindsay knew she had already involved herself. Smiling, she kissed the little ballerina's cheek, then set her down.

Tomorrow, Lindsay decided, we'll see if she can dance.

Lindsay began to wonder if the rain would last forever. It was warm—even cozy—in her bed, but the night wore on, and she was still wide awake. It was odd, she thought, because usually the patter of lingering rain and the soft quilt around her would have induced sleep. She thought perhaps it was leftover tension from the recital which kept her mind alert.

It had gone well, she recalled, pleased. The little ones, shaky posture and all, had been as appealing as she had hoped, and the older girls had demonstrated all the poise and grace she could have asked of them. If only she could lure some boys into class! She sighed. But she had to put that out of her mind. The recital had gone well, her students were happy. Some of them showed potential. But soon her thoughts drifted to the dark-haired girl, Ruth.

Lindsay had recognized ambition there but wondered if she would find talent. Remembering Ruth's eyes and the need and vulnerability she had seen there, she hoped she would. She wants to dance Dulcinea, she remembered with a wistful smile. Lindsay felt a small ache, knowing how many hopes could be dashed to the ground in the world of dance. She could only hope Ruth's weren't, for something in the young, poignant face had touched a chord in her. There had been a day not so long ago when dancing Dulcinea had been only a wish for Lindsay as well. She thought perhaps she had come full circle.

Lindsay closed her eyes, but her mind continued to race.

She briefly considered going down to the kitchen for some tea or hot chocolate. She sighed into the darkness. The noise would disturb her mother. Mae slept lightly, especially in the rain. Lindsay knew how difficult it was for her mother to deal with all the disappointments she had been handed. And the tragedy.

Mae's aching hip would be a continual reminder of the death of her husband. Lindsay knew that Mae had not always been happy, but her father had been so quietly supportive. His loss had been hard on Mae, who had awakened from a coma confused and in pain, unable to understand how he could have been taken from her. Lindsay knew her mother could never forget her husband's death, her own injuries and painful therapy and the abrupt end of her daughter's career.

And now that Mae was finally accepting Dad's death, Lindsay reflected, and could get around a bit more, she thought of nothing but Lindsay's return to professional dancing.

Lindsay rolled to her side, curling her arm under her pillow. The rain splashed on the window glass, excited by the wind. What would it take to resign her mother to the inevitable, she wondered. What would it take to make her happy? Would she ever be able to do both? The look on her mother's face as she had stood at the base of the stairs that afternoon came back to her. With the image came the familiar helplessness and guilt.

Rolling onto her back, Lindsay stared at the ceiling. She had to stop thinking about it. It was the rain, she decided, just the rain. To ease her insomnia, she began to go over the details of the day.

What an afternoon it had been. The varied complications now brought on a smile. Still, for a Friday class in which older girls were always thinking about their Saturday night dates and the younger ones were just thinking about Saturday, it had gone fairly well. And everything had worked out, except for that blasted car!

The thought of her broken-down car pushed the memory of the man in the rain back into Lindsay's mind. Frowning, she turned her head so that she faced the closet. In the near-perfect darkness, it was impossible to see the door itself, much less what was inside it. But Lindsay continued to frown. I wonder, she thought, if he'll come back for his jacket.

He had been so rude! Indignation welled up again, replacing her earlier depression. She much preferred it. He was so superior? *If you're going to go out in the rain...* In her mind she mimicked his low, controlled voice.

A wonderfully appealing voice, she reflected. Too bad it has to come out of such an unappealing man. Clumsy, she thought, fuming all over again. And he had the nerve to call me clumsy! She rolled onto her stomach and pounded the pillow before placing her head on it. I hope he does come back for his jacket, she decided.

This time I'll be ready for him. It gave her a great deal of pleasure to imagine a variety of situations in which she returned the borrowed jacket. Haughtily, disdainfully, benevolently…she would hold the upper hand and humiliate the objectionable man whose eyes and cheekbones now haunted her. When next they met, it would not be raining. She would not be at a disadvantage—soaking wet and sneezing. She would be witty, poised…devastating. She smiled to herself as she drifted off to sleep.

Chapter 3

Rain had accumulated in puddles. The morning sun glistened on their surfaces in a splash of colors, while beads of moisture still clung to the grass. There was just a trace of fog misting over the ground. Andy turned up the car heater to combat the chill as he watched Lindsay walk through the front door of her house. She was, to him, the most gorgeous creature in the world. In point of fact, Andy felt Lindsay was beyond the real world. She was too delicate, too ethereal to be of the earth.

And her beauty was so pure, so fragile. It tied his stomach into knots when he saw her. It had been so for fifteen years.

Lindsay smiled and lifted a hand in greeting as she moved down the concrete walk toward the car. In her smile he saw the affection, the friendship she had always offered to him. Andy returned both the smile and the wave. He had no illusions about his relationship with Lindsay. Friendship and no more. It would never be anything else. Not once in all the time he had known her had she encouraged him beyond the borders of friendship.

She's not for me, Andy mused as Lindsay swung through the gate. But he felt the familiar surge when she opened the car door and slid in beside him. Her scent was always the same, light and fresh with a touch of the mysterious. He always felt too big when she was beside him. Too broad, too clumsy.

Lindsay smiled into his wide, square-jawed face and kissed him with quick friendliness. "Andy, you're a lifesaver." She studied his face, liking it as always; the dependable dark eyes, the strong bones, the slightly disheveled brown hair reminiscent of a family dog. And like a family pet, he made her feel comfortable and just a little maternal. "I really appreciate your driving me to the studio this way."

He shrugged broad shoulders. Already the surge had mellowed into the familiar warmth he felt whenever she was near. "You know I don't mind."

"I know you don't," she acknowledged as he pulled away from the curb. "So I appreciate it even more." As was her habit, she slid sideways in the seat as she spoke. Personal contact was vital to her. "Your mom's coming by to spend some time with mine today."

"Yeah, I know." Andy drove down the street with the relaxed attention of one who had followed the same route uncountable times. "She's going to talk her into taking that trip to California this winter."

"I really hope she does." For a moment Lindsay allowed her mind to linger on her mother's restless, unhappy face. "She could use a change."

"How's she doing?"

Lindsay let out a long sigh. There was nothing she felt she could not discuss with Andy. She'd had no closer friend since childhood. "Physically, so much better. There's a great improvement even in the last three months, but otherwise…" She linked her fingers together, then turned her hands palms up, a gesture she used as others used a shrug. "Frustrated, angry, restless. She wants me to go back to New York to dance. She can't see it any other way. It's tunnel vision; she's refused to accept the fact that picking up where I left off is virtually impossible. Three years away, three years older." She shook her head and lapsed into thoughtful silence. Andy gave her a full minute.

"Do you want to go back?"

She looked back at him now, and though the frown brought a line between her brows, it was one of concentration and not annoyance. "I don't know. I don't think so. I did it all once, and I'm very content here, but…" She sighed.

"But?" Andy turned left and absently waved to a pair of youngsters on bicycles.

"I loved it when I was doing it, even though so much of the life is brutal. I loved it." She smiled, relaxing against the seat again. "Past tense, you see. But Mother continually pushes it into the present. Even if I wanted it—wanted it desperately—the chance that the company would have me back is so—so slim." Her eyes wandered to the familiar houses. "So much of me belongs here now. It feels right, being home. Do you remember that night we snuck into the Cliff House?" Her eyes were alight again, laughing. Andy responded with a grin.

"I was scared to pieces. I still swear I saw the ghost."

Lindsay's laugh was a light, bubbling sound. "Ghost or no ghost, it's the most fantastic place I've ever seen. You know, it was finally sold."

"I'd heard." Andy shot her a look. "I remember you swearing you'd live there one day."

"We were young," she murmured, but the sadness she felt at the memory was warm and not unpleasant. "I wanted to live high up above the town and feel important. All those marvelous rooms stacked on top of each other, and those endless corridors," she recalled out loud.

"The place is a labyrinth," he remarked unromantically. "There's been a lot of work going on up there."

"I hope they haven't ruined the atmosphere."

"What, spider webs and field mice?"

Lindsay wrinkled her nose. "No, idiot, the stateliness, the magnificence, the arrogance. I've always imagined it with the gardens blooming and the windows wide open for parties."

"The place hasn't had a window open in more than a decade, and the garden has the toughest weeds in New England."

"You," she said gravely, "have no vision. Anyway," she continued, "the girl I'm seeing this morning is the niece of the man who bought the place. Know anything about him?"

"Nope. Mom might; she's always up on the town's latest gossip."

"I like the girl," Lindsay mused, conjuring up a picture of Ruth's poignant beauty. "She has rather a lost look. I'd like to help her."

"You think she needs help?"

"She seemed like a bird who wasn't quite certain

whether the hand held out to her would squeeze or stroke. I wonder what the uncle's like."

Andy pulled into the studio parking lot. "How much could you find wrong with the man who bought the Cliff House?"

"Very little, I'm sure," she agreed, slamming her door behind her as Andy slammed his.

"I'll take a look at your car," he volunteered, and moving to it, lifted the hood. Lindsay walked to stand beside him. She scowled at the engine.

"It looks dreadful in there."

"It might help if you'd have it serviced once in a while." He grimaced at the grime-coated engine, then gave a disgusted look at the spark plugs. "You know, there are things that need to be replaced other than gas."

"I'm a mechanical failure," Lindsay said carelessly.

"You don't have to be a mechanic to take minimal care of a car," Andy began, and Lindsay groaned.

"A lecture. It's better to plead guilty." She threw her arms around his neck and kissed both his cheeks. "I'm incompetent. Forgive me."

Lindsay watched the grin flash just as she heard another car pull into the lot. With her arms still around Andy's neck, she turned her head. "That must be Ruth," she thought aloud before releasing him. "I really appreciate your checking out the car, Andy. If it's anything terminal, try to break it to me gently."

Turning around to greet Ruth, Lindsay was struck dumb. The man who approached with the girl was tall and dark. Lindsay knew how his voice would sound before he spoke. Just as she knew his taste in jackets.

"Marvelous," she said just under her breath. Their

eyes locked. She decided he was not a man who surprised easily.

"Ms. Dunne?" There was a hesitant question in Ruth's voice. Shock, distress and annoyance were all easily read on Lindsay's face. "You did say I should be here at nine?"

"What?" Lindsay stared a moment. "Oh, yes," she said quickly. "I'm sorry. I've had some car trouble; I was a bit preoccupied. Ruth, this is my friend Andy Moorefield. Andy, Ruth…"

"Bannion," Ruth supplied, visibly relaxing. "And my uncle, Seth Bannion."

Andy discouraged handshakes by holding out his grimy palms and grinning.

"Ms. Dunne." Seth's tone was so bland, Lindsay thought perhaps he hadn't recognized her after all. A glimpse of his face, however, scotched the theory. Recognition was mixed with mockery. Still, the handshake was unquestionably polite, his fingers making firm but brief contact with hers. Two can play at this game, she decided.

"Mr. Bannion." Her tone was politely distant. "I appreciate your coming with Ruth this morning."

"My pleasure," he returned. Lindsay eyed him suspiciously.

"Let's go inside," she said directly to Ruth. Moving toward the building, she waved a quick farewell in Andy's direction, then dipped into her jacket pocket for the keys.

"It's nice of you to see me early this way, Ms. Dunne," Ruth began. Her voice was much as it had been the night before: low with a faint tremor that betrayed nerves barely under control. Lindsay noted that she clung to her uncle's arm. She smiled, touching the girl's shoulder.

"It helps me to see students individually the first time." She felt the slight resistance and casually removed her hand. "Tell me," she went on as she unlocked the studio door, "whom did you study under?"

"I've had several teachers." As she answered, Ruth stepped inside. "My father was a journalist. We were always traveling."

"I see." Lindsay glanced up at Seth, but his expression remained neutral. "If you'll just make yourself comfortable, Mr. Bannion," she said, matching his seamless politeness, "Ruth and I will work at the barre for a few moments."

Seth merely gave Lindsay a nod, but she noticed that he lightly touched Ruth's hand before he moved to a seat.

"The classes are on the small side," she began as she slipped out of her jacket. "In a town this size, I suppose we have a fairly good number of students, but we're not turning them away in droves." She smiled at Ruth, then drew white leg warmers over her dark green tights. She wore a chiffon overskirt in a shade of sea green. Lindsay realized abruptly that the color was identical to Seth's eyes. She scowled as she reached for her ballet shoes.

"But you like to teach, don't you?" Ruth stood a few feet from her. Lindsay looked up to see her, slim and uncertain in a rose pink leotard that enhanced her dark coloring. Lindsay cleared her expression before she rose.

"Yes, I do. Barre exercises first," she added, gesturing to Ruth as she herself moved to the mirrored wall. Placing her hand on the barre, she indicated for Ruth to stand in front of her. "First position."

Both figures in the mirror moved simultaneously.

Both women were poised together, of nearly identical height and build. One was all light, the other stood as a dark shadow, waiting.

"Grand plié."

With seemingly no effort, they dipped into deep knee bends. Lindsay watched Ruth's back, her legs, her feet for posture, positioning, style.

Slowly she began to take Ruth through the five positions, working her thoroughly. The *pliés* and *battements* were well-executed, she observed. Lindsay could see by the gesture of an arm, the movement of a leg, the love Ruth had for the dance. She remembered herself a decade before, achingly young, full of dreams and aspirations.

She smiled, recognizing a great deal of herself in Ruth. It was easy to empathize with the girl and in their joint motions to forget everything else. As her body stretched, her mind moved in close harmony.

"Toe shoes," she said abruptly, then walked away to change the CD. As she did, her eyes passed over Seth. He was watching her, and she thought there might have been something soothing in his look had it not been so uncompromisingly direct. Still, she met his eyes levelly as she slipped Tchaikovsky into the player. "We'll be about a half hour yet, Mr. Bannion. Shall I make you some coffee?"

He didn't answer with the immediacy she expected from a casual question. The ten seconds of silence left Lindsay oddly breathless. "No," he paused, and she felt her skin grow warm. "Thank you."

When she turned away, the muscles that had been loosened at the barre were taut again. She swore under her breath but wasn't certain if she cursed Seth or herself. After gesturing for Ruth to stand in the center of the room, Lindsay walked back to the barre. She would start *adagio,* slow, sustained steps, looking for balance and style and presence. Too often in her students she found a desire only for the flash: dizzying *pirouettes, fouettés, jetés.* The beauty of a long, slow move was forgotten.

"Ready?"

"Yes, Ms. Dunne."

There was nothing shy about the girl now, Lindsay thought. She caught the light in Ruth's eyes.

"Fourth position, *pirouette,* fifth." The execution was clean, the line excellent. "Fourth position, *pirouette, attitude.*" Pleased, Lindsay began to take a slow circle around Ruth. "*Arabesque.* Again. *Attitude,* hold. *Plié.*"

Lindsay could see that Ruth had talent, and more important, she had endurance and drive. She was further gifted with the build and face of a classical dancer. Her every move was an expression of her love for the art, and Lindsay responded to her involvement. In part, Lindsay felt pain for the sacrifices and self-denial that lay ahead for Ruth, but her joy overpowered it. Here was a dancer who would make it. Excitement began to course through Lindsay's body. *And I'm going to help her,* she thought. There's still quite a bit she needs to learn. She doesn't yet know how to use her arms and hands. She has to learn to express more emotion through her face and body. But she's good—very, very good....

Nearly forty-five minutes had passed. "Relax," Lindsay said simply, then walked over to switch off the CD player. "Your several teachers appear to have done a good job." Turning back, she saw the anxiety had returned to Ruth's eyes. Instinctively, she moved to her, placing her hands on her shoulders. The withdrawal was unspoken, but feeling it, Lindsay removed her hands. "I don't have to tell you that you've a great deal of talent. You're not a fool."

She watched her words sink in. The tension seemed to dissolve from Ruth's body. "It means everything to have you say it."

Surprise lifted Lindsay's brows. "Why?"

"Because you're the most wonderful dancer I've ever seen. And I know if you hadn't given it up, you'd be the most famous ballerina in the country. I've read things, too, that said you were the most promising American dancer in a decade. Davidov chose you for his partner, and he said you were the finest Juliet he ever danced with, and…" She stopped abruptly, ending the uncharacteristically long speech. Color deepened her cheeks.

Though sincerely touched, Lindsay spoke lightly to ease the embarrassment. "I'm very flattered. I don't hear nearly enough of that sort of thing around here." She paused, resisting the instinctive move to touch the girl's shoulder again. "The other girls will tell you I can be a very difficult teacher, very demanding and strict with my advanced students. You'll work hard."

"I won't mind." The gleam of anticipation had returned.

"Tell me, Ruth, what do you want?"

"To dance. To be famous," she answered immediately. "Like you."

Lindsay gave a quick laugh and shook her head. "I only wanted to dance," she told her. For a moment, the amusement flickered out. "My mother wanted me to be famous. Go, change your shoes," she said briskly. "I want to talk to your uncle now. Advanced class on Saturday is at one, *pointe* class at two-thirty. I'm a demon on punc-

tuality." Turning, she focused on Seth. "Mr. Bannion…
shall we use my office?"

Without waiting for an answer, Lindsay walked to
the adjoining room.

Chapter 4

Because she wanted to establish her authority from the outset, Lindsay moved behind her desk. She felt neat and competent, light-years away from the first time she had met Seth. With a gesture for him to do likewise, she sat. Ignoring the instruction, Seth stood, scanning the photographs on her wall. She saw that he had focused on one of herself and Nick Davidov in the final act of *Romeo and Juliet*.

"I managed to get my hands on a poster from this ballet and sent it to Ruth some years back. She has it in her room still." He turned back but didn't move to her. "She admires you tremendously." Though his tone was even, Lindsay understood he felt the admiration implied responsibility. She frowned, not because she was loath to take it, but because he gave it to her.

"As Ruth's guardian," she began, circling around his

statement, "I feel you should know precisely what it is she'll be doing here, what's expected of her, when the classes are set and so forth."

"I believe you're the expert in this field, Ms. Dunne." Seth's voice was quiet, but Lindsay wasn't certain his mind was on his words. Again his eyes roamed her face inch by inch. It was odd, she thought, that his manner and tone could be so formal while his gaze was so personal. She shifted, suddenly uncomfortable.

"As her guardian…"

"As her guardian," Seth interrupted, "I'm aware that studying ballet is as necessary to Ruth as breathing." He came closer now, so that she had to tilt her head back to keep her eyes on his. "I'm also aware that I have to trust you…to an extent."

Lindsay lifted a brow curiously. "To what extent is that?"

"I'll know better in a couple of weeks. I like my information to be more complete before I make a decision." The eyes that were fixed on her face narrowed ever so slightly. "I don't know you yet."

She nodded, miffed without knowing precisely why. "Nor I you."

"True." He took the statement without a change of expression. "I suppose that's a problem that will solve itself in time. It's difficult for me to believe that the Lindsay Dunne I saw dance Giselle is clumsy enough to fall into puddles."

She sucked in her breath, staring at him in outraged amazement. "You nearly ran me down!" All the restraint she had practiced that morning vanished. "Anyone who comes barreling down a residential street in the rain that way should be arrested."

"Fifteen miles an hour isn't considered barreling," he countered mildly. "If I'd been doing the speed limit, I *would* have run you down. You weren't looking where you were going."

"Most people take a little care to learn the streets when they move into a new neighborhood," Lindsay retorted.

"Most people don't go for walks in rain storms," he returned. "I've an appointment shortly," he continued before she could answer. "Shall I write you a check for Ruth's tuition?"

"I'll send you a bill," she told him icily, walking past him to open the door.

Seth followed her, then pausing, crowded her into the jamb as he turned to face her again. Their bodies brushed in brief, potent contact. Every coherent thought veered out of Lindsay's brain. Tilting her head, she stared up at him, surprised and questioning, while her body reacted with instinctual knowledge.

For a moment he stayed, his eyes again making their slow, intruding study before he turned and walked to Ruth.

Off and on during the day, Lindsay's thoughts returned to Seth Bannion. What sort of man was he? On the surface he appeared to be conventional enough. But there was something more beneath. It wasn't just the glimpse of his temper she had witnessed in their first meeting. She had seen something in his eyes, felt something in the touch of his body. It was an energy that went further than the physical. She knew that volcanoes were usually calm and well-mannered on the surface but that there was always something hot and dangerous underneath.

It's nothing to me, she reminded herself, but her thoughts drifted back to him more often than she liked. He interested her. And so did his niece.

Lindsay watched Ruth during her first two classes, looking for more than technique and movement. She wanted to discover attitude and personality. Outgoing herself, Lindsay found it difficult to understand the guards the girl had built. She made no move to reach out to any of her fellow students nor to accept any overtures made to her. She was not unfriendly nor impolite, simply distant. It would be her fate, Lindsay knew, to be labeled a snob. But it isn't snobbery, Lindsay mused as she took her class through *glissades.* It's overwhelming insecurity. Lindsay recalled the instant withdrawal when she had laid her hands on Ruth's shoulders. She remembered how Ruth had been clinging to Seth before the morning session. He's her anchor at the moment; I wonder if he knows it, she mused. How much does he know about her doubts and her fears and the reason for them? How much does he care?

Lindsay demonstrated a move, her body lifting effortlessly to *pointe,* her arms rising slowly. His doubts about her training seemed to Lindsay inconsistent with his patience in sitting through the morning session.

It annoyed her that once again he had insinuated himself into her thoughts. Thrusting him out, Lindsay concentrated fully on the last of her classes. But even as her final student dashed through the front door, leaving her alone, her defenses slipped. She remembered the exploring way he had looked at her and the quiet, even texture of his voice.

Trouble, she thought as she stacked CDs. *Complications*. I'm beginning to enjoy life without complications. She glanced around with a satisfied smile.

My studio, she thought chauvinistically. I'm making something out of it. It might be small and filled with girls who won't dance to anything but top-forty rock after they hit sixteen, but it's mine. I'm making a living doing something I enjoy. What else could anyone want? Irresistibly, her eyes were drawn down to the CD she still held in her hand. Without hesitation, she inserted it into the player.

She loved her students, and she loved teaching them, but she also loved the empty studio. She had found satisfaction in the past three years of instructing, but there was something private—something nourishing—in dancing for the sheer sake of it. It was something her mother had never understood. To Mae, dancing was a commitment, and obsession. To Lindsay, it was a joy, a lover.

Ruth had brought back memories of Dulcinea. It had always been a favored role of Lindsay's because of its enthusiasm and power. Now, as the music poured into the room, she remembered vividly the flow of movement and the strength.

The music was fast and richly Spanish, and she responded to it with verve. Her body came to life with the need to dance. The challenge of the story came back to her to be expressed with sharp arm movements and *soubresauts*. There was energy and youth in the short, quick steps.

As she danced, the mirror reflected the gently flowing chiffon, but in Lindsay's mind, she wore the stiff tutu in black lace and red satin. There was a full-blossomed rose behind her ear and a Spanish comb in her hair. She was Dulcinea, all spirit, all challenge, with the energy to dance endlessly. As the music built toward the finish, Lindsay began her *fouettés*. Around and around with speed and style she twirled herself. It seemed she could go on forever, like the ballerina on a music box, effortlessly spinning to the tune. And as the toy stopped with the music, so did she. She threw a hand over her head and the other to her waist, styling for the sassy ending.

"Bravo."

With both hands clasped to her speeding heart, she whirled. There, straddling one of her small, wooden chairs, was Seth Bannion. She was breathing heavily, both from the exertion of the dance and from the shock of discovering she had not been alone. Her eyes were huge, still dark with excitement, her skin wildly flushed.

The dance had been for herself alone, but she felt no infringement on her privacy. There was no resentment that he had shared it with her. Even her initial surprise was fading to be replaced by an inner knowledge that he would understand what she had been doing and why. She didn't question the feeling, but stood, waiting as he rose and moved to her.

He kept his eyes on hers, and something more than breathlessness began to flutter inside her breast. The look was long and personal. Her blood, already warmed from the dance, heated further. She could feel it tingle under the surface of her skin. There was a feathery dryness in her throat. She lifted one of the hands she still held against her breast and pressed it to her lips.

"Magnificent," he murmured with his eyes still locked on hers. He took the hand she had pressed to her lips and brought it to his own. Her pulse was still racing at her wrist, and his thumb grazed it lightly. "You make it seem so effortless," he commented. "I hardly expect you to be out of breath."

The smile he gave her was as potent as it was un-expected. "I feel I should thank you, even though the dance wasn't for me."

"I didn't...I wasn't expecting anyone." Her voice was as jumpy as her nerves, and Lindsay sought to discipline them both. She began to remove her hand from his and was surprised when Seth resisted, holding her fingers an extra moment before releasing them.

"No, I could see you weren't." He took yet another careful scan of her face. "I'd apologize for intruding, but I'm not in the least bit sorry to have been your au-dience." He possessed considerably more charm than Lindsay had given him credit for. It made it difficult to separate her response to the dance from her response to him. She thought the slight wings at the tips of his brows were fascinating. Only when the left one tilted up did she realize she'd been staring and that he was amused by it. Annoyed with her own lack of sophistication, she turned to the CD player.

"I don't mind," she told him carelessly. "I always worked better with an audience. Was there something you wanted to talk to me about?"

"My knowledge of ballet is limited. What was the dance from?"

"Don Quixote." Lindsay slipped the CD back into its case. "Ruth reminded me of it last night." She faced Seth again with the CD held between them. "She intends to dance Dulcinea one day."

"And will she?" Seth took the CD from her hands, setting it aside as if impatient with the barrier.

"I think so. She has exceptional talent." Lindsay gave him a direct look. "Why did you come back here?"

He smiled again, a slow, somehow dashing smile she knew women found difficult to resist. "To see you," he said and continued to smile as surprise reflected clearly on her face. "And to talk about Ruth. It simply wasn't possible this morning."

"I see." Lindsay nodded, prepared to become the instructor again. "There is quite a bit we need to discuss. I'm afraid I thought you weren't terribly interested this morning."

"I'm very interested." His eyes were on hers again. "Have dinner with me."

It took Lindsay a moment to react, as her mind had jumped forward to plans for Ruth. "Dinner?" She gave him an ingenuous stare as she tried to decide how she felt about the idea of being with him. "I don't know if I want to do that."

His brows lifted at her bluntness, but he nodded. "Then you apparently haven't any great objection. I'll pick you up at seven." Before she could comment, Seth walked back to the door. "I already know the address."

When she had bought it, Lindsay had thought the pelican gray dress would be clean and sophisticated. It was made of thin, soft wool and was closely tailored with a mandarin collar. Critically studying herself in it, she was pleased. This was a far different image than the dripping, babbling mess who had sat in a roadside puddle, and more different, still, from the dreamy, absorbed dancer. The woman who stared back at Lindsay from the glass was a confident, mature woman. She felt as comfortable with this image as she felt with all her other roles. She decided that this aspect of Lindsay Dunne would deal most successfully with Seth Bannion. Lindsay brushed her long mane of hair over one shoulder and braided it loosely as she thought of him.

He intrigued her, perhaps because she hadn't been able to pigeonhole him, as she often did with the people she met. She sensed he was complex, and complexities always had interested her. Or perhaps, she thought, fastening thick, silver hoops to her ears, it was just because he had bought the Cliff House.

Moving to the closet, Lindsay took out his jacket and folded it. It occurred to her suddenly that it had been some time since her last real date. There had been movies and quick dinners with Andy, but thinking back on them, she decided those times hardly counted as dates. Andy's like my brother, she mused, unconsciously toying with the collar of Seth's jacket. His scent still clung to it, faint but unmistakably male.

How long has it been since I went out with a man? she wondered. Three months? Four? Six, she decided with a sigh. And in the past three years, no more than a handful of times. Before that? Lindsay laughed and shook her head. Before that, a date had been the next performance scheduled.

Did she regret it? For a moment she studied herself seriously in the glass. There was a young woman there whose fragile looks were deceptive, whose mouth was generous. No, she'd never regretted it. How could she? She had what she wanted, and whatever she had lost was balanced on the other end of the scale. Glancing up, she saw the reflection of her toe shoes in the mirror as they hung over her bed. Thoughtfully, she stroked the collar of Seth's jacket again before gathering it up with her purse.

Her heels clicked lightly on the stair treads as she came down to the main floor. A quick glance at her watch assured her that she had a few minutes to spare. Setting down the jacket and her purse, Lindsay walked back toward her mother's rooms.

Since Mae's return from the hospital, she had been confined to the first floor of the house. Initially, the stairs had been too much for her to manage, and afterward, the habit of avoiding them had set in. The arrangement afforded both women privacy. Two rooms off the kitchen had been converted to serve as Mae's bedroom and sitting room. For the first year, Lindsay had slept on the sofa in the living room to be within calling distance. Even now she slept lightly, ever alert for any disturbance in the night.

She paused at her mother's rooms, hearing the low drone of the television. After knocking softly, she opened the door.

"Mother, I..."

She stopped when she saw Mae sitting in the recliner. Her legs were propped up as she faced the television, but her attention was focused on the book in her lap. Lindsay knew the book well. It was long and wide and leather-bound to endure wear. Nearly half of its oversized pages were crammed with clippings and photos. There were professional critiques, gossip column tidbits and interviews, all expounding on Lindsay Dunne's dancing career. There was the earliest story from the *Cliffside Daily* to her final review in the *New York Times*. Her professional life—and a good portion of her personal one as well—were bound in that book.

As always, when she saw her mother poring over the scrapbook, Lindsay was struck by waves of guilt and helplessness. She felt her frustration rise as she stepped into the room.

"Mother."

This time Mae glanced up. Her eyes were lit with excitement, her cheeks flushed with it. "'A lyrical dancer,'" she quoted without looking back at the clipping, "'with the beauty and grace of a fairy tale. Breathtaking.' Clifford James," Mae continued, watching Lindsay as she crossed the room. "One of the toughest dance critics in the business. You were only nineteen."

"I was overwhelmed by that review," Lindsay remembered, smiling as she laid her hand on her mother's shoulder. "I don't think my feet touched ground for a week."

"He'd say the same thing if you went back today."

Lindsay shifted her attention from the clipping and met her mother's eyes. A thin thread of tension made its way up her neck. "Today I'm twenty-five," she reminded her gently.

"He would," Mae insisted. "We both know it. You..."

"Mother." Sharply, Lindsay cut her off, then, appalled by her own tone, crouched down beside the chair. "I'm sorry, I don't want to talk about this now. Please." She lifted their joined hands to her cheek, and sighing, wished there could be more between them than the dance. "I've only another minute or two."

Mae studied her daughter's dark, expressive eyes and saw the plea. She shifted restlessly in her chair. "Carol didn't say anything about your going out tonight."

Reminded that Andy's mother had spent part of the day with her mother, Lindsay rose and began a cautious explanation. "I'm not going out with Andy." She straightened the line of her dress.

"No?" Mae frowned. "Who, then?"

"The uncle of a new student of mine." Lindsay brought her head up to meet Mae's eyes. "She has potential, a truly natural talent. I'd like you to see her."

"What about him?" Mae brushed off the thought of Lindsay's student and stared down at the open scrapbook.

"I don't know him very well, of course. He's bought the Cliff House."

"Oh?" Mae's attention returned. She was aware of Lindsay's fascination with the house.

"Yes, they've just recently moved in. It seems Ruth was orphaned a few months ago." She paused, remembering the sadness lurking in the girl's eyes. "She interests me very much. I want to speak to her uncle about her."

"So you're having dinner."

"That's right." Annoyed at having to justify a simple date, Lindsay moved to the door. "I don't suppose I'll be very late. Would you like anything before I go?"

"I'm not a cripple."

Lindsay's eyes flew to her mother's. Mae's mouth was set, her fingers gripped tight on the edges of the book. "I know."

Then there was a silence between them that Lindsay felt unable to break. Why is it, she wondered, that the longer I live with her, the wider the gap? The doorbell sounded, overloud in the quiet. Studying her daughter, Mae recognized the indecision. She broke the contact by looking back at the pages in her lap.

"Good night, Lindsay."

She tasted failure as she turned to the door. "Good night."

Briskly, Lindsay walked down the hall, struggling out of the mood. There was nothing I could have done differently, she told herself. Nothing I could have altered. Suddenly she wanted escape, she wanted to open the front door, to step outside and to keep going until she was somewhere else. Anywhere else. Someplace where she could take her time discovering what it was she really wanted of herself. Lindsay pulled open the door with a hint of desperation.

"Hi." She greeted Seth with a smile as she stepped back to let him in. The dark suit was perfect for his lean, elegant build. Still, there was something slightly sinful about his face. It was dark and narrow and knowing. Lindsay found she liked the contrast. "I suppose I need a coat; it's turned cold." She walked to the hall closet to take out a coat of dark leather. Seth took it from her.

Wordlessly, she allowed him to slip the coat over her while she wondered about basic chemistry. It was odd, she thought, that one person should have such a strong physical reaction to another. Wasn't it strange that nearness or a touch or just a look could increase the heartbeat or raise the blood pressure? Nothing else was required— no personal knowledge, no amiability—just that chance mixture of chemicals. Lindsay didn't resist when Seth turned her to face him. They stood very close, eyes holding, as he brought his hand from her shoulder to adjust the collar of her coat.

"Do you think it's strange," she asked thoughtfully, "that I should be so strongly attracted to you when I thought you were quite horrible the first time I met you, and I'm still not completely sure you're not?"

His grin was different from his smile, she noted. The smile was slow, while the grin was a quick flash. All of his features responded at once. "Are your sentences always so frank and so convoluted?"

"Probably." Lindsay turned away, pleased to have seen the grin. "I'm not very good at dissimulating, and I suppose I talk as I think. Here's your jacket." She handed it to him, dry and neatly folded. Her smile came easily. "I certainly didn't expect to return it to you under these circumstances."

Seth took it, glancing at it briefly before bringing his eyes back to hers. "Did you have other circumstances in mind?"

"Several," Lindsay answered immediately as she picked up her purse. "And you were extremely uncomfortable in all of them. In one, you were serving a ten-year stretch for insulting dancers on rainy afternoons. Are we ready?" she asked, holding out her hand to him in a habitual gesture. His hesitation was almost too brief to measure before he accepted it. Their fingers interlocked.

"You're not what I expected," Seth told her as they stepped out into the chill of the night.

"No?" Lindsay took a deep breath, lifting her face to try to take in all the stars at once. "What did you expect?"

They walked to the car in silence, and Lindsay could smell the spicy aroma of mums and rotting leaves. When they were in the car, Seth turned to her to give her another of the long, probing looks she had come to expect of him.

"The image you were portraying this morning was

more in line with what I expected," he said at length. "Very professional, very cool and detached."

"I had fully intended to continue along those lines this evening," Lindsay informed him. "Then I forgot."

"Will you tell me why you looked ready to run for your life when you answered the door?"

She lifted a brow. "You're very perceptive."

With a sigh, Lindsay sat back against the seat. "It has to do with my mother and a constant feeling of inadequacy." She twisted her head until her eyes met his. "Perhaps one day I'll tell you about it," she murmured, not pausing to ponder why she felt she could. "But not tonight. I don't want to think about it anymore tonight."

"All right." Seth started the car. "Then perhaps you'll let a new resident in on who's who in Cliffside."

Lindsay relaxed, grateful. "How far away is the restaurant?"

"About twenty minutes," he told her.

"That should about do it," she decided, and she began to fill him in.

Chapter 5

Lindsay felt comfortable with Seth. She told him amusing stories because she liked the sound of his laughter. Her own mood of panic and desperation was gone. As they drove, she decided she wanted to know him better. She was intrigued and attracted, and if something volcanic erupted, she'd risk it. Natural disasters were rarely dull.

Lindsay knew the restaurant. She had been there once or twice before when a date had wanted to impress her. She knew that Seth Bannion wouldn't feel the need to impress anyone. This was simply the sort of restaurant he could choose: quiet, elegant, with superior food and service.

"My father brought me here once," Lindsay remembered as she stepped from the car. "On my sixteenth birthday." She waited for Seth to join her, then offered her hand. "I hadn't been allowed to date until then, so he took me out on my birthday. He said he wanted to be my first date." She smiled, warmed by the memory. "He was always doing things like that...small, incredible things." Turning, she found Seth watching her. Moonlight showered over both of them. "I'm glad I came. I'm glad it was with you."

He gave her a curious look, then trailed a finger down her braid. "So am I."

Together they walked up the steps that led to the front door.

Inside, Lindsay was attracted to the long, wide window that revealed an expanse of the Long Island Sound. Sitting in the warm, candlelit restaurant, she could all but hear the waves beat against the rocks below. She could almost feel the cold and the spray.

"This is a wonderful place," she enthused as they settled at their table. "So elegant, so subdued, yet open to all that power." There was a smile on her lips as she turned back to Seth. "I like contrasts, don't you?" The candlelight caught the dull gleam of silver at her ears. "How dull life would be if everything fit into a slot."

"I've been wondering," Seth countered as his eyes flickered from the thick hoops to the delicate planes of her face, "exactly where you fit in."

After a quick shake of her head, Lindsay looked back out the window. "I often wonder that myself. You know yourself well, I think. It shows."

"Would you like something to drink?"

Lindsay turned her head at Seth's question and saw a waiter hovering at his elbow. "Yes." She smiled at him before she gave her attention back to Seth. "Some white wine would be nice, I think. Something cold and dry."

His eyes remained on hers while he ordered. There's something quietly tenacious in the way he looks at me, Lindsay decided, like a man who's finished one page of a book and intends to go on reading until the end. When they were alone, the silence held. Something fluttered up her spine, and she drew in a long breath. It was time to establish priorities.

"We need to talk about Ruth."

"Yes."

"Seth." Nonplussed that his look didn't waver, Lindsay added authority to her voice. "You have to stop looking at me that way."

"I don't think so," he disagreed mildly.

Her brow arched at his reply, but a hint of amusement touched her mouth. "And I thought you were so scrupulously polite."

"I'm adaptable," he told her. He was relaxed in his chair, one arm resting over the back as he studied her. "You're beautiful. I enjoy looking at beauty."

"Thank you." Lindsay decided she would grow used to his direct gaze before the evening was over. "Seth," she leaned forward, pushed by her own thoughts, "this morning, when I watched Ruth, I knew she had talent. This afternoon in class I was even more impressed."

"It was very important to her to study with you."

"But it shouldn't be." Lindsay continued quickly as she again observed the slight narrowing of his eyes. "I'm not capable of giving her everything she needs. My school's so limited in what it can offer, especially to a girl like Ruth. She should be in New York, in a school where her training could be more centered, more intense."

Seth waited while the waiter opened and poured their

wine. He lifted his glass, studying the contents carefully before speaking. "Aren't you capable of instructing Ruth?"

Lindsay's brows shot up at the tone of the question.
When she answered, her voice was no longer warm. "I'm
a capable instructor. Ruth simply needs discipline and
advantages available elsewhere."

"You're easily annoyed," Seth commented, then
sipped his wine.

"Am I?" Lindsay sipped hers as well, trying to remain as pragmatic as he. "Perhaps I'm temperamental,"
she offered and felt satisfied with the cool tone. "You've
probably heard dancers are high-strung."

Seth shifted his shoulders. "Ruth plans to take more
than fifteen hours of training a week with you. Isn't
that adequate?"

"No." Lindsay set down her glass and again leaned
close. If he asked questions, she concluded, he couldn't
be totally unreasonable. "She should be taking classes
every day, more specialized classes than I could possibly offer because I simply don't have any other students
with her abilities. Even if I could instruct her one on one,
it wouldn't be enough. She needs partnering classes. I
have four male students, all of whom come in once a
week to polish their football moves. They won't even
participate in the recitals."

A sound of frustration escaped. Her voice had become
low and intense in her need to make him understand.
"Cliffside isn't the cultural center of the east coast. It's
a small Yankee town." There was an inherent, unrehearsed beauty in the way her hands gestured to accent
her words. Music was in the movement, silent and sweet.
"People here are basic, they're not dreamers. Dancing

has no practical purpose. It can be a hobby, it can be an enjoyment, but here it isn't thought of as a career. It's not thought of as a life."

"Yet you grew up here," Seth pointed out, then added more wine to the glasses. It shimmered gold in the candlelight. "You made it a career."

"That's true." Lindsay ran a fingertip around the rim of her glass. She hesitated, wanting to choose her words carefully. "My mother was a professional dancer, and she was very...strict about my training. I went to a school about seventy miles from here. We spent a great deal of time in the car coming and going." Again she looked up at Seth, but the smile was beginning to play around her mouth. "My teacher was a marvel, a wonderful woman, half French, half Russian. She's almost seventy now and not taking students or I'd plead with you to send Ruth to her."

Seth's tone was as calm and undisturbed as it had been at the start of the conversation. "Ruth wants to study with you."

Lindsay wanted to scream with frustration. She took a sip of wine until the feeling passed. "I was seventeen, Ruth's age, when I went to New York. And I'd already had eight years of intense study in a larger school. At eighteen I started with the company. The competition for a place is brutal, and training is..." Lindsay paused, then laughed and shook her head. "It's indescribable. Ruth needs it, she deserves it. As soon as possible if she wants to be a serious dancer. Her talent demands it."

Seth took his time in answering. "Ruth is little more than a child who's just been through a series of unhappy events." He signaled the waiter for menus. "New York will still be there in three or four years."

"Three or four years!" Lindsay set the menu down without glancing at it. She stared at Seth, incredulous. "She'll be twenty."

"An advanced age," he returned dryly.

"It is for a dancer," Lindsay retorted. "It's rare for one of us to dance much past thirty. Oh, the men steal a few extra years with character parts, or now and again there's someone spectacular like Fonteyn. Those are the exceptions, not the rules."

"Is that why you don't go back?" Lindsay's thoughts stumbled to a halt at the question. "Do you feel your career is over at twenty-five?"

She lifted her glass, then set it down again. "We're discussing Ruth," she reminded him, "not me."

"Mysteries are intriguing, Lindsay." Seth picked up her hand, turning it over to study her palm before he brought his eyes back to hers. "And a beautiful woman with secrets is irresistible. Have you ever considered that some hands were made for kissing? This is one of them." He took her palm to his lips.

Lindsay's muscles seemed to go fluid at the contact. She studied him, frankly fascinated with the sensations. She wondered what it would feel like to have his lips pressed to hers, firmly, warmly. She liked the shape of his mouth and the slow, considering way it smiled. Abruptly, she brought herself out of the dream. *Priorities,* she remembered.

"About Ruth," she began. Though she tried to pull her hand away, Seth kept it in his.

"Ruth's parents were killed in a train accident barely six months ago. It was in Italy." There was no increased pressure on her fingers, but his voice had tightened. His eyes had hardened. Lindsay was reminded of how he had looked when he had loomed over her in the rain. "Ruth was unusually close to them, perhaps because they traveled so much. It was difficult for her to form other attachments. You might be able to imagine what it was like for a sixteen-year-old girl to find herself suddenly orphaned in a foreign country, in a town they'd been in for only two weeks."

Lindsay's eyes filled with painful sympathy, but he continued before she could speak. "She knew virtually no one, and as I was on a site in South Africa, it took days to contact me. She was on her own for nearly a week before I could get to her. My brother and his wife were already buried when I got there."

"Seth, I'm sorry. I'm so terribly sorry." The need to comfort was instinctive. Lindsay's fingers tightened on his as her other hand reached up to cover their joined ones. Something flickered in his eyes, but she was too overwhelmed to see it. "It must have been horrible for her, for you."

He didn't speak for a moment, but his study of her face deepened. "Yes," he said at length, "it was. I brought Ruth back to the States, but New York is very demanding, and she was very fragile."

"So you found the Cliff House," Lindsay murmured.

Seth lifted a brow at the title but didn't comment. "I wanted to give her something stable for a while, though I know she's not thrilled with the notion of settling into a house in a small town. She's too much like her father. But for now, I feel it's what she needs."

"I think I can understand what you're trying to do," Lindsay said slowly. "And I respect it, but Ruth has other needs as well."

"We'll talk about them in six months."

The tone was so final and quietly authoritative that Lindsay had closed her mouth before she realized it. Annoyance flitted over her face. "You're very dictatorial, aren't you?"

"So I've been told." His mood seemed to switch as she looked on. "Hungry?" he asked and smiled with slow deliberation.

"A bit," she admitted, but she frowned as she opened the menu. "The stuffed lobster is especially good here."

As Seth ordered, Lindsay let her eyes drift back out to the Sound. Clearly, she could see Ruth alone, frightened, stunned with grief, having to deal with the loss of her parents and the dreadful details that must have followed. Too well could she recall the panic she had felt upon being notified of her own parents' accident. There was no forgetting the horror of the trip from New York back to Connecticut to find her father dead and her mother in a coma.

And I was an adult, she reminded herself, already having been on my own for over three years. I was in my hometown, surrounded by friends. More than ever, she felt the need to help Ruth.

Six months, she mused. *If I can work with her individually, the time wouldn't be completely wasted. And maybe, just maybe, I can convince Seth sooner. He's got to understand how important this is for her. Losing my temper isn't going to get me anywhere with a man like this,* she acknowledged, *so I'll have to find some other way.*

On a site in South Africa, Lindsay reflected, going back over their conversation. Now what would he have been doing in South Africa? Even before she could mull over the possibilities, a jingle of memory sounded in her brain.

"Bannion," she said aloud and sent his eyebrow up in question. "S. N. Bannion, the architect. It just came to me."

"Did it?" He seemed mildly surprised, then broke a breadstick in half. He offered her a share. "I'm surprised you've had time to delve into architecture."

"I'd have to have been living in a cave for the past ten years not to know the name. What was it in... *Newsview?* Yes, *Newsview,* about a year ago. There was a profile of you with pictures of some of your more prestigious buildings. The Trade Center in Zurich, the Mac-Afee Building in San Diego."

"Your memory's excellent," Seth commented. The candlelight marbled over her skin. She looked as fragile as porcelain with eyes dark and vivid. They seemed to smile at him.

"Flawless," Lindsay agreed. "I also recall reading several tidbits about you and a large portion of the female population. I distinctly remember a department store heiress, an Australian tennis pro and a Spanish opera star. Weren't you engaged to Billie Marshall, the newscaster, a few months ago?"

Seth twirled the stem of his glass between his fingers. "I've never been engaged," he answered simply. "It tends to lead to marriage."

"I see." Absently, she chewed on the breadstick. "And that isn't one of your goals?"

"Is it one of yours?" he countered.

Lindsay paused, frowning. She took his parry quite seriously. "I don't know," she murmured. "I suppose I've never thought of it in precisely that way. Actually,

I haven't had a great deal of time to think of it at all. Should it be a goal?" she thought aloud. "Or more of a surprise, an adventure?"

"So speaks the romantic," Seth observed.

"Yes, I am," Lindsay agreed without embarrassment. "But then, so are you or you'd never have bought the Cliff House."

"My choice of real estate makes me a romantic?"

Lindsay leaned back, still nibbling on the breadstick. "It's much more than a piece of real estate, and I've no doubt you felt that, too. You could have bought a dozen houses, all more conveniently located and in less need of repair."

"Why didn't I?" Seth asked, intrigued with her theory.

Lindsay allowed him to top off her glass again but left it untouched. The effect of the wine was already swirling pleasantly in her head. "Because you recognized the charm, the uniqueness. If you were a cynic, you'd have bought one of the condos twenty miles further up the coast which claim to put you in touch with genuine New England scenery while being fifteen convenient minutes from the Yankee Trader Mall."

Seth laughed, keeping his eyes on her while their meal was served. "I take it you don't care for condos."

"I detest them," Lindsay agreed immediately. "Arbitrarily, I'm afraid, but that's strictly personal. They're perfect for a great number of people. I don't like…" She trailed off, hands gesturing as if to pluck the word from the air. "Uniformity," she decided. "That's strange, I suppose, because there's so much regimentation in my career. I see that differently. Individual expression is so vital. I'd so much rather someone say I was different than I was beautiful." She glanced down at the enormous serving of lobster. "*Innovative* is such a marvelous word," she stated. "I've heard it applied to you."

"Is that why you became a dancer?" Seth speared a delicate morsel of lobster into melted butter. "To express yourself?"

"I think it might be that because I was a dancer, I craved self-expression." Lindsay chose lemon over butter. "Actually, I don't analyze myself often, just other people. Did you know the house was haunted?"

"No." He grinned. "That wasn't brought up during settlement."

"That's because they were afraid you'd back out." Lindsay speared a piece of lobster. "It's too late now, and in any case, I think you'd enjoy having a ghost."

"Would you?"

"Oh, yes, I would. Tremendously." She popped the lobster into her mouth, leaning forward. "It's a romantic, forlorn creature who was done in by a narrow-minded husband about a century ago. She was sneaking off to see her lover and was careless, I suppose. In any case, he dropped her from the second-floor balcony onto the rocks."

"That should have discouraged her adulterous tendencies," Seth commented.

"*Mmm,*" she agreed with a nod, hampered by a full mouth. "But she comes back now and again to walk in the garden. That's where her lover was waiting."

"You seem rather pleased about the murder and deceit."

"A hundred years can make almost anything romantic. Do you realize how many of the great ballets deal with death yet remain romantic? *Giselle* and *Romeo and Juliet* are only two."

"And you've played both leads," Seth said. "Perhaps that's why you emphathize with a star-crossed ghost."

"Oh, I was involved with your ghost before I danced either Giselle or Juliet," Lindsay sighed, watching the stars glitter over the water's surface. "That house has fascinated me for as long as I can remember. When I was a child, I swore I'd live there one day. I'd have the gardens replanted, and all the windows would glisten in the sun." She turned back to Seth. "That's why I'm glad you bought it."

"Are you?" His eyes ran the length of her slender throat to the collar of her dress. "Why?"

"Because you'll appreciate it. You'll know what to do to make it live again." His gaze paused briefly on her mouth before returning to her eyes. Lindsay felt a tingle along her skin. She straightened in her chair. "I know you've done some work already," she continued, feeling the Cliff House was a safe dinner topic. "You must have specific plans for changes."

"Would you like to see what's been done?"

"Yes," she answered immediately, unable to pretend otherwise.

"I'll pick you up tomorrow afternoon." He looked at her curiously. "Did you know you've an outrageous appetite for someone so small?"

Lindsay laughed, at ease again, and buttered a roll.

The sky was a deep, dark blue. The stars were low and bright, glimmering through a cloudy sky. Lindsay could feel the autumn wind shiver against the car as Seth drove along the coast. It added excitement to the romance of moonlight and wine.

The evening, she decided, had been much more pleasant than she had anticipated. From the first moment, she had enjoyed being with him. It surprised her that he could make her laugh. Lindsay knew there were times between dealing with her work and her mother that she became too serious, too intense. It was good to have someone to laugh with.

By unspoken agreement, they had steered away from controversial topics, keeping the conversation as light and palatable as the meal. She knew they would lock horns again over Ruth; there was no escaping it. Their desires for her were so totally diverse that no solution could be reached without a battle. Or two. But for the moment, Lindsay felt calm. Even as she wondered about the eye of the storm, she accepted it.

"I love nights like this," she said on a sigh. "Nights when the stars hang low and the wind talks in the trees. You'd hear the water from the east side of your house." She turned to him as she spoke. "Did you take the bedroom with the balcony that hangs over the Sound? The one that has an adjoining dressing room?"

Seth turned to her briefly. "You seem to know the house well."

Lindsay laughed. "You could hardly expect me to resist exploring the place when it was just sitting there waiting."

Ahead, a few twinkling lights outlined Cliffside against the darkness. "Is that the room you've taken?"

"The huge stone fireplace and lofty old ceiling would have been enough by themselves, but the balcony... Have you stood on it during a storm?" she demanded. "It must be incredible with the waves crashing and the wind and lightning so close." Her eyes were trained on him so that she saw the tilt of his smile when it began.

"You like to live dangerously."

She wondered how his hair would feel between her fingers. Her eyes widened at the route her thoughts had taken. Carefully, she laced her fingers in her lap. "I suppose," she began, going back to his comment. "Perhaps I never have, except vicariously. Cliffside isn't exactly fraught with danger."

"Tell that to your ghost."

Lindsay chuckled. "*Your* ghost," she corrected as he pulled up in front of her house. "You've absolute claim on her now." While she spoke, Lindsay stepped from the car. The wind fluttered over her face. "It's truly fall now," she mused, looking about her at the quiet house. "We'll have a bonfire in the square. Marshall Woods will bring his fiddle, and there'll be music until midnight." She smiled. "It's a big event in town. I suppose it must seem very tame to someone who's traveled as much as you have."

"I grew up in a dot on the map in Iowa," he told her as they passed through the gate.

"Did you really?" Lindsay mulled over the information. "Somehow I pictured you growing up in a city, very urbane, very sophisticated. Why didn't you go back?" She stood on the first step of the porch and turned to him again.

"Too many memories."

With the height of the step and her evening shoes, Lindsay stood nearly level with him. There was a jolt of surprise in finding her eyes and mouth lined up with his. In his irises were tiny amber flecks. Without thinking, she counted them.

"There are thirteen," she murmured. "Six in one and seven in the other. I wonder if it's bad luck."

"If what's bad luck?" Her eyes were direct on his, but he could see her mind drift off, then snap back at his question.

"Oh, nothing." Lindsay brushed off the question, embarrassed by her lapse. "I have a tendency to day-dream." Amusement moved over Seth's face. "Why are you smiling?"

"I was thinking back on the last time I walked my girl to her door with the front porch light shining behind her and her mother inside. I think I was eighteen."

Lindsay's eyes brightened with mischief. "It's a comfort to know you were eighteen once. Did you kiss her good-night?"

"Naturally. While her mother peeked through the living room drapes."

Slowly, Lindsay twisted her head and studied the dark, empty windows. With an arching brow, she turned back. "Mine's probably gone to bed by now," she decided. Laying her hands on his shoulders, Lindsay leaned forward to touch her lips lightly, quickly, to his.

In an instant of contact, everything changed. The bare brushing of lips was cataclysmic. Its effect rocketed through her with such velocity that she gasped. Carefully she drew away, still keeping her hands on his shoulders as they studied each other.

Her heart was knocking against her ribs as it had when she had stood in the wings before a difficult *pas de deux*. Anticipation soared through her. But this duet was unrehearsed and older than time. She dropped her eyes to his mouth and felt a hunger that was essentially physical.

They came together slowly, as if time would stop for them. There was a certainty as they slipped into each other's arms, as of old lovers reacquainting rather than meeting for the first time. Their lips touched and parted, touched and parted, as they experimented with angles. His hands slid inside her coat, hers inside his jacket. Warmth grew as the wind swirled a few autumn leaves around them.

Seth caught her bottom lip between his teeth to halt her roaming mouth. The tiny nick of pain shot trembles of desire through her. Passion flared. The slow, experimental kisses became one desperate demand. Her tongue moved with his. The hunger intensified, promising only to increase with each taste. Lindsay curved her arms up his back until she gripped his shoulders. She pressed hard against him as he took his mouth from hers to move it to the slender arch of her throat. His hair feathered against her cheek. It was soft and cool, unlike the heat of his mouth, and it seemed to draw her fingers into it.

She felt him tug the zipper of her dress down until his hands touched the naked skin of her back. They roamed, trailing down to her waist and up to the nape of her neck, flashing flames along the journey. The longing for him swelled so urgently that Lindsay trembled with it before his mouth at last returned to hers.

Her emotions began to swirl, rising to compete with the physical need. The onslaught made her dizzy, the intensity frightening her. She was discovering frailties she had not known she possessed. Struggling back to the surface, Lindsay brought her hands to his chest to push herself away. Seth freed her lips, though he kept her close in his arms.

"No, I..." Lindsay closed her eyes briefly, drawing back the strength she had always taken for granted. "It was a lovely evening, Seth. I appreciate it."

He watched her in silence a moment. "Don't you think that little speech is a bit out of place now?" Barely moving, he rubbed her lips with his.

"Yes, yes, you're right, but…" Lindsay turned her head and breathed deep of the cool, evening air. "I have to go in. I'm out of practice."

Seth took her chin in his hand, turning her face back to his. "Practice?"

Lindsay swallowed, knowing she had allowed the situation to get out of hand and having little idea how to regain control. "Please, I've never been any good at handling this sort of thing, and…"

"What sort of thing is that?" he asked her. There was no lessening of his grip on her, no weakening in the strength of his eyes.

"Seth." Her pulse was beginning to beat wildly again. "Please, let me go in before I make a total fool of myself."

All the uncertainty of her emotions beamed from her eyes. She saw anger flash in his before he crushed her mouth in a swift, powerful kiss.

"Tomorrow," he said and released her.

Breathless, Lindsay ran her hand through her hair. "I think I'd better not…."

"Tomorrow," he said again before he turned and walked back to his car.

Lindsay watched its taillights disappear. *Tomorrow,* she thought and trembled once in the chill of the night air.

Chapter 6

Because she arose late, it was past noon before Lindsay finished her barre and changed. She was determined to keep her afternoon at the Cliff House casual and dressed accordingly in a rust-colored jogging suit. Tossing the matching jacket over her arm, Lindsay bounded down the stairs just as Carol Moorefield let herself in.

Mrs. Moorefield was as unlike her son as night and day. She was petite and slender, with sleek brunette hair and sophisticated looks that never seemed to age. Andy's looks came straight from his father, a man Lindsay had seen only in photographs, as Carol had been a widow for twenty years.

When her husband had died, she had taken over his florist business and had run it with style and a keen business sense. She was a woman whose opinion Lindsay valued and whose kindness she had grown to depend on.

"Looks like you're geared up to do some running," Carol commented as she closed the front door behind her. "I'd think you'd want to rest up after your date last night."

Lindsay kissed the lightly powdered cheek. "How'd you know I'd had a date? Did Mother call you?"

Carol laughed, running a hand down the length of Lindsay's hair. "Naturally, but I could have told her. Hattie MacDonald," she supplied with a jerk of her head to indicate the house across the street. "She saw him pick you up and gave me the early bulletin."

"How nice that I made the Saturday evening information exchange," Lindsay said dryly.

Carol turned into the living room to drop her purse and jacket on the sofa. "Did you have a nice time?"

"Yes, I...yes." Lindsay suddenly found it necessary to retie her tennis shoes. Carol studied the top of her head but said nothing. "We had dinner up the coast."

"What sort of man is he?"

Lindsay looked up, then slowly began to tie her other shoe. "I'm not completely sure," she murmured. "Interesting, certainly. Rather forceful and sure of himself, and just a little formal now and again, and yet..." She recalled his attitude toward Ruth. "And yet, I think he can be very patient, very sensitive."

Hearing the tone, Carol sighed. Though she, too, knew Lindsay was not for Andy, a tiny part of her heart still hoped. "You seem to like him."

"Yes..." The word came out in a long, thoughtful stretch. Laughing, Lindsay straightened. "At least, I think I do. Did you know he's S. N. Bannion, the architect?"

At the rate Carol's brows rose, Lindsay knew this was

news. "Is he really? I thought he was going to marry some Frenchwoman, a race car driver."

"Apparently not."

"Well, this is interesting," Carol decided. She placed her hands on her hips as she did when she was truly impressed. "Does your mother know?"

"No, she…" Lindsay glanced back over her shoulder toward her mother's rooms. "No," she repeated, turning back. "I'm afraid I upset her last night. We haven't really spoken yet this morning."

"Lindsay." Carol touched her cheek, seeing the distress. "You mustn't let this sort of thing worry you."

Lindsay's eyes were suddenly wide and vulnerable. "I never seem to be able to do the right thing," she blurted out. "I owe her…"

"Stop it." Carol took her by the shoulders and gave them a brisk, no-nonsense shake. "It's ridiculous for children to go through life trying to pay back their parents. The only thing you owe Mae is love and respect. If you live your life trying to please someone else, you'll make two people unhappy. Now—" she stroked Lindsay's hair again and smiled "—that's all the advice I have for today. I'm going to go talk Mae into a drive."

Lindsay threw her arms around Carol's neck and gave one desperate squeeze. "You're so good for us."

Pleased, Carol squeezed back. "Want to come?" she invited. "We can drive for a while and have a fussy little lunch somewhere."

"No, I can't." She drew away. "Seth is picking me up soon to take me through his house."

"Ah, your Cliff House." Carol gave a knowledgeable nod. "This time you'll be able to wander about in broad daylight."

Lindsay grinned. "Do you think it'll lose some of its charm?"

"I doubt it." Carol turned to start down the hall. "Have fun, and don't worry about getting home to fix supper. Your mother and I will eat out." Before Lindsay could speak, the doorbell rang. "There's your young man," Carol announced and disappeared around the corner.

Lindsay turned to the door in a flurry of nerves. She had told herself that her response to Seth the night before had been abetted by the mood of the evening. It had been aided by her own lack of male companionship and his well-reported experience. It had been a moment only, nothing more. She told herself that now it was important to remember who he was and how easily he drew women. And how easily he left them.

It was important to channel their association into a careful friendship right from the outset. There was Ruth to think of. Lindsay knew that if she wanted what was right for Ruth, she had to keep her involvement with Ruth's uncle amicable. Like a business relationship, she decided, placing a hand on her stomach to quiet jarred nerves. Lightly friendly, no strings, nothing personal. Feeling herself settle, Lindsay opened the door.

He wore dark brown chinos and a bone-colored, crewneck sweater. His raw physicality hit Lindsay instantly. She had known one or two other men who possessed this elemental sexual pull. Nick Davidov was one, and a choreographer she had worked with in the company was another. She recalled, too, that for them there had been women—never *a* woman—in their lives. Be careful, her brain flashed. *Be very careful.*

"Hi." Her smile was friendly, but the wariness was in her eyes. She slipped a small, canvas purse over her shoulder as she pulled the door shut behind her. Habitually, she offered her hand. "How are you?"

"Fine." With a slight pressure on her fingers, he stopped her from continuing down the porch steps. They stood almost precisely where they had stood the night before. Lindsay could all but feel the lingering energy in the air. Looking at him, she met one of his long, searching gazes. "How are you?"

"Fine," she managed, feeling foolish.

"Are you?" He was watching her carefully, deeply.

Lindsay felt her skin warm. "Yes, yes, of course I am." Annoyance replaced the guardedness in her eyes. "Why shouldn't I be?"

As if satisfied by her answer, Seth turned. Together they walked to his car. A strange man, Lindsay decided, unwittingly more intrigued than ever. Smiling, she shook her head. A very strange man.

As she started to slip into the car, she spotted three small birds chasing a crow across the sky. Amused, she followed their progress, listening to the taunting chatter. The crow arched toward the east and so did the trio of birds. Laughing, she turned, only to find herself in Seth's arms.

For a moment Lindsay lost everything but his face. Her being seemed to center on it. Her mouth warmed as his eyes lingered on hers. In invitation, her lips parted, her lids grew heavy. Abruptly she remembered what she had promised herself. Clearing her throat, she drew away. She settled herself in the car, then waited until she heard Seth shut the door before she let out a long, shaky breath.

She watched him move around the car to the driver's side. I'll have to start out in control of the situation and

stay that way, she decided. She turned to him as he slid
in beside her, and opted for bright conversation.

"Have you any idea how many eyes are trained on us
at this moment?" she asked him.

Seth started the car but left it idling. "No, are there
many?"

"Dozens." Though the car doors were closed, she lowered her voice conspiratorially. "Behind every curtain
on the block. As you can see, I'm totally unaffected
by the attention, but then, I'm a trained performer and
used to center stage." Mischief was in her eyes. "I hope
it doesn't make you nervous."

"Not a bit," Seth returned. In a quick move, he pinned
her back against the seat, taking her mouth in a rapid,
thrilling kiss. Though quick, it was thorough, leaving no
portion of her mouth unexplored, no part of her system
unaffected. When he drew away, Lindsay was breathing
jerkily and staring. No one, she was certain, had ever
felt what she was feeling at that moment.

"I hate to put on a dull show, don't you?" The words
were low and intimate, stirring Lindsay's blood.

"Mmm," she answered noncommittally and slid cautiously away from him. This was not the way to stay in
control.

The Cliff House was less than three miles from Lindsay's, but it stood high above the town, high above the
rocks and water of the Sound. It was built of granite. To
Lindsay's fascinated imagination, it seemed hewn from
the cliff itself, carved out by a giant's hand. It was un-
refined and fierce, a wicked castle perched at the very
edge of the land. There were many chimneys, doors and
windows, as the size of the place demanded them. But
now, for the first time in more than a dozen years, Lind-

say saw the house live. The windows sparkled, catching the sun, then holding it or tossing it back. There were no flowers yet to brighten the serious face of the house, but the lawn was neatly tended. And to her pleasure, there was smoke curling and drifting from the several chimneys. The driveway was steep and long, starting out from the main road, curving along the way and ending at the front of the house.

"It's wonderful, isn't it?" Lindsay murmured. "I love the way it has its back turned to the sea, as if it isn't concerned with any power but its own."

Seth stopped the car at the end of the drive, then turned to her. "That's a rather fanciful thought."

"I'm a rather fanciful person."

"Yes, I know," Seth observed, and leaning across her, unlatched her door. He stayed close a moment so that the slightest move would have brought their mouths together. "Strangely, on you it's attractive. I've always preferred practical women."

"Have you?" Something seemed to happen to Lindsay when he was close. It was as if many threads, thin but impossibly strong, wound their way around her until she was helpless. "I've never been very good at practicalities. I'm better at dreaming."

He twisted the end of a strand of her hair around his fingers. "What sort of dreams?"

"Foolish ones mostly, I suppose. They're the best kind." Quickly she pushed the door open and stepped outside. Closing her eyes, she waited for her system to drift back to normal. When she heard his door shut, she opened them again to study the house. Casual, friendly, she reminded herself and took a deep breath.

"Do you know," she began, "the last time I walked

here, it was about midnight and I was sixteen." She smiled, remembering, as they moved up the narrow walk toward a skirting porch. "I dragged poor Andy along and crawled through a side window."

"Andy." Seth paused at the front door. "That's the weight-lifter you were kissing in front of your studio."

Lindsay lifted a brow, acknowledging the description of Andy. She said nothing.

"Boyfriend?" Seth asked lightly, jiggling the keys in his palm as he studied her.

Lindsay kept her look bland. "I outgrew boyfriends a few years back, but he's a friend, yes."

"You're a very affectionate friend."

"Yes, I am," she agreed. "I've always considered the two words synonymous."

"An interesting outlook," Seth murmured and unlocked the door. "No need to crawl in a side window this time." He gestured her inside.

It was as awesome as Lindsay remembered. The ceilings in the entrance hall were twenty feet high with the rough beams exposed. A wide staircase curved to the left, then split in two and ran up opposing sides of an overhanging balcony. The banister was polished mirror-like, and the treads were uncarpeted.

The dusty, peeling wallpaper Lindsay remembered had been stripped away to be replaced by a new fabric of rich cream. A long, narrow Persian carpet was spread on the oak-planked floor. The sun was muted, reflected on the prisms of a tiered chandelier.

Without speaking, she walked down the hall to the first doorway. The parlor had been completely restored. There was a bold floral print on one wall, offset by the lacquered pearl-colored tones of the others. Lindsay took a slow tour of the room. She stopped by a small, eighteenth-century table, touching it lightly with a fingertip.

"It's wonderful." She glanced at the thinly striped brocade of the sofa. "You knew precisely what was needed. I could almost have pictured this room with a Dresden shepherdess on the mantel—and there it is!" She walked over to study it, moved by its delicacy. "And French carpets on the floor...." Lindsay turned back with a smile that reflected all her pleasure with the room. Hers was a fragile, timeless beauty suited to the antiques and silks and brocades that now surrounded her. Seth took a step closer. Her perfume drifted to him. "Is Ruth here?" she asked.

"No, not at the moment." He surprised them both by reaching out to run a fingertip down her cheek. "She's at Monica's. This is the first time I've seen you with your hair down," he murmured, moving his fingers from her skin to her hair, where he tangled them in its length. "It suits you."

Lindsay felt the threads of desire reaching out for her and stepped back. "I had it down the first time we met." She smiled, ordering herself not to be foolish. "It was raining, as I remember."

Seth smiled back, first with his eyes, then with his lips. "So it was." He closed the distance between them again, then trailed a finger down her throat. Lindsay shivered involuntarily. "You're amazingly responsive," he said quietly. "Is that always true?"

Heat was rushing through her, pulsing where his flesh touched hers. Shaking her head, she turned away. "That's not a fair question."

"I'm not a fair man."

"No," Lindsay agreed and faced him again. "I don't

think you are, at least not in your dealings with women. I came to see the house, Seth," she reminded him briskly. "Will you show it to me?"

He moved to her again but was suddenly interrupted. A small, trim man with a dark, silver-speckled beard appeared in the doorway. The beard was full, beautifully shaped, growing down from his ears to circle his mouth and cover his chin. It was all the more striking as it was the only hair on his head. He wore a black, three-piece suit with a crisp, white shirt and a dark tie. His posture was perfect, militarily correct, his hands at ease by his sides. Lindsay had an immediate impression of efficiency.

"Sir."

Seth turned to him, and the tension seemed to slip from the room. Lindsay's muscles relaxed. "Worth." He nodded in acknowledgement as he took Lindsay's arm. "Lindsay, Worth. Worth, Ms. Dunne."

"How do you do, miss?" The slight bow was European, the accent British. Lindsay was captivated.

"Hello, Mr. Worth." Her smile was spontaneously open and friendly as was the offering of her hand. Worth hesitated with a brief glance at Seth before accepting it. His touch was light, a bare brushing of her fingertips.

"You had a call, sir," he said, returning his attention to his employer. "From Mr. Johnston in New York. He said it was quite important."

"All right, get him back for me. I'll be right in." He turned to Lindsay as Worth backed from the room. "Sorry, this shouldn't take long. Would you like a drink while you wait?"

"No." She glanced back to where Worth had stood. It was easier, she decided, to deal with Seth when he slipped into a formal attitude. Smiling, she wandered back to the window. "Go ahead, I'll just wait here."

With a murmur of assent, Seth left her.

It took less than ten minutes for Lindsay's curiosity to overpower her sense of propriety. This was a house she had explored in the dead of night when cobwebs and dust had been everywhere. It was impossible for her to resist exploring it when the sun was shining on a polished floor. She began to wander, intending to limit her tour to the main hall.

There were paintings to admire and a tapestry that took her breath away. On a table sat a Japanese tea set so thin, she thought it might shatter under her gaze. Too intrigued by the treasures she was discovering to remember her resolution to keep to the hall, she pushed open the door at the end of it and found herself in the kitchen.

It was a strange, appealing mixture of scrupulous efficiency and old-fashioned charm. The appliances were built-in, with stainless steel and chrome glistening everywhere. The counters were highly lacquered wood. The dishwasher hummed mechanically while a quiet little fire crackled in a waist-high hearth. Sunlight poured through the window illuminating the vinyl-covered walls and planked floors. Lindsay made a sound of pure appreciation.

Worth turned from his activity at a large butcher block table. He had removed his jacket, replacing it with a long, white, bibbed apron. An expression of astonishment ran across his face before he folded it into its habitual placid lines.

"May I help you, miss?"

"What a wonderful kitchen!" Lindsay exclaimed and let the door swing shut behind her. She turned a circle, smiling at the shining copper-bottomed kettles and pans that hung over Worth's head. "How clever Seth must be to have blended two worlds into one so perfectly."

"To be sure, miss," Worth agreed crisply. "Have you lost your way?" he asked and carefully wiped his hands on a cloth.

"No, I was just wandering a bit." Lindsay continued to do so around the kitchen while Worth stood correctly and watched her. "Kitchens are fascinating places, I think. The hub of the house, really. I've always regretted not learning to cook well."

She remembered the yogurts and salads of her professional dancing days, the occasional binges at an Italian or French restaurant, the rarely used refrigerator in her apartment. Eating had been something often overlooked in the crammed course of a day. Cooking had been out of the question.

"I'm baffled by anything more complex than a tuna casserole." She turned to Worth, still smiling. "I'm sure you're a marvelous cook." Lindsay stood just to the side of the window. The afternoon sun shone strong on her face, accentuating the fine bones and delicate complexion.

"I do my best, miss. Shall I serve you coffee in the parlor?"

Lindsay held back a sigh. "No, thank you, Mr. Worth. I suppose I'll just wander back and see if Seth is finished."

As she spoke, the door swung open and Seth walked through. "I'm sorry that took so long." The door closed soundlessly behind him.

"I barged into your kitchen without thinking." After casting a quick, apologetic glance at Worth, she moved to Seth. "Things have changed a bit since the last time I was here."

Some silent male message passed over her head between Seth and Worth before he took her arm to lead her through the door. "And you approve?"

She pushed her hair off her shoulder as she turned her face up to his. "I should reserve judgment until I see the rest, but I'm already captivated. And I *am* sorry," she continued, "about just walking into the kitchen that way. I got involved."

"Worth has a policy about women in the kitchen," Seth explained.

"Yes," Lindsay agreed wryly. "I think I know what the policy is. *Keep out.*"

"Very perceptive."

They moved through the downstairs rooms; the library, where the original paneling had been restored and polished to a glossy finish; a sitting room stripped of wallpaper and as yet unfinished; to Worth's quarters, spartan in cleanliness.

"The rest of the main level should be finished off this winter," Seth commented as they started up the staircase. Lindsay let her fingers trail over the banister. *How could wood feel this smooth?* she mused. "The house was solidly built, and there's generally only small bits of repair and redesigning to do," Seth continued.

The banister, she reflected, would have known the touch of countless palms and an occasional bottom. She grinned, thinking what a thrill it would be to slide all the way down from the third floor.

"You love this place," Seth stated, pausing at the landing, catching Lindsay between the banister and himself.

They were close, and she tilted her head until she could meet his eyes. "Why?"

It was obvious he wanted an answer that was specific rather than general. Lindsay thought it through before speaking. "I think because it's always seemed so strong, so eternal. There's a fairy tale quality about it. Generation after generation, era after era, it endures."

Turning, Lindsay walked along the railing that overhung the first floor. Below, the line and space of the main hall ran parallel. "Do you think Ruth will adjust to living here? That she'll come to accept being settled in one place?"

"Why do you ask?"

Shrugging, Lindsay turned and began to walk with Seth down the hall. "Ruth interests me."

"Professionally."

"And personally," Lindsay countered, glancing up at his tone. "Are you against her dancing?"

He stopped at a doorway to fix her with one of his lengthy looks. "I'm not at all certain your definition of dancing and mine are the same."

"Maybe not," she acknowledged. "But perhaps Ruth's definition would be more to the point."

"She's very young. And," he added before Lindsay could retort, "my responsibility." Opening the door, he guided her inside.

The room was unmistakably feminine. Pale blue Priscilla curtains fluttered at the windows, and the shade was repeated in the counterpane. There was a white brick fireplace with a brass fan-shaped screen in front of the hearth. English ivy trailed from a brass pot on a piecrust table. Lining the walls were framed pictures of ballet stars. Lindsay saw the poster Seth had spoken of. Her Juliet to Davidov's Romeo. Memories flooded back.

"There's no doubt about whose room this is," she murmured, glancing at the pink satin ribbons on the bureau. She looked up to study Seth's chiseled features. He is a man, accustomed to seeing things exclusively from a man's perspective, she realized. He could easily have settled Ruth in a boarding school and sent her generous checks. Had it been difficult to make room for a girl and a girl's unique needs in his life?

"Are you a generous man on the whole, Seth," she asked curiously, "or is it selective?"

She saw his brow lift. "You have a habit of asking unusual questions." Taking her arm, he began to lead her back down the hall.

"And you've a talent for evading them."

"This is the room that should interest your ghost," Seth smoothly changed the subject.

Lindsay waited for Seth to open the door, then stepped inside. "Oh, yes!" She walked to the center and turned a quick circle. Her hair followed in a slow arch. "It's perfect."

Deep, curved window seats were cushioned in burgundy velvet, the shade picked up in the pattern of a huge Oriental rug. The furniture was old, heavy Victorian, gleaming from Worth's attentiveness. Nothing could have suited the high, wide room more. There was a blanket chest at the foot of the four-poster bed and pewter candlesticks on either side table.

"It's because you're an architect, I suppose," Lindsay said, admiringly. "You seem to know exactly what's needed."

The fireplace was stone and massive, sending images

of thundering flames through Lindsay's mind. On a long, dark night the fire would roar, then crackle, then sizzle as the hours passed. She had a vivid flash of herself curled in the huge bed with Seth's body warming hers. A bit stunned by the clarity of the vision, she turned to wander about the room.

Too soon, she told herself. *Too fast.* Remember who he is. Silently she juggled the unexpected and unwanted emotions. At the French doors she paused, pushing them both open to step out. A rush of wind met her.

There was the raw sound of water against rock, the scent of salt in the chilling air. Lindsay watched the clouds scrambling across the sky chased by the wild wind. She walked to the rail and looked down. The drop was sheer and deadly. The fierce waves battered the jagged rocks, receding only to gather force to strike again. Lost in the wild excitement of the scene, Lindsay was not fully aware of Seth close behind her. When he turned her toward him, her response was as unrestrained and inevitable as the moving clouds above, the pounding surf below.

Her arms reached up to circle his neck as he drew her close. They came together. Her mouth molded to his, the hunger instant. She didn't hesitate but answered the intimacies of the kiss, exploring with her tongue until his taste mixed with hers. When he touched her, she trembled, not from fear or resistance, but from pure pleasure.

His hand slid under her shirt, trailing briefly along her rib cage. He cupped her breast; she was small and his hand was large. Slowly, while he took the kiss deeper, he traced his finger over the swell. As she had longed to do, she tangled her fingers in his hair. There was an impossible surge of need. It ran through her quickly—

a river changing course. The current was irresistible, dragging her along into more turbulent waters. His fingers warmed against her skin as they roamed, spreading waves of delight.

When he took his mouth from hers to ravage the cord of her neck, Lindsay felt her body suffused by a sudden heat. The chill of the wind was a shock to her face and only increased the excitement. His teeth brought tiny ripples of pain to blend with the pleasure. The sound of the surf echoed in her brain, but through it she heard him murmur her name. When his mouth returned to claim hers, she welcomed it eagerly. Never had desire been so quick, so all-consuming.

Seth tore his mouth from hers, bringing his hands to her shoulders to keep her close. His eyes locked on hers. In them, Lindsay recognized anger and passion. A fresh tremor of excitement sped up her spine. She would have melted back into his arms had he not held her away.

"I want you." The wind tossed his hair around his face. His brows were lowered, accentuating the slight upsweep at the tips.

Lindsay could hear her heartbeat increase to roar in her brain like the waves below. She was courting danger and knew it, but the extent of it began to seep through. "No." She shook her head even as she felt the flush of desire on her cheeks. "No." The ground was unsteady under her feet. She moved away to grip the rail and breathe deep of the cold, sea air. It left her throat raw and tingling. Abruptly, Seth took her arm and spun her around.

"What the hell do you mean, no?" His voice was deadly low.

Lindsay shook her head again. The wind threw her

hair into her eyes, and she tossed it back, wanting to see him clearly. Something in his stance was as untamed and fierce as the surf below them. This was the volcano. It drew her, tempted her. "Just that," she said. "What happened just now was unavoidable, but it won't go beyond that."

Seth came closer. A strong hand took hold of the back of her neck. Lindsay could feel the weight and texture of each separate finger. "You don't believe that."

His mouth lowered swiftly to hers, but instead of demand, he used persuasion. He traced his tongue between her lips until they parted on a sigh. He plundered, but gently, devastatingly. Lindsay gripped his arms to keep her balance. Her breath was as trapped as it would have been had she tumbled over the edge of the balcony to cartwheel through the air to the rocks below.

"I want to make love with you." The movement of his lips against hers shot an ache of desire through her. Lindsay struggled away.

For a moment she didn't speak but stood, catching her breath and watching him. "You have to understand," she began, then paused for her voice to steady. "You have to understand the kind of person I am. I'm not capable of casual affairs or one-night stands." Again she tossed her hair from her eyes. "I need more than that. I haven't your sophistication, Seth, I can't—I won't—compete with the women you've had in your life."

She turned to move away, but he took her arm again, keeping her facing toward him. "Do you really think we can walk away from what's already between us?"

"Yes." The word came out sharply as doubts crowded her. "It's necessary."

"I want to see you tonight."

"No, absolutely not." He was close, and Lindsay backed away.

"Lindsay, I'm not going to let this pass."

She shook her head. "The only thing between us is Ruth. Things would be simpler if we'd both remember that."

"Simple?" He caught a strand of her hair. A half smile played around his mouth. "I don't think you're the sort of woman who'd be satisfied with simplicity."

"You don't know me," she retorted.

He smiled fully now, and releasing her hair, took her arm to lead her firmly into the house. "Perhaps not, Lindsay," he agreed pleasantly, "but I will." The iron determination of his tone was not lost on Lindsay.

Chapter 7

It had been almost a month since Ruth had joined Lindsay's school. The weather had turned cold quickly, and already there was a hint of snow in the air. Lindsay did her best to keep the school's ancient furnace operating to its fullest capacity. With a shirt tied loosely at the waist over her leotard, she taught the final class of the day.

"*Glissade, glissade. Arabesque* on *pointe.*" As she spoke, Lindsay moved up and down the line of students, watching each critically for form and posture. She was pleased with her advanced *pointe* class. The students were good, possessing a firm understanding of music and movement. But the longer Ruth remained in the class, the more she stood apart from the others.

Her talent is so far above the ordinary, Lindsay thought, studying her for posture and flow. *She's being wasted here.* The now-familiar frustration overcame her, bordering on anger. And the look in her eyes, she thought as she signaled to one of the girls to keep her chin lifted, says, *"I want."* How do I convince Seth to let her go for it—and to let her go for it now before it slips away?

At the thought of Seth, Lindsay's attention wavered from her students. It locked on the last time she had seen him. If she were honest with herself, she'd admit that she'd thought of him over and over again these past weeks. She wanted to tell herself that the physical attraction she felt for him would fade. But remembering the strength, remembering the speed, she knew it was a lie.

"Tendu," Lindsay instructed and folded her arms over her chest. Still the memories of his touch, of his taste, lingered. Often she had caught herself wondering what he was doing—when she was drinking coffee in the morning, when she was alone in the studio in the evening, when she woke without cause in the middle of the night. And she had forced herself to resist the urge to question Ruth.

I will not make a fool of myself over this man, she thought.

"Brenda, hands." Lindsay demonstrated, fingers flowing with a movement of her wrist. The ringing of the phone caught her by surprise. She gave her watch a frown. No one ever called the studio during class. Instantly the thought rushed through her mind: *Mother.*

"Take over, Brenda." Without waiting for a reply, she raced back to her office and grabbed the phone.

"Yes, Cliffside School of Dance." Her heart fluttered in her throat.

"Lindsay? Lindsay, is that you?"

"Yes, I…" Her hand paused on its way to her lips.

"Nicky." There was no mistaking the musical Russian accent. "Oh, Nick, how wonderful to hear your voice!" Monica's piano playing continued smoothly. Lindsay cupped her hand over her ear as she sat. "Where are you?"

"In New York, of course." There was a laughing lilt to his voice which she had always loved. "How is your school progressing?"

"Very well. I've worked with some very good dancers. In fact, there's one in particular I want badly to send up to you. She's special, Nick, beautifully built, and…"

"Later, later." As he cut off Lindsay's enthusiastic report of Ruth, she could almost see the quick brushing-away gesture that would have accompanied the words. "I've called to talk about you. Your mother does well?"

Lindsay's hesitation was barely a sigh. "Much better. She's been getting around on her own for some time now."

"Good. Very good. Then when are you coming back?"

"Nick." Lindsay moved her shoulders, then glanced at the wall at the photograph of herself dancing with the man on the other end of the phone. Three years, she mused. It might as well be thirty. "It's been too long, Nick."

"Nonsense. You're needed."

She shook her head. He had always been dictatorial. Perhaps, she thought, it's my fate to tangle with domineering men. "I'm not in shape, Nick, not for the merry-go-round. There's young talent coming up." Her mind drifted back to Ruth. "*They're* needed."

"Since when are you afraid of hard work and competition?"

The challenge in his voice was an old ruse that made

Lindsay smile. "We're both aware that teaching dance for three years is entirely different from performing for three years. Time doesn't stand still, Nick, not even for you."

"Afraid?"

"Yes. A little, yes."

He laughed at the confession. "Good, the fear will push you to dance better." He broke in on her exasperated laugh. "I need you, *ptichka,* my little bird. I've almost finished writing my first ballet."

"Nick, that's wonderful! I had no idea you were working on anything."

"I have another year, perhaps two, to dance. I have no interest in character parts." During the slight pause, Lindsay heard the murmur of girls as they changed into their outdoor shoes. "I've been offered the directorship of the company."

"I can't say I'm surprised," Lindsay returned warmly. "But I am pleased, for you and for them."

"I want you back, Lindsay, back in the company. It can be arranged, you know, with some strings pulled."

"I don't want that. No, I…"

"There is no one to dance my ballet but you. She is Ariel, and Ariel is you."

"Oh, Nick, please." Lifting a hand, she pinched the bridge of her nose between her thumb and forefinger. She had put the world he was offering behind her.

"No, no argument, not over the phone." She shook her head silently and shut her eyes. "When I've finished the ballet, I'm coming to Cliffdrop."

"Cliffside," Lindsay corrected. She opened her eyes as a smile came to her lips.

"Side, drop, I'm Russian. It's expected. I'll be there

in January," he continued, "to show you the ballet. Then you'll come back with me."

"Nick, you make it sound so simple."

"Because it is, *ptichka*. In January."

Lindsay took the dead receiver from her ear and stared at it. How like Nick, she mused. He was famous for his grand, impulsive gestures, his total dedication to the dance. And he's so brilliant, she thought, replacing the receiver. So confident. He'd never understand that some things can be tucked away in a memory box and still remain precious and alive. For Nick it was all so simple.

She rose and walked over to study the photograph. It's the company first, last and always. But for me there are so many other factors, so many other needs. I don't even know what they are, only that I have them. She folded her arms across her chest, hugging her elbows. Maybe this was the time of decision. A flutter of impatience ran through her. I've been coasting for too long, she accused. Shaking herself back to the moment, Lindsay walked into the studio. Students were still milling about, reluctant to leave the warmth of the school for the cold outside. Ruth had returned to the barre alone to practice. In the mirror, her eyes followed Lindsay across the room. Monica looked up with her cheerful smile.

"Ruth and I are going to do a pizza and a movie. Want to come?"

"Sounds great, but I want to do a little more work on the staging for *The Nutcracker*. Christmas will be here before we know it."

Monica reached out to touch her hand. "You work too hard, Lindsay."

Lindsay squeezed Monica's hand, meeting the grave,

concerned eyes. "I've just been giving that some thought." Both women glanced up as the door opened. A blast of cold air whooshed in with Andy. His normally pale complexion was reddened with cold, his huge shoulders hunched against it.

"Hi!" Lindsay held out her hands to take both of his. She chafed at the chill. "I didn't expect to see you tonight."

"Looks as though I timed it pretty well." He gave a quick look around as students pulled slacks and sweaters over their leotards. He greeted Monica casually; she, in turn, seemed to nod almost hopefully in Andy's direction.

"Hello, Andy," she seemed to stammer at last.

Ruth watched the simple exchange from across the room. It was so obvious, she thought, to everyone but the three of them. He was crazy in love with Lindsay, and Monica was crazy in love with him. She had seen Monica flush with anticipation the moment Andy had entered the studio. He, on the other hand, had seen only Lindsay. How strange people are, she reflected as she executed a *grand plié*.

And Lindsay. Lindsay was everything Ruth ever hoped to be: a true ballerina, confident, poised, beautiful, with something elusive in her movements. Ruth thought she moved not like a butterfly or bird, but like a cloud. There was something light, something free, in each step, in each gesture. It wasn't with envy that Ruth watched her, but with longing. And she did watch her, closely, continually. And because she did so, Ruth felt she was growing to know Lindsay well.

Ruth admired Lindsay's openness, her free flow of

emotions. She had warmth, which drew people to her. But there was more playing beneath the surface, much more, Ruth felt, than Lindsay was in the habit of revealing. Ruth doubted whether those hidden passions were often fully released. It would take something strong, like the dance itself, to release them.

As Ruth pondered these thoughts, the door opened again, and her uncle strode into the studio.

A smile sprang to Ruth's lips along with a greeting. She halted the latter to play the observer once more.

The jolt of the eye contact between Seth and Lindsay was quick and volcanic. Its flare was so short that had she not been watching so intensely, she would have missed it. But it was real and potent. She paused a moment, frowning thoughtfully at her mentor and her uncle. This was unexpected, and she didn't know how she felt about it. The attraction between them was as patently obvious to her as Monica's for Andy and Andy's for Lindsay.

Amazing, she decided, that none of them seemed aware of the emotions at play among the four of them. She remembered the awareness in her parents' eyes when they had looked at each other. The vision brought both warmth and sadness. Ruth badly wanted to feel a part of that kind of love again. Without speaking, she moved to the corner of the room to remove her toe shoes.

The moment Lindsay had looked over and seen Seth, she had felt the power. It flooded her, then ebbed so swiftly she was certain that her legs had dissolved below the knees. No, the attraction hadn't faded. It had doubled. Everything about him was instantly implanted in her brain: his wind-tousled hair, the way he left his sheepskin jacket unbuttoned to the cold, the way his eyes seemed to swallow her the moment he stepped inside.

It seemed impossible that without even an effort she could completely obliterate everyone else from her consciousness. They might have stood alone, on an island, on a mountaintop, so complete was her absorption with him.

I've missed him, she realized abruptly. It's been twenty-six days since I've seen him, spoken to him. A month ago I didn't know he existed, and now I think about him at all sorts of odd, unexpected times. Her smile began of its own volition. Though Seth didn't return it, Lindsay stepped forward, extending her hands.

"Hello. I've missed seeing you."

The statement came spontaneously and without guile. She took Seth's hands as he studied her face.

"Have you?" He asked the question quietly, but the demand in his tone reminded Lindsay to use caution.

"Yes," she admitted. She took her hands from his and turned. "You know Monica and Andy, don't you?" Monica stood near the piano stacking sheet music, but Lindsay approached her now and claimed the task. "You don't have to bother with that," she said. "You and Ruth must be starving, and you'll miss that movie if you stay around too long." She rambled, annoyed with herself. Why, she asked herself, don't I ever think before I speak? She lifted her hand in farewell as loitering students trickled out. "Have you eaten, Andy?"

"Well, no, actually, that's why I stopped by." He glanced at Seth. "I thought maybe you'd like to grab a hamburger and take in a movie."

"Oh, Andy, that's sweet." She stopped shuffling music to smile at him. "But I've got some work to finish up.

I've just turned down a similar offer from Monica and Ruth. Why don't you switch to pizza and go with them?"

"Sure, Andy." Monica spoke up rapidly, then struggled with a flush. "That'd be fun, wouldn't it, Ruth?"

At the entreaty in Monica's liquid brown eyes, Ruth smiled and nodded. "You weren't coming by for me, were you, Uncle Seth?" Ruth rose, pulling on jeans.

"No." He watched his niece's head disappear inside a bulky sweater, then pop through the neck opening. "I came to have a few words with Lindsay."

"Well, we should get out of your way." Monica moved with a grace unexpected in a large-boned girl. There was an athletic swing to her gait softened by her own early years at the barre. Grabbing her coat, she looked back at Andy. Her smile wasn't reserved, but hesitant. "Coming, Andy?" She saw the quick glance he aimed at Lindsay. Her heart sank.

"Sure." He touched Lindsay's shoulder. "See you tomorrow."

"Night, Andy." Rising on her toes, she gave him a light kiss. "Have a good time." The statement was made to all three. Andy and Monica walked to the door, both battling depression. Ruth trailed after them, a smile lurking at her mouth.

"Good night, Uncle Seth, Ms. Dunne." She pulled the studio door firmly shut behind her.

Lindsay stared at the closed panel a moment, wondering what had caused the gleam in Ruth's eyes. It had been mischief, pure and simple, and though it pleased her to see it, Lindsay wondered at its cause. Shaking her head, she turned back to Seth.

"Well," she began brightly, "I suppose you want to discuss Ruth. I think…"

"No."

Lindsay's thoughts paused in midstream, then backed up. "No?" she repeated. Her expression was one of genuine bafflement until Seth took a step closer. Then she understood. "We really should talk about her." Turning away, she wandered to the room's center. In the wall of mirrors, she could see their reflections. "She's far more advanced than any of my other students, far more dedicated, far more talented. Some were born to dance, Seth. Ruth is one of them."

"Perhaps." Casually, he shrugged out of his jacket and laid it on top of the piano. She knew instinctively that tonight he wouldn't be easy to deal with. Her fingers plucked at the knot in her shirt. "But it's been one month, not six. We'll talk about Ruth next summer."

"That's absurd." Annoyed, Lindsay turned to face him. It was a mistake, she discovered, as the reality of him was far more potent than the mirror image. She turned away again and began to pace quickly. "You make it sound as though this is a whim she'll outgrow. That's simply unrealistic. She's a dancer, Seth. Five months from now she'll still be a dancer."

"Then waiting shouldn't be a problem."

His logic caused Lindsay to close her eyes in a spurt of fury. She wanted badly to reason with him calmly. "Wasted time," she said with quiet control. "And in this situation, wasted time is a sin. She needs more—so much more—than I can give her here."

"She needs stability first." There was annoyance just under the surface of his voice. It mirrored Lindsay's own sentiments as the glass did their bodies.

"She has something," she tossed back, gesturing with both arms in frustration. "Why do you refuse to see it?

It's rare and beautiful, but it needs to be nurtured, it needs to be disciplined. It only becomes more difficult to do that as time goes on."

"I told you before, Ruth's my responsibility." His voice had sharpened to a fine edge. "And I told you I didn't come to discuss Ruth. Not tonight."

Lindsay's intuition repressed her retort. She'd get nowhere with him now, not this way, and it was possible to ruin the chance of any further opportunity. To win for Ruth, she needed patience.

"All right." She took a deep breath and felt her temper recede. "Why did you come?"

He walked to her, taking her firmly by the shoulders before she could move away. "You missed seeing me?" he asked as his eyes bored into hers in the glass.

"In a small town like this it's rare to go nearly a month without seeing someone." She tried to step away, but his fingers tightened.

"I've been working on a project, a medical center to be built in New Zealand. The drawings are nearly finished now."

Because the idea intrigued her, Lindsay relaxed. "How exciting that must be—to create something out of your head that people will walk in, live in, work in. Something that's solid and lasting. Why did you become an architect?"

"Buildings fascinated me." He began a slow massage of her shoulders, but her interest was focused on his words. "I wondered why they were built in certain ways, why people chose different styles. I wanted to make them functional and appealing to the eye." His thumb trailed up the nape of her neck and awakened a myriad of nerve endings. "I've a weakness for beauty."

Slowly, while Lindsay's eyes were glued to the mirror, he lowered his mouth to tease the freshly aroused skin. A breath trembled through her lips to be sucked back in at the contact.

"Seth…"

"Why did you become a dancer?" His question interrupted her protest. He kneaded her muscles with his fingers and watched her in the mirror. He caught the desire flickering in her eyes.

"It was all there ever was for me." Lindsay's words were husky, clouded with restrained passion. She found it hard to concentrate on her own words. "My mother spoke of nothing else as far back as I can remember."

"So you became a dancer for her." He lifted a hand to her hair and drew out a pin.

"No, some things are meant to be. This was meant for me." His hand trailed up the side of her neck to bury itself in her hair. He drew out another pin. "It would have been dancing for me regardless of my mother. She only made it more important sooner. What are you doing?" She placed a hand over his as he began to withdraw another pin.

"I like your hair down, where I can feel it."

"Seth, don't…"

"You always wear it up when you're teaching, don't you?"

"Yes, I…" The weight of her hair pushed against the remaining pins until they fell to the floor. Her hair tumbled free in pale blond clouds.

"School's out," he murmured, then buried his face in its thickness.

Their reflection showed her the sharp contrast of his hair against hers, of his tanned fingers against the ivory skin of her throat. There was a magic about watching him brush the hair from her neck and lower his mouth while feeling his lips and fingers on her skin. Fascinated, she watched the couple in the wall of the mirrors. When he turned her so that flesh and blood faced flesh and blood, she felt no lessening of the trance. Totally involved, she stared up at him.

He lowered his mouth, and though her lips hungered, he feathered kisses along her jawline. His hands moved greedily through her hair while he teased her face with promising kisses. Lindsay began to burn for the intimacy that comes with the joining of mouth to mouth. But even as she turned her head to find his lips, he drew her away.

Waves of heat rose from her toes, concentrating in her lungs until she was certain they would explode from the pleasure. With his eyes locked on hers, Seth slowly untied the knot in her shirt. Barely touching her, he ran his fingers up her shoulders, lingering only a heartbeat away from the swell of her breasts. Gently, he pushed the shirt from her until it drifted soundlessly to the floor.

There was something stunningly sexual in the gesture. Lindsay felt naked before him. He had destroyed all her barricades. There was no longer room for illusions. Stepping forward, she rose on her toes to take his mouth with hers.

The kiss started slowly, luxuriously, with the patience of two people who know the pleasure they can bring to each other. The mouth is for tasting, and they assuaged a hunger that had grown sharp and deep with fasting. They supped without hurry, as if wanting to prolong the moment of full contentment.

Lindsay took her lips from his to explore. There was a hint of roughness at his jawline from the day's growth of beard. His cheekbones were long and close to his skin. Below his ear his taste was mysteriously male. She lingered there, savoring it.

His hands were on her hips, and his fingers trailed along the tops of her thighs. She shifted so that he might touch her more freely. On a long, gradual journey, he brought his hand to her breast. Her leotard was snug, hardly an intrusion between his palm and her flesh.

Their lips joined in a hot, desperate demand as their bodies strained, one against the other. His arms swept her closer, nearly bringing her off the floor. There was no longer comfort, no longer leisure, but the pain was exquisite.

As from down a long tunnel, Lindsay heard the ringing of the bell. She burrowed deeper into Seth. The ringing came again, and yet again, until its meaning sunk into her consciousness. She moved against him, but he caught her closer.

"Let it ring, damn it." His mouth took hers, swallowing the words.

"Seth, I can't." Lindsay struggled through the mists in her brain. "I can't…my mother."

He swore richly but loosened his hold. Pushing away, Lindsay rushed to answer the phone.

"Yes?" Passing a hand through her hair, she tried to gather enough of her wits to remember where she was.

"Miss Dunne?"

"Yes. Yes, this is Lindsay Dunne." She sat on the corner of her desk as her knees trembled.

"I'm sorry to disturb you, Miss Dunne. This is Worth. Might I find Mr. Bannion there?"

"Worth?" Lindsay slowly let air in and out of her lungs. "Oh, yes. Yes, he's here. Just a moment."

Her movements were slow and deliberate as she set the receiver beside the phone and rose. For a moment she stood in the doorway of her office. He was turned toward her, and his eyes met hers instantly as if he'd been waiting for her return. Lindsay stepped into the studio, resisting the need to clasp her hands together.

"It's for you," she told him. "Mr. Worth."

Seth nodded, but there was nothing casual in the way he took her shoulders as he passed. Briefly, they stood side by side. "I'll only be a moment."

Lindsay remained still until she heard the murmur of his voice on the phone. Whenever she finished a difficult dance, she always took a few moments to breathe. It was concentrated breathing, in-out, deep and slow, not the unconscious movement of air in the lungs. She took time to do so now. Gradually, she felt the flow of blood decrease, the hammer of her pulse quiet. The tingle just under her skin faded. Satisfied that her body was responding, Lindsay waited for her mind to follow suit.

Even for a woman who enjoyed taking risks, Lindsay knew the idiocy of her behavior. With Seth Bannion, the odds were too highly stacked against her. She was beginning to realize that she contributed to those odds. She was too attracted to him, too vulnerable to him. It didn't seem to matter that she had known him for only a matter of weeks.

Slowly, she walked to the shirt that lay on the floor. She stooped just as a movement in the mirror caught her eye. Again, her eyes locked with Seth's in the glass. Chilled pinpricks spread over her skin. Lindsay rose and turned. Now, she knew, was not the time for fantasies and illusions.

"A problem on a site," he said briefly. "I need to

check some figures at home." He crossed to her. "Come with me."

There was no mistaking what he meant. To Lindsay, the simplicity and directness were overpoweringly seductive. With careful movements, she slipped back into her shirt.

"No, I can't. I've work to do, and then..."

"Lindsay." He halted her with a word and a hand to her cheek. "I want to sleep with you. I want to wake up with you."

She let out a long breath. "I'm not accustomed to dealing with this sort of thing," she murmured. She ran a hand through her loosened hair, then her eyes lifted to his again and held. "I'm very attracted to you. It's a bit beyond what I've felt before and I don't know quite what to do about it."

Seth's hand moved from her cheek to circle her throat. "Do you think you can tell me that and expect me to go home alone?"

Lindsay shook her head and put a decisive hand to his chest. "I tell you that, I suppose, because I'm not sophisticated enough to keep it to myself. I don't believe in lies and pretense." A faint line appeared between her brows as she continued. "And I don't believe in doing something I'm not totally sure is what I want. I'm not going to sleep with you."

"But you are." He put his hand over hers, capturing the other at the same time. "If not tonight, tomorrow; if not tomorrow, the day after."

"I wouldn't be so smug if I were you." Lindsay shook off his hands. "I'm never very obliging when told what I'm going to do. I make my own decisions."

"And you made this one," Seth said easily, but temper flared in his eyes. "The first time I kissed you. Hypocrisy doesn't suit you."

"Hypocrisy?" Lindsay held the words back a moment, knowing she would stutter. "The precious male ego! Refuse a proposition and you're a hypocrite."

"I don't believe *proposition* is a fully accurate term."

"Go sit on your semantics," she invited. "And do it elsewhere. I've got work to do."

He was quick. He grabbed her arm, jerking her against him before the command to step away could shoot from her brain to her feet. "Don't push me, Lindsay."

She pulled at her arm. It remained in his grip. "Aren't you the one who's pushing?"

"It appears we have a problem."

"*Your* problem," she tossed back. "I'm not going to be another set of blueprints in your file. If I decide I want to go to bed with you, I'll let you know. In the meantime, our main topic of conversation is Ruth."

Seth made an intense study of her face. Her cheeks had flushed with temper, her breath came quickly. A hint of a smile played on his mouth. "Right now you look a bit as you did when I watched you dance Dulcinea, full of passion and spirit. We'll talk again." Before Lindsay could comment, he gave her a long, lingering kiss. "Soon."

She managed to gather her wits as he crossed to the piano to retrieve his jacket. "About Ruth…"

He shrugged into his coat, all the time watching her. "Soon," he repeated and strode to the door.

Chapter 8

On Sundays Lindsay had no set schedule. Six days a week her time was regimented, given over to classes and paperwork and her mother. On Sunday she broke free.

It was late morning when she wandered downstairs. The aroma of coffee was strong, drawing her into the kitchen. She could hear her mother's slow, uneven movements before she pushed open the door.

"Morning." Lindsay crossed the linoleum floor to kiss Mae's cheek, then studied her neat, three-piece suit. "You're all dressed up." Pleasure warmed her voice. "You look wonderful."

Mae smiled as she touched her hair with a fussy hand. "Carol wanted to have lunch at the country club. Do you think my hair's all right?"

"It's lovely." Lindsay's heart lightened as she watched her mother preen again. "But you know it's your legs everybody looks at. You've got great legs."

Mae laughed, a sound Lindsay had waited a long time to hear. "Your father always thought so." The tone was sad again. Lindsay slipped her arms around Mae's neck.

"No, don't, please." She held her close a moment, willing away the gloom. "It's so good to see you smile. Dad would want you to smile." When she felt Mae sigh, she held her closer. If it were possible, she would have transfused some of her own strength into her. Mae patted Lindsay's back, then drew away.

"Let's have coffee." She moved to sit at the table. "My legs might look good, but they're still attached to this hip, and they get tired easily."

Lindsay watched as her mother carefully settled herself, then turned to the cupboard. It was important to keep Mae's mood on the upswing. "I worked late yesterday with the girl I've been telling you about, Ruth Bannion." Lindsay poured two cups of coffee before walking to the refrigerator for milk. She added a generous dose to her mother's and left her own black. "She's exceptional, truly exceptional," she continued as she walked over to join Mae. "I've cast her as Carla in *The Nutcracker.* She's a shy, introverted girl who seems really confident only when she's dancing." Thoughtfully, Lindsay watched the steam curl up from the surface of her coffee. "I want to send her to New York, to Nick. Her uncle won't even discuss it." Not for four and a half more months, she thought grimly. Stubborn, immovable… "Are all men mules?" Lindsay demanded, then swore as she scalded her tongue with a sip of steaming coffee.

"For the most part," Mae told her. Her own coffee sat

cooling in front of her. "And for the most part, women seem to be attracted to mules. You're attracted to him."

Lindsay glanced up, then stared back down at the coffee. "Well...yes. He's a bit different from the men I've known. His life doesn't center around dancing. He's traveled almost everywhere. He's very sure of himself and arrogant in a very controlled sort of way. The only other man I've known who has that sort of confidence is Nick." She smiled, remembering, and her hands floated with the words. "But Nicky has that passionate Russian temper. He throws things, he moans, he shrieks. Even his moods are elaborately orchestrated. Seth is different. Seth would just quietly snap you in two."

"And you respect him for that."

Lindsay looked up again, then laughed. It was the first time she remembered she and her mother having an in-depth discussion on anything that didn't directly involve dancing. "Yes," she agreed. "As ridiculous as it sounds, I do. He's the sort of man who commands respect without demanding it, if you know what I mean." Lindsay sipped her coffee with more caution. "Ruth adores him. It shows in her face whenever she looks at him. The lonely look is fading from her eyes and I'm sure it's his doing." Her voice softened. "He's very sensitive, I think, and very much in control of his emotions. I think if he loved someone, he'd be very demanding because he wouldn't invest his emotions easily. Still, if he weren't so stubborn, I'd send Ruth to Nick. A year's training in New York, and I'm sure she'd be chosen for the *corps*. I mentioned her to him, but..."

"To Nick?" Mae interrupted Lindsay's verbal thoughts. "When?"

She brought herself back with a mental curse. It

hadn't been an oversight that she had neglected to mention Nick's call. She had wanted to avoid a topic that brought pain to both of them. Now she shrugged and spoke casually between sips. "Oh, a couple of days ago. He called the studio."

"Why?"

Mae's question was quiet and unavoidable. "To see how I was, to ask after you." The flowers Carol had brought the week before were wilting in the bowl on the table. She rose, taking them with her. "He was always very fond of you."

Mae watched her daughter as she tossed the faded flowers into the trash. "He asked you to come back."

Lindsay placed the bowl in the sink and began to rinse it. "He's excited about a new ballet he's written."

"And he wants you for it." Lindsay continued to rinse the bowl. "What did you tell him?"

She shook her head, wanting only to avoid another strained argument. "Mother, please."

There was silence for a moment with only the sound of water splashing in the sink. It warmed Lindsay's hands.

"I've been thinking I might go to California with Carol."

Surprised by both the statement and the calm tone of her mother's voice, Lindsay turned without switching off the faucet. "That would be wonderful for you. You'd miss the worst of the winter."

"Not for the winter," Mae countered. "Permanently."

"Permanently?" Lindsay's face clouded with confusion. Behind her the water danced against the glass bowl. Reaching back, she twisted the handle of the faucet. "I don't understand."

"She has people there, you know." Mae rose to get more coffee, motioning a protest as Lindsay moved to do it for her. "One of them, a cousin, found a florist who was selling out. Good location. Carol bought it."

"She bought it?" Astonished, Lindsay sat down again. "But when? She hasn't said a word. Andy hasn't said anything either; I just saw him…."

"She wanted everything settled first." Mae interrupted Lindsay's disbelief. "She wants me to be her partner."

"Her partner?" Lindsay shook her head, then pressed fingers to both temples. "In California?"

"We can't go on this way, Lindsay." Mae limped back to the table with her coffee. "Physically, I'm as good as I'm going to be. There's no need for me to be pampered or for you to worry about me anymore. Yes, you do," she continued, even as Lindsay opened her mouth to object. "I'm a long way from where I was when I came out of the hospital."

"I know. I know that, but California…." She sent Mae a helpless look. "It's so far away."

"It's what we both need. Carol told me I was pressuring you, and she's right."

"Mother…"

"No, I do, and I'll keep right on doing it as long as we're living in each other's pockets this way." After a long breath, Mae pursed her lips. "It's time…for both of us. I've only wanted one thing for you. I haven't stopped wanting it." She took Lindsay's hands, studying the long, graceful fingers. "Dreams are stubborn things. I've had the same one all my life…first for me, then for you. Maybe that's wrong. Maybe you're using me as an excuse not to go back." Even as Lindsay shook her head, she continued. "You took care of me when I needed you, and I'm grateful. I haven't shown it always because the dream got in the way. I'm going to ask you something one last time." Lindsay remained silent, waiting. "Think about what you have, who you are. Think about going back."

There was nothing Lindsay could do but nod. She had thought about it, long and painfully two years before, but she wouldn't shut the door between herself and her mother; it had just worked its way open. "When would you go?"

"In three weeks."

Letting out a quick breath at the reply, Lindsay rose. "You and Carol will make great partners." She suddenly felt lost, alone and deserted. "I'm going for a walk," she said swiftly before the emotions could show on her face. "I need to think."

Lindsay loved the beach when the air hinted at winter. She wore an ancient peacoat against the bite of the cold, and with her hands in her pockets, she walked the low, slow arch of rock and sand. Above the sky was calm and unrelentingly blue. The surf was wild. There was more than the scent of the sea, there was the taste of it. Here the wind blew free, and she felt it would clear her mind.

She had never considered that her mother would make a permanent move away from Cliffside. *She wasn't sure how she felt about it.* A gull swooped low over her head, and Lindsay stopped to watch it wing its way over the rocks. Three years, she thought. Three years of being wrapped up in a routine. She wasn't certain that she could function without it. Bending over, she picked up a smooth, flat stone. It was sand-colored, speckled with black, the size of a silver dollar. Lindsay brushed it clean, then dropped it into her pocket. She kept her hand over it, absently warming it as she walked.

She thought over each stage of her life since her return to Cliffside. Casting her mind back, she recalled her years in New York. Two different lives, Lindsay mused, hunching her shoulders. Perhaps I'm two different people. As she tossed back her head, she saw the Cliff House. It was high above her and still perhaps a quarter of a mile off, but it warmed her as she warmed the stone.

Because it's always there, she decided, because you can depend on it. When everything else goes haywire, it stays constant. Its windows shimmered in the sun as she watched. Puffs of smoke curled, just as they should, from several chimneys. Lindsay sighed, hugging herself.

From far down the beach a movement caught her eye. Seth was walking toward her. He must have come down the beach steps from the house. Shielding her eyes with her hands, she watched him. She was smiling before she was aware of it. Why does he do this to me? she wondered with a shake of her head. Why am I always so terribly glad to see him? He walks with such confidence. No wasted motion, no superfluous movement. I'd like to dance with him, something slow, something dreamy. She felt the tug and sighed. I should run before he gets any closer.

She did. Toward him.

Seth watched her coming. Her hair lifted and streamed behind her. The wind pinched pink into her cheeks. Her body seemed weightless, skimming over the sand, and he was reminded of the evening he had come upon her dancing alone. He wasn't aware that he had stopped walking.

When she reached him, her smile was brilliant. She held out her hands in greeting. "Hi." Rising on her toes, she brushed his mouth with a quick kiss. "I'm so glad to see you. I was lonely." Her fingers laced with his.

"I saw you from the house."

"Did you?" She thought he looked younger with his hair ruffled by the wind. "How did you know it was me?"

There was the faintest of frowns in his eyes, but his voice was untroubled. "The way you move."

"No greater compliment for a dancer. Is that why you came down?" It felt good to feel his hands again, to see the solemn, studying look in his eyes. "To be with me?"

Only his eyebrow moved—in a slight upward tilt—before he answered. "Yes."

"I'm glad." She smiled warmly, without reservation. "I need someone to talk to. Will you listen?"

"All right."

In silent agreement, they began to walk.

"Dancing has always been in my life," Lindsay began. "I can't remember a day without classes, a morning without the barre. It was vital to my mother, who had certain limitations as a dancer, that I go further. It was very fortunate for everyone that I wanted to dance and that I could. It was important to us in different ways, but it was still a bond."

Her voice was quiet but clear against the roar of the sea. "I was only a bit older than Ruth when I joined the company. It's a hard life; the competition, the hours, the pressure. Oh God, the pressure. It begins in the morning, the moment your eyes open. The barre, classes, rehearsals, more classes. Seven days a week. It's your life; there's nothing else. There can't be anything else. Even after you begin to ease your way out of the *corps,* you can't relax. There's always someone behind you, wanting your place. If you miss a class, one class, your body knows it and tortures you. There's pain—in the muscles, the tendons, the feet. It's the price necessary to maintain that unnatural flexibility."

She sighed and let the wind buffet her face. "I loved it. Every moment of it. It's difficult to understand how it feels to be standing there in the wings before your first solo. Another dancer knows. And when you dance, there isn't any pain. You forget it because you have to. Then, the next day, it starts again.

"When I was with the company, I was completely wrapped up in myself, in my work. I rarely thought of Cliffside or anyone here. We were just going into rehearsals for *Firebird* when my parents had the accident." She paused here, and though her voice thickened, it remained steady. "I loved my father. He was a simple, giving man. I doubt if I thought of him more than a dozen times that last year in New York. Have you ever done something, or not done something, that you periodically hate yourself for? Something you can't change, ever?"

"Something that wakes you up at three o'clock in the morning?" Seth slipped an arm around Lindsay's shoulders and drew her closer to him. "A couple of times."

"My mother was in the hospital a long time." For a moment she turned her face into his shoulder. It was more difficult to speak of it than she had anticipated. "She was in a coma, and then there were operations, therapy. It was long and painful for her. There were a lot of arrangements I had to make, a lot of papers I had to go through. I found out they'd taken a second mortgage on the house to finance my first two years in New York." A deep breath helped to hold back tears. "I'd been there, totally fixated on myself, totally involved with my own ambitions, and they were putting up their home."

"It must have been what they wanted to do, Lindsay. And you succeeded. They were obviously proud of you."

"But you see, I just took it from them without any thought, without any gratitude."

"How can you be grateful for something you know nothing about?" he pointed out.

"Logic," Lindsay murmured as a gull screamed over their heads. "I wish I could be more logical. In any case," she continued, "when I came back, I opened the school to keep myself sane and to help with the finances until my mother was well enough for me to leave. At that time I had no plans for staying."

"But your plans changed." Her steps had slowed, and Seth shortened his stride to suit hers.

"The months piled up." Absently, Lindsay pushed at the hair that fluttered into her line of vision. "When my mother finally got out of the hospital, she still needed a great deal of care. Andy's mother was a lifesaver. She split her time between her shop and the house so that I could keep the school going. Then there came a point when I had to face things as they were. Too much time had gone by, and there wasn't an end yet in sight."

She walked for a moment in silence. "I stopped thinking about going back to New York. Cliffside was my home, and I had friends here. I had the school. The lives of professional dancers are very regimented. They take classes every day which is far different from teaching them. They eat a certain way, they think a certain way. I simply stopped being a professional dancer."

"But your mother wouldn't accept that."

Surprised, Lindsay stopped walking and looked up at him. "How did you know?"

He brushed the hair from her cheek. "It isn't difficult."

"Three years, Seth." She shrugged her shoulders. "She isn't being realistic. I'll be twenty-six soon; how can I go back and attempt to compete with girls Ruth's age? And if I could, why should I torture my muscles, destroy my feet and starve myself a second time? I don't even know if I'm capable. I loved it there…and I love it here." She turned to watch the surf spray high over the rocks. "Now my mother plans to move away permanently, to start fresh, and I know, to force me to make a decision. A decision I thought I'd already made."

His hands came to her shoulders, the fingers light and strong. "Do you resent her moving away where you can't take care of her anymore?"

"Oh, you're very perceptive." Lindsay leaned back against him a moment. There was comfort there. "But I want her to be happy—really happy—again. I love her, not in the same uncomplicated way I loved my father, but I do love her. I'm just not sure I can be what she wants."

"If you think being what she wants will pay her back, you're wrong. Life doesn't work that neatly."

"It should." Lindsay frowned at the foaming spray. "It should."

"Don't you think it might be boring if it did?" His voice was quiet and controlled above the screams of the gulls and the roar of the waves. Lindsay was glad, very glad, she had run toward him and not away. "When is your mother leaving?"

"In three weeks."

"Then give yourself some time after she's gone to decide where your life's heading. There's too much pressure on you now."

"I should have known you'd be logical." She turned to him and was smiling again. "Usually, I resent that kind of advice, but this time it's a relief." She slipped her arms around his waist and buried her face in his chest. "Will you hold me? It feels so good to depend on someone else for just a minute."

She seemed very small when his arms came around her. Her slightness appealed to his protective instincts. Seth rested his cheek on the top of her head and watched the water war against the rocks.

"You smell of soap and leather," Lindsay finally murmured. "I like it. A thousand years from now I'll remember you smelled of soap and leather." She lifted her face and searched deep in his eyes. I could fall in love with him, she thought. He's the first man I could really fall in love with.

"I know I'm crazy," she said aloud, "but I want you to kiss me. I want so badly to taste you again."

Their mouths met slowly to linger, to savor. They drew away once, far enough to see the need mirrored in each other's eyes, then they joined again, flame for flame. The taste and texture of his mouth was familiar now, but no less exciting. Lindsay clung to him. Their tongues teased only, hinting of what could be. The well of desire was deeper than she had known, and its waters more treacherous. For a moment she gave herself to him utterly. Promises trembled on her lips.

Quickly, Lindsay pushed away, shaking her head.
She placed a hand to her head, smoothing her hair back
from her face as she took a long breath.

"Oh, I should stay away from you," she whispered.
"Very far away."

Seth reached up to cup her face in his hand. "It's too
late for that now." Passion was still dark in her eyes. With
only the slightest pressure, he brought her back a step.

"Maybe." She placed her hands on his chest but neither pushed away nor drew closer. "In any case, I asked
for this."

"If it were summer," he said and trailed his fingers
down her throat, "we'd have a picnic here, late at night
with cold wine. Then we'd make love and sleep on the
beach until dawn came up over the water."

Lindsay felt the tremors start at her knees. "Oh yes,"
she said on a sigh. "I should stay away from you." Turning, she sprinted for a clump of rocks. "Do you know
why I like the beach best in early winter?" she called
out as she scrambled to the top.

"No." Seth walked over to join her. "Why?"

"Because the wind is cold and alive, and the water can
be mean. I like to watch it just before a storm."

"You enjoy challenges," Seth remarked, and Lindsay
looked down at him. The height gave her a unique perspective. "Yes, I do. So do you, as I recall. I read that
you're quite a parachutist."

He held a hand up to her, smiling as their fingers
touched. Lindsay wrinkled her nose and jumped lightly
to the sand. "I only go as far off the ground as I can
without apparatus," she said and cocked a brow. "I'm
not about to go leaping out of a plane unless it's parked
at the airport."

"I thought you enjoyed a challenge."

"I also enjoy breathing."

"I could teach you," Seth offered, drawing her into his arms.

"You learn to do a *tour en l'air,* and I'll learn to jump. Besides…" Lindsay struggled from his arms as a recollection struck her. "I remember reading that you were teaching some Italian countess to free fall."

"I'm beginning to think you read entirely too much." Seth grabbed her hand and pulled her back.

"I'm surprised you've had time to build anything with such an active social life."

His grin was a quick, youthful flash. "I'm a firm believer in recreation."

"Hmm." Before Lindsay could mull over an answer, a flash of red caught her eye from a short distance down on the beach. "It's Ruth," she said, twisting her head.

Ruth raised her hand once hesitantly as she crossed the sand toward them. Her hair hung loose over a scarlet jacket. "She's a lovely girl." Lindsay turned to face Seth again. She saw as he, too, watched Ruth, but there was a frown in his eyes. "Seth?" He looked down at her. "What is it?" she asked with concern.

"I might have to go away for a few weeks. I worry about her; she's still so fragile."

"You don't give her enough credit." Lindsay tried to ignore the sudden sense of loss his words gave her. *Go away?* Where? When? She focused on Ruth and forced the questions away. "Or yourself," she added. "You've built a relationship. A few weeks won't damage it or Ruth."

Before he could answer, Ruth had joined them.

"Hello, Ms. Dunne." Her smile had become more

relaxed since the first time Lindsay had seen it. There was a welcome sparkle of excitement in her eyes. "Uncle Seth, I've just come from Monica's. Her cat had kittens last month."

Lindsay laughed. "Honoria is single-handedly responsible for the feline population explosion in Cliffside."

"Not single-handedly," Seth commented dryly, and Lindsay laughed again.

"She had four," Ruth continued. "And one of them... well..." She glanced from Seth to Lindsay, catching her bottom lip between her teeth. Silently, she pulled open the snaps of her jacket and revealed a tiny bundle of orange fur.

Lindsay let out an inevitable squeal as she reached out and took the velvety kitten from Ruth. She buried her nose in its fur. "He's beautiful. What's his name?"

"Nijinsky," Ruth told her and turned her dark eyes to her uncle. "I'd keep him upstairs in my room where he wouldn't be in Worth's way. He's little and won't be any trouble," she rushed on hopefully.

Lindsay looked up as Ruth spoke. Animation had lit her eyes. In Lindsay's experience with her, only dancing had brought that much life to her face. "Trouble?" she said, automatically allying herself with the girl. "Of course he won't be any trouble. Just look at that face." She pushed the kitten into Seth's hands. Seth took a finger and tilted the kitten's face upward. Nijinsky mewed and settled down to sleep again.

"Three against one," Seth said as he scratched the furry ears. "Some might consider that foul play." He gave the kitten back to Ruth, then ran a hand down her hair. "Better let me handle Worth."

"Oh, Uncle Seth." Cradling the kitten, Ruth tossed her

free arm around Seth's neck. "Thank you! Ms. Dunne, isn't he wonderful?"

"Who?" Her eyes danced above Ruth's head. "Nijinsky or Seth?"

Ruth giggled. It was the first time Lindsay had heard the uniquely girlish sound from her. "Both of them. I'm going to take him in." She snapped the small bundle back inside her jacket and began to jog across the sand. "I'll sneak some milk from the kitchen," she called back behind her.

"Such a small thing," Lindsay murmured, watching the bright red jacket disappear down the stretch of sand. She turned to Seth with a nod of approval. "You did that very well. She thinks she persuaded you."

Seth smiled and caught at Lindsay's wind-tossed hair. "Didn't she?"

Lindsay returned his smile and gave in to the urge to touch his cheek. "I like knowing you're a soft touch." She dropped her hand. "I have to go."

"Lindsay." He held her still when she tried to turn away. "Have dinner with me." The look in his eyes was intimate. "Just dinner. I want you with me."

"Seth, I think we both know we wouldn't just have dinner. We'd both want more."

"Then we'll both have more," he murmured, but when he drew Lindsay into his arms, she resisted.

"No, I need to think." For a moment she rested her forehead against his chest. "I don't think clearly when you're touching me. I need some time."

"How much?" He put his hand under her chin to lift her face.

"I don't know." The tears that sprang to her eyes

stunned them both. Astonished, Lindsay brushed at them. Seth lifted a finger and trapped one on the tip.

"Lindsay." His voice was gentle.

"No, no, don't be kind. Yell at me. I'll get control of myself if you yell at me." She put both hands to her face and took deep breaths. Quite suddenly, she knew what had brought on the tears. "I have to go. Please let me go, Seth. I need to be alone."

From the pressure of his hands, she was afraid he would refuse. "All right," he said after a long moment. "But I'm not known for my patience, Lindsay."

She didn't respond but turned and fled. Fleeing with her was the realization not only that she could fall in love with Seth Bannion, but that she already had.

Chapter 9

They drove to the airport in the early afternoon. Andy drove with Lindsay beside him and both their mothers in the back seat. The trunk was cramped with luggage. Even after the three weeks of helping her mother prepare for the move, a cloud of disbelief hung over Lindsay. Already, boxes had been shipped ahead to California, and the house she had grown up in was on the market.

When it was sold, she knew her last ties to her childhood would go with it. It's for the best, she thought as she listened to her mother and Carol chatter in the rear seat. Everything I need will fit into the spare room at the school. It'll be more convenient for me, and there isn't any doubt that it's best for Mother.

She watched a plane gliding toward the ground and knew they were almost there. Her thoughts seemed to drift with the aircraft. Since the day Mae had announced her plans, Lindsay hadn't functioned at top level. Too many emotions had surfaced that day. She had tried to lock them away until she could deal with them rationally, but they had been too powerful. Again and again, they had escaped to haunt her dreams, or worse, to catch her unprepared in the middle of a class or conversation. She hadn't wanted to think about Seth, but she had: once when Monica had innocently brought up his name, again when Ruth had smuggled the kitten into class and dozens of other times when something reminded her of him.

It was odd how she could no longer walk into a room where he had been without associating it with him. Even her own studio reminded her of Seth.

After the initial shock had settled, Lindsay had explored the adventure of being in love. It didn't make her light-headed, as some songs promised, but it did make her less attentive to ordinary things. She hadn't lost her taste for food, but sleep had become a problem. She wasn't walking on clouds, but found herself, instead, waiting for the storm to hit. It was not falling in love that dictated her reactions, she decided, but the person with whom she had chosen to fall in love.

Chosen, Lindsay repeated silently, paying no attention as Andy worked his way through airport traffic. If I could have chosen who I'd fall in love with, it would've been someone who adored me, someone who thought I was perfection and whose life would be totally devoted to making mine Utopia.

Oh, no you wouldn't have, she corrected. Her window reflected the ghost of her smile. That would've bored me to death in a week. Seth suits me entirely too well. He's totally in command of himself, very cool, yet sensitive. Trouble is, he's a man who's made a career out of avoiding commitments…except for Ruth. She sighed and touched her own reflection with a fingertip. And there's another problem. It's difficult to be so totally opposed to something that's so important to both of us. How can we get closer when we're on opposite sides of a sixty-foot fence?

It was Andy's voice that brought Lindsay's mind back to present company. Disoriented, she glanced about to see that they had parked and that the others were already climbing out of the car. Quickly, Lindsay got out and tried to catch up with the conversation.

"…since we've already got our tickets and a car waiting at LAX," Carol finished as she pulled a suitcase and tote bag from the trunk.

"You will have to check all this baggage," Andy reminded her, easily hefting three more cases with a garment bag slung over his shoulder. "Catch the trunk, will you, Lindsay?" he asked absently as she was left with only her own purse and a cosmetic case.

"Sure."

Carol winked at Mae as Lindsay slammed the trunk shut and pulled out the keys. The wind billowed the hem of her coat. Glancing up, she scanned the sky. "It'll be snowing by nightfall."

"And you'll be trying on new bathing suits," Lindsay grumbled obligingly as she tried to move the two women along. The air was sharp and stung her cheeks.

Inside the terminal, there was the usual last-minute confusion about locating tickets and securing boarding passes. After checking the luggage, Andy began a detailed verbal listing of the do's and don'ts his mother was to follow.

"Keep the baggage checks in your wallet."

"Yes, Andy."

Lindsay caught the gleam in Carol's eye, but Andy continued to frown.

"And don't forget to call when you get to L.A."

"No, Andy."

"You have to set your watch back three hours."

"I will, Andy."

"And don't talk to strange men."

Carol hesitated. "Define strange," she demanded.

"Mom." His frown turned up into a grin before he enveloped her in a crushing hug.

Lindsay turned to her mother. She wanted it over quickly, without strain. But when they faced each other, her glib parting speech became lost. She was a child again, with words running riot in her mind. Instead of trying to sort through them, she threw her arms around her mother's neck.

"I love you," she whispered, shutting her eyes tight on tears. "Be happy. Please, please, be happy."

"Lindsay." Her name was a softly spoken sigh. After a moment, Mae drew away. They were of the same height, and their eyes were level. It was strange, but Lindsay couldn't remember the last time her mother had looked at her with such total concentration. Not at the dancer, but at her daughter.

"I love you, Lindsay. I might've made mistakes," Mae sighed with the admission. "But I always wanted the best for you—what I thought was the best. I want you to know I'm proud of you."

Lindsay's eyes widened, but her throat closed on any response. Mae kissed both her cheeks, then, taking the case from her hands, turned to say goodbye to Andy.

"I'm going to miss you," Carol said on a quick, energetic hug. "Go after that man," she whispered in Lindsay's ear. "Life's too short." Before Lindsay could answer, she, too, had kissed her. She walked with Mae through the gate.

When they were gone, Lindsay turned to Andy. Tears dampened her lashes, but she managed to prevent them from rolling down her cheeks. "Should I feel like an orphan?"

He smiled and slipped an arm around her. "I don't know, but I do. Want some coffee?"

Lindsay sniffled, then shook her head. "Ice cream," she said positively. "A great big ice cream sundae because we should be celebrating for them." She linked her arm with his as they began to walk away from the gate. "I'm treating."

Carol's weather forecast was right on the mark. An hour before sunset, the snow began. It was announced by Lindsay's evening students as they arrived for class. For several moments she and her students stood in the cold of the opened doorway and watched it fall.

There was always something magical about the first snow, Lindsay thought. It was like a promise, a gift. By midwinter, snow would bring grumbling and complaints, but now, fresh and soft and white, it brought dreams.

Lindsay continued the class, but her mind refused to settle. She thought of her mother landing in Los Angeles. It would still be afternoon there, and sunny. She thought of the children here in Cliffside who would be dragging their sleds out of attics and storerooms and sheds in preparation for tomorrow's rides. She thought of taking a long, solitary walk on the snowy beach. She thought of Seth.

It was during the break between classes, when her students were changing shoes for *pointe* class, that Lindsay went to the door again. The wind had picked up, and it tossed snow into her face. There were six inches or more on the ground already, and it was falling thickly. At that rate, Lindsay calculated, there would be well over a foot before the class was finished. Too risky, she decided, and shut the door.

"No *pointe* class tonight, ladies." Rubbing her arms to restore circulation, she moved back into the room. "Who has to call home?"

It was fortunate that the majority of Lindsay's advanced students drove or car pooled to class. Arrangements were soon made for the younger ones to be dispatched, and after the obligatory confusion, the studio was cleared. Lindsay took a deep breath before turning to Monica and Ruth.

"Thanks. That exodus would've taken twice the time if you hadn't helped." She looked directly at Ruth. "Have you called Seth?"

"Yes. I'd already made plans to stay at Monica's tonight, but I checked in."

"Good." Lindsay sat down and began to pull a pair of corduroy slacks over her tights and leg warmers. "I'm afraid this is going to turn into a solid blizzard in another hour or so. I want to be home with a cup of hot chocolate by then."

"I like the sound of that." Monica zipped up a down-filled parka, then pulled on the hood.

"You look ready for anything," Lindsay commented. She was carefully packing toe and ballet shoes into a tote bag. "What about you?" she asked Ruth as she pulled a ski cap down over her ears. "Ready?"

Ruth nodded and joined the women as they walked to the door. "Do you think classes will be on schedule tomorrow, Ms. Dunne?"

Lindsay opened the door, and the three of them were buffeted by the wind. Wet snow flew into their faces. "Such dedication," Monica mumbled, lowering her head to force her way across the parking lot.

By tacit agreement, all three began by clearing off Monica's car, sharing the broom Lindsay had brought with her from the studio. In short order, the car was unearthed, but before they could turn to give Lindsay's the same attention, Monica let out a long groan. She pointed to the left front tire.

"Flat," she said dully. "Andy told me it had a slow leak. He told me to keep air in it. Shoot." She kicked the offending tire.

"Well, we'll punish you later," Lindsay decided. She stuck her hands in her pockets, hoping to keep her fingers warm. "Right now, I'll take you home."

"Oh, but Lindsay!" Distress poured from Monica's eyes. "It's so far out of your way."

Lindsay thought a moment, then nodded. "You're right," she said briskly. "Guess you'll have to change that tire. See you tomorrow." Hefting the broom over her shoulder, she started toward her car.

"Lindsay!" Monica grabbed Ruth's hand, and the two ran after the departing figure. Along the way, Monica scooped up a fistful of snow and laughingly tossed it at Lindsay's ski cap. Her aim was flawless.

Lindsay turned, unconcerned. "Want a lift?" The expression on Ruth's face had her bubbling with laughter. "Poor thing, she thought I meant it. Come on." Generously, she handed Monica the broom. "Let's get moving before we're buried in this stuff."

In less than five minutes Ruth was sandwiched between Lindsay and Monica in the front seat. Snow swirled outside the windshield and danced in the stream of the headlights. "Here goes," Lindsay said and took a deep breath as she put the car in first.

"We were in a snowstorm once in Germany." Ruth tried to make herself smaller to avoid cramping Lindsay as she drove. "We had to travel on horseback, and when we reached the village, we were snowbound for three days. We slept on the floor around a fire."

"Got any other bedtime stories?" Monica asked. She closed her eyes against the rapidly falling snow.

"There was an avalanche," Ruth supplied.

"Terrific."

"We haven't had one of those here in years," Lindsay stated as she crept cautiously along.

"I wonder when the snow plows will be out." Monica frowned at the street, then at Lindsay.

"They've already been out; it's just hard to tell. They'll be busy tonight." Lindsay shifted, keeping her eyes on the road. "See if that heater's warmed up yet. My feet are freezing."

Obediently, Ruth switched it on. There was a blast of cold air. "I don't think it's ready," she hazarded, switching it off again. Out of the corner of her eye, Lindsay caught the smile.

"You're just smug because you've battled avalanches."

"I did have on pile-lined boots," Ruth admitted.

Monica wriggled her toes inside her thin loafers. "She's a smart aleck," she said conversationally. "The reason she gets away with it is because she does it with such innocence. Look." She pointed upward and to the right. "You can just see the lights of the Cliff House through the snow."

The urge was irresistible; Lindsay glanced up. The faint brightness of artificial light shone through the curtain of snow. She felt almost as though she were being pulled toward it. The car skidded in response to her inattention. Monica shut her eyes again, but Ruth chattered away, unconcerned.

"Uncle Seth's working on drawings for a project in New Zealand. It's beautiful, even though it's only pictures. You can tell it's going to be fabulous."

Cautiously, Lindsay turned the corner toward Monica's house. "I suppose he's pretty busy these days."

"He closes himself up in his office for hours," Ruth agreed. She leaned forward to try the heater again. This time the air was tepid. "Don't you love winter?" she asked brightly. Monica moaned, and Lindsay burst out laughing. "She is a smart aleck," she agreed. "I might not have noticed if you hadn't pointed it out."

"I didn't detect it myself all at once," Monica told her. She was beginning to breathe a bit easier as they made their way slowly down the block toward her house. When they pulled up in her driveway, Monica heaved a sigh of relief. "Thank goodness!" She shifted in her seat, crushing Ruth as she leaned toward Lindsay. Ruth found she liked the companionable discomfort. "Stay here tonight, Lindsay. The roads are awful."

Lindsay shrugged off the concern. "They're not that bad yet." The heater was humming along nicely now, and she felt warm and confident. "I'll be home in fifteen minutes."

"Lindsay, I'll worry and bite my nails."

"Good grief, I can't be responsible for that. I'll call you the minute I get home."

"Lindsay…"

"Even before I fix the hot chocolate."

Monica sighed, recognizing defeat. "The very minute," she ordered sternly.

"I won't even wipe my feet on the way to the phone."

"Okay." She climbed out of the car and stood amidst the thickly falling snow as Ruth followed. "Be careful."

"I will. Good night, Ruth."

"Good night, Lindsay." Ruth bit her lip at the slip in propriety, but Monica was already closing the door. No one else had noticed. Ruth smiled as she watched Lindsay's headlights recede.

Lindsay backed slowly out of the driveway and headed up the road. She switched on the radio to fill the void left by Monica and Ruth. The roads, as Monica had said, were awful. Though her wipers were working at top speed, they afforded her only scant seconds of vision before the windshield was covered again. It took every bit of her concentration and skill to keep the car from sliding. She was a good driver and knew the roads intimately, yet there was a small knot of tension at the base of her neck. Lindsay didn't mind it. Some people work best under pressure, and she considered herself one of them.

She pondered a moment on why she had refused Monica's invitation. Her own house would be dark and quiet and empty. The refusal had been automatic, and now she found herself regretting it. She didn't want to brood or to be alone. She was tired of thinking.

For a moment she vacillated between going ahead and going back. Before she could reach a firm decision, a large, black shape darted into the road ahead of her. Lindsay's brain barely had enough time to register that the shape was a dog before she was whipping the wheel to avoid a collision.

Once the skid had begun, she had no control. As the car spun, spitting up snow from the wheels, she lost all sense of direction. There was only the blur of white. Firmly, she controlled panic and resisted the urge to slam on the brakes. The fear that bubbled in her throat had no time to surface. It happened fast. The car struck something hard, and there was no slow-motion interlude before it slammed to a halt. She felt a flash of pain and heard the music on the radio turn to static before there was only the silence and the dark....

Lindsay moaned and shifted. There was a fife and drum corps marching inside her head. Slowly, because she knew she'd have to eventually, she opened her eyes.

Shapes floated and dimmed, then swam into focus. Seth frowned down at her. She felt his fingers on the side of her head where the pain was concentrated. Lindsay swallowed because her throat felt dry, but her voice was still husky when she spoke.

"What are you doing here?"

He raised a brow. She watched the change in the slant of its tip. Without speaking, he lifted her lids one at a time and studied her pupils carefully.

"I had no idea you were a complete idiot." The words were calmly spoken. In her dazed state, Lindsay didn't detect the edge of temper. She started to sit up, only to have him place his hand on her shoulders to hold her down. For the moment, she lay back without protest. She was, she discovered, on the sofa in his parlor. There was a fire in the hearth; she could hear its crackle and smell the hint of wood smoke. Its flames cast shadows into a room lit only by two muted china lamps. There was a needleworked pillow under her head, and her coat was still buttoned. Lindsay concentrated on each trivial fact and sensation until her mind began to come to order.

"That dog," she said, abruptly remembering. "Did I hit that dog?"

"What dog?" Impatience was evident in Seth's voice, but she plunged on.

"The dog that jumped out in front of the car. I think I missed him, but I can't be sure...."

"Do you mean to tell me that you ran into a tree to avoid hitting a dog?" If Lindsay had possessed all her faculties, she would have recognized the danger of the icy calm. Instead, she reached up gingerly to finger the ache at her temple.

"Is that what I hit? It feels more like I ran into an entire forest."

"Lie still," he ordered, leaving Lindsay staring as he strode from the room.

Cautiously, she persuaded her body into a sitting position. Her vision remained clear, but her temple throbbed abominably. Leaning her head back against the cushions, she closed her eyes. As a dancer, she was used to pain and to coping with it. Questions began to form in her mind. Lindsay let them shape and dissolve and regroup until Seth came back into the room.

"I thought I told you to lie still."

Lindsay opened her eyes and gave him a wan smile. "I'll do better sitting up, really." She accepted the glass and pills he thrust at her. "What are these?"

"Aspirin," he muttered. "Take them." Her brow lifted

at the command, but the ache in her head persuaded her to give in gracefully. Seth watched her swallow before he walked across the room to pour brandy. "Why the hell didn't you stay at Monica's?"

Lindsay shrugged, then leaned back against the cushion again. "I was asking myself that same question when the dog jumped into the road."

"And you hit the brakes in a snowstorm to avoid running into him." The disgust was ripe in his tone. Lindsay opened one eye to stare at his back, then closed it again.

"No, I turned the wheel, but I suppose it amounts to the same thing. I didn't think, though I imagine I'd have done the same thing if I had. In any case, I don't think I hit him, and I'm not damaged much, so there's little harm done."

"Little harm done?" Seth paused in the act of handing her a brandy. The tone of his words caused both of her eyes to open. "Do you have any idea what might have happened to you if Ruth hadn't called and told me you'd driven her to Monica's?"

"Seth, I'm not really very clear on what happened other than that I lost control of my car and hit a tree. I think you'd better clear up the basic facts before we argue."

"Drink some of this." He gave her the brandy snifter. "You're still pale." He waited until she obeyed, then went back to pour his own. "Ruth phoned to let me know she was safe at Monica's. She told me you'd driven them, then insisted on driving yourself home."

"I didn't insist, exactly," Lindsay began, then, noting Seth's expression, she shrugged and sampled the brandy again. It wasn't the hot chocolate she had envisioned, but it was warming.

"Monica was quite naturally worried. She said you'd be driving past shortly and asked, since I've such a good view of the road, if I'd keep a lookout for you. We assumed there wouldn't be much traffic in this miserable weather." He paused to drink, then swirled the remaining brandy while he looked at her. Faint color was returning to her cheeks. "After I hung up, I went to the window, just in time, it seems, to see your headlights. I watched them veer, then circle, then stop dead." After setting the brandy down, he thrust his hands into his pockets. "If it hadn't been for that phone call, you could very well still be in that car unconscious. Thank God you at least had enough sense to wear your seat belt, otherwise you'd have a great deal more than a bump on your head."

She bristled defensively. "Listen, I hardly intended to knock myself unconscious, and I..."

"But you did," Seth inserted. His tone was quiet and clipped.

"Seth, I'm trying very hard to be grateful, as I assume it was you who got me out of the car and up to the house." She drank the rest of her brandy, then set down the snifter. "You're making it difficult."

"I'm not interested in your gratitude."

"Fine, I won't waste it, then." Lindsay rose. The movement was too swift. She had to dig her nails into her palms to drive away the dizziness. "I'd like to call Monica so she won't be worried."

"I've already called." Seth watched the color the brandy had restored drain. "I told her you were here, that you had car trouble. It didn't seem necessary to tell her what kind. Sit down, Lindsay."

"That was very sensible of you," she returned. "Perhaps I could impose further on you to drive me back to Monica's."

Seth walked to her, placed his hands on her shoulders, and meeting her angry eyes, shoved her back down on the sofa. "Not a chance. Neither one of us is going back out in that storm."

Lindsay lifted her chin and aimed a glare. "I don't want to stay here."

"At this point, I don't think you have much choice," he retorted.

Lindsay shifted, crossing her arms over her chest. "I suppose you'll have Worth make up a room in the dungeon."

"I might," he agreed. "But he's in New York seeing to some business for me." He smiled. "We're quite alone."

Lindsay tried to make an unconcerned gesture with her shoulders, but the movement came off as a nervous jerk. "It doesn't matter; I can walk to Monica's in the morning. I suppose I could use Ruth's room."

"I suppose."

She rose, but more slowly than the first time. The throbbing was down to a dull ache, easily ignored. "I'll go up, then."

"It's barely nine." The hand on her shoulder was light but enough to stop her. "Are you tired?"

"No, I…" The truth was out before she thought to prevaricate.

"Take off your coat." Without waiting for her response, he began undoing the buttons himself. "I was too preoccupied with trying to bring you around to worry about it before." As he slipped the coat from her shoulders, his eyes came back to hers. Gently, he touched a finger to the bruise on her temple. "Hurt?"

"Not much now." Lindsay's pulse rate had quickened. There was no use trying to blame it on the shock of the accident. Instead, she admitted to the feelings that were beginning to swim inside her and met his eyes directly. "Thank you."

He smiled as he ran his hands up her arms, then back down to her fingers.

A moan escaped when he lifted both of her hands to kiss the insides of her wrists. "Your pulse is skittish."

"I wonder why," she murmured. Pleased, Seth gave a low laugh as he released her hands.

"Have you eaten?"

"Eaten?" Lindsay's mind tried to focus on the word, but her senses were still dominating her system.

"Food," Seth supplied. "As in dinner."

"Oh, no, I've been at the studio since this afternoon."

"Sit down, then," he ordered. "I'll go see if Worth left anything palatable."

"I'll come with you." She placed her hand on his to halt his objection. "Seth, we dancers are a sturdy breed. I'm fine."

He studied her face critically, then nodded. "All right, but my way." In an unexpected move, he swept her up in his arms. "Humor me," he said, anticipating her objection.

Lindsay found the sensation of being pampered delicious and settled back to enjoy it. "Have you eaten?"

Seth shook his head. "I've been working.... Then I was distracted."

"I've already thanked you," Lindsay pointed out. "I won't apologize on top of it. It was the dog's fault anyway."

Seth nudged open the kitchen door with his shoulder.

"It wouldn't be an issue if you'd done the sensible thing and stayed at Monica's."

"There you go, being logical again." Lindsay heaved a sigh as he set her down at the kitchen table. "It's a nasty habit, but I'm certain you could break it." She smiled up at him. "And if I'd stayed at Monica's, I wouldn't be here right now being waited on. What are you going to fix me?"

Seth captured her chin in his hand and examined her closely. "I've never known anyone like you."

His voice was brooding, so she touched his hand with hers. "Is that good or bad?"

He shook his head slowly, then released her. "I haven't made up my mind."

Lindsay watched him walk to the refrigerator. It was hard for her to believe how much she loved him—how complete and solid the love had already become.

And what do I do about it? she asked herself. Do I tell him? How embarrassing that would be for him, and how completely I would ruin what seems to be the beginning of a great friendship. Isn't love supposed to be unselfish and understanding? Spreading her fingers on the table's surface, she stared at them. But is it supposed to hurt one minute and make you feel like flying the next?

"Lindsay?"

She looked up sharply, suddenly aware that Seth had spoken to her. "I'm sorry." She smiled. "I was daydreaming."

"There's a platter of roast beef, a spinach salad and a variety of cheeses."

"Sounds terrific." Lindsay stood, holding up a hand to quiet his protest. "I'm off the critical list, I promise.

I'll trust you to put all that together while I set the table." She walked to a cupboard and began searching.

"How do you feel about washing dishes?" Lindsay asked while Seth made after-dinner coffee.

"I've given the subject very little thought." He glanced back over his shoulder. "How do you feel about it?"

Lindsay leaned back in her chair. "I've just been in an accident. Very traumatic. I doubt whether I'm capable of manual labor just yet."

"Can you walk into the other room?" he asked dryly. He lifted a tray. "Or shall I take the coffee in and come back for you?"

"I'll try." Lindsay pushed herself away from the table. She held open the door and allowed Seth to pass through.

"Actually, most people wouldn't bounce back as quickly as you have." They moved down the hall together. "You took a pretty good whack, from the size of the bump on your head. And from the look of your car, you're lucky it wasn't more."

"But it wasn't," Lindsay pointed out as they came to the parlor. "And please, I don't want to know about my car until I have to. That could send me into severe depression." Sitting on the sofa, she gestured for Seth to set the tray on the table in front of her. "I'll pour. You take cream, don't you?"

"Mmm." Seth moved over to toss another log on the fire. Sparks shot out before the log hissed and caught. When he came back to her, Lindsay was pouring her own cup. "Are you warm enough?"

"Oh yes, the fire's wonderful." She sat back without touching her coffee. "This room's warm even without it." Snug and relaxed, she allowed her eyes to wander and appreciate. "When I was a teenager, I used to dream about sitting here just like this…a storm outside, a fire in the grate and my lover beside me."

The words tumbled out without thought. The moment they had, Lindsay's cheeks went wild with color. Seth touched the back of his hand to her face.

"A blush is something I didn't expect to see on you." Lindsay caught the hint of pleasure in his voice. She shifted away.

"Maybe I'm feverish."

"Let me see." Seth turned her back to face him. Firmly, he held her still, but the mouth that lowered to her brow was gentle as a whisper. "You don't seem to be." One hand trailed up to the pulse at her throat. His fingers pressed lightly. "Your pulse isn't steady."

"Seth…" She let his name trail off into silence as he slid a hand under her sweater to caress her back. He ran a fingertip along the path where the leotard gave way to flesh.

"But perhaps you're too warm with this heavy sweater."

"No, I…" Before she could prevent him, he had expertly slipped it over her head. Her skin was rosy warm beneath.

"That's better." He kneaded her bare shoulders briefly, then turned back to his coffee. Every nerve in Lindsay's body had been awakened. "What else did you dream about?" As he drank, his eyes sought hers. Lindsay wondered if her thoughts were as transparent as she feared.

"About dancing with Nicky Davidov."

"A realized dream," Seth commented. "Do you know what fascinates me about you?"

Intrigued, Lindsay shook her head. At her stern orders, her nerves began to settle. "My stunning beauty?" she suggested.

"Your feet."

"My feet!" She laughed on the words, automatically glancing down at the canvas slip-ons she wore.

"They're very small." Before Lindsay had any notion of his intent, he had shifted her feet into his lap. "They should belong to a child rather than a dancer."

"But I'm lucky enough to be able to support them on three toes. A lot of dancers can only use one or two. Seth!" She laughed again as he slipped her shoes off.

The laughter stilled as he trailed a finger down her instep. Incredibly, she felt a fierce rush of desire. It poured into her, then spread like wildfire through her system. Her quiet moan was involuntary and irrepressible.

"They appear very fragile," Seth commented, cupping her arch in his palm. "But they must be strong." Again he lifted his eyes to hers. His thumb trailed over the ball of her foot, and she shuddered. "And sensitive." When he lifted her feet and kissed both of her ankles, Lindsay knew she was lost.

"You know what you do to me, don't you?" she whispered. It was time to accept what had to be between them.

There was a gleam of triumph in his eyes as he lifted his head again. "I know that I want you. And that you want me."

If it were only that simple, Lindsay thought. If I didn't love him, we could share each other with total freedom, without regrets. But I do love him, and one day I'll have to pay for tonight. There was a light flutter of fear in her chest at the thought of what the price might be.

"Hold me." She went into his arms and clung. "Hold

me." While the snow lasts, she told herself, we're alone. There's no one else in the world, and this is our time. There's no tomorrow. There's no yesterday.

She tilted back her head until she could see his face. With a fingertip, she slowly traced the curves and angles until she knew every inch was carved in her memory.

"Love me, Seth," she said with her eyes wide. "Make love with me."

There was no time for a gentleness neither of them wanted. Passion sets its own rules. His mouth was avid, burning on hers before her words had dissolved in the air. His hunger was unbearably arousing. But she sensed he was in control, still the captain of their destiny. There was no fumbling as he undressed her. His hands caressed her as each layer of clothing was removed, inciting desire wherever they touched. When she struggled to release the buttons of his shirt, he helped her. There was fire and need and spiraling pleasure.

Touching him, exploring the taut flesh of his chest and shoulders, Lindsay felt yet a new sensation. It was one of possession. For now, for the moment, he belonged to her, and he owned her absolutely. And they were flesh to flesh without barriers, naked and hungry and tangled together. His mouth roamed down feverishly to taste her breast, then lingered there, savoring, while his hands brought her trembling delight. His tongue was excitingly rough. As he nuzzled, she moved under him, powered by needs that grew in velocity and strength.

Her breath came in whimpers as she urged his lips back to hers. They came on a slow journey, pausing at her throat, detouring to her ear until she was near madness for the taste of him. Ravenously, she took his mouth with hers, shuddering now with a passion more all-consuming than anything she had ever experienced. In the dance, she remained one unit. The pleasure and dreams were hers and within her control. Now, she was joined to another, and pleasure and dreams were a shared thing. The loss of control was a part of the ecstasy.

She felt strong, more powerful than it seemed possible for her to be. Her energy was boundless, drawn from the need to have, the need to give. Their passion flowed sweet as honey; she was molten in his arms.

Chapter 10

Lindsay dreamed she was lying in a big, old bed, wrapped in quilts and in her lover's arms. It was a bed that knew their bodies well, one she had awakened in morning after morning over the years. The sheets were Irish linen and soft as a kiss. The quilt was an heirloom she would pass on to her daughter. The lover was a husband whose arms became only more exciting over the years. When the baby cried, she stirred, but lazily, knowing that nothing could disturb the tranquil beauty in which she lived. She snuggled deep into the arms that held her and opened her eyes. Still dreaming, she smiled into Seth's.

"It's morning," she murmured and found his mouth warm and soft and delightful. She ran her fingertips down his spine, smiling when his lips became more insistent. "I've got to get up," she whispered, nestling as his hand cupped her breast. She could still hear the faint, plaintive cry of the baby.

"Uh-uh." His lips moved to her ear. Slowly, his tongue began to awaken her fully. Passion rekindled the night's embers.

"Seth, I have to, she's crying."

With a halfhearted oath, Seth rolled over and reached down to the floor. Rolling back, he plopped Nijinsky the cat on Lindsay's stomach. She blinked, disoriented and confused as the kitten mewed at her, making sounds like a baby. The dream shattered abruptly.

Lindsay reached up to drag a hand through her hair and took a long breath.

"What's the matter?" Seth tangled his hand in her hair until she opened her eyes.

"Nothing." She shook her head, stroking the kitten so that he purred. "I was dreaming. It was silly."

"Dreaming." He brushed his lips over her naked shoulder. "About me?"

Lindsay turned her head until their eyes met again. "Yes." Her lips curved. "About you."

Seth shifted, bringing her to rest in the curve of his shoulder. Nijinsky moved to curl at their feet. He circled twice, pawed the quilt, then settled. "What was it about?"

She burrowed into the column of his throat. "My secret." His fingers were trailing soothingly over her shoulder and upper arm.

I belong to him, she thought, *and can't tell him.* Lindsay stared at the window, seeing that though the snow was thinning, it fell still. There's only the two of us, she reminded herself. Until the snow stops, there's just we two. *I love him so desperately.* Closing her eyes, she ran her hand up his chest to his shoulder. There were muscles there she wanted to feel again. With a smile, she pressed her lips against his throat. There was today. *Only today.* She moved her mouth to his, and their lips joined.

Their kisses were short, quiet tastes. The rush—the desperation—of the night before had mellowed. Now desire built slowly, degree by degree. It smoldered, it teased, but it didn't overpower. They took time to enjoy. Seth shifted so that she lay across his chest.

"Your hands," he murmured as he brought one to his lips, "are exquisite. When you dance, they seem to have no bones." He spread his hand over hers, palm to palm.

Her hair cascaded around her shoulders to fall on his. In the soft, morning light it was as pale as an illusion. Her skin was ivory with touches of rose just under the surface. It was a fragile, delicately boned face, but the eyes were vivid and strong. Lindsay lowered her mouth and kissed him, long and lingeringly. Her heartbeat quickened as she felt his hunger build.

"I like your face." She took her mouth from his to softly kiss his cheeks and eyelids and jaw. "It's strong and just a bit wicked." She smiled against his skin, remembering. "You terrified me the first time I saw you."

"Before or after you ran out in the road?" He trailed one hand up her back while the other stroked her hair. It was a lazy, comfortable loving.

"I did not run out in the road," Lindsay nipped at his chin. "You were driving too fast." She began to plant kisses down the length of his chest. "You looked awfully tall when I was sitting in that puddle."

She heard him chuckle as he ran a hand down the arch of her back, then slowly reacquainted himself with the slight flare of her hips, the long length of her thighs.

He shifted, and they moved as one until their positions were reversed. The kiss deepened. The touch of hands to flesh was still gentle but more demanding now. Conversation lapsed into a soft slumber. Passion rose like a tropical wave, warm and steep. It crested, then receded....

Dressed in jeans and a flannel shirt borrowed from Ruth's wardrobe, Lindsay skipped down the main stairway. There was a chill in the house which told her the fires had yet to be lit. Only the one in the master bedroom crackled. The first stage of her plan was to start one in the kitchen hearth. She hummed an impromptu tune as she pushed open the door.

It surprised her that Seth was there ahead of her. She could smell the coffee.

"Hi!" Walking over, she wrapped her arms around his waist, resting her cheek on his back. "I thought you were still upstairs."

"I came down while you were using Ruth's barre." Turning, he gathered her close. "Want some breakfast?"

"Maybe," she murmured, nearly exploding with joy at the simple intimacy. "Who's going to fix it?"

He tilted her chin. "We both are."

"Oh." Her brows lifted. "I hope you like cold cereal and bananas. That's my specialty."

Seth grimaced. "Can't you do anything with an egg?"

"I make really pretty ones at Easter time."

"I'll scramble," he decided, then kissed her forehead. "Can you handle toast?"

"Possibly." With her head resting against his chest, she watched the snow fall.

The trees and lawn resembled a stage set. The white

blanket on the ground lay completely unmarred. The evergreen shrubs Seth had planted were wrapped in their own snowy coats; towering above them nearby, the trees stood as snow-covered giants. And still it fell.

"Let's go outside," Lindsay said impulsively. "It looks wonderful."

"After breakfast. We'll need more wood, in any case."

"Logical, logical." Lindsay wrinkled her nose at him. "Practical, practical." She let out a quick cry when he tugged her earlobe playfully.

"Architects have to be logical and practical, otherwise buildings fall down and people get upset."

"But your buildings don't look practical," Lindsay told him. She watched him as he walked to the refrigerator. Who, exactly, was this man she was in love with? Who was the man who had laid claim to her emotions and her body? "They always look beautiful, never like those steel and glass boxes that rob cities of their character."

"Beauty can be practical, too." He turned back with a carton of eggs in one hand. "Or perhaps it's better to say practicality can be beautiful."

"Yes, but I should think it more difficult to make a really good building appealing to the eye as well as functional."

"If it isn't difficult, it's hardly worth the trouble, is it?"

Lindsay gave a slow nod. That she understood. "Will you let me see your drawings of the New Zealand project?" She wandered to the bread box. "I've never seen the conception of a building before."

"All right." He began to break eggs into a bowl.

They prepared and ate the meal in easy companionship. Lindsay thought the kitchen smelled of family; coffee and toast and singed eggs. She logged the scent in her memory file, knowing it would be precious on some future morning. When they had eaten and set the kitchen to rights, they piled on layers of outdoor clothing and left the house.

Lindsay's first step took her thigh-deep in snow. Laughing, Seth gave her a nudge that sent her sprawling backward. She was quickly up to her shoulders. The sound of his laughter hit the wall of snow and bounced back, accentuating their solitude.

"Maybe I'd better put a bell around your neck so I can find you," he called out, laughing.

Lindsay struggled to stand up. Snow clung to her hair and crusted her coat. Seth's grin widened as she scowled at him. "Bully," she said with a sniff before she began to trudge through the snow.

"The wood pile's over here." Seth caught her hand. After giving token resistance, Lindsay went with him.

Their world was insular. Snow tumbled from the sky to disappear into the thick blanket around them. She could barely hear the sea. Ruth's boots came to her knees, but with every step, snow trickled inside the tops. Her face was rosy with cold, but the view outbalanced every discomfort.

The whiteness was perfect. There was no glare to sting the eyes, nor any shadows to bring variations in shade. There was simply white without relief, without obstruction.

"It's beautiful," Lindsay murmured, pausing as they reached the woodpile. She took a long, sweeping view. "But I don't think it could be painted or photographed. It would lose something in the duplication."

"It'd be flat," Seth told her. He stacked wood into her arms. Lindsay's breath puffed out in front of her as she gazed beyond his shoulder.

"Yes, that's it exactly." The agreement pleased her. "I'd rather remember it than see it in one dimension." With Seth alongside, she made slow progress to the back door. "But you must be an expert at visualizing reality from a flat drawing."

"You've got it backwards." They stacked the wood behind the utility room door. "I make drawings from a reality I visualize."

Lindsay stopped a moment, a bit breathless from the exertion of wading through thigh-deep snow. "Yes." She nodded. "I can understand that." Studying him, she smiled. "You've snow on your eyelashes."

His eyes searched hers questioningly. She tilted her head, inviting the kiss. His lips lowered to touch hers, and she heard him suck in his breath as he lifted her into his arms.

He carried her over the threshold and through the door. When he continued through the utility room into the kitchen, Lindsay roused herself to object. "Seth, we're covered with snow. It's going to drip everywhere."

"Yep."

They were in the hall, and she pushed the hair from her eyes. "Where are you going?"

"Upstairs."

"Seth, you're crazy." She bounced gently on his shoulder as he climbed the main staircase. "We're making a mess. Worth's going to be very upset."

"He's resilient," Seth stated, turning into the master bedroom. He placed Lindsay onto the bed. From her reclining position she pushed herself up onto her elbows.

"Seth." He had removed his coat and was working on his boots. Lindsay's eyes widened, half in amusement, half in disbelief. "Seth, for goodness sake, I'm covered with snow."

"Better get out of those wet things, then." He tossed his boots aside, then moved to her to unbutton her coat.

"You're mad," she decided, laughing as he drew off her coat and tossed it on the floor to join his boots.

"Very possibly," he agreed. In two quick tugs, he had removed her boots. The thick wool socks she wore were stripped off before he began to massage warmth back into her feet. He felt her instant response to his touch.

"Seth, don't be silly." But her voice was already husky. "Snow's melted all over the bed."

With a smile, he kissed the balls of her feet and watched her eyes cloud. Moving to her side, he gathered her into his arms. "The rug is dry," he said as he lowered her. Slowly, his fingers following his mouth, he undid the buttons of her shirt. Beside them, the fire he had built before breakfast sizzled.

He parted her shirt, not yet removing it. With a tender laziness he began kissing her breasts while Lindsay floated on the first stage of pleasure. She sighed once, then, touching his cheek with her hand, persuaded his mouth to hers. The kiss began slowly, but the quality changed without warning. His mouth became desperate on a groan that seemed to come from somewhere deep inside him. Then he was tugging at the rest of her clothes, impatient, tearing the seam in Ruth's shirt as he pulled it from Lindsay's shoulder.

"I want you more than before," he mumbled as his teeth and lips grew rough at her neck. "More than yesterday. More than a moment ago." His hands bruised as they took possession of her body.

"Then have me," she told him, drawing him closer, wanting him. "Have me now."

Then his mouth was on hers and there were no more words.

The phone woke Lindsay. Drowsily, she watched Seth rise to answer it. He wore the forest green robe he had slipped on when he had rebuilt the fire. She had no sense of time. Clocks were for a practical world, not for dreams.

She stretched slowly, vertebra by vertebra. If forever could be a moment, she would have chosen that one. She felt soft and warm and well-loved. Her body was heavy with pleasure.

Lindsay watched Seth without hearing the words he spoke into the phone. He stands so straight, she thought and smiled a little. And he so rarely uses gestures with his words. Gestures can betray feelings, and his are very private. He holds his own leash. Her smile sweetened. And I like knowing I can take him to the end of it.

His voice intruded into her musings as snatches of his conversation leaked through. It's Ruth, she realized, distracted from her concentrated study of his face. After sitting up, Lindsay drew the quilt around her shoulders. Before she looked to the window, she knew what she would see. The snow had stopped while they slept. She waited for Seth to hang up the phone.

She managed to smile at him while her mind worked feverishly to gather impressions; the way his hair fell over his forehead, the glint of the sun on it as light spilled through the window, the straight, attentive way he stood.

Her heart seemed to expand to hold new degrees of love. She fought to keep her face composed.

Don't spoil it, she ordered herself frantically. *Don't spoil it now.* It seemed to Lindsay that Seth was studying her with even more than his usual intensity. After a long moment, he crossed to where she sat on the floor, cocooned by quilts and pillows.

"Is she coming home?" Lindsay asked when Seth replaced the receiver.

"She and Monica are driving over shortly. The county's been on the ball, it seems, and the roads are nearly clear."

"Well." Lindsay pushed at her hair before she rose, still tented by the quilt. "I suppose I'd better get ready, then. It seems I'll have evening classes."

There was a sudden outrageous desire to weep. Lindsay battled against it, bundling herself up in the quilt as she gathered her clothes. Be practical, she instructed. Seth is a practical man. He'd hate emotional scenes. She swallowed hard and felt control returning. While slipping into her tights and leotard, she continued to talk.

"It's amazing how quickly these road crews work. I can only hope they didn't bury my car. I suppose I'll have to have it towed. If it's only a minor disaster, I shouldn't be without it for long." Dropping the quilt, she slipped her sweater over her head. "I'll have to borrow Ruth's brush," she continued, pulling her hair out from the collar. Suddenly, she stopped to face Seth directly. "Why do you just look at me?" she demanded. "Why don't you say something?"

He stood where he was, still watching her. "I was waiting for you to stop babbling."

Lindsay shut her eyes. She felt completely defenseless. She had, she realized, made an utter fool of herself. This was a sophisticated man, one used to casual affairs and transitory relationships. "I'm simply no good at this sort of thing," she said. "I'm not good at it at all." He reached for her. "No, don't." Quickly, she jerked away. "I don't need that now."

"Lindsay." The annoyance in his tone made it easier for her to control the tears.

"Just give me a few minutes," she snapped at him. "I hate acting like an idiot." With this, she turned and fled the room, slamming the door behind her.

In fifteen minutes Lindsay stood in the kitchen pouring Nijinsky a saucer of milk. Her fine hair was brushed to fall neatly down her back. Her nerves, if not quiet, were tethered. Her hands were steady.

The outburst had been foolish, she decided, but maybe it had helped ease her into the first stage of her return to the outside world.

For a moment she lost herself in a dream as she gazed out on the world of white. She knew, though he made no sound, the moment Seth stepped into the room. Lindsay took an extra second, then turned to him. He was dressed in dark brown corduroy slacks and a V-neck sweater over a pale blue shirt. She thought he looked casually efficient.

"I made some coffee," she said in a carefully friendly voice. "Would you like some?"

"No." He came toward her purposefully; then, while she was still wondering what he would do, he brought her close. His hands circled her upper arms. The kiss was searing and long and enervating. When he drew her away, Lindsay's vision dimmed and then refocused.

"I wanted to see if that had changed," he told her while his eyes seemed to spear into hers. "It hasn't."

"Seth…" But his mouth silenced hers again. Protest became hungry response. Without thought, she poured every ounce of her feelings into the kiss, giving him all. She heard him murmur her name before he crushed her against him. Again, all was lost. The flashes of paradise came so swiftly, Lindsay could only grasp at them without fully taking hold. Drawn away again, she stared up at him, not seeing, only feeling.

Another woman, she thought dazedly, would be content with this. Another woman could continue to be his lover and not hurt for anything else. Another woman wouldn't need so much from him when she already has so much. Slowly, Lindsay brought herself back. The only way to survive was to pretend she was another woman.

"I'm glad we were snowbound," she told him, pulling gently from his arms. "It's been wonderful being here with you." Keeping her voice light, she walked back to the coffeepot. When she poured, she noticed her hand was no longer steady.

Seth waited for her to turn back, but she continued to face the stove. "And?" he said, slipping his hands into his pockets.

Lindsay lifted the coffee cup and sipped. It was scalding. She smiled when she turned. "And?" she repeated. The hurt was thudding inside her throat, making the word painful.

His expression seemed very much as it had the first time she had seen him. Stormy and forbidding. "Is that all?" he demanded.

Lindsay moistened her lips and shrugged. She clung

to the cup with both hands. "I don't think I know what you mean."

"There's something in your eyes," he muttered, crossing to her. "But it keeps slipping away. You won't let me know what you're feeling. Why?"

Lindsay stared into the cup, then drank again. "Seth," she began calmly and met his eyes again. "My feelings are my business until I give them to you."

"Perhaps I thought you had."

The hurt was unbelievable. Her knees trembled from it. His eyes were so steady, so penetrating. Lindsay took her defense in briskness. "We're both adults. We were attracted to each other, we have been for some time...."

"And if I want more?"

His question scattered her thoughts. She tried to draw them back, tried to see past the guard that was now in his eyes. Hope and fear waged war inside her. "More?" she repeated cautiously. Her heart was racing now. "What do you mean?"

He studied her. "I'm not certain it's an issue if I have to explain it."

Frustrated, Lindsay slammed her cup back on the counter. "Why do you start something and not finish it?"

"Exactly what I'm asking myself." He seemed to hesitate, then lifted a hand to her hair. She leaned toward him, waiting for a word. "Lindsay..."

The kitchen door swung open in front of Ruth and Monica.

"Hi!" Ruth's greeting trailed off the moment she took in the situation. She searched quickly for a way to back out, but Monica was already passing her to go to Lindsay.

"Are you okay? We saw your car." Concern dominated her tone as she reached out to touch her friend. "I knew I should've made you stay."

"I'm fine." She gave Monica a kiss for reassurance. "How're the roads now?"

"Pretty good." She jerked her head at Ruth. "She's worried about missing class."

"Naturally." Lindsay gave her attention to the girls until her pulse leveled. "That shouldn't be a problem."

Attracted by Ruth's voice, Nijinsky wandered over to circle her legs until she obliged him by picking him up. "Are you sure you feel up to it?"

Lindsay read the knowledge in Ruth's eyes and reached for her cup again. "Yes. Yes, I'm fine." Automatically she went to the sink for a cloth to wipe up the coffee she had spilled. "I guess I should call a tow truck."

"I'll see to it." Seth spoke for the first time since the interruption. His tone was formal and distant.

"That isn't necessary," Lindsay began.

"I said I'll see to it. I'll take you all to the studio when you're ready." He walked from the room, leaving the three of them staring at the swinging door.

Chapter 11

Monica and Ruth rode in the back of Seth's car on the drive to the studio. Ruth was conscious of a definite, pronounced tension between her uncle and Lindsay. Whatever was between them, she concluded, had hit a snag. Because she was fond of both of them, Ruth did her best to ease the strained atmosphere. "Is Worth due back tonight?"

Seth met her eyes briefly in the rearview mirror. "In the morning."

"I'll fix you coq au vin tonight," she volunteered, leaning forward onto the front seat. "It's one of my best dishes. But we'll have to eat late."

"You have school tomorrow."

"Uncle Seth." Her smile was tolerant. "I'm graduating from high school, not elementary school.

"Monica showed me her brother's yearbook last

night," she continued, turning her attention to Lindsay. "The one from the year you and Andy graduated."

"Andy looked great in his football jersey, didn't he?" Lindsay shifted in her seat so that she faced Ruth.

"I liked your picture best." She pushed her hair back over her shoulder. Lindsay saw that all her shyness had fled. Her eyes were as open and friendly as her smile. "You should see it, Uncle Seth. She's on the steps leading into the auditorium. She's doing an *arabesque*."

"Smart aleck Tom Finley told me to do a little ballet."

"Is that why you were sticking out your tongue?"

Lindsay laughed. "It added to the aesthetic value of the photograph."

"It sounds like a good likeness," Seth commented, turning both Lindsay's and Ruth's attention to himself. "The *arabesque* was in perfect form, I imagine. You could dance in the middle of an earthquake."

Lindsay kept her eyes on his profile, not certain if he was praising her or criticizing her. "It's called concentration, I suppose."

"No." Seth took his eyes from the road long enough to meet her gaze. "It's called love. You love to dance. It shows."

"I don't think there's a better compliment," Ruth said. "I hope someone says that to me one day."

All the things she wanted to say raced through Lindsay's mind, but none would remain constant. Instead, she laid her hand on the back of his. Seth glanced at their hands, then at Lindsay. "Thank you," she said.

Her heart caught when he turned his hand over to grip hers. He brought it to his lips. "You're welcome."

Ruth smiled at the gesture, then settled back as they turned into the school parking lot. Someone had made a halfhearted attempt to clear the snow, and Lindsay knew immediately that it must have been the neighborhood kids.

"Someone's here," Ruth commented when she spotted the sleek foreign car parked in the lot.

Lindsay absently glanced away from Seth as he stopped the car. "I wonder who…" The words stumbled to a halt, and her eyes widened. She shook her head, certain she was wrong, but climbed slowly out of the car. The man in the black overcoat and fur hat stepped away from the studio door and walked to her. The moment he moved, Lindsay knew she wasn't mistaken.

"Nikolai!" Even as she shouted his name, she was racing through the snow. She saw only a blur of his face as she flung herself into his arms. Memories poured over her.

He had held her before; the prince to her Giselle, the Don to her Dulcinea, Romeo to her Juliet. She had loved him to the fullest extent of friendship, hated him with the pure passion of one artist for another, worshipped his talent and despaired of his temper. As he held her again, everything they had shared, everything she had felt in her years with the company, flooded back to her. The wave was too quick and too high. Weeping, she clung to him.

Nick laughed, pulling her away to give her a boisterous kiss. He was too absorbed with Lindsay to hear Ruth's reverently whispered *"Davidov"* or to see Seth's concentrated study.

"Hello, *ptichka,* my little bird." His voice was high and rich with Russian inflection. Lindsay could only shake her head and bury her face in his shoulder.

The meeting was unexpected, whipping up her already heightened emotions. But when he drew her away again, she saw through her blurred vision that he was precisely the same. Though he had a deceptively innocent boy's face, he could tell ribald jokes and swear in five languages. His thickly lashed blue eyes crinkled effectively at the corners. His mouth was generous, romantically shaped, and there was the charm of two slight dimples when he smiled. His hair was dark blond, curling and thick. He left it tousled to his advantage. He skimmed under six feet, making him a good partner for a dancer of Lindsay's size.

"Oh, Nick, you haven't changed." Lindsay touched his face with both hands. "I'm so, so glad you haven't."

"But you, *ptichka,* you have changed." The potent choirboy grin lit his face. "You are still my little bird, my *ptichka,* but how is it you are still more beautiful?"

"Nick." Tears mixed with laughter. "How I've missed you." She kissed his cheeks, then his mouth. Her eyes, washed with tears, were shades deeper. "What are you doing here?"

"You weren't home, so I came here." He shrugged at the simplicity. "I told you I'd come in January. I came early."

"You drove from New York in all this snow?"

Nikolai took a deep breath and looked around. "It felt like Russia, your Connecticut. I like to smell the snow." His eyes alit on Seth and Ruth. "Your manners are revolting, *ptichka,*" he said mildly.

"Oh, I'm sorry! I was so surprised...." She felt flustered and brushed at her tears with the back of her hand. "Seth, Ruth, this is Nikolai Davidov. Nicky, Seth and Ruth Bannion. She's the dancer I told you about."

Ruth stared at Lindsay. In that moment, she became Lindsay's willing slave.

"A pleasure to meet friends of Lindsay's." He shook hands with Seth. A small line appeared between his brows as he studied him. "You are not perhaps the architect Bannion?"

Seth nodded while Lindsay watched the men measure each other. "Yes."

Nick beamed with pleasure. "Ah, but I have just bought a house of your design in California. It's on the beach with many windows so that the sea is in the living room."

He's so effusive, Lindsay thought of Nick. So different from Seth, and yet they remind me of each other.

"I remember the house," Seth acknowledged. "In Malibu?"

"Yes, yes, Malibu!" Obviously delighted, Nick beamed again. "I'm told it's early Bannion, reverently, as though you were long dead."

Seth smiled as people invariably did with Nick. "The more reverently, the higher the market value."

Nikolai laughed offhandedly, but he had caught the expression in Lindsay's eyes when she looked at Seth. So, he thought, that's the way the wind blows. "And this is the dancer you want to send me." He turned his attention to Ruth, taking both hands in his. He saw a small, dark beauty—with good bones and narrow hands—who trembled like a leaf. The face would be exotic with the right makeup and lighting, he decided. And her size was good.

"Mr. Davidov." Ruth struggled not to stutter. To her, Nikolai Davidov was a legend, a figure larger than life.

To be standing toe to toe with him, her hands held by his, seemed impossible. The pleasure was excruciating.

He chafed her hands, and his smile was personal. "You must tell me if Lindsay's manners are always so appalling. How long does she usually keep her friends standing out in the cold?"

"Oh, blast!" Lindsay fumbled for her keys. "You completely stun me by popping up from nowhere, then expect me to behave rationally." She pushed open the front door. "I was right," she told him over her shoulder, "you haven't changed."

Nikolai wandered past her into the room's center without speaking. Pulling off his gloves, he tapped them idly against his palm as he surveyed the studio. Ruth hung on his every movement.

"Very good," he decided. "You've done well here, *ptichka*. You have good students?"

"Yes." Lindsay smiled at Ruth. "I have good students."

"Have you found a teacher to run your school when you come back to New York?"

"Nick." Lindsay paused in the act of unbuttoning her coat. "I haven't agreed to come back."

"That is nonsense." He dismissed her objection with a flick of the wrist. It was a gesture Lindsay remembered well. An argument now would be heated and furious. "I must be back in two days. I direct *The Nutcracker*. In January I begin staging for my ballet." As he spoke, he shrugged out of his coat. He wore a simple gray jogging suit and looked, to Ruth's mind, magnificent. "With you as my Ariel, I have no doubt as to its success."

"Nick…"

"But I want to see you dance first," he said over her protest, "to make certain you haven't gone to pot."

"Gone to pot?" Incensed, Lindsay tossed her coat over a chair. "You'll be writing Russian phrase books long before I go to pot, Davidov."

"That's yet to be seen." He turned to Seth as he slipped off his hat. "Tell me, Mr. Bannion, do you know my *ptichka* well?"

Seth turned his eyes to Lindsay, holding them there until she flushed. "Fairly well." His gaze slid back to Nikolai. "Why?"

"I wonder if you could tell me if she has kept her muscles as well-exercised as her temper. It's important that I know how much time I must spend whipping her back into shape."

"Whipping me back into shape!" Knowing she was being maneuvered didn't prevent Lindsay from falling into the trap. "I don't need you or anyone to whip me into shape."

"Okay." He nodded as he looked down at her feet. "You need toe shoes and tights, then."

Lindsay turned on her heel and headed for her office. Still fuming, she slammed the door behind her. Nick grinned at Seth and Ruth.

"You know her very well," Seth commented.

Nikolai gave a quick chuckle. "As I know myself. We are very much the same." Reaching into a deep pocket of his coat, he produced a pair of ballet shoes. He sat on a chair to change into them. "You've known Lindsay long?" Nikolai knew he was prying and realized from the lift of Seth's brow that the bluntness had been acknowledged.

He is a private, self-contained man, Nikolai decided.

But his thoughts are on Lindsay. If it was a man who was keeping her from resuming her profession, he wanted to know it and to understand the man. He concluded that Seth wouldn't be an easy man to understand. Complications, he knew, appealed to Lindsay.

"A few months," Seth answered at length. The artist in him recognized an extraordinarily beautiful man. The sensitive face held just enough puckishness to keep it from being too smooth. It was a face easily cast as a fairy-tale prince. A difficult face to dislike. Seth slipped his hands into his pockets. He, too, felt a desire to understand the man.

"You worked together for some time in New York."

"I've had no better partner in my career," he said simply. "But I could never say so to my *ptichka*. She works best when her passions are aroused. She has great passions." He smiled as he rose. "Like a Russian."

Lindsay came back into the room wearing black tights and a leotard with white leg warmers and *pointe shoes*. Her chin was still lifted.

"You've put on some weight," Nikolai commented as he gave her willow slim figure a critical survey.

"I'm a hundred and two," she said defensively.

"You'll need to drop five pounds," he told her as he walked to the barre. "I'm a dancer, not a weight-lifter." He *pliéd* while Lindsay caught her breath in fury.

"I don't have to starve myself for you anymore, Nick."

"You forget, I'm director now." He smiled at her blandly and continued to warm up.

"You forget," she countered, "I'm not with the company now."

"Paperwork only." He gestured for her to join him.

"We'll leave you two alone." Lindsay turned to Seth

as he spoke. Nikolai watched the contact of their eyes. *This man gives nothing away,* he decided. "And give you some privacy."

"Please," Nikolai interrupted Lindsay's response. "You must stay."

"Yes, Nick never could perform without an audience." She smiled, reaching out to touch Seth's hand. "Don't go."

"Please, Uncle Seth." Enraptured by the possibility of watching her two favorite artists perform impromptu, Ruth clung to Seth's arm. Her eyes were dark with excitement.

Seth hesitated. He looked once at Lindsay, long and deep. "All right."

The formality was back in his tone and troubled her. Why, she thought as she walked to join Nikolai, was the closeness between them so elusive? She spoke to Nick casually as they loosened and warmed their muscles, but he noted how often her eyes drifted to Seth's reflection in the glass.

"How long have you loved him?" he murmured in a voice only Lindsay could hear. She glanced up sharply. "You could never hold a secret from me, *ptichka*. A friend often sees more clearly than a lover."

"I don't know." Lindsay sighed, feeling the weight of it settle on her. "Sometimes it feels like forever."

"And your eyes are tragic." He stopped her from turning away by placing a hand to her cheek. "Is love so tragic, my little bird?"

Lindsay shook her head, trying to dispel the mood. "What sort of question is that from a Russian? Love is meant to be tragic, isn't it?"

"This isn't Chekhov, *ptichka*." After patting her

cheek, he walked to the CD player. "Perhaps Shakespeare would suit you." He glanced up from the CDs he sifted through. "Do you remember the second *pas de deux* from *Romeo and Juliet?*"

Lindsay's eyes softened. "Of course I do. We rehearsed endlessly. You pulled my toes when they cramped, then threw a sweaty towel at me when I missed a *sauté*."

"Your memory is good." He inserted the CD and programmed the selection. "Come then, dance with me now, *ptichka,* for old times and for new." Nikolai held out his hand. There was magic when they came together.

Their fingers touched, then parted. Lindsay felt it instantly: the youth, the hope, the poignancy of first love. Her steps were instinctive. They flowed with the music and paired fluidly with Nick's. When he lifted her the first time, she felt as though she was lost forever in the music, in the emotion.

Ruth watched them, hardly daring to breathe. Although the dance looked deceptively simple, her training gave her a complete appreciation of its intricacies and difficulties. It was romance in its purest form: a man and a woman irresistibly drawn together, testing the waters of new love. The music vibrated with the emotion of a love deep and doomed. It shone naked in Lindsay's eyes when she looked at Davidov. Here was not the teasing sauciness of her Dulcinea, but the vulnerabilities of a girl loving for the first time. And when they knelt on the floor, fingertips reaching for fingertips, Ruth's heart nearly burst from the glory of it.

For several seconds after the music ended, the dancers remained still, eyes locked, fingers just touching.

Then Davidov smiled, and moving close, pulled her to him. She trembled lightly under his palm.

"It seems you haven't gone to pot after all, *ptichka*. Come back with me. I need you."

"Oh, Nick." Drained, she laid her head on his shoulder. She had forgotten the depth of the pleasure that was hers when she danced with him. And yet, the very essence of the dance had intensified her feelings for Seth.

If she could have gone back to the snowbound house, cut off from all in the world but him, she would have done so blindly. Her mind seemed almost drugged with wants and doubts. She clung to Nick as if he were an anchor.

"She was not too bad." Over Lindsay's head, he grinned at Seth and Ruth.

"She was wonderful," Ruth responded in a voice husky with feeling. "You were both wonderful. Weren't they, Uncle Seth?"

Slowly, Lindsay lifted her head. When she looked up at him, her eyes were still brimming with love. "Yes."

Seth watched her, but there was no expression on his face. "I've never seen two people move together more perfectly." He stood, lifting his coat as he did so. "I have to go." He laid his hand on Ruth's shoulder as he heard her murmur of disappointment. "Perhaps Ruth could stay. There's only an hour or so before her class."

"Yes, of course." Lindsay stood, uncertain how to deal with the distance that was suddenly between them. Her body still quivered with emotions that belonged to him. "Seth…" She said his name, knowing nothing else.

"I'll pick her up tonight." He shifted his attention to Nikolai, who had risen to stand beside Lindsay. "A pleasure meeting you, Mr. Davidov."

"And for me," Nikolai responded. He could feel the vibrations of distress from Lindsay as Seth turned away.

She took a step, then stopped herself. The night had been her dream, the dance her fantasy. She closed her eyes tight as the door shut behind him.

"Lindsay." Nick touched her shoulder, but she shook her head furiously.

"No, please. I—I have to make some phone calls." Turning, she fled into her office.

Nick sighed as the door clicked shut. "We are an emotional lot, dancers," he commented as he turned to Ruth. Her eyes were dark and wide and young. "Come, then, you will show me why Lindsay would send you to me."

Stunned, Ruth stared at him. "You want—you want me to dance for you?" Her limbs turned to lead. Never would she be able to lift them.

Nick nodded briskly, suddenly all business. "Yes." His eyes drifted to the closed door as he moved back to the CD player. "We will give Lindsay the time she needs for her phone calls, but we need not waste it. Change your shoes."

Chapter 12

Ruth couldn't believe what was happening. As she hurried to exchange boots for ballet shoes, her fingers seemed numbed and unable to function. *Davidov* wanted to see her dance. It was a dream, she was certain. The fantasy was so long-standing and far-fetched that she was positive she would wake up at any moment in her high, soft bed at the Cliff House.

But she was sitting in Lindsay's studio. To reassure herself, Ruth put her mind to work fiercely, checking and rechecking all points of reference while her hands tugged at the boots. There was the long, inescapable wall of mirrors; the shining, always spotless wood floor. She looked at the familiar sheet music piled on the piano, the CDs scattered on the stand. The struggling plant Lindsay had nursed so carefully sat in front of the east window. Ruth could see that another leaf had wilted. She could hear the click and hum of the heater, which had been switched on. The fan whirred softly.

Not a dream, she told herself. This was real. Her trembling hand slipped the favored ballet shoes onto her feet. She rose, daring at last to look at Davidov.

He should have been undistinguished in the plain gray jogging suit, but he wasn't. Ruth, despite her youth, recognized that certain men could never be ordinary. Some drew notice without effort. It was more than his face and physique, it was his aura.

When he had danced with Lindsay, Ruth had been transported. He was no teenage Romeo but twenty-eight, perhaps at the zenith of his career as a dancer. But she had believed him because he had exuded tender youth and the wonder of first love. No one would question any role Nick Davidov chose to portray. Now she tried to see the man but was almost afraid to look. The legend was very important to her. She was still young enough to want indestructible heroes.

She found him remarkably beautiful, but the demand of his eyes and the slight crookedness of his nose prevented it from being too smooth a face. Ruth was glad without knowing why. Now she could see only his profile as he poured over Lindsay's collection of CDs. There was a faint gleam of perspiration on his forehead testifying to the exertion of the dance he had just completed. His eyebrows were lowered, and though he studied the CD insert in his hand, Ruth wondered if his mind was on it. He seemed distant, in a world of his own. She thought perhaps that was how legends should be: remote and unapproachable.

Yet Lindsay had never been, she reflected. And Davidov had not seemed so at first. He had been friendly, she remembered. He had smiled at her.

Perhaps he's forgotten about me, she thought, feeling small and foolish. Why should he want to see me dance? Her spine straightened with a surge of pride. He asked, she reminded herself. He *ordered,* was more accurate. And he's going to remember me when I'm finished, she determined as she walked to the barre to warm up. And one day, she thought, taking first position, I'll dance with him. Just as Lindsay did.

Without speaking, Davidov set down the CD he was holding and began to pace the studio. His movements were those of a caged animal. Ruth lost her timing in simple awe. She'd been wrong; he hadn't forgotten about her, but his thoughts were focused on the woman behind the office door. He hated the look of hurt and desolation he had seen in Lindsay's eyes as she had rushed from the room.

What a range of emotions her face had held in one short afternoon, Nick mused. He'd watched Lindsay and enjoyed her surprised joy when she had seen him outside for the first time. Her eyes had brimmed with feeling. Being an emotional man, Davidov understood emotional people. He admired Lindsay's abilities to speak without words and to speak passionately.

There had been no mistaking Lindsay's feelings for Seth Bannion. He had seen it instantly. And though Seth was a controlled man, Nikolai had felt something there, too—a slight current, like a soft breath in the air. But Seth had left Lindsay without an embrace or a touch and barely a word. Nikolai felt he would never understand restrained Americans and their hesitancy to touch each other.

Still, he knew the cool departure would have hurt Lindsay. But it wouldn't have devastated her. She was too strong for that. There was something more, he was certain, something deeper. His impulses urged him to walk through the office door and demand to know the problem, but he knew Lindsay needed time. So he would give it to her.

And there was the girl.

He turned to watch Ruth warming up at the barre. The sun, slanting through the windows, flashed in the mirrors. It glowed around Ruth as she brought her leg up to an almost impossible ninety-degree angle. She held it there poised, effortlessly.

Nikolai frowned, narrowing his eyes. When he had looked at her outside, he had seen a lovely girl with exotic features and good bones. But he had seen a child, not yet out of the schoolroom; now he saw a beautiful woman. A trick of the light, he thought, taking a step closer. Something stirred inside him which he quickly suppressed.

Ruth moved, and the angle of the sun altered. She was a young girl again. The tension in Nick's shoulders evaporated. He shook his head, smiling at his own imagination. Sternly professional again, he walked over and selected a CD.

"Come," he said commandingly. "Take the room's center. I'll call the combination."

Ruth swallowed, trying to pretend it was every day that she danced in front of Nikolai Davidov. But she found that even taking a step from the barre was impossible. Nikolai smiled, suddenly recognizing the girl's nervousness.

"Come," he said again with more gentleness. "I rarely break the legs of my dancers."

He was rewarded by a quick, fleeting smile before Ruth walked to the center of the studio. Programming the CD selection, he began.

Lindsay had been right. Nikolai saw that within moments, but the pace of his instructions remained smooth and steady. Had Ruth been able to study him, she might have thought him displeased. His mouth was sternly set, and his eyes held an unfathomable, closed look. Those who knew him or had worked with him would have recognized unswerving concentration.

Ruth's initial terror had passed. She was dancing, and she let the music take her. An *arabesque,* a *soubre-saut,* a quick, light series of *pirouettes.* She gave what he demanded her to give without question. When the instructions stopped, so did she, but only to wait. She knew there would be more. She sensed it.

Nick moved back to the CD player without a glance or a word for Ruth. He sifted quickly through the CDs until he found what he wanted. "*The Nutcracker.* Lindsay does it for Christmas?" It was more of a statement than a question, but Ruth answered it.

"Yes." Her voice came strong and smooth with no more trembling nerves. She was the dancer now, the woman in control.

"You're Carla," he said with such casual confidence that Ruth thought Lindsay must have told him she had been cast in the role. He gave the combination quickly. "Show me," he demanded and folded his arms.

* * *

Inside her office, Lindsay sat silently at her desk. Nikolai's instructions to Ruth came clearly enough through the closed door, but they didn't register. She was astonished by the depth of the pain. And it kept coming—wave after wave of it. She had been so certain that she could cope with the end of her idyll with Seth, just as she had coped with the snow. She hadn't realized how much hurt there would be.

The hideous battle with tears had almost passed. She could feel the outrageous need to shed them lessen. She had sworn when she had given herself to Seth that she would never regret it and never weep. She was comforted by the knowledge that there would be memories when the pain subsided—sweet, precious memories. She had been right, she was convinced, not to have thrown herself into his arms confessing her love as she had longed to do. It would have been unbearable for both of them. She had made it easy on him by giving a casual tone to their time together. But she hadn't expected the coldness or the ease with which he had walked out of her studio—and her life. She had thought for a moment, standing in his kitchen and again in the car driving to the studio, that perhaps she had been wrong after all. Imagination, Lindsay told herself with a quick shake of her head. Wishful thinking.

What had been between them had been wonderful: now it was over. That's what she had said to Seth, that's what she would have to remember.

She straightened, trying desperately to act with the same dispassion she had seen in Seth's eyes as he had turned to leave the studio. But her hands tightened into fists as emotions rose again to clog her throat. Will I stop loving him? she wondered despairingly. Can I?

Her eyes drifted to the phone, and she uncurled her hand and touched the receiver. She longed to phone him, just to hear his voice. If she could just hear him say her name. There must be a dozen excuses she could manufacture.

Idiot! She scolded herself and squeezed her eyes tightly shut. He's hardly had time to drive across town, and already you're prepared to make a fool of yourself.

It will get easier, she told herself firmly. It has to.

Rising, Lindsay moved to the window. Ice had formed along the edges of the pane. Behind the school was a high, sloping hill that curved into a narrow field. Already more than a dozen children were sledding madly. They were much too far away for her to hear the screams and laughter that must have echoed in the clear air. But she could sense the excitement, the freedom. There were trees here and there, mantled as they should be, heavy with snow and glistening in the strong sunlight.

Lindsay watched for a long time. A blur of red flew down the hill, then slowly made the trudge back to the summit. A flash of green followed to overturn halfway down and tumble to the bottom. For a moment Lindsay wanted almost desperately to run out and join them. She wanted to feel the cold, the sharp bite of snow as it hurled into her face, the breath-stealing surge of speed. She wanted the long, aching trudge back to the top. She felt too warm—too isolated—behind the window glass.

Life goes on, she mused, leaning her brow against the cool glass. And since it won't stop for me, I'd better keep up with the flow. There isn't any backing away from it, no hiding from it. I have to meet it head on. Then she heard the evocative music of *The Nutcracker*.

And this is where I begin.

Lindsay went to her office door, opened it and walked into the studio.

Neither Nikolai nor Ruth noticed her, and not wanting to disturb them, Lindsay came no farther into the room but stood watching Ruth who, smiling a dreamy half smile, moved effortlessly and gracefully to Nikolai's command. Nick watched without comment.

No one, Lindsay decided, could tell by looking at him just what was going on in his head.

It was part of his character to be as open as the wind one moment, as mysterious as the sphinx the next. Perhaps that was why he attracted women, she thought. Suddenly it occurred to her that he was not so very different from Seth. But it was not what she wanted to ponder at the moment, and she turned back to watch Ruth.

How young she was! Hardly more than a child despite her wise and tragic eyes. For her there should be high school proms, football games and soft summer nights. Why should the life of a seventeen-year-old be so complicated?

Lindsay pressed her fingers to her temple, trying to remember herself at the same age. She'd already been in New York, and life had been simple but very, very demanding, both for the same reason. Ballet. It was going to be the same for Ruth.

Lindsay continued to watch her dance. For some, she decided, life is not meant to be easy. She thought of herself as much as Ruth. For some it's meant to be hard, but the rewards can be so, so sweet. Lindsay remembered the incredible exhilaration of dancing on stage, the culmination of hours of work and rehearsals, the payment for all the pain and all the sacrifice. Ruth would have it as well. She was destined to. Lindsay shunned the knowledge that in order to secure what she felt was Ruth's right, she herself would have to face Seth. And in facing him, she would have to be very strong. There would be time enough to think of that in the nights ahead when she was alone. She was certain that in a few days she could cope, that she would be able to deal with her own emotions. Then she would speak to Seth about Ruth.

When the music ended, Ruth held the final position for several seconds. As she lowered her arms, the next movement began, but Nick didn't speak to her. He gave no instruction, no comment, but went instead to switch off the CD player.

Ruth, her breath coming quickly, moistened her lips. Now that the dance was finished and she could relax her concentration, every other part of her tensed. Her fingers, which had been superbly graceful during the dance, now began to tremble.

He thinks I was dreadful, and he'll tell me so, she agonized. *He'll feel sorry for me and say something pacifying and kind.* Both alternatives were equally horrifying to her. A dozen questions came to her mind. She wished for the courage to voice them but could only grip one hand with the other. It seemed to her that her very life was hanging in the balance, waiting for one man's opinion, one man's words.

Davidov looked over suddenly and locked eyes with her. The intensity of his gaze frightened her, and she gripped her hands together more tightly. Then the mask was gone, and he smiled at her. Ruth's heart stopped.

Here they come, she thought dizzily. Those kind, terrible words.

"Mr. Davidov," she began, wanting to stop him before he could begin. She would prefer a quick, clean cut.

"Lindsay was right," he interrupted her. "When you come to New York, come to me."

"To you?" Ruth repeated stupidly, not certain she had heard him correctly, not daring to believe.

"Yes, yes, to me." Nikolai appeared amused by Ruth's response. "I know a few things about ballet."

"Oh, Mr. Davidov, I didn't mean…" She came to him then, propelled by horrified distress. "I was just…I only meant…"

Nikolai took her hands to quiet her disjointed explanation. "How large your eyes are when you're confused," he said, giving her hands a quick squeeze. "There's still much I haven't seen, of course." He dropped her hands to take her chin and begin a thorough impassive study of her face. "How you dance on *pointe*," he continued. "How you dance with a partner. But what I've seen is good."

She was speechless. Good from Davidov was the highest of accolades.

Lindsay moved forward then, and Nikolai looked up from his study of Ruth's face. *"Ptichka?"* Releasing the girl's chin, he went to Lindsay.

Her eyes were composed and dry without any trace of red, but her face was pale. Her hand was not lifeless in his; the fingers interlocked, but they were cold. He placed his other hand over them as if to warm them.

"So, you're pleased with my prize student." There was the slightest of signals, a glimpse in her eyes there, then gone, that said what had happened was not now to be discussed.

"Did you doubt I would be?" he countered.

"No." She smiled, turning her face to Ruth. "But I'm sure she did." Lindsay looked back at Nick, and the smile was wry. "You're every bit as intimidating as your reputation, Nikolai Davidov."

"Nonsense." He shrugged off Lindsay's opinion and shot Ruth a grin. "I'm as even-tempered as a saint."

"How sweetly you lie," Lindsay said mildly. "As always."

To this he merely grinned at her and kissed her hand. "It's part of my charm."

His comfort and his friendship were easing the pain. Lindsay pressed his hand to her cheek in gratitude. "I'm glad you're here." Then, releasing his hand, she walked to Ruth. "You could use some tea," she suggested but restrained herself from touching the girl's shoulder. She wasn't yet certain the gesture would be welcomed. "Because if memory serves me, your insides are shaking right now. Mine were the first time I danced in front of him, and he wasn't nearly the legend he is now."

"I've always been a legend, *ptichka*," Nikolai corrected. "Ruth is merely better schooled in the art of respect than you were. This one," he told Ruth with a jerk of the thumb at Lindsay, "likes to argue."

"Especially with the mighty," Lindsay agreed.

Ruth laughed a breathy, relieved, wondering sound. Could all this really be happening? she wondered. Am I actually standing here with Dunne and Davidov being treated as a professional? Looking into Lindsay's eyes, Ruth saw understanding and the faintest hint of sadness. *Uncle Seth,* she remembered abruptly, ashamed of her own self-absorption. She recalled how crushed Lindsay had looked when Seth had closed the studio door behind him. Tentatively, she reached out and touched her mentor's hand.

"Yes, please, I would like some tea now."

"Russian tea?" Nikolai demanded from across the room.

Lindsay gave him a guileless smile. "Rose hips."

He made a face. "Perhaps vodka, then?" His brow rose in mild question.

"I wasn't expecting any Russian celebrities," Lindsay apologized with a smile. "There's a possibility I could dig up a diet soda."

"Tea is fine." He was studying her again, and Lindsay knew his thoughts had drifted. "Later I'll take you out for dinner, and we'll talk." He paused when Lindsay eyed him suspiciously. "Like old times, *ptichka*," he told her innocently. "We have much to catch up on, don't we?"

"Yes," Lindsay agreed cautiously, "we do." She started to go back into her office to make the tea, but Ruth stopped her.

"I'll do it," she volunteered, recognizing that they could speak more openly without her standing between them. "I know where everything is." She darted quickly away before Lindsay could assent or decline.

Casually Nikolai slipped a CD at random from its case and inserted it into the player. The quiet romance of Chopin was enough to help insure a more private conversation. "A lovely girl," he said. "I congratulate you on your judgment."

Lindsay smiled, glancing at the door that Ruth had left partly ajar. "She'll work harder than ever now after what you said to her. You'll take her into the company,

Nick," she began, suddenly eager, wanting to seal Ruth's happiness. "She…"

"That isn't a decision to be made in the snap of a finger," he interrupted. "Nor is it only mine to make."

"Oh, I know, I know," she said impatiently, then grabbed both of his hands. "Don't be logical, Nick, tell me what you feel, what your heart tells you."

"My heart tells me you should come back to New York." He held her fingers tighter as she started to withdraw them from his. "My heart tells me you're hurt and confused and still one of the most exquisite dancers I've ever partnered."

"We were talking about Ruth."

"You were talking about Ruth," he countered. *"Ptichka."* The quiet sound of his voice brought her eyes back to his. "I need you," he said simply.

"Oh, don't." Lindsay shook her head and closed her eyes. "That's not fighting fair."

"Fair, Lindsay?" He gave her a quick shake. "Right or wrong isn't always fair. Come, look at me." She obeyed, letting his direct, blue eyes look deep into hers. "This architect," he began.

"No," Lindsay said quickly. "Not now, not yet."

She looked pale and vulnerable again, and he lifted a hand to her cheek. "All right. Then I'll ask you this: Do you think I would want you back in the company, dancing the most important role of my first ballet, if I had any doubts about your talent?" She started to speak, but a lift of his brow halted her. "Before you talk of sentiment and friendship, think."

Taking a deep breath, Lindsay turned away from him and walked to the barre. She knew Nikolai Davidov and understood his utter selfishness when dancing was involved. He could be generous, giving, charmingly self-less personally. When it suited him. But when the dance was involved, he was a strict professional. Ballet held the lion's share of his heart. She rubbed the back of her neck, now tense again. It all seemed too much to think about, too much to cope with.

"I don't know," she murmured. Nothing seemed as clear or as certain as it had only hours before. Turning back to Nick, Lindsay lifted both hands, palms up. "I just don't know."

When he came to her, she lifted her face. He could see that hurt was still mixed with confusion. The shrill whistle of the teakettle in her office momentarily drowned out Chopin. "Later we'll talk more," he decided and slipped an arm around her. "Now we'll relax before your classes begin."

They walked across the room to join Ruth in Lindsay's office. Stopping, she gave him a quick kiss. "I am glad you're here."

"Good." He gave her a hug in return. "Then after class you can buy me dinner."

Chapter 13

On the day after Christmas, snow lay in drifts on the side of the road. Thick icicles glinted from eaves of houses while multitudes of tiny ones clung to tree branches. The air was crisp and cold, the sunlight thin.

Restless and more than a little bored, Monica walked to the town park. The playground looked abandoned and pitiful. Brushing the snow off a wooden swing, she sat down. She kicked at the snow with her boots and set herself in motion. She was worried about Lindsay.

There had been a change, a change of some magnitude. It had started right after the first snow of the season. She was not sure whether it had been brought about by the time Lindsay had spent with Seth or the visit from Nick Davidov. Moodiness was simply not a characteristic trait of Lindsay's. But time had passed, and the moodiness remained. Monica wondered if she was more sensitive to Lindsay's mood because her own was so uncertain.

Monica had been shocked to realize that the long-standing crush she had on Andy had developed into full-blown love. She had hero-worshipped him from the first day he had come home with her brother wearing his high school football jersey. She had been ten to his fifteen. Ironically, the major obstacle in her path was the person she felt closest to: Lindsay.

Why couldn't Lindsay see how crazy Andy was about her? Monica leaned far back in the swing, enjoying the flutter in her stomach as the sky tilted with her movements. It was pale blue. Why hadn't he told her? Monica pushed harder.

During the years of Lindsay's absence from Cliffside, Monica had been a love-struck teenager whom Andy had treated kindly with absent pats on the head. Since Lindsay's return, he hadn't appeared to notice that his friend's little sister had grown up. No more, Monica thought grouchily, than Lindsay had noticed Andy's heart on his sleeve.

"Hi!"

Turning her head, Monica got a quick glimpse of Andy's grin before she flew forward. On the backswing, it was still there. She dragged her feet on the ground and slowed. "Hi," she managed as he settled in her line of vision.

"You're up early for a Saturday," he commented, idly running his hand down the chain of the swing. "How was your Christmas?"

"Fine—good." She cursed herself and tried to speak coherently. "You're up early, too."

Andy shrugged, then sat on the swing beside her.

Monica's heart trembled. "Wanted a walk," he murmured. "Still giving piano lessons?"

Monica nodded. "I heard you were expanding the flower shop."

"Yeah, I'm adding a whole section of house plants."

Monica studied the hands on the chains of the swing beside her. It was amazing that such large and masculine hands could arrange flowers with incredible delicacy. They were gentle hands. "Aren't you opening today?"

"This afternoon, for a while, I thought." He shrugged his broad shoulders. "Doesn't look like anybody's up but you and me." He turned his head to smile at her. Monica's heart cartwheeled.

"I—I like getting up early," she mumbled.

"Me, too." Her eyes were soft and vulnerable as a puppy's.

Monica's palms were hot in the December air. She rose to wander restlessly around the playground.

"Do you ever think about moving away from Cliffside?" she asked after a short silence.

"Sure." Andy pushed off the swing to walk with her. "Especially when I'm down. But I don't really want to leave."

She looked up at him. "I don't, either." Her foot kicked an abandoned ball half-buried in the snow. Stooping, Monica picked it up. Andy watched the thin winter sunlight comb through her hair. "I remember when you and my brother used to practice in the backyard." She tossed the small ball lightly. "Sometimes you'd throw me one."

"You were pretty good, for a girl," Andy acknowledged and earned a scowl. He laughed, feeling lighter than he had when he started on his walk. Monica always made him feel good. As she tossed the ball up again, he grabbed it. "Want to go out for one?"

"Okay." She jogged across the snow, then ran laterally, remembering the moves from years before. Andy drew back, and the ball sailed toward her in a sweeping arch. Perfectly positioned, she caught the ball handily.

"Not bad," Andy yelled. "But you'll never score."

Monica tucked the ball under her arm. "Watch me," she yelled back and raced through the trampled snow.

She ran straight for him, then veered off to the left before he could make the touch. Her agility surprised him, but his reflexes were good. He turned, following her zigzagging pattern. Caught up in the chase, he threw himself out, nipping her by the waist and bringing her down. They hit the snow with a muffled thud. Instantly horrified, Andy rolled her over. Her face was pink under a coating of snow.

"Oh, wow, Monica, I'm sorry! Are you okay?" He began to brush the snow from her cheeks. "I wasn't thinking. Did I hurt you?"

She shook her head but hadn't yet recovered the breath to speak. He lay half across her, busily brushing the snow from her face and hair. Their breath puffed out and merged. She smiled at his expression of horrified concern, and their eyes met. Suddenly Andy gave way to impulse and placed a light, hesitant kiss on her lips.

"Sure you're okay?" His taste was much sweeter than Monica had imagined. She tasted it again when he lowered his mouth a second time.

"Oh, Andy!" Monica threw her arms around his neck and rolled until he was positioned beneath her. Her lips descended to his, but there was nothing light or hesitant about her kiss. Snow slipped down Andy's collar, but he ignored it as his hand went to the back of her head to prolong the unexpected. "I love you," she said as her mouth roamed his face. "I love you so much."

He stroked her hair. Monica felt weightless. He seemed determined to lie there forever as Monica, soft and scented, clung to his neck. Then he sat up, still cuddling her, and looked down at her eyes, dark and wet and beautiful. He kissed her again. "Let's go to my house." His arm went around her shoulders to draw her close to his side.

Driving by, Lindsay passed Andy and Monica and absently lifted her hand in a wave. Neither of them saw her. Her mind crowded with thoughts, she drove on toward the Cliff House. She had to speak with Seth. Time, she felt, was running out for her, for them, for Ruth. Nothing seemed to be going the way it should…not since the afternoon the first snow had stopped.

Seth had gone away almost immediately to his New Zealand site and hadn't returned until a few days before Christmas. He hadn't written or called, and while Lindsay hadn't expected him to, she had hoped for it nonetheless. Missing him was painful. She wanted to be with him again, to recapture some of the happiness, some of the closeness they had shared. Yet she knew that once they had spoken, they could be farther apart than ever. She had to convince him, by whatever means possible, to let Ruth go. Her last conversation with Nick had persuaded her that it was time to press for what was needed, just as it had convinced her it was time to make a final decision about her own life. She wanted Ruth in New York with her.

She took the long curve of Seth's driveway slowly, watching the house as the road rose. Because her heart was thumping inside her chest, she took an extra moment to breathe after she stopped the car. She didn't want to make a fool of herself when she saw Seth again. Ruth's chances depended on her being strong enough to convince him that she knew what the girl needed.

Lindsay got out of the car, nervously clutching her purse in both hands as she walked to the front door. Relax, she told herself. She couldn't allow her feelings for him to ruin what she had come to do.

The wind pinched color into her face, and she was grateful. She had braided her hair and coiled it neatly at her neck so the wind wouldn't disturb it. Composure, at the moment, was vital to her. She knew that the memories of what she had shared with Seth were dormant and would overwhelm her the moment she stepped into the house. She lifted a gloved finger and pushed the doorbell. The wait was mercifully short before Worth answered.

He was dressed much as before. The dark suit and tie were impeccable. The white shirt crisp. The beard was neatly trimmed, his expression inscrutable.

"Good morning, Miss Dunne." There was nothing in his voice to indicate his curiosity at her early call.

"Good morning, Mr. Worth." Lindsay could prevent her hands from nervously twisting her bag, but some of her anxiety escaped into her eyes. "Is Seth in?"

"He's working, I believe, miss." Politely he moved back to allow her entrance into the warmth of the house. "If you'd care to wait in the parlor, I'll see if he can be disturbed."

"Yes, I...please." She bit her lip as she followed his

straight back. Don't start babbling, she admonished herself.

"I'll take your coat, miss," he offered as she stepped over the parlor threshold. Wordlessly, Lindsay slipped out of it. The fire was crackling. She could remember making love with Seth here for the first time while the fire hissed and the mantel clock ticked away the time they had together.

"Miss?"

"Yes? Yes, I'm sorry." She turned back to Worth, suddenly aware that he had been speaking to her.

"Would you care for some coffee while you wait?"

"No, nothing. Thank you." She pulled off her gloves and walked to the window. She wanted to regain her composure before Seth joined her. Setting the purse and gloves on a table, she laced her fingers.

It was difficult waiting there, she discovered, in the room where she had first given her love to him. The memories were painfully intimate. Priorities, she reminded herself. I have to remember my priorities. In the window glass she could see just the ghost of her reflection: the trimly cut gray trousers, the burgundy mohair sweater with its full, cuffed sleeves. She looked composed, but the composure, like the woman in the glass, was all illusion.

"Lindsay."

She turned, thinking herself prepared. Seeing him again sent a myriad of feelings washing over her. But the most dominant was an all-encompassing joy. She smiled, filled with it, and crossed the room to him. Her hands sought him without hesitation.

"Seth. It's so good to see you."

She felt his hands tighten on hers before he released

them to say, "You're looking well," in a casually distant tone that had her battling back the words that trembled on her tongue.

"Thank you." Turning, she walked to the fire, needing to warm herself. "I hope I'm not disturbing you."

"No." Seth stayed where he was. "You're not disturbing me, Lindsay."

"Did things go well in New Zealand?" she asked, facing him again with a more reserved smile. "I imagine the weather was different there."

"A bit," he acknowledged. He moved closer then but kept a safe distance between them. "I have to go back after the first of the year for a few weeks. Things should settle down when that's over. Ruth tells me your house is sold."

"Yes." Lindsay tugged at the collar of her sweater, wishing she had something to fill her hands. "I've moved into the school. Everything changes, doesn't it?" He inclined his head in agreement. "There's plenty of room there, of course, and the house seemed terribly empty when I was alone. It'll be simpler to organize things when I go to New York...."

"You're going to New York?" he interrupted her sharply. Lindsay saw his brows draw together. "When?"

"Next month." She roamed to the window, unable to keep still any longer. "Nick starts staging his ballet then. We reached an agreement on it, finally."

"I see." Seth's words came slowly. He studied the long slope of her neck until she turned back to him. "Then you've decided to go back."

"For one performance." She smiled, trying to pretend it was a casual conversation. Her heart was knocking at her ribs. "The premiere performance is going to be televised. I've agreed, since I was Nick's most publicized partner, to dance the lead for it. The reunion aspect will bring it more attention."

"One performance," Seth mused. He slipped his hands into his pockets as he watched her. "Do you really believe you'll be able to stop at that?"

"Of course," Lindsay tried to say evenly. "I've a number of reasons for doing it. It's important to Nick." She sighed. Thin rays of sunlight passed through the window and fell on her hair. "And it's important to me."

"To see if you can still be a star?"

She lifted her brow with a half laugh. "No. If I'd had that sort of ego, things would've been different all along. That part of it wasn't ever important enough to me. I suppose that's why my mother and I couldn't agree."

"Don't you think that'll change once you're back living in that kind of world again?" There was an edge to his voice which brought a frown to Lindsay. "When you danced with Davidov in the studio, everything you were was bound up in it."

"Yes, that's as it should be." She closed some of the distance between them, wanting him to understand. "But dancing and performing aren't the same thing always. I've had the performing," she reminded him. "I've had the spotlight. I don't need it anymore."

"Simple enough to say here now. More difficult after you've stood in the spotlight again."

"No." Lindsay shook her head. "It depends on the reasons for going back." She stepped to him, touching the back of his hand with her fingers. "Do you want to know mine?"

He studied her for a long, silent moment, then turned

away. "No. No, I don't believe I do." He stood facing the fire. "What if I asked you not to go?"

"Not to go?" Her voice reflected her confusion. She walked to him, laying her hand on his arm. "Why would you?"

Seth turned, and their eyes met. He didn't touch her. "Because I'm in love with you, and I don't want to lose you."

Lindsay's eyes widened. Then she was in his arms, clinging with all her strength. "Kiss me," she demanded. "Before I wake up."

Their lips met with mutual need, tasting and parting to taste again until the sharp edge of hunger had subsided. She pressed her face into his shoulder a moment, hardly daring to believe what she had heard. She felt his hands roam down the softness of her sweater, then under it and upon the softness of her skin.

"I've missed touching you," he murmured. "There were nights I could think of nothing else but your skin."

"Oh, Seth, I can't believe it." She tangled both hands in his hair as she drew her face away from his shoulder. "Tell me again."

He kissed her temple before he drew her close again. "I love you." She felt his body relax as she heard his sigh. "I've never said that to a woman before."

"Not even an Italian countess or a French movie star?" Lindsay's voice was muffled against his throat.

He pulled her away far enough so that their eyes could meet, then he held her there with a look deep and intent. "No one's ever touched me the way you have. I could say I've spent my life looking for someone like you, but I haven't." He smiled, running his hands up her arms until they framed her face. "I didn't know there was anyone like you. You were a surprise."

"That's the nicest thing anyone's ever said to me." She turned her face and kissed the palm of his hand. "When I knew I loved you, I was afraid because it meant needing you so much." She looked at him, and everything in his face pulled at her. He had laid claim not only to her heart and body, but to her mind as well. The depth of it seemed awesome. Suddenly she pressed against him, her pulse speeding wildly. "Hold me," she whispered, shutting her eyes. "I'm still afraid."

Her mouth sought his, and the kiss that ensued was electric. They took each other deep until neither could rise to the surface alone. It was a kiss of total dependence. They held each other and gave.

"I've been half-alive since you walked out of the studio that day," she confessed. The planes of his face demanded the exploration of her fingertips. "Everything's been flat, like the photograph of the snow would have been."

"I couldn't stay. You had told me that what had happened between us had been nice. Two adults, alone, attracted to each other. Very simple." He shook his head, pulling her closer possessively. "That caught me by the throat. I loved you, I needed you. For the first time in my life, it wasn't simple."

"Can't you tell when someone's lying?" she asked softly.

"Not when I'm trying to deal with being in love."

"If I had known…" Her voice trailed as she nestled, listening to the sound of his heartbeat.

"I wanted to tell you, but then I watched you dance. You were so exquisite, so perfect." He breathed in her scent again, holding her close. "I hated it. Every second I watched you go further away."

"No, Seth." She silenced him with her fingertips on his lips. "It's not like that. It's not like that at all."

"Isn't it?" He took her by the shoulders, holding her away. "He was offering you a life you could never share with me. He was offering you your place in the lights again. I told myself I had to do the right thing and let you walk away. I've stayed away from you all these weeks. But I knew the moment I saw you standing here today that I couldn't let you go."

"You don't understand." Her eyes were sad and pleading. "I don't want that life again, or the place in the lights, even if I could have it. That's not why I'm going back to do this ballet."

"I don't want you to go." His fingers tightened on her shoulders. "I'm asking you not to go."

She studied him for a moment with all the emotion still brimming in her eyes. "What if I asked you not to go to New Zealand?"

Abruptly he released her and turned away. "That's not the same thing. It's my job. In a few weeks it would be over and I'd be back. It's not a life-ruling force." When he turned back to her, his hands were balled in his pockets. "Would there be room for me and for children in your life if you were prima ballerina with the company?"

"Perhaps not." She came closer but knew from the look in his eyes that she dared not touch him. "But I'll never be prima ballerina with the company. If I wanted it with all my heart, it still couldn't be. And I don't want it. Why can't you understand? I simply haven't the need for it. I won't even officially be with the company for this performance. I'll have guest status."

This time it was she who turned away, too filled with emotions to be still. "I want to do it, for Nick, because he's my friend. Our bond is very special. And for myself. I'll be able to close out this chapter of my life with something beautiful instead of my father's death. That's important to me; I didn't know myself how important until recently. I have to do it, or else I'd live forever with regrets."

In the silence a log shifted and spewed sparks against the screen.

"So you'll go, no matter how I feel."

Lindsay turned slowly. Her eyes were dry and direct. "I'll go, and I'll ask you to trust me. And I want to take Ruth."

"No." His answer came immediately and with an edge. "You ask for too much. You ask for too damn much."

"It isn't too much," she countered. "Listen to me. Nick asked for her. He watched her dance; he tested her here, and he wants her. She could have a place in the *corps* by summer, Seth, she's that good. Don't hold her back."

"Don't talk to me about holding her back." Fury licked at the words. "You've described to me the life she'd lead, the physical pain and emotional anguish, the pressures, the demands. She's a child. She doesn't need that."

"Yes, she does." Lindsay paced back to him. "She's not a child; she's a young woman, and she needs it all if she's going to be a dancer. You haven't the right to deny her this."

"I have every right."

Lindsay breathed deeply, trying to keep control. "Legally, your right will run out in a few months. Then you'll put her into a position of having to go against your wishes. She'll be miserably unhappy about that, and it could be too late for her. Nikolai Davidov doesn't volunteer to train every young dancer he runs across. Ruth is special."

"Don't tell me about Ruth!" His voice rose, surprising her. "It's taken nearly a year for her to begin to be happy again. I won't push her into the kind of world where she has to punish herself every day just to keep up. If it's what you want, then take it. I can't stop you." He took her by the arm and pulled her to him. "But you won't live out your career vicariously through Ruth."

Color fled from Lindsay's face. Her eyes were huge and blue and incredulous. "Is that what you think of me?" she whispered.

"I don't know what I think of you." His face was as alive with fury as hers was cold with shock. "I don't understand you. I can't keep you here; loving you isn't enough. But Ruth's another matter. You won't keep your spotlight through her, Lindsay. You'll have to fight for that yourself."

"Let me go, please." This time it was she who possessed the restraint and control. Though she trembled, her voice was utterly calm. When Seth had released her, she stood for a moment, studying him. "Everything I've told you today is the truth. Everything. Would you please have Worth bring my coat now? I have classes very soon." She turned to the fire; her back was very straight. "I don't think we have anything more to say to each other."

Chapter 14

It was very different being the student rather than the teacher. Most of the women in Lindsay's classes were years younger than her; girls, really. Those who had reached their mid- and late twenties had been on the professional circuit all along. She worked hard. The days were very long and made the nights easier to bear.

The hours were filled with classes, then rehearsals and yet more classes. She roomed with two members of the company who had been friends during her professional days. At night she slept deeply, her mind dazed with fatigue. In the morning her classes took over her body. Her muscles grew familiar with aches and cramps again as January became February. The routine was the same as it had always been: impossible.

The studio window was darkened by an ice storm, but no one seemed to notice as they rehearsed a dance from the first act of Davidov's *Ariel*. The music was fairylike, conjuring up scenes of dusky forests and wild flowers. It was here that the young prince would meet Ariel. Mortal and Sprite would fall in love. The *pas de deux* was difficult, demanding on the female lead because of its combinations of *soubresauts* and *jetés*. High-level energy was required while keeping the moves light and ethereal. Near the end of the scene, Lindsay was to leap away from Nikolai, turning in the air as she did so in order to be facing him, teasingly, when she touched ground again. Her landing was shaky, and she was forced to plant both feet to prevent a spill. Nick cursed vividly.

"I'm sorry." Her breath came quickly after the exertion of the dance.

"Apologies!" He emphasized his anger with a furious flick of his hand. "I can't dance with an apology."

Other dancers in the room glared at Lindsay with varying degrees of sympathy. All of them had felt the rough edge of Davidov's tongue. The pianist automatically flipped back to the beginning of the suite.

Lindsay's body ached from a twelve-hour, punishing day. "My feet hardly touch the ground in the whole third scene," she tossed back at him. Someone handed her a towel, and gratefully she wiped sweat from her neck and brow. "I haven't got wings, Nick."

"Obviously."

It amazed her that his sarcasm wounded. Usually it touched off anger, and the row that would ensue would clear the air. Now she felt it necessary to defend herself. "It's difficult," she murmured, pushing loosened wisps of hair behind her ear.

"Difficult!" He roared at her, crossing the room to stand in front of her. "So it is difficult. Did I bring you here to watch you do a simple pirouette across the stage?" His hair curled damply around his face as his eyes blazed at her.

"You didn't bring me," she corrected, but her voice was shaky, without its usual strength. "I came."

"You came." He turned away with a wide gesture. "To dance like a truck driver."

The sob came too quickly for her to prevent it. Appalled, she pressed her hands to her face. She had just enough time to see the stunned look on Nikolai's face before she fled the room.

Lindsay let the door to the rest room slam behind her. In the far corner was a low bench. Lindsay curled up on it and wept as if her heart would break. Unable to cope any longer, she let the hurt pour out. Her sobs bounced off the walls and came back to her. When an arm slipped around her, Lindsay turned into it, accepting the offered comfort blindly. She needed someone.

Nikolai rocked and stroked her until the passion of her tears lessened. She had curled into him like a child, and he held her close, murmuring in Russian.

"My little dove." Gently he kissed her temple. "I've been cruel."

"Yes." She used the towel she had draped over her shoulders to dry her eyes. She was drained, empty, and if the pain was still there, she was too numb to feel it.

"But always before, you fight back." He tilted her chin. Her eyes were brilliant and wet. "We are very volatile, yes?" Nikolai smiled, kissing the corners of her mouth. "I yell at you, you yell at me, then we dance."

To their mutual distress, Lindsay buried her face in his shoulder and began to cry again. "I don't know why I'm acting this way." She took deep breaths to stop herself. "I hate people who act this way. It just all seems so crazy. Sometimes it feels like it's three years ago and nothing's changed. Then I see girls like Allyson Gray." Lindsay sniffed, thinking of the dancer who would take over the part of Ariel. "She's twelve years old."

"Twenty," Nikolai corrected, patting her hair.

"She makes me feel forty. And the classes seem hours longer than they ever did before."

"You're doing beautifully; you know that." He hugged her and kissed the top of her head.

"I feel like a clod," she said miserably. "An uncoordinated clod."

Nikolai smiled into her hair but kept his voice sympathetic. "You've lost the five pounds."

"Six," she corrected, and sighing, wiped her eyes again. "Who has time to eat? I'll probably keep on shrinking until I disappear." She glanced around, then her eyes widened. "Nick, you can't be in here, this is the ladies' room."

"I'm Davidov," he said imperially. "I go anywhere."

That made her laugh, and she kissed him. "I feel like a total fool. I've never fallen apart at a rehearsal like that before."

"It's not any of the things we talked about." He took her shoulders, and now his look was solemn. "It's the architect."

"No," she said too quickly. Only his left brow moved. "Yes." She let out a long breath and closed her eyes. "Yes."

"Will you talk about it now?"

Opening her eyes, Lindsay nodded. She settled back in the curve of his shoulder and let the silence hang for a moment. "He told me he loved me," she began. "I thought, this is what I've waited for all my life. He loves me, and life's going to be perfect. But love isn't enough. I didn't know that, but it's not. Understanding, trust... love is a closed hand without those."

She paused in silence, remembering clearly every moment of her last meeting with Seth. Nikolai waited for her to continue. "He couldn't deal with my coming back for this ballet. He couldn't—or wouldn't—understand that I had to do it. He wouldn't trust me when I told him it was only for this one time. He wouldn't believe that I didn't want this life again, that I wanted to build one with him. He asked me not to go."

"That was selfish," Nikolai stated. He frowned at the wall and moved Lindsay closer to him. "He's a selfish man."

She smiled, thinking how simple it had been for Nick to demand that she come. It seemed she was caught between two selfish men. "Yes. But perhaps there should be some selfishness in love. I don't know." She was calm now, her breathing steady. "If he had believed me, believed that I wasn't going back to a life that would exclude him, we might have come to an understanding."

"Might?"

"There's Ruth." A new weight seemed to drag on her heart. "There was nothing I could say that would convince him to send her here. Nothing that could make him see that he was depriving her of everything she was, everything she could be. We argued about her often, most violently the last time I saw him."

Lindsay swallowed, feeling some of the pain return. "He loves her very much and takes his responsibility for her very seriously. He didn't want her to deal with the hardships of the life we lead here. He thinks she's too young, and…" Lindsay was interrupted by a Russian curse she recognized. It lightened her mood a little, and she relaxed against him again. "You'd see it that way, of course, but for an outsider, things look differently."

"There is only one way," he began.

"Davidov's," Lindsay supplied, adoring him for his perfect confidence.

"Naturally," he agreed, but she heard the humor in his voice.

"A non-dancer might disagree," she murmured. "I understand how he feels, and that makes it harder, I suppose, because I know, regardless of that, that Ruth belongs here. He feels…" She bit her lip, remembering. "He thinks I want to use her, to continue my career through her. That was the worst of it."

Davidov remained silent for several moments, digesting all Lindsay had told him, then adding it to his own impressions of Seth Bannion. "I think it was a man very hurt who would say that to you."

"I never saw him again after that. We left each other hurting."

"You'll go back in the spring, when your dance is over." He tilted her face. "You'll see him then."

"I don't know. I don't know if I can." Her eyes were tragic. "Perhaps it's best to leave things as they are, so we don't hurt each other again."

"Love hurts, *ptichka,*" he said with a broad shrug. "The ballet hurts you, your lover hurts you. Life. Now, wash your face," he told her briskly. "It's time to dance again."

Lindsay faced herself at the barre. She was alone now in a practice room five stories above Manhattan. It was night, and the windows were black. On the CD player, the music came slowly, a piano only. Turning out, she began to lift her right leg. It seemed straight from the hip to the toe, one long line. Keeping her eyes locked on her eyes in the mirror, she took the leg behind her into an *attitude* position, then rose slowly onto her toe. She held it firm, refusing to let her muscles quiver, then brought her leg back painstakingly on the return journey. She repeated the exercise with her left leg.

It had been nearly a week since her outburst at rehearsal. Every night since then she had used the practice room when everyone had gone. An extra hour of reminding her body what was expected of it, an extra hour of keeping her mind from drifting back to Seth. *Glissade, assemblé, changement, changement.* Her mind ordered, and her body obeyed. In six weeks she would be performing for the first time in more than three years. For the last time in her life. She would be ready.

She took herself into an achingly slow *grand plié,* aware of each tendon. Her leotard was damp from her efforts. As she rose again, a movement in the mirror broke her concentration. She would have sworn at the interruption, but then her vision focused.

"Ruth?" She turned just as the girl rushed toward her. Enveloped in a tight hug, Lindsay was thrown back to the first time they had met. She had touched Ruth's shoulder and had been rejected. How far she's come, Lindsay thought, returning the hug with all her strength. "Let me look at you." Drawing away, Lindsay framed her face. It was animated, laughing, the eyes dark and bright. "You look wonderful. Wonderful."

"I missed you. I missed you so much!"

"What are you doing here?" Lindsay took her hands,

automatically chafing the cold from them. "Seth. Is Seth with you?" Hoping, fearing, she looked to the doorway.

"No, he's at home." Ruth saw the answer to the question she harbored. She was still in love with him. "He couldn't get away right now."

"I see." Lindsay brought her attention back to Ruth and managed a smile. "But how did you get here? And why?"

"I came by train," Ruth answered. "To study ballet."

"To study?" Lindsay became very still. "I don't understand."

"Uncle Seth and I had a long talk a few weeks ago before he went back to New Zealand." She unzipped her corduroy jacket and slipped out of it. "Right after you'd left for New York, actually."

"A talk?" Lindsay moved to the CD player to switch off the music. She used a towel to dry her neck, then left it draped over her shoulders. "What about?"

"About what I wanted in my life, what was important to me and why." She watched Lindsay carefully remove the CD from the player. She could see the nerves in the movements. "He had a lot of reservations about letting me come here. I guess you know that."

"Yes, I know." Lindsay slipped the disc back into its case.

"He wanted what was best for me. After my parents were killed, I had a hard time adjusting to things. The first couple of months, he dropped everything just to be with me when I needed him. And even after, I know he rearranged his life, his work, for me." Ruth laid her coat over the back of a wooden chair. "He's been so good to me."

Lindsay nodded, unable to speak. The wound was opening again.

"I know it was hard for him to let me come, to let me make the choice. He's been wonderful about it, taking care of all the paperwork with school, and he arranged for me to stay with a family he knows. They have a really great duplex on the East Side. They let me bring Nijinsky." She walked to the barre, and in jeans and sneakers, began to exercise.

"It's so wonderful here." Her expression shone radiant as Lindsay watched it in the glass. "And Mr. Davidov said he'd work with me in the evenings when he has time."

"You've seen Nick?" Lindsay crossed over so that they both stood at the barre.

"About an hour ago. I was trying to find you." She smiled, her head dipping below Lindsay's as she bent her knees. "He said I'd find you here, that you come every evening to practice. I can hardly wait until the ballet. He said I could watch it from backstage if I wanted."

"And, of course, you do." Lindsay touched her hair, then walked to the bench to change her shoes.

"Aren't you terribly excited?" Ruth did three *pirouettes* to join her. "Dancing the lead in Davidov's first ballet."

"Once," Lindsay reminded her, undoing the satin ribbons on her shoes.

"Opening night," Ruth countered. Clasping her hands together, Ruth looked down at Lindsay. "How will you be able to give it up again?"

"It's not again," she corrected. "It's *still*. This is a favor for a friend, and for myself." She winced, slipping the shoe from her foot.

"Hurt?"

"Oh, God, yes."

Ruth dropped to her knees and began to work Lindsay's toes. She could feel the tension in them. With a sigh Lindsay laid her head against the wall and closed her eyes.

"Uncle Seth's going to try to come spend a few days with me in the spring. He isn't happy."

"He'll miss you." The cramps in Lindsay's feet were subsiding slowly.

"I don't mean about that."

The words caused Lindsay to open her eyes. Ruth was watching her solemnly, though her fingers still worked at the pain. "Did he say anything? Did he send a message?"

Ruth shook her head. Lindsay shut her eyes again.

Chapter 15

Lindsay found that a three-year absence hadn't made her any less frantic during the hours before a performance. For the past two weeks she had endured hours of interviews and photography sessions, questions and answers and flashing cameras. The reunion of Dunne and Davidov for a one-time performance of a ballet he himself had written and choreographed was news. For Nick and for the company, Lindsay made herself available for any publicity required. Unfortunately, it added to the already impossibly long days.

The performance was a benefit, and the audience would be star-studded. The ballet would be televised, and all proceeds would be donated to a scholarship fund for gifted young dancers. Publicity could encourage yet more donations. For this, Lindsay wanted success.

If the ballet was well-received, it would be incorporated into the program for the season. Nick would broaden himself immeasurably in the world of dance. For him, and for herself, Lindsay wanted success.

There had been a phone call from her mother and a visit from Ruth in her dressing room. The phone call had had a warm tone, without pressures.

Mae was as pleased about the upcoming performance as she could have been; but to Lindsay's surprise and delight, her own responsibilities and new life demanded that she remain in California. Her heart and thoughts would be there with Lindsay, she promised, and she would view the ballet on television.

The visit from Ruth had been a breath of fresh air. Ruth had become star-struck at the mechanics of backstage life. She was a willing slave for anyone who asked. Next year, Lindsay thought, watching her bustle about carrying costumes and props, she would be fussing over her own costumes.

Taking a hammer, she took a new pair of toe shoes, sat on the floor and began to pound them. She would make them supple before sewing on the ribbons. Her costumes hung in order in the closet. Backstage cacophony accompanied the sound of hammer against wood. There was makeup and hair styling yet to be seen to, and dressing in the white tutu for the first act. Lindsay went through each process, aware of the video cameras that were recording the preperformance stage of the ballet. Only her warmups were done in private, at her insistence. Here, she would begin to focus the concentration she would need to carry her through the following hours.

The pressure in her chest was building as she walked down the corridor toward the wings at stage left. Here, she would make her entrance after the opening dance by the forest ensemble. The music and lights were already on her. She knew Nick would be waiting in the wings at stage right, anticipating his own entrance. Ruth stood beside her, gently touching her wrist as if to wish her luck without speaking the words. Superstitions never die in the theater. Lindsay watched the dancers, the women in their long, bell-like white dresses, the men in their vests and tunics.

Twenty bars, then fifteen, and she began taking long, slow breaths. Ten bars and then five. Her throat went dry. The knot in her stomach threatened to become genuine nausea. The cold film on her skin was terror. She closed her eyes briefly, then ran onto the stage.

At her entrance, the rising applause was a welcome wave. Lindsay never heard it. For her, there was only the music. Her movements flowed with the joy of the first scene. The dance was short but strenuous, and when she ran back into the wings, beads of moisture clung to her brow. She allowed herself to be patted dry and fed a stingy sip of water as she watched Nick take over the second scene. Within seconds, he had the audience in the palm of his hand.

"Oh yes," Lindsay breathed, then turned to smile at Ruth. "It's going to be perfect."

The ballet revolved around its principals, and it was rare for one or both of them not to be onstage. In the final scene the music slowed and the lights became a misty blue. Lindsay wore a floating knee-length gown. It was here that Ariel had to decide whether to give up her immortality for love; to marry the prince, she had to become mortal and renounce all her magic.

Lindsay danced alone in the moonlit forest, recall-ing the joy and simplicity of her life with the trees and flowers. To have love—mortal love—she had to turn her back on everything she had known. The choice brought great sadness. Even as she despaired, falling on the ground to weep, the prince entered the forest. He knelt beside her, touching her shoulder to bring her face to his.

The *grand pas de deux* expressed his love for her, his need to have her beside him. She was drawn to him, yet afraid of losing the life she had always known, afraid of facing death as a mortal. She soared with freedom, through the trees and the moonlight that had always been hers, but again and again, she was pulled back to him by her own heart. She stopped, for dawn was breaking, and the time for decision had come.

He reached out to her, but she turned away, uncertain, frightened. In despair, he started to leave her. At the last moment, she called him back. The first rays of sunlight seeped through the trees as she ran to him. He lifted her into his arms as she gave him her heart and her life.

The curtain had closed, but still Nick held her. Their pulses were soaring, and for the moment, they had eyes only for each other.

"Thank you." And he kissed her softly, as a friend saying goodbye.

"Nick." Her eyes filled with emotion after emotion, but he set her down before she could speak.

"Listen," he ordered, gesturing to the closed curtain. The sound of applause battered against it. "We can't keep them waiting forever."

Flowers and people. It seemed that no more of either could be crammed into Lindsay's dressing room. There was laughter, and someone poured her a glass of champagne. She set it down untasted. Her mind was already drunk with the moment. She answered questions and smiled, but nothing seemed completely in focus. She was still in costume and makeup, still part Ariel.

There were men in tuxedos and women in sparkling evening dress mingling with elves and wood sprites. She had spoken to an actor of star magnitude and a visiting French dignitary. All she could do was hope her responses had been coherent. When she spotted Ruth, Lindsay hailed her, the look in her eyes entreating.

"Stay with me, will you?" she asked when the girl managed to plow her way through the crowd. "I'm not normal yet; I need someone."

"Oh, Lindsay." Ruth threw her arms around her neck. "You were so wonderful! I've never seen anything more wonderful."

Lindsay laughed and returned the hug. "Just bring me down. I'm still in the air." She was interrupted by the assistant director, who brought more flowers and champagne.

It was more than an hour before the crowd thinned. By then, Lindsay was feeling the weariness that follows an emotional high. It was Nick, who had managed to work his way out of his own dressing room to find her, who cleared the room. Seeing the telltale signs of fatigue on her face, he reminded those remaining of a reception being held at a nearby restaurant.

"You must go so *ptichka* can change," he said jovially, patting a back and nudging it out the door. "Save us some champagne. And caviar," he added, "if it's Russian."

Within five minutes, only he and Ruth joined Lindsay in the flower-filled room.

"So," he addressed Ruth, coming over to pinch her chin. "You think your teacher did well tonight?"

"Oh, yes." Ruth smiled at Lindsay. "She did beautifully."

"I mean me." He tossed back his hair and looked insulted.

"You weren't too bad," Lindsay informed him.

"Not too bad?" He sniffed, rising to his full height. "Ruth, I would ask you to leave us a moment. This lady and I have something to discuss."

"Of course."

Before Ruth could step away, Lindsay took her hand. "Wait." From her dressing table she took a rose, one that had been thrown at her feet after the performance. She handed it to Ruth. "To a new Ariel, another day."

Wordlessly, Ruth looked down at the rose, then at Lindsay. Her eyes were eloquent, though she could only nod her thanks before she left the room.

"Ah, my little bird," Nick took her hand and kissed it. "Such a good heart."

She squeezed his fingers in return. "But you will cast her in it. Three years, perhaps two."

He nodded. "There are some who are made for such things." His eyes met hers. "I will never dance with a more perfect Ariel than I have tonight."

Lindsay leaned forward so that their faces were close. "Charm, Nick, for me? I had thought I was through with bouquets tonight."

"I love you, *ptichka*."

"I love you, Nicky."

"Will you do me one last favor?"

She smiled, leaning back in her chair again. "How could I refuse?"

"There is someone else I would like you to see to-night."

She gave him a look of good-humored weariness. "I can only pray it's not another reporter. I'll see whomever you like," she agreed recklessly. "As long as you don't expect me to go to that reception."

"You are excused," he said with a regal inclination of his head. He went to the door, and opening it, turned briefly to look at her.

She sat, obviously exhausted in the chair. Her hair flowed freely over the shoulders of the thin white gown, her eyes exotic with their exaggerated lines and coloring. She smiled at him, but he left without speaking again.

Briefly, Lindsay closed her eyes, but almost instantly a tingle ran up her spine. Her throat went dry as it had before her first dance of the ballet. She knew who would be there when she opened her eyes.

She rose when Seth closed the door behind him, but slowly, as if measuring the distance between them. She was alert again, sharply, completely, as if she had awakened from a long, restful sleep. She was suddenly aware of the powerful scent of flowers and the masses of color they brought to the room. She was aware that his face was thinner but that he stood straight and his eyes were still direct and serious. She was aware that her love for him hadn't lessened by a single degree.

"Hello." She tried to smile. Formal clothing suited him, she decided as she laced her fingers together. She remembered, too, how right he had looked in jeans and a flannel shirt. There are so many Seth Bannions, she mused. And I love them all.

"You were magnificent," he said. He came no closer to her but stood, seeming to draw every inch of her through his eyes. "But I suppose you've heard that too often tonight."

"Never too often," she returned. "And not from you." She wanted to cross the room to him, but the hurt was still there, and the distance was so far. "I didn't know you were coming."

"I asked Ruth not to say anything." He came farther into the room, but the gap still seemed immense. "I didn't come to see you before the performance because I thought it might upset you. It didn't seem fair."

"You sent her...I'm glad."

"I was wrong about that." He lifted a single rose from a table and studied it a moment. "You were right, she belongs here. I was wrong about a great many things."

"I was wrong, too, to try to push you too soon." Lindsay unlaced her fingers, then helplessly, she laced them again. "Ruth needed what you were giving her. I don't think she'd be the person she is right now if you hadn't had those months with her. She's happy now."

"And you?" He looked up again and pinned her with his gaze. "Are you?"

She opened her mouth to speak, and finding no words, turned away. There on the dressing table was a half-filled bottle of champagne and her untouched glass. Lindsay lifted the glass and drank. The bubbles soothed the tightness in her throat. "Would you like some champagne? I seem to have plenty."

"Yes." He took the last steps toward her. "I would."

Nervous now that he stood so close, Lindsay looked around for another glass. "Silly," she said, keeping her back to him. "I don't seem to have a clean glass anywhere."

"I'll share yours." He laid a hand on her shoulder,

gently turning her to face him. He placed his fingers over hers on the stem. He drank, keeping his eyes on hers.

"Nothing's any good without you." Her voice broke as he lowered the glass. "Nothing."

His fingers tightened on hers, and she saw something flash in his eyes. "Don't forgive me too quickly, Lindsay," he advised. The contact was broken when he placed the glass back on the table. "The things I said…"

"No. No, they don't matter now." Her eyes filled and brimmed over.

"They do," he corrected quietly. "To me. I was afraid of losing you and pushed you right out of my life."

"I've never been out of your life."

She would have gone to him then, but he turned away. "You're a terrifying person to be in love with, Lindsay, so warm, so giving. I've never known anyone like you." When he turned back, she could see the emotions in his eyes, not so controlled now, not so contained. "I've never needed anyone before, and then I needed you and felt you slipping away."

"But I wasn't." She was in his arms before he could say another word. When he stiffened, she lifted her face and found his mouth. Instantly, the kiss became avid and deep. The low sound of his breath sent pleasure through her. "Seth. Oh, Seth, I've been half-alive for three months. Don't leave me again."

Holding her close, he breathed in the scent of her hair. "You left me," he murmured.

"I won't again." She lifted her face so that her eyes, huge and brilliant, promised him. "Not ever again."

"Lindsay." He reached up to frame her face. "I can't…

I won't ask you to give up what you have here. Watching you tonight…"

"You don't have to ask me anything." She placed her hands on his wrists, willing him to believe her. "Why can't you understand? This isn't what I want. Not now, not anymore. I want you. I want a home and a family."

He looked at her deeply, then shook his head. "It's difficult to believe you can walk away from this. You must have heard that applause."

She smiled. It should be so simple, she thought. "Seth, I pushed myself for three months. I worked harder than I've ever worked in my life to give one performance. I'm tired; I want to go home. Marry me. Share my life."

With a sigh, he rested his forehead on hers. "No one's ever proposed to me before."

"Good, then I'm the first." It was so easy to melt in his arms.

"And the last," he murmured between kisses.

* * * * *